THE
VILLA

BOOKS BY CLARE BOYD

THE
VILLA

CLARE BOYD

bookouture

Published by Bookouture in 2022

An imprint of Storyfire Ltd.
Carmelite House
50 Victoria Embankment
London EC4Y 0DZ

www.bookouture.com

ISBN: 978-1-80314-199-2
eBook ISBN: 978-1-80314-198-5

This book is a work of fiction. Names, characters, businesses, organizations, places and events other than those clearly in the public domain, are either the product of the author's imagination or are used fictitiously. Any resemblance to actual persons, living or dead, events or locales is entirely coincidental.

PROLOGUE

The bungalow smelt of old socks and strange people and of failure. Was this what my life had amounted to?

The girls were trying their best to like it.

'I love this big window, Mumma!' Libby cried, pressing her nose against the enormous picture window.

'It doesn't even open,' I said, my palms flattened upon it. A wall of glass that symbolised my new entrapment in a life I had never wanted. I couldn't pretend for the girls' sake. Their enthusiasm was phoney and rather Pollyanna-ish, and it was irritating me.

It was plain this house was a devastating downgrade from Hugh's beautiful high-ceilinged apartment in London that we'd moved from. I yearned for its corniced elegance and the smell of its polished parquet floor. He had kept it in the divorce. Because he was a bastard. It had been in his family for two generations, but that shouldn't have counted for anything. It had become the girls' home. *My* home. After everything he'd put us through, we deserved it.

I'd never wanted to move to the country. It wasn't me. The square patch of scrubland at the back of the house was a burden for some other woman; the close of five houses was the soulless and depressing address of someone I looked down on and felt sorry for; the neighbours' bottle of wine and 'Welcome to Your New Home' card was the sort of gesture a suburban housewife would be moved by. Not this woman standing here with her two promising children. Not this woman who'd vowed she'd never go backwards as her father had. Not us. Not me. Never me.

All the same, I wiped away a grateful tear as I stood the greetings card on the low brick mantel, hoping it wouldn't burst into flames when I turned on the five-bar gas fire below it.

'Mum! Mum! Look what I found!' Emma called out. I followed her voice through the varnished, sticky-looking kitchen to a small utility room – which I grudgingly quite liked the idea of, having never had one – and out into the garden. Emma was emerging from a shed pulling a red Radio Flyer.

'Oh, I love those!' I cried, genuinely thrilled by it. 'Libby! Libby!'

Libby came hopping out, pulling on her new green welly boots.

'Look what your sister found,' I said to her.

'Get in, quick!' Emma said, as though someone might take it from them.

She pulled Libby through the side gate and around to the front of the house, and wheeled her up and down the empty road. She went so fast, Libby tumbled out. But she climbed back in again, wanting more. Then they swapped places, and Libby dragged her sister along, puffing and panting up the slight incline. Emma whistled, lying back with her knees flopped open, telling her how boring it was to go so slow. The faster Libby tried to go, the more she giggled. Emma began shouting at her, saying how useless she was. They argued, made up and carried on.

I leant into the side of the open front door and brought my

cigarettes out from my pocket. As I smoked, I watched them and felt happy. They were at lovely ages, ten and seven, the sweet spot of childhood. There was freedom here that they wouldn't have had in Clapham, and the thought helped me to breathe again. I was as free to do as I pleased as they were. And I had the blood money Hugh had given me, which I wasn't sure yet what to do with. I wouldn't fritter it. I had more dignity than that.

That night, quite late, after unpacking our clothes, we got into the car, drove to the local off-licence and rented *Crocodile Dundee* on VHS. The jaunt was fun. Hugh would have disapproved of it: the late hour and the spontaneity. But I didn't have to care what he thought any more.

Back at the house, the three of us sat in a cosy row on the two-seater sofa in front of the telly. We jostled for elbow space and scorched our tongues on the too-hot tinned tomato soup in mugs. There was no cream to cool the burnt-orange liquid, and the white rolls from the corner shop were stale, but it didn't matter. We were together, glued to each other as an unbreakable trio. Nobody else in the whole world mattered. We were all we needed.

ONE

LIBBY, 2022

Hot and stressed and eager to get to France, Libby followed Emma along the airport corridors towards the gate, doing absolutely everything her sister said, bumping into her if she stopped abruptly, herding her mum and the gang back into the slipstream of her wheelie suitcase, picking up a dropped something or other. Key responsibilities.

It had been a long time since she had been in an airport, and she had forgotten how people pushed and rushed, and how bungling she was. Her beach bag was weighed down by three holiday reads, two supersize packets of batteries, a half-finished jumper, and her daughters' magazines and sweets. Amber and Hazel probably wouldn't even read the magazines they'd begged for. Their phones were too gripping – life itself couldn't compete.

She dropped the load at her feet, letting the conveyor carry her along, enjoying a brief rest. Emma turned back to her, picked up her bag and ushered her along. Behind them, the rest of the family rebelled by stopping in a clump.

'My God, what have you got in this?' Emma said, hefting it on her shoulder before slipping her arm through Libby's, practically dragging her away from the others. 'Libby. How am I going to last two weeks with her?'

They both glanced back at their mum. Even under a rather eccentric floppy hat, she was deceptively pretty and harmless-looking. Her round face was shaped by sweet high cheekbones, permanently pink like a child flushed from the outdoors; her wide eyes were a sharp golden-brown; her thick white-blonde hair swept off her face and down her back.

'It'll be all right when we get there,' Libby puffed, out of breath, wondering whether *she* could survive two weeks with *Emma*.

'Look, she wants to sit next to us on the plane, but whatever it is she wants to tell us, I'm not sure I'm ready. I think I'd prefer to be by that pool with a large glass of wine.'

'She has something to tell us?' Libby's stomach flipped. The squeak of her wheelie case cut out for a second, and her step faltered.

'It's probably nothing.'

'Oh, right.' She pushed her fingernails into her wrist.

'Anyway, let's get Patrick to sit with us on the plane and tell Mum that the kids are dying for her to sit with them.'

'Good plan,' Libby replied vaguely. Saying 'good plan' to her sister was always a safe bet. Emma was wedded to her good plans, and it was easier to go along with her, whether the plan was good or not. This time, she doubted it was. Their mother was stubborn, and unlikely to want to change the seating arrangements, particularly if she had something to tell them.

Looking behind her again to check on everyone, Libby noticed that Amber had stepped off the conveyor and was standing at a vending machine. At the next opportunity, Libby jumped off and switched back to join her daughter, suddenly needing some water too. By the time they had fiddled around with the machine and handed out a bottle each to the other two children, she had lost sight of Emma.

She scoured the crowds, left to right, up and down, searching urgently for her older sister's blonde head, always much shinier and cleaner than her own fuzzy mess, but seeing only a blur of faces. In Emma's absence, Libby would have to shift a gear and concentrate on gate numbers and boarding times. She preferred to let other people take control of the practical stuff. If she'd had Connor with her, she would have turned to him.

Missing him more than ever, she conjured him up in her head and thought back to the weekend before he'd left for Costa Rica.

'Can't you pack me in there too?' she had pleaded gently, sitting cross-legged on their duvet next to his rucksack, watching him put a laptop, a phone charger, two green earplugs and a small tube of suncream into neat places inside it.

'You guys could still come with me.' He had rolled his second pair of swimming trunks into another zipped pocket.

The reasons why she had said no in the first place had flickered in her mind like a faulty sign, but she'd said, 'They don't have Tetley's out there. I'd never cope.'

His eyes had fallen to his bare feet, which he had positioned exactly parallel to one another, with his toes stretched wide on the carpet, as though he were anchoring himself to the floor, ready to stretch into an aggressive yogic sun salute. Her fingers had been interlocked around a mug that was emblazoned with the bright yellow slogan, 'CHICKEN NUGGET LOVER'. Its bowl-like rim had not strayed too far from her mouth in between sips.

Tea was a comfort. Her life was full of it: Friday nights of tea and chocolate in front of the telly; Saturday morning fry-ups with more tea; tea and knitting projects that went nowhere; tea when the girls got home from their faceless, factory-like secondary school. Compared to Costa Rica, perhaps her woolly, tea-drowned life seemed small and aimless to him. This ordinariness, her coasting along cosily like this, paled into insignificance next to his beach-hut days in Playa Santa Teresa, sand in his toes, the roll of a wave under his board, and a cold bottle of beer at sunset; exotic bird calls and strong coffee as he plotted his 'dystopian environmentalist science fiction' novel, as he called it.

'Emma's gone to the loo,' her mum said, waggling boarding passes in her face, jolting her forward four weeks and into the present. Standing eagerly in front of Libby, Nora was rounded and soft and owl-eyed. She flicked her hair behind her shoulders like a young girl brimming with excitement about their upcoming adventure. France wasn't as far-flung as Costa Rica, but it was damn exciting nevertheless. 'We're meeting her at the gate. Follow me.'

As she trailed after her mother, Libby's mind drifted off again. Her thoughts were usually somewhere else, anywhere else but in the here and now. She imagined Connor in the photograph he had sent by text, placing a mug of coffee on his rickety writing desk that looked out through an opening on to jungle. In that strange, distant life, he would be finishing his book this time, having not done so in Morocco the year before. Or in Portugal the year before that. Or in Patagonia five years ago. Previous experience told her he would again come home early without a completed manuscript, missing his 'two little sidekicks', Amber and Hazel, too much. And then a few months later, he would disappear again. That was how it rolled with Connor. There would barely be enough time to get angry or sad about the money he was channelling into this dream of his before he'd fill his tired rucksack and be gone. Like lighting a wood burner in summer, which Libby sometimes liked to do, she had known that allowing him to go to Costa Rica and miss this family holiday had felt a little bit wrong.

'Follow Granny Nor-Nor, girls,' she said, wafting her arms in her mother's general direction.

She let them go on ahead, admiring the three children: her two girls and Emma's son, Eliot. Even the backs of them warmed her heart. In front of them, her mother floated through the crowds with purpose. She had a full figure, a poised deportment and a soft, comfy step, which made her seem light and elegant, like a matriarchal sylph. Libby noted how trim she had become.

She guessed they'd been spending too much time together for her to have noticed it before now. Since Connor had left, her mum, who lived around the corner, had dropped by every day for a cup of mid-morning tea, or a movie after supper, or a sunny weekend stroll out through the back gate and into the woods. She was never any trouble. When she stayed over on a week night, she wouldn't linger for breakfast or get in the way of their routine in their small space, and always unloaded the dishwasher. Libby had enjoyed her company.

The toilets were coming up on their left, and she stopped, deciding she might go one more time before boarding. By the time she came out, there was a commotion going on.

'Mum!' Hazel said. '*There* you are! Come on! Stop being so slow. Granny Nor-Nor and Auntie Emma have had an argument.'

'I can't even leave them alone long enough to have a wee?'

They hurried to the gate to find Amber sitting next to Nora, with no sign of Emma and the others.

'Everything okay, Mum?'

Nora unplugged an earbud from her ear and Amber took the other one out of her own. 'We've been listening to Amber's spa music to calm us down,' Nora said. Her big eyes were watery and wounded. A huge plane wheeled down the runway behind her, making her look very small.

Amber showed Libby the Spotify playlist she'd titled 'Calm the F**k Down' and grinned wickedly at her.

'Where's Emma?' Libby asked.

'She won't sit with us,' her mum said, sighing, rotating her hand in the air like the Queen and waving it in the direction of the other side of the lounge.

Three rows across, with their backs to them, Emma was sitting by Patrick. Next to them, Eliot was bent over his phone, wearing big red headphones.

'What happened?' Libby asked.

'Oh, you know, I'm in trouble with her.'

Amber fixed her earbud back into her ear.

'I'm sure you're not, Mum,' Libby said.

'I can't say anything right.'

'You know how het up she gets about her schedule.'

'All I wanted to do was to sit between you on the plane and share a glass of bubbly.'

'Oh, Mum. That would be lovely!'

'But *she* plainly doesn't want to.'

'Of course she does.'

Libby felt bad that she hadn't been more forthright with Emma about the seating plan, and regretted not asking her to leave it as it was. She knew how uppity their mum could be when she felt rejected.

'Hmm,' Nora said. 'I don't know where she gets her stubbornness from, I really don't.'

Libby stared at her, waiting for a wry smile or a sheepish knowing glance, but there was nothing, not a hint of irony. Nora genuinely did not recognise herself in Emma. But there was more under the surface of this tiff between them, Libby could sense it. Tenderly she placed a hand on her mum's arm and dropped her voice a little. 'Is it also because you wanted to tell us something?'

Abruptly Nora stood up, making Libby jump. She gathered all her hair into her hands and twisted it onto the top of her head, revealing her face as a beautiful milky moon. 'Why do you say that?' Her voice had lost its sweetness.

Libby felt a sucking sensation inside her. She wanted it to stop, and so she backtracked. 'Just something Emma said. I must've misunderstood.'

'Yes.' Her mother's brown eyes were like saucers rimmed in gold.

'I'll go and give her these,' Libby said, taking out some batteries from her bag and skulking away across enemy lines.

When Emma saw her approaching, she launched right in. 'Did she say sorry?'

'Er, yeah, sort of.'

Patrick stood up and gestured to his seat. Libby shook her head. 'No, no, you stay there, but thanks,' she said. She couldn't look at him in case he spotted her shiftiness.

Emma huffed. 'Don't lie. She doesn't even know what she did wrong. She called the kids morons!'

Patrick chipped in. 'That wasn't exactly how she put it.'

'She said she didn't want to sit next to the kids because they would be on their phones like morons for the whole journey and she couldn't bear to sit there without anybody talking to her. I mean, I didn't want to point out that Eliot's actually reading a book on his phone!'

Libby looked over at Eliot, whose thumb was pressing madly at a screen button as a racing car drove through a narrow pass.

'Gaming can be very educational too,' she said.

'Oh dear! Right?' Emma had the grace to burst out laughing. 'I don't know why I let her wind me up, I really don't. I probably went in a bit strong,' she admitted, looking to Patrick to confirm this. Libby silently urged him not to fall into the trap of agreeing.

Patrick, still standing politely, and ever the diplomat, said, 'Airports bring out the worst in all of us.'

'In *Mum*. All her cloak-and-dagger stuff around this holiday is really getting to me. I can't bear it.'

Libby decided to sit down in the seat Patrick had vacated. 'What cloak-and-dagger stuff? What am I missing here?'

Emma exhaled. 'Okay, okay. Look, I barely know more than you do, but apparently she wants to tell us all something. She didn't say anything to you because she knew you'd worry.'

'Well, now I *am* worried.'

'Point proven.'

'But you're not?' Libby said, looking around at their mother, who was bopping along to something on Amber's playlist.

Emma tightened her ponytail. 'Honestly, I don't know what to think.'

'Weirdly,' Libby said, 'I thought something was up when I saw the photos of the villa online. It must've cost an absolute fortune. Where's she getting the money from?' She looked up at a passing pilot in a smart uniform and thought he looked the type to have the answer.

'We've been wondering about that too, haven't we?' Emma nudged Patrick. 'Then there was that email. I mean, come on, you have to admit it was bizarre.' She scrolled through her phone and thrust it at Libby. 'What's that creepy photo of Grandpa Morris all about?'

Libby absently took the phone. It had been over a month since the email drama had died down, and she was reluctant to re-engage. But she skim-read the email now, hoping for clues about the secret Emma thought their mother was keeping.

Dear Emma,

Your grandfather owned a toyshop in a small town and worked his fingers to the bone to pay for me to eat. This family holiday in France would have been beyond his wildest dreams. It gives me such pride and pleasure to know that I am able to pass on his legacy, not in monetary terms – he lost everything himself – but as an echo of his staunch work ethic. It was what he always wanted, for me to work hard and better myself, to achieve where he had failed. I attach a photograph of him. I wish you had known him for longer. He was a great man.

With love always,

Mum x

Eyes still on the screen, Libby said, 'Dad told me once that Grandpa was a horrible old man who was too lazy to run the toyshop properly.' As she spoke, she sneakily scrolled down to read Emma's original email. The one that had prompted their mum's emotionally charged response.

Dear Mum,

Thanks so much for sending the link for the holiday. What a stunning villa! Have you won the lottery? Sorry I didn't respond earlier. Summer term has been incredibly busy, as ever, and I do find it a struggle to get through all my emails at the end of the day. On the holiday front, I've had to weigh up the commitments we have in July, which are considerable. As you know, Eliot has his swimathon coming up. And I'm opening the school to a summer holiday camp, which will need overseeing, but I do have a deputy to whom I can delegate, allowing me two weeks off. On balance, we feel the dates would work for us, with a bit of juggling, and we would like to accept your kind offer.

With much love,

Emma x

Seeing it from her mum's point of view now, Libby handed

back the phone. 'It doesn't explain how she's affording this holiday, though.'

'The money's either come from a dear dead aunt we never knew about, or she's marrying a millionaire.' Emma sliced the air with her hand decisively. 'I'm hoping she's going to tell us she's stinking rich, and that she's going to BACS us a massive chunk of money each. And then Pat and I can build a resistance pool in our back garden for Eliot.' She chortled. 'Not that it would fit.'

'Nooo, you think?' Libby's thoughts ran riot with fantasies of their wealthy mother giving them handouts whenever they wanted something. She dreamt of adding an extension to their tiny terraced cottage for her knitting business. It would have floor-to-ceiling shelves stuffed with wools of every colour. And they'd lease-purchase a car that didn't break down every week. Maybe even a convertible. And they'd buy a puppy. She'd always wanted one.

'Remember how cagey she was about where she'd been the other week?' Emma continued. 'That's not the first time. Not that I'm policing where she's going or anything, but, you know, I wondered if she was internet-dating and didn't want to say – she's probably run out of octogenarians to snog in the village or something.'

'Stop it!' Libby laughed guiltily.

Patrick brought them down to earth. 'Or maybe she's been saving for years and has scraped just enough for the villa?'

'Her theatre pension can't be enough for even that,' Libby said.

'She's wilier than she makes out,' Patrick said enigmatically.

'Do you know something we don't, Patrick?' Emma asked, staring up at him.

'No, nothing,' he replied, pinching the end of his nose and shuffling his feet. 'I think we're getting ahead of ourselves, that's all. I'm sure the reality is much less interesting.'

'Ugh! So all I've got to look forward to is her flirting with the air steward and hearing her tell him about how much I screamed as a baby and how perfectly angelic Libby was?' Emma asked.

'Yup. I imagine that's as good as it's going to get,' Patrick replied.

The three of them grinned at each other. Libby quietly questioned whether Patrick was using his psychoanalyst's professional nous to gauge their mother, or whether he really did know something. Before she could ask him, the tannoy announced the boarding of flight BA724 to Nice. Emma hopped up and they followed her into the queue.

Once they were in the sky, looking out on to a billowy platform of pinkish clouds, they ordered a glass of champagne each. Emma tried to lead their mother into a confession, but she wasn't forthcoming.

'Isn't this marvellous?' Nora bubbled. Her spirits had been lifted by her bonding with the steward, to whom she had predictably told stories of Emma's tantrums in supermarkets and Libby's cute cooing at old ladies. It seemed that Patrick, whose wise bald head was bobbing about four rows ahead, had read their mum better than they had. Like old times, she had simply wanted to have her daughters to herself and tell random strangers about their childhood, as though they had never grown up.

Softened by the champagne, Emma appeared to have relaxed a little.

When her mum nodded off for ten minutes, Libby's imagination began to run wild. She feared some French dude was going to show up at the villa and announce both his engagement to Nora and their move to Provence. Or worse. Perhaps she was moving somewhere even further away, with an Australian or

Saudi Arabian, embarking on an exotic retirement far away from them.

Projecting a future without her mum around the corner left Libby feeling panicked. Who would drop by for a cup of tea and put the world to rights with her? Who would she turn to for a hug when Connor was being difficult or absent, or when the girls were driving her mad? Who would bake her infamous inedible biscuits when she screwed up her life?

When her mum woke up, Libby squeezed her hand needily.

A smile spread slowly across Nora's sleepy face. She leant over and kissed Libby's cheek and lingered there, smelling her as though she were freshly baked pie. 'Hmm, I love you so much, my darling.' Her own cheek was cushiony, and Libby was comforted by its familiar give, and that specific smell of hers. Never of perfume, only of skin and hair and Mum. Without knowing anything concrete, she refused to contemplate her mother's new life.

Emma gestured to her champagne glass. 'Another one?'

Libby nodded enthusiastically. 'Why not.'

'Want one, Mum?' Emma said.

'Oh okay,' Nora said weakly, with a wan smile. 'You only live once.'

TWO

EMMA

Stepping off the plane and into the dense, burning heat of France with her mother by her side was like moving into a different dimension. The molecules in the air fought to keep Emma back, melting her skin, stuffing up her lungs. She kept walking across the tarmac, wanting to love the sunshine – and her mother – more, but feeling claustrophobic. It had been a long while since she had spent this much time with Nora, and her whole being was rejecting the closeness.

'Darling, are you okay?' her mum asked as they took their place at the end of the snaking queue for the rental car company. While Libby and Patrick were milling about in arrivals, keeping the kids out of the heat, Emma had opted to deal with the car, knowing that if she let Libby or Mum do it, the family would somehow end up squeezed into a three-wheeler with a sidecar, or in a stretch limo with fluorescent lights under the chassis.

'I'm fine, why?' she said.

'Darling, "fine" doesn't mean anything. What are you *feeling* right now?' Nora drew her shoulders back and pressed her fist into her diaphragm. How she loved drawing attention to her diaphragm!

'I'm feeling absolutely nothing, Mum. I'm standing in a queue in forty-degree heat, thinking about whether or not the car will have inbuilt sat nav or whether we'll have to use Google.'

'Whereas I'm simply grateful to be here with you,' her mother replied with a sad lilt.

Everything Nora said was like a spike in Emma's side, whether she meant it as one or not. To reconnect with the Emma her mother never saw or appreciated, she turned her thoughts back to work. Meditatively she envisaged her leather slip-ons planted firmly on the blue nylon carpet of her office, and recalled Samarth's tall, reassuring figure on the other side of her desk.

'Any feelings either way?' he had asked her, his hand slung in his pocket appealingly. He had been waiting to hear what she thought of his mid-morning snack suggestions for his Year 6 students during SATs week. On her desktop, alongside budget spreadsheets and a half-finished weekly newsletter, was the website image of the villa's swimming pool. As the azure blue caught her eye, an edgy, unspecified uneasiness slid through her. Outside in the playground, Eliot's head of red hair ducked a football. *There's something I want to tell everyone*, her mother had written in the email above the link.

Samarth stood there patiently. There was a sense that everything was flying at her, that she was having to bat it all away for a second while she ordered her thoughts. Under her chair, she pushed down the back of one of her shoes with the heel of the other, kicking it off absently. She considered sharing with Samarth her torn feelings about the holiday, telling him a few of the funny, ghastly stories about her mother to illustrate why she was reluctant to go. She thought better of it. If he had seen the shots of the vast bedrooms with views of the shimmering Mediterranean, he would have considered her very ungrateful.

'Sorry, yes,' she said, clicking the photograph closed while her toes felt about for her shoe. 'Let's walk and talk.' She had zipped past him and out of her office towards the gym to meet the caretaker about a leak.

'Orange squash and KitKats?' Samarth recapped, following her.

'Perhaps some healthier snacks instead, like those fruit twists, or some actual fruit, and apple juice, don't you think?'

'The thing is,' he said, stopping by the coat pegs, forcing her to stop too, ruffling his hair into an artful mess, 'they've been working so hard, and they'll be so excited about getting something they're not usually allowed.'

Despite the school governors' edict to hire more male teachers, Emma had not employed Samarth because he was a man, nor had she been swayed by his toffee-smooth skin and gorgeous open face. She had taken him on because he was by far the smartest and most enthusiastic teacher they had interviewed. But she missed his predecessor, the retired Mrs Bright – yes, her actual name – she missed her experienced pair of hands and her fleshy, rosy face that would never bring about an unnerving tummy flutter.

'No, it'll just give them a sugar rush and they'll crash horribly. And there's Michael's ADHD to think about,' she said, picking up a stray shoe, recognising it instantly as Elizabeth Clark's due to the ladybird studs. The adornments were against school regulation, but Emma turned a blind eye to them because of Elizabeth's home circumstances. She put the shoe neatly back in its designated cubbyhole. It would be a mistake to believe that Emma was black-and-white about rules. She valued her pupils as individuals who needed bespoke care.

'Emma, is everything okay today? You seem...' Samarth had paused to hang up a cardigan with a chewed sleeve. It belonged to Alfie Moore, and it reminded her to nominate him for the Kindness Award, having witnessed him taking such good care of Mary when she'd fallen over today.

'I seem what?'

'Preoccupied?'

'Not at all. I've got to meet John about this bloody leak, that's all,' she said, stalking away, leaving Samarth scratching the back of his hand. She felt his big, hopelessly kind brown eyes on her and imagined he would be judging her for being a meanie. Just as her mother would have.

Mrs Bright had never questioned her, fully understanding that it was Emma's job to be the sensible one, and sometimes the killjoy. How else had her school been awarded Ofsted Outstanding? It didn't matter how many times Samarth might flutter those thick black lashes over those insanely beautiful eyes of his – or how many imaginary sighs her mother might make in her mind – Emma would not compromise her standards.

She would maintain them on this holiday too. In the same way that she managed Michael's mood swings and Year 6's sugar intake and her giddiness about Samarth's eyes, she would keep up her barriers – or boundaries, as Patrick liked to call them – and protect herself from her mother's crafty ability to reach right inside her head and pull out her worst feelings about herself.

Feeling the scorch of the sun, she took out her Factor 50 suncream, smeared it on her arms and face and offered some to her mother.

'No, thank you, darling,' Nora said, shaking her head, whipping off her silly floppy hat and tilting her face up to the sky. 'I want all the vitamin D I can get.'

Emma was agog. All her life, her mother had hidden under wide brims or in the shade of tree boughs, wearing SPF 50 on cloudy days, remaining enviably unblemished and peachy pale.

Yet, here she was, challenging the sun to wrinkle her. Emma stared at her shiny, translucent skin and long wavy locks, unnerved by this exposing gesture, indecent in a way.

'Can I borrow that then?' she asked sensibly, pointing to the hat.

Her mother stepped closer and stuck it on Emma's head. Because of her ponytail, it didn't fit, so Nora gently pulled out Emma's hair elastic and tucked a loose lock behind her ear. 'There,' she said softly. Her fingers brushed her daughter's cheek. 'You look just like me now.'

A prickle of tears came sharply into Emma's eyes, strange and inexplicable. 'I wish,' she said, smiling shyly.

When her mother replied, there was a watery gurgle in her throat. 'I need to make a quick call. I'll be back in a min, okay, darling?'

And off she went, leaving Emma alone under the hat, feeling both loved and vulnerable. The emotional barriers she'd put in place only a few minutes before had been shoved over. At the first hurdle, she had stumbled. And yet she wasn't so sure it was wholly a bad thing.

THREE

NORA

'This is going to be harder than I thought.'

Not long to go.

'I think I'll feel better once we're all gathered in the villa.'

A captive audience.

'Not captives at all. I'm going to make sure it's the best two weeks of their lives.'

You're being very brave about this.

'You mustn't give anything away. They're already asking questions. And I need to do this in my own way.'

You can absolutely trust me.

'Yes, I suppose I can.'

Try to relax.

'Impossible.'

I love you.

'Oh. Goodness. Don't say that when you don't mean it.'

But I do mean it.

'That's awful.'

Call me when it's done.

'I'll say goodbye now, then.'

But he hung up before she could.

FOUR

EMMA

Nora returned from her phone call in bright spirits and spoke in loud, broken French to the orange-uniformed Frenchman, who had a higgledy-piggledy mouth with a gold tooth, and a gold badge embossed with his name, Gabon.

'I'm sorry, but we have no booking under that name,' he told them.

'What?' Emma cried. 'My mother booked a seven-seater, didn't you, Mum?'

'I did.'

'Do you have the email confirmation?' Gabon asked.

Emma searched through the emails on Nora's phone, but couldn't find the confirmation. This felt like the beginning of the end. The whole damned reason she hadn't wanted to come on this holiday. It would be one disaster after another, she just knew it. The villa probably didn't even exist!

'Mum, there isn't an email confirmation – in your *thousands* of unopened emails.'

'*Non?*' Nora said in her best flirty French.

Emma wanted to kill her. 'Do you have any more available cars?'

'You are lucky. We have two cars remaining, mesdames. An orange Peugeot Partner van and a Fiat 500. Unless you want to wait until this evening, when we'll have a fleet of Renault people carriers returning.'

Panic burst inside Emma. 'We can't wait until this evening!'

Mum spoke over her. 'Ooh, marvellous! I've always wanted to drive one of those darling little Fiats! *Quelle couleur?*'

'*Rouge, madame! C'est bon?*' Gabon tapped into his computer.

'But Mum, we need a people carrier.'

'The Peugeot? Is this big?' Nora asked in an outrageous French accent, widening her arms to explain 'big'. Then she giggled, and Emma winced, amazed that she could still embarrass her this much.

'For five,' Gabon replied, then added, 'You are two sisters, *non?*'

'*Vous êtes méchant, monsieur!*' Nora cackled.

He winked. 'Five seats in this Fiat is good, yes?'

'I think so. Me, Libby and the girls can go in the Fiat, and you and Patrick and Eliot can go in the van.'

'Rent two cars?' Emma asked.

'Why not?'

'Because it costs twice as much?'

Gabon clicked his tongue and twisted his screen to show her the figures. 'A little more, *oui.*'

'It's a ridiculously expensive way of doing it,' Emma said.

A reasonably priced sensible people carrier was what she'd asked her mother to book. She glanced over to the other rental company. Its metal shutter was down. Behind them, people were waiting, hot and bothered. 'Oh God, okay, we'll take whatever you've got. But I'm not happy about it. I'll be complaining to your managers.'

'Boff!' Nora said. 'Ignore her, monsieur. *Nous aimons la France.* We love everything about it.'

She was flirting with the man, and Emma was now convinced that their hunch was right: that she was in love with someone hopelessly inappropriate, married or famous or uberwealthy. Or all three? When Nora was in a relationship, she was always happier. Sex was high on her agenda. She'd always talked about it with a cringeworthy openness, insisting it was what made life worth living.

One of Emma's earliest memories was of walking in on her mother having sex with her boyfriend of the month. Their naked bodies had seemed to be locked in an angry tussle. Remembering it gave her a little shudder. She herself would never dream of putting Eliot through anything like that. Although, conveniently, she and Patrick didn't have a sex life to walk in on. This thought was followed by an ill-timed and thrilling image of falling into bed with Samarth. Her Year 6 teacher! *Eliot's* teacher! She decided she was an even worse person than her mother thought she was, and blamed Nora for that too.

Patrick laughed his head off when he saw the metallic orange minivan. 'We'll be like French farmers. *Très authentique!* I love it!'

'Can we just not do the whole franglais thing? It'll drive me mad.'

'Hon-he-hon! *Mais non, ma chérie.* You no like my *français*?'

Emma tried not to laugh. '*Tu es un cornichon,*' she said.

'This is a super-embarrassing car, Mum.' Eliot slouched down in the back, putting his swimming goggles on his forehead so that it looked like he had two sets of eyes.

After half an hour, Emma turned off the autoroute. They trundled along the satisfyingly straight rural roads listening to

French pop on the radio. She had decided it was good to tune
Eliot's ear into the language. But the station kept going fuzzy,
and Emma blamed the bent aerial and then, inevitably, her
mother. Everything about the vehicle annoyed her.

She checked in her rear-view mirror to make sure Libby was
still following them. The sight made her smile. The four of
them looked huge inside their tiny red car. It was like the illus-
tration in the story Emma read to her reception children about
four elephants squeezed into a Mini.

'I can't wait to see the villa!' Eliot yelped from the back
suddenly.

'It's hard to believe it's going to be as amazing as those
photos,' Emma said.

'I bet it is!' Eliot stuck his head through the gap between the
seats.

'Sit back, monkey,' Emma said.

'She's certainly picked a lovely part of the world.' Patrick
sighed contentedly.

However lovely the south of France was, Emma couldn't
relax until they arrived at the villa. And she couldn't switch off
from work. She was constantly wondering how Samarth would
get on with the logistics of the summer camp next week, and
hoped he would contact her if he was worried about anything,
even if he thought it was a small thing. If you saw small problems as warnings, you could stave off the bigger ones.

A flash of her mother turning her face to the sun earlier
came to mind. A small thing – it was only suncream – but it was
the abandon of it that had rattled her. Her mum didn't do abandon, especially when it came to sunscreen and wrinkle preven-
tion. She worked hard at her appearance. The way she moved
was like a dancer: controlled, meticulous, designed to look
effortless.

It was true that Nora was still quite beautiful, and it
wouldn't be a surprise if some old French creep had fallen for

her. A little churlishly, Emma felt their mum owed them to *not* run off with someone, to stick around in her dotage, be there for her grandchildren in the way she hadn't been there for Libby and Emma as children; make up for lost time. She totted up the many au pairs they'd had during Nora's touring days with various theatre companies. At least two a year for ten years. As a costume designer, their mother had spent many months away. Emma and Libby had liked their Eastern European or South American carers, who had been fun and pretty – except Vangelija from Macedonia, who had been surly (and pretty) – but they had been no substitute for their mum. Nobody was. Even though she had always been a royal pain in Emma's backside.

After getting lost a few times, they slowed down alongside a yellow-painted stucco house with a low terracotta roof, and pulled over outside its black metal gate, on which a tanned man in a suit leant. Frédéric, the rental agent, she guessed.

'Are we here?' Eliot squealed.

Mortified by their van, Emma introduced herself to Frédéric through the window. He smiled and waved them towards the double garage further along, pointing a clicker. The words 'Villa Papillon', painted in white italics, slowly disappeared upwards with the black roller door. Libby pulled in next to them. Before the engines were even off, the kids had jumped out, yapping like puppies.

'Oh my God,' Patrick breathed as they walked out of a side door from the garage.

The villa was extraordinary. It was carved into the cliff face, and its three storeys of Roman-style arched windows and balconies towered over the sea. A series of crazy-paved terraces jutted out at angles over the water: one with a small pool and a pool house, another with two loungers pointed at the sun,

another holding an outdoor dining table sheltered by a semicircular tunnel of cream canvas.

A flight of stone steps carved out of the rock wound down to
the bay, disappearing into the water. Emma imagined walking
down them until her head was submerged, stepping directly
onto the ocean floor in a wondrous secret underworld.

The kids ran towards it – even Amber, who generally
slouched – stopping to lean over the flimsy railings and squint at
the view. The sun was low, ready to drop behind the sea, which
rippled and glistened in the bay. The waves slipped up and
down their private jetty and lapped against the red rocks.

Nora stood between Emma and Libby and wrapped her
arms around their waists. Putting her head on Libby's shoulder,
she said, 'What do you think, darlings?'

'Out of this world,' Libby exclaimed.

Emma exhaled. 'I can't quite believe we're going to be
staying here.'

Nora glanced at her with a brief arch of one eyebrow. 'Not
bad for a toyshop owner's daughter, is it?'

Emma refused to rise to it, and instead broke away and
hurried to follow Frédéric, who was trying a series of keys in the
lock of the lavender-blue front door, demurely positioned on the
side of the house and sheltered by a striped awning. As she
waited for him to slowly work through each key, Emma decided
that this villa couldn't possibly be their holiday home. Her mum
had made a mistake. They weren't the sort of family to stay in a
place like this, even if it was only for two weeks.

Finally, one of the keys worked and he showed them inside.

It was beautifully cool, the perfect antidote to the hellish-
ness of queuing in the heat.

They took their shoes off and left sweaty footprints across
the limestone floor, following Frédéric, nodding as he explained
the various modern features of the house: how to work the television built into the kitchen units; how to operate the power

shower settings, ranging from 'massage' to 'light rain'; how to open the windows in the gymnasium. Various sitting rooms could be found on each level, where there were plumped sofas or chaises longues, arched windows, wrought-iron balconies, whitewashed walls and sea views.

Emma raised her eyebrows and stole a look at Patrick. He was standing with one hand resting on his bald head, completely flummoxed. They had all seen the photographs of the villa, but nothing compared to being inside it. Nora added her own snippets of information, but the rest of them remained largely silent, apart from the odd awestruck 'Wow!'

In each room, Emma was expecting the appearance of a surprise guest who might offer a large manicured hand for them to shake, revealing a Seamaster wristwatch, and introduce himself as their holiday benefactor.

Cautiously she peered into the master bedroom, which took up the whole of the top floor. There was a four-poster bed and an adjoining bathroom with a double sink, gold taps and a terra-cotta marble bath. Still no sign of a surprise suitor. Nora put her bag on the bed, claiming it as hers. She winked mysteriously at Emma, perhaps enjoying her bafflement, and Emma again resisted the urge to ask her how the hell they could afford to stay in a place like this.

On the floor below Nora's, there was an extraordinarily large corner room with a balcony that wrapped around the two banks of windows. It was so beautiful, her heart fluttered. 'Can Patrick and I have this one?' she asked her sister.

'Of course,' Libby said.

Next door, there was a smaller adjoining child's room, with two single beds.

'That can be yours, Eliot. Then we're right here through this secret little door.'

Emma glanced at Patrick. He jangled some change in his pocket and his gaze flicked over the sumptuous bed. In a room like this, some might think it a marital crime to lie chastely next to one another. Emma dreaded the effort it would take to have sex. After so long going without, it would be weird. Almost icky. She wanted to relax. Eliot being nearby and within earshot would put a stop to it.

Amber chose the bedroom across the hall from them. It had an en suite bathroom, and hanging above the cushioned headboard of the super-king bed, there was a vast acrylic canvas: a modern, impressionistic portrait of a girl, whose pale mouth and skin blended with the background, disappearing almost completely. Her eyes were piercing blue and seemed to stare right at Emma, as though seeking to communicate a message that she couldn't utter from her almost-there lips. Emma tried not to see her as a knowing onlooker, silently aware of great change around the corner.

Twisting down a circular staircase, they trooped to the lower level, where they were shown the gym and the two remaining bedrooms. These were smaller, but still bright and elegantly decorated, sandwiched next to each other. Libby and Hazel took them. Nobody said anything about the clattering noise from the air conditioning.

When they had been little, Emma had always bagsied the top bunk and Libby had never complained. If Libby refused to fight for what she wanted, what was Emma supposed to do about it? Maybe she liked these rooms, separate from the rest of them. Who knew what went on in that dreamy head of hers?

After Frédéric had left, Nora said to the kids, 'Get your cozzies on! Patrick's already in. I want to hear your bombs from here!' The three of them scuttled off to get changed.

Peeved that Patrick had gone in without her, Emma said, 'He didn't waste any time, did he?'

'Relax, darling. He's allowed a swim without your permission. Ha ha!'

Ha-bloody-ha, Emma thought.

'Supper is at seven,' Nora declared. 'Why don't you two unpack and relax for a bit, and give yourselves time to get ready.'

Emma checked her watch. 'But that doesn't give us much time to go to the supermarket.'

'I've got a chef for tonight,' their mother said casually.

'A *chef?*' Libby and Emma spluttered in unison.

'It didn't cost as much as you think. Anyway, I don't want anyone fussing around the kitchen or having to clear up tonight. It'll be too much to cope with on top of everything else.' She reached out to Emma and Libby and put a hand on each of their forearms, squeezing gently. Emma guessed it was meant to be a reassuring gesture, but it was loaded.

'What is it, Mum?' she asked. She didn't want to wait a second more for Nora's news.

In the breeze from the open window, her mother's white-blonde hair fluttered behind her shoulders and her golden-brown eyes looked bigger and rounder than ever. 'I want to tell you when we're all together. I don't want any drama.'

Nora Fitz? Not wanting *drama?* It was unheard of, and Emma mentally shrank away from its connotations.

'Great. Fine. I might have a bath then,' she said, avoiding Libby's eye, picturing her cheeks rosy with anxiety.

Whatever the news was tonight, Emma would cope better than Libby. Not that it was a competition.

I'll be fine. I'm always fine, she thought.

And she'd look after Libby, too.

She had spent her whole childhood withstanding their mother's crises: the divorce, the unsuitable boyfriends, the ever-rotating au pairs. And look where she was now. A head teacher! You didn't get to that position by being porous and weak.

When she went upstairs to unpack, she started to obsessively fret about the summer camp at school, which she couldn't imagine running smoothly without her. Breaking a promise to herself that she would stay away from her computer, she emailed Samarth about a few things he might have forgotten.

By the time she was out of the bath, she was already more relaxed. And Samarth had emailed back.

Don't worry, Emma. I've got this. Let go! Be free! You deserve the break more than anyone I know. Sam x

Let go! Be free! Cheeky bugger! She grinned to herself. She couldn't help enjoying the kiss and the shortening to 'Sam' as a sign-off, and she appreciated his concern. There were times when she thought he was the only person in the world who truly understood how hard she worked to give those kids the best education money couldn't buy. And she didn't mean in terms of grades only. She meant holistically, socially, emotionally.

Now that Patrick specialised in psychoanalysing teens, he was weighed down with the daily emergencies of his young patients' heartbreaking mental health problems, and barely noticed how important and challenging it was to keep healthy children happy too.

Emma stepped onto the balcony and looked out on to the silvery water, taking in a great lungful of warm Mediterranean air. A bottle of champagne had been left in a bucket on the table. She popped the cork and poured herself a glass, feeling quite decadent. Go ahead, Mother! Entertain us with your big reveal! she thought.

She would try to sit back and enjoy the performance.

When she stepped back into the room to get changed into the dress she'd laid out on top of the sheets, she noticed how huge and comfortable and luxurious the bed looked. Maybe sex with Patrick wouldn't be such a bad idea after all, she thought naughtily.

FIVE

NORA

I put on my make-up with extra care, using more blusher than usual and a new gold eyeshadow. On the dressing table, carefully arranged, were the mementos I had brought from home. A silver hairbrush that had once been my mother's, an enamel pill box, a triptych of photographs of my girls and my grandchildren, and an ordinary-looking exercise book, with bent corners and some scribbles across the marble-patterned cover. This last item appeared the least interesting, yet it was the most important of all. I laid a hand on top of it before sliding it into a shallow drawer of the table.

Eliot knocked, then came in and sat cross-legged on the stool next to me. It was lovely to have him all to myself for a change. He had brought his swimming goggles and plucked at their rubber strap. His red hair was cut into a sensible short back and sides, reminding me of snapshots of my older cousins in the fifties. In the sun, his white, almost blue skin had already freckled into large blotches, which were too clunky for his delicate features.

'Fancy a cheeky swim before supper?' I asked him. It would be one way of putting off the task ahead.

'I don't really feel like it, Nor-Nor. Do you mind?'

I smiled at him. 'My darling boy, of course I don't.'

Quietly he watched me apply my mascara.

'Your hands are all shaky,' he said.

'Silly old hands,' I laughed.

'My hands go like that before I do my races.'

'Ah, yes. A marvellous actor friend of mine – he's dead now...' I paused to recollect.

Eliot squeezed my hand, saying simply, 'Sorry he died.'

'He had a good life, sweetheart.' I remembered his side-splittingly funny rendition of a rude joke about a drunk man and a twenty-pound note, and I contemplated my own passing and what would linger in people's memories about me when I was dead. The exercise book in the drawer by my knees came to mind.

Not that.

Better would be my costumes memorialised in the stills taken on the productions I'd worked on. Mostly they were black and white, printed up in the newspapers alongside reviews of the plays. I would sometimes be credited, some-times remembered. When my father had been alive, I had shown him them and he had remarked that they were like the little dresses I had hand-sewn once for the dolls in the toyshop. It hadn't been a compliment. I shuddered at the memory.

'I'm sorry, petal, but it's not always about what *you* want,' he had said, stumbling over the stack of games in the window display to whip the dolls out of sight, comically fast. In the yellow light of the anti-glare window film, I had sobbed angry tears as I pushed their china limbs back into their original dresses, into the hideous frilly lace, confused that Dad hadn't been able to appreciate how much more fashionable and modern mine were. For the first time in my life, I had looked down on him for not recognising what was obvious to me. At ten years old, I had felt superior to him. Which was odd, when you thought about it.

I patted Eliot's hand. 'You're a sweet darling, d'you know that?' I said, and kissed his knuckles, inhaling the familiar scent of chlorine. 'Well, anyway, this actor chap told me how to stop stage fright, or in your case, swim gala fright. You have to notice your breath and slow it down. Do it with me now, Eliot. In through the nose, that's right, hold it, and out through the mouth. And again. Focus on all the positive things, really bring them to life in your head and say, "All will be well".'

And I did the same: the sea's eternal movement, my grand-children's beautiful smiles, my two daughters' big hearts. My gaze turned away from the past and also from what lay ahead this evening, and I felt at one with the moment.

'Hold your hand out now, Nor-Nor,' Eliot ordered.

'Steady as a rock. See? Now off you go and get ready for supper.'

After I'd shooed Eliot out – my gorgeous boy – I dressed in my stiff white cotton kaftan edged with gold brocade, which made me feel like a film star. I'd bought it decades ago with my own money – a tenner – for the main character to wear in a fringe production at the Finborough. Or was it the Union? I can't remember. Either way, the play had been written by a young bipolar playwright who'd killed herself two days after her rave reviews came out. The disappointment of success has brought many to their knees! But depression was commonplace in the industry. I was so lucky never to have suffered from it, and felt desperate for those many talented friends of mine who had struggled with it all their lives. My father had always warned me that life could be cruel, as it had been to him.

As I stood in front of the mirror, I closed my eyes and breathed in through the nose and out through the mouth before assessing my reflection. My hair was pushed back, still damp at the roots, and my skin shone from the moisture in the air.

All will be well.

By the time I'd gathered myself and mentally whizzed through the key points of my speech, I was a little late downstairs. I passed Emma in the kitchen and could instantly tell she had low blood sugar. She had that furtive look in her eyes and was hovering around Maria, the old Italian chef, who wore a pinny and had large bosoms.

Emma was pretending to help, and I wondered whether Maria was pretending she couldn't understand English. I knew I would if I were her.

How I had struggled when Emma had come into the world; how exhausting and angry she had been from the moment she had first drawn breath: red gummy screams, eyes fused shut, dry with fury, as though she were the only baby in the world to know hunger and injustice. Then, typically, perversely, after all that protest, she would not take the breast. My beautiful breast, my young swollen breast that I was offering into her tiny mouth to give her my milk, my sustenance, my lifeblood. She'd fuss and twist as though it disgusted her, as though I wasn't living up to her expectations, as though I was her first and terrible disappointment. When she did finally latch on, when I was in tears and fearful of her starving to death, she'd suck from me with that greedy, urgent draw, draining me of everything I had. I swear when she got what she wanted, she radiated self-satisfaction; contented finally, having made me cry.

'Come on, Emma darling, let's go and sit with the others.'

As though in a dream, I descended the steps with my difficult daughter, down to the first-level terrace.

'You okay, Mum?' Emma asked.

I must have paused on one of the steps. 'Sorry, yes. Ha!'

The table we moved towards stood on a rocky outcrop that had been tamed and levelled. Palm trees and pot plants and floral climbers softened the edges. Smart black and white floor tiles were underfoot. Outdoor lamps and candles in tall glass holders lent the scene a stage-like ambience, a theatrical setting onto which I would tread heavily.

I sat at the head. The table was laid with a cream tablecloth and bone-handled antique silverware. A stone balustrade surrounded us snugly and the canopy curved above us. It was quite magical, like being out at sea on a yacht. My heart was beating fast, making me feel quite sick. Sicker than usual. I'd wanted everything to be absolutely perfect, but now I had what I wanted, I wasn't sure it was right. It all appeared too lovely for what I was about to say.

These darling faces of mine sent shivers of love through me. I watched them eagerly, greedily, casting my mind back to them as yelling, squirming babies – except Patrick, of course, whom I hadn't known – and I longed to stop time right here and now.

To my right, Libby's mat and knife and fork were skew-whiff, shoved aside to make room for her elbows. Her chin was buried in the heels of her hands as she listened earnestly to Patrick, who sat on her right. I brushed my hand down her fleshy spine so that she sat up straight, which she did without breaking her concentration. But there was little I could do about her hair. It was what we might call 'big' hair, wild loopy curls, almost growing outwards rather than down. She refused to tame it. But her cheeks were soft, full and shiny like a baby's, with two gorgeous dimples and ridiculously long eyelashes.

Emma sat on my left. She had the rounded Fitz face, but her curves were muscular, honed and hardened by self-discipline. I slyly questioned whether all the running was for the benefit of her Year 6 teacher – whatshisname – whom she talked about rather too often. I'd seen him at Eliot's assemblies and couldn't blame her for having a crush. When it came to weaknesses for pretty young men, I was a fine one to talk. Guilt punched at my heart, interrupting its rhythm.

She had pulled her chair close to Eliot, smothering him as usual – helicopter parenting, as they call it these days. Eliot was leaning away from her and over Hazel to watch something on Amber's phone. Amber and Hazel's faces were wonderfully rosy and squidgy – Fitz through and through – and both had huge bundles of hair, but Amber had Connor's darker colouring. I was glad Connor wasn't here.

Please. Stop time. I spoke to the stars above me and the sea below, to the universe, asking them to make an exception for me. For my family. Look at them, for God's sake! They were worth bending astrophysics for, weren't they? I cowered at the vastness of everything, knowing it was no good to beg. How could I do this to them? How could this be happening to me?

By the time Maria had bustled about and served up the bouillabaisse and crusty bread, I had lost my appetite, in spite of it being my favourite dish. It wasn't unusual these days. Even when I did eat, I might throw it up or end up on the loo. I'd spent the last few months making sure I visited Libby before or after mealtimes, so that she wouldn't notice. She thought I was dieting to look good in my swimsuit. I'd told so many lies to my darling Libby.

My hands fluttered and jigged so much I knocked over the bottle of red, which Emma caught expertly before it spilled.

I noticed how she and Libby glanced at each other. They had discussed me, I knew it. Emma was the one to launch right in. 'So, Mum. What's this secret of yours?'

'Oh darling, nothing. I mean, it's not nothing, but I'm, well, let's just enjoy pudding first.'

'Mum, you can tell us anything, you know that, don't you?' Libby said.

Sweet thing, with her big weepy eyes. I was her everything. As a baby, she had reached her chubby arms out to me and had never let me go, had never wanted to be held by other people, had clung to my legs as soon as she could walk. She didn't have a bad bone in her body. A lump formed in my croaky old throat. 'Yes, I do know that. And I do have...' The words caught.

A horrible rap song blared out from Amber's phone. The children giggled and Emma snapped, 'Can we have phones away now, please?'

It was said with such force that Amber stared agog at her aunt and then at her mum, looking for salvation. For a change, Libby didn't offer it up. She said, 'Yes, come on, Amber. Turn it off.' Amber sulked.

I waited for a hush before saying, 'Darlings, I've got some rather tiresome news.'

Their attentive faces broke me. My resolve wobbled. But not enough to stop me. I'd fight on. I had been brought up to tell the truth. Cowardice wasn't an option.

'We're here... well, partly we're here to swim and laugh and dance, right, kids?' My laugh fell flat. All eyes were on me, glinting in the candlelight. There was a stilted, nightmarish breath-holding. I would plough on. 'The thing is, and I don't want you to be sad or to worry about me, but I'm afraid it's all rather boring. Boring, or, I suppose, grisly. Not grisly in a gory way, more that it's... Oh gosh, this is not going how I wanted it to go.' The words I'd planned out scrambled into a mess in my head. So I just said it how it was. 'Look. I'm afraid I've got cancer, darlings. That's the thing.'

The horror etched on each and every dear face seemed to extinguish the candlelight that had danced innocently in their eyes only two minutes before.

'What?' Emma said, as if she genuinely hadn't heard me.

I took a sip of red to fortify myself. 'I've got cancer. Stomach cancer.'

There was more to tell them, but their dismayed silence was a body blow.

Emma sounded desperate when she said, 'But you don't look ill, Mum.'

'You look lovely, actually,' Libby said, a little raspy.

'Looks can be deceiving,' I replied.

I glanced away from them, suddenly quite overcome, blinking back the tears, hearing the silence around me. I suppose it was to be expected that they'd doubt what they didn't want to believe, but I had imagined immediate hugs and sweetness and sympathy.

'What stage is it at?' Emma said, barely audibly.

'The doctors said that...' I looked at Eliot's pale face and paused.

Libby interrupted. 'Maybe we should talk about this later.'

And Emma looked over at the children, checking herself. 'Yes.'

'No,' I said, in a deep, gravelly voice. 'Sorry,' I added, more gently. 'I want *everyone* to know the truth.' That last word was a shard in my throat, and I coughed, spluttering into my napkin. Libby stood up and stroked my back and told Hazel to refill the water jug in the kitchen. 'Libby, I'm fine. I'm really absolutely fine.' Already they were treating me differently. I hated it. 'Coughing is not a symptom of stomach cancer, for God's sake!'

'Go on, Hazel. I'd like some too,' Libby said.

'No, we don't need any bloody water.' I slammed the table. Eliot jumped. Hazel froze on the spot, with the jug hanging from her hand, dripping its leftovers onto the tiles. 'Please sit down,' I said. She did as I asked.

The stiff fronds of the palm trees scratched and twisted against each other in the wind, and I recalled a line from a play. Breaking the silence, I spoke on an exhale. '"Do you see that tree? It is dead but it still sways in the wind with the others. I think it would be like that with me. That if I died I would still be part of life in one way or another", and so I—'

'You're going to *die*?' Eliot interrupted.

'It's a quote from a play,' Patrick said, calmly, as though this answered his son's question. Eliot ignored him and stared right at me, his tongue flicking into the corners of his lips nervously, his skin glowing whiter than ever. The red of his hair seemed to burn like furious flames from his brain. The hurt in his eyes dragged me into his soul, kicking and screaming with remorse. It was his darling face that stopped me from going through with the rest of my speech, and my plan for full disclosure instantly disintegrated.

I backtracked. 'No, no, darling! No! I'm not going to *die*. I'll have some chemo, scare you with my bald head and be absolutely fine. I didn't mean to worry everyone so much. I was just quoting from *The Three Sisters*. Because it's beautiful, don't you think?'

Unable to look any of them in the eye, I dropped my gaze to my lap, over which I smoothed the folds of material, creased where the cotton had been clamped between my knees.

'It's a brilliant play. I'll take you to see it one day, Eliot,' Emma said, her tone dead.

Eliot pushed back his chair and stood rod-straight. 'I'm not feeling very well.' He darted off and Emma rose to go after him.

I blocked her before she could get any further. 'I'll go,' I said.

She hesitated. I expected combat. Her gaze was searching, mistrustful, but she stepped aside, sighing. 'Yes, okay.'

My concern for Eliot, as much as I loved him, wasn't the only reason I left the table. I'd lost my nerve. It would be impossible to tell them absolutely everything tonight.

SIX

LIBBY

'I really hope Eliot's all right in there with Mum,' Emma said, looking up at the villa accusingly.

Libby was patient with her. 'Why wouldn't he be, Em?'

'It's just...' Emma got up.

Tugging her down gently by the sleeve, Libby said, 'They'll be fine.'

Finding out why her sister was anxious about them was beyond Libby. She was trying to hold it together, feeling a cold stickiness in the folds of her elbows and behind her knees, thrown sideways by her mother's news. Her head had been shaken and rattled; dozens of questions were fighting for space in there.

She moved into Eliot's vacated chair next to her daughters. Amber was tossing her switched-off phone from one hand to the other and Hazel was staring at her doing it.

'Are you okay, sweethearts?' she asked them, stilling Amber's hands. Her elder daughter's eyes flicked up to meet hers briefly, and in that split second Libby saw the fear. Instant shadows appeared beneath them, but her pale, full lips didn't move to speak.

Hazel sniffed, scooting closer to Libby. 'Will Granny Nor-Nor be okay?'

Libby's heart pounded in her chest as she told them what they would want to hear. 'By the sounds of it, she'll have some chemotherapy to zap all the bad cells and make them healthy, and then she'll be back on form, driving your Auntie Emma mad for decades to come.' She winked at her sister.

Emma found a way to laugh. 'She does drive me totally crackers. But I love her to bits.'

'She's the best granny ever,' Hazel said, nuzzling into Libby's arm.

Amber said, 'Can I get down? I need to speak to my friends.'

'Stay, please, darling,' Libby urged gently. 'Talk to us.'

'I'm fine, Mum. They'll think I'm airing them.' Before Libby could reply, she was off, bent over her phone as she went.

Patrick topped up their glasses. Hazel glugged her water down and begged Libby to let her watch a film on her iPad. 'Please!'

'Off you go then,' Libby sighed. What more could she tell them? She was as poleaxed as they were. My God, Mum has cancer, she thought.

'They're being ages. I'm going inside,' Emma said, getting up again, frowning at their mother's bedroom window.

Less tolerantly than before, Libby said, 'Why are you so worried about them?'

'Mum's upset. And ever since Spain, I don't know, I worry more.'

'He doesn't remember that holiday,' Patrick said firmly.

'Trouble is, the rest of us do,' Emma replied.

Libby certainly did.

'Two for poo!' Eliot had yelled gleefully as he had stepped across the threshold of the poky hacienda, proud of the eye-watering smell coming from his pants. At two and a half, he had not been fully potty-trained, which was normal enough for his age, but Granny Nor-Nor had decided to take it on herself to get him there. Every time it had happened, she'd lifted his slippery little body out of the algae-edged above-ground pool, dangled him over it, then shoved him towards the poo. She'd blamed Emma for being too soft on him. Libby had felt so sorry for both her sister and Eliot, and had helped Emma scoop out the poos before their mum could spot them. Sometimes with nervous giggling.

'It was awful on every level,' she said now. 'But it was such a long time ago.' She was surprised Emma was holding onto it.

Emma rubbed the corner of her forehead. 'I never told you the full story, did I?'

Patrick groaned. 'Is this really the time for potty-gate?'

'Well, she can't be trusted alone with him,' Emma shot back.

'Mum, you mean?' Libby asked, half laughing. 'Are you serious?'

Patrick sustained a long, loaded look with Emma, exchanging a private marital communication.

'It doesn't matter now.' Emma swept her wine glass up and put it to her lips. 'But if they're not down in five minutes, you go up, Patrick.'

Libby let it go for the time being. Gathering details of this past feud between her mother and sister was not a priority. Her brain was full enough. *Oh my God. Oh. My. God. Mum has cancer.* She couldn't take it in. She could hardly believe it.

'I'm going down to the water for a bit,' Emma said, pouring more wine.

Libby and Patrick watched her jog down the steps.

'Are you going to abandon me too, Patrick?' Libby joked. It was unfair on Emma, but she was trying to find lightness from somewhere, desperate to smother the stinging terror that was scrabbling around inside her.

'Now that you've played the victim card, how could I?' he teased back.

Libby lifted her glass to his. 'Cheers. To the worst announcement ever. And curses to the no-show of the dishy French dude!'

With a sad, sympathetic smile, he put his glass to hers. 'Curses indeed.'

They sat quietly for a while. The sound of the cicadas was a reminder of how far away from home they were. The villa seemed to be teetering on the very edge of the world. Its luxury had become a shadowy version of what it had been half an hour before.

At last Patrick spoke. 'Ever since Spain, we've held your mum at arm's length, tended to control how much she sees of Eliot. We invite her to his galas or class assemblies or afternoon tea out somewhere nice, that kind of thing, but it has been monitored and managed heavily. And way more formal than your mother would have liked.'

'Oh.' Libby was taken aback. 'I didn't know.'

'I regret it now.' Patrick sighed. 'Now that she's ill.' His almost-gone hair and his muted skin tone gave him a transparent, ghostly appearance. He looked out to Emma by the water. Her toes were dipped in, and the top of her head shone with a silver moonlit halo.

'But Mum worships Eliot.'

'They've put each other on a pedestal, but it's not cosy, you know?'

'I'm not sure she was ever going to be a cosy granny.'

Patrick paused before responding, pressing his thumbnail into his bottom lip. 'I think Emma overreacted. After Spain.'

Libby waited for him to explain what had happened, beyond what she knew already, but he didn't, and she didn't ask. Her mum's cancer was all she could cope with.

She counted back the months to the first time Nora had unnecessarily over-explained her absence on a Tuesday afternoon. She'd come out with a bungled story, exaggerated hand gestures, little eye contact and a louder than usual voice, as though projecting to the back of the theatre. It was obvious now that it had been a performance.

'It must be over three months that she's known. How did I miss the signs?'

Patrick's eyes shot up to her mum's window. 'We all missed them.'

Libby chewed on the soft inside of a piece of bread left by Amber on her side plate. 'There have been days she's looked a bit peaky in the mornings, but I just put it down to tiredness because she said she hadn't been sleeping well. I mean, who does these days?'

'She's lost quite a bit of weight, too.'

'I see her too often to notice,' Libby lied defensively, ashamed of herself for ignoring her mother's weight loss. In the light of his confession, it came out like a rebuke. 'Sorry... I just meant, Emma's at school and so busy, and...' She trailed off.

Patrick smiled at her kindly. 'Libby. I know what you meant.'

Libby blushed. 'I feel so stupid. I should have asked Mum more questions.'

'Don't be hard on yourself. Your mother is a master of deception.' His eyes wandered upwards for another quick scan of the window. His and Emma's watchfulness was beginning to spook Libby.

'You know, it's been well over five minutes. Do you want to go up and check on him?'

'I might, actually. Do you mind?' He stretched his arms above his head.

'Not at all.'

'The micromanaging is ingrained,' he admitted self-depre-catingly, pushing his chair in. Holding onto it still, he turned his attention to the lone figure of Emma by the water. 'Best to give her some space, you think?' he asked.

'Wise.'

'Everyone's probably a bit frazzled tonight. Try not to over-think everything, okay? We'll get some hard facts to work with tomorrow.'

'Yes. Thanks, Patrick.'

Her overthinking was already in full flow, yet she appreci-ated Patrick's recognition of her tendency to worry.

'Hard facts sound good.' Emma's voice made Libby jump. Her sister was suddenly behind her, ascending the steps.

Patrick stopped. 'Hi. I was just off to check on Eliot.'

'Oh. I was going to do that.'

'It's fine, honestly. I'm ready for bed now anyway. And you two probably need to talk.'

Again that look between them that reminded Libby of the mention of Spain.

'Call me if he needs me, won't you?' Emma said to Patrick. With an anxious expression on her face, she let him go. Then she sat down opposite Libby, poured the last of the wine and sighed. 'So, about Mum. We need to find out (a) what stage it's at,' she counted off the list on her fingers, '(b) how long she's known, (c) whether she's having an operation to remove the tumour, and (d) how long her chemo plan is. And what the prognosis is, in terms of recovery and survival.'

With each bent-back finger, Libby felt incrementally reas-sured that Emma would take charge. Her own fingers trembled as she reached for her wine glass. 'Tonight?' she asked. The mere thought of hearing the truth terrified her. She took out her needles and neon-pink wool and continued with Hazel's sweater.

'That's incredible,' Emma said.

At first, amidst the general despondency, Libby wondered what her sister was referring to. Her needles had a life of their own and she'd forgotten she was in charge of them. 'Thanks,' she said, stretching the knitting out.

'When are you going to get that Instagram page up and running?'

'Amber started one for me a while back.'

'And?'

'I don't know, I never look.'

'Ugh, Libs. You're hopeless.' Emma launched into one of her sisterly lectures about how Libby should set up a proper knitting business; how to do this and that and how not to do the other. As usual, Libby listened vaguely and nodded, while waiting patiently for the moment she could change the subject.

During this well-meant but unwelcome careers advice, she caught sight of their mum and Eliot waving down at them from his bedroom balcony. Nora had her arm around her grandson's shoulder protectively. His face was squashed into her bosom.

'Emma? Don't you think it's time to put him to bed?' she called down.

Emma snorted good-naturedly. 'Don't go anywhere. I'll maybe bring Mum back down and we can talk properly.'

'Sending vibes of patience and forgiveness,' Libby whispered, grinning.

After Emma had gone inside, Libby continued knitting. Enjoying the peace, she stared out to sea as she worked the rows and contemplated life.

There was an empty seat next to her where Connor should have been. She pictured him there, handsome, almost beautiful, looking good for his fifty-one years, with his shoulder-length hair shot with grey, his weathered cheekbones and coat-hanger shoulders. He would be patting the oversized pockets of his artisanal cotton jacket, permanently littered with crumpled Rizlas and the grit of old marijuana leaves. He'd probably roll a cigarette right about now. But he wasn't in the seat. He wasn't there for them, for her. He was nowhere near, too busy catching waves on a faraway beach. Thousands of miles away at such a crucial time. It was typical of him to somehow unconsciously pre-empt a massive family crisis and conveniently sidestep it. She wanted to scream the news across the water at him and make him feel bad for not being there with her.

Emma returned to the table alone.

'Everything okay?' Libby asked.

'Mum got a call. She said she'd come down in a minute.'

'Oh, good.' But she wasn't sure it was. An overwhelming weight of tiredness cloaked her. 'Was Eliot upset?'

Emma pressed two fingers into the space between her eyebrows as she sat down next to Libby. 'He seemed fine, actually. Apparently Mum explained the science bit behind the chemotherapy and he felt better.'

'I wish she'd make *us* feel better.'

'Same. I hate not knowing.'

White muslin curtains billowed out of Nora's open French windows, caught on a breeze, then settled inside again.

'Do you think she'd prefer us to go up?' Libby asked.

Emma sighed heavily. 'Let's wait a bit. It's nice out here.'

There was a sense that the two of them were prolonging their time alone. The mention of Spain had left an unfinished sentence in the air between them, an important train of thought that had gone missing. For a time, they talked around it. Libby heard how anxious Eliot had been about his SATs, which he'd aced. How sporty he was – he had raised £458.34 for his upcoming 5K swim in aid of the gym roof! – how good at bloody everything he was.

She decided it was lucky she loved her nephew as much as she did. She was unable to compete on behalf of her daughters, and confessed that she was worried about Amber's phone use and that Hazel's school attendance was abysmal. Moving on to Connor's novel, she was proud to tell Emma that he was fully immersed, absolutely determined to finish it this time.

Inevitably, their conversation circled back to their mother's diagnosis, but she had not reappeared at the dinner table and neither of them had again suggested they go upstairs to her room.

It was time to broach the subject they had been avoiding.

'Tell me what happened in Spain, Em,' Libby said softly, resting her elbows on the table and her chin on her hands.

Emma adjusted her necklace, rotating it until its clasp was out of sight. 'Do you really want to know?'

Libby nodded.

Emma breathed in, puffing out her chest, and then exhaled. 'You remember how Eliot pooed all over the bloody place? Anywhere but in the actual bloody potty?'

'We became the most excellent pooper-scooper team.'

A smile twitched on her lips briefly. 'Well, on the last day of the holiday, I caught Mum with Eliot in that horrible downstairs bathroom – remember it, with the dead pot plant in the shower? – smearing his skid-marked, wee-soaked pants into his tearful little face.'

'What?' Libby was absolutely horrified. 'You actually saw that?'

'Afraid so.'

'That's *awful*,' she said in disbelief. 'Why have you never told me?'

'Oh, I don't know. I guess I was just ashamed of the whole thing. You'd never had any of those problems with Amber, and I felt like such a failure as a mum.'

'Oh Emma! You weren't a failure!' Libby reached over to touch her hand.

'To be fair to Mum, there was an era when it was considered okay to do that whole pants-in-the-face thing. That's how I've rationalised it anyway. You know, as a generational thing.'

'Hmm. Yes,' Libby said doubtfully.

'But being here on holiday with her again has kind of triggered me a bit.'

Over the years, Libby had assumed it had been Emma's obsessive dedication to St Thomas's Primary School that had widened the wedge between her mum and her sister. Nora was always complaining that Emma never picked up the phone when she called, never wanted to see her, while Emma would joke to Libby that St Thomas's would fall into special measures if she answered every time their mum rang. Her policy was to take roughly two out of ten of her calls. Libby probably picked up about eight or even nine out of ten. She couldn't switch off her 'what if' button when she saw Nora's number flash up. It seemed to take on a special ringtone, slightly dragging and high-pitched, pleading with her.

Only last week, her mum had called in floods of tears, barely able to take a breath, saying how lonely she was. Libby had ditched her loaded trolley in the middle of the supermarket aisle and rushed around to the close. When she got there, she found Nora kneeling in the front garden in her long white nightie, her bare feet blackened with soil, planting some begonias.

'What are you doing here?' she had barked.

'I was worried about you.'

'Shh, listen, can you hear that? My little friend has come back to me.' She pointed up into the silver birch tree that Libby and Emma had climbed as kids. 'He hasn't been around lately. Those horrible crows have been scaring him off. I feed him worms and little titbits. Here, little Robin Redbreast,' she cooed. 'Aah, his birdsong is like music – the canary of the garden.'

Libby had driven away feeling like a child who'd never grown up, annoyed with herself for being dragged into her mother's drama.

There was a bang from one of the shutters on the house as the wind picked up.

'I wish you'd told me all this,' Libby said.

'Well. Anyway, as I said, it really doesn't matter now.' Emma's eyes scooted up to their mum's bedroom window once more. 'Look, her light is still on.'

Libby checked her watch. It was midnight. 'Doesn't look like she's coming down, though.'

Emma yawned. 'Maybe I'll knock on her door on the way to bed, see if she wants to join me and Eliot at the market tomorrow morning. I could talk to her properly then. When we're feeling less exhausted.'

'Won't it be difficult with Eliot there?'

'Oh no. He'll scamper around the stalls spending his pocket money and practising his French, and Mum and I can trail behind him.'

'Do you want me to go with you?' Libby asked, yawning too, hoping Emma would say no. She would go if her sister needed moral support, but she wasn't keen. As much as she enjoyed browsing the fresh produce, she hated getting up at 6 a.m. On holiday, it felt wrong not to lie in on a Sunday morning. But more than anything, she felt uncomfortable about pestering their mum about her prognosis. Part of her really didn't want to know yet.

'Do you mind if I go on my own?' Emma said.

Libby tried not to show how relieved she was. 'Not at all. I tell you what, I'll go to the supermarket instead and stock up the fridge. Patrick can look after the girls.'

'Great. It's a plan. I'll ask her now.'

'Say goodnight to her for me,' Libby said as they both stood. She felt a little hurt that their mum hadn't come down to talk to them and a little guilty that she hadn't been up to see her.

Emma wrapped her arms around her, and they stood for a while in a long goodnight hug. Libby felt closer to her sister than she had in years, and thankful for her now in the face of

Nora's news. The openness of their chat had reminded her of how much they shared. All their lives they'd shouldered so much of their mum's emotional baggage. And they might have more of it to carry tomorrow.

SEVEN

NORA

'It was a disaster.'

Oh.

'I couldn't go through with it.'

How much did you tell them?

'The cancer bit.'

That's a big bit.

'I couldn't do the rest.'

I should be there.

'It would have complicated things.'

I could have been a support.

'There's certainly none of that here.'

You're bad at asking for it.

'I don't need anyone, you know that.'

I remember reading that somewhere.

'I was a girl when I wrote that.'

That girl is still in there.

'I shouldn't have let you read it. She's best forgotten about.'

No. She's not. She needs so much. So much love she never got.

'And you can give it to her?'

Yes. I am the only one who can. You need me. And you know it.

EIGHT

LIBBY

Libby was wide awake. Her quandary was suspended in the thick heat of the room. The air conditioning had been noisy, so she had turned it off. Now she wondered whether the noise would have been more bearable than the temperature, or whether the greatest problem of all was the tussle in her mind. She wanted to call Connor and tell him the news, but she was too annoyed he wasn't here, blame on the tip of her tongue.

After an hour of wriggling around, throwing the sheet off and on and applying wet flannels to her forehead and wrists, she turned on the bedside light and finally dialled his number.

'Mum has stomach cancer,' she blurted tearfully, almost before he had said hello. Her heart lurched. There was a background noise of wind and waves, like a conch shell to her ear.

'I'm so sorry, Libby.' There was a throaty croak to his voice when he spoke her name.

'She says she's going to be okay, but she was a bit vague. Emma's going to find out more in the morning.'

She waited for him to say something more. But he didn't. Then she realised that he was crying, that he couldn't talk until he had gathered himself. She loved him dearly for caring, for loving her mum as much as she did, for being sensitive enough to know how big this was. It mattered to her and she was glad she'd called. But she couldn't cry herself. Not until she knew more about the prognosis, until she knew what she should be crying for. For the cancer diagnosis alone? Or worse? For something Emma might find out tomorrow?

'I can't believe I'm so far away when this is going on. I should be there. I'm so sorry for not being there. I'm so sorry.'

While she listened to him say how sorry he was, she pictured him sitting on his surfboard on the sand, his bare tanned shoulders wide and strong, his grey eyes squinting out at the crashing waves.

'You couldn't possibly have known,' she said, trying ever so hard to keep the accusation out of her voice. She didn't want her upset to get mixed up in his guilt. 'Tell me about what you've been up to. I could do with the escapism.'

Needing no encouragement, he described the surf tour he was on the way back from, naming beaches with the worst rip tides and using surf jargon to describe his near-death experiences. She couldn't relate to any of it and stopped listening. As though she were on a boat on the sea in his line of vision, her thoughts drifted away from him towards the burning horizon.

There was only one thing on her mind.

'I'm going to fly over on the next available flight,' Connor said, and she wondered whether she had missed a whole chunk of his side of the conversation.

'No, Connor. That's crazy. We can't afford it. It'll clean us out.'

'I'll use the cut-up credit card.'

'But then there's nothing left for an emergency.'

'And this isn't one?'

'She's going to be fine.'

'Libby, I want to be there.'

After hanging up, she felt giddy. She guessed this was the

upside of being with someone enigmatic and unreliable like Connor. She had never truly pinned him down, had spent their whole relationship hooked into the abstract idea of doing so, and whenever she won his attention, she felt grateful, validated and simultaneously ashamed. No modern woman worth her salt needed a man's attention to boost her self-esteem. But this was the point: she didn't feel like a woman who was worth anything, let alone salt. He wasn't making this grand gesture because he wanted to spend time with her; he was flying over because her mum had cancer.

Mum. Had. Cancer. Oh. My. God.

What if Nora didn't want Connor to be here? This worry reared up and got her by the throat. It wasn't logical, she told herself. Her mum loved Connor; they were sparring partners, friends. Because of her affection for him, she had insisted their villa holiday would not disrupt his plans to finish his book. Or so Libby had thought up until this very moment. Was that feasible, considering what she knew now? Why would her mum have wanted him to miss this, knowing what the implications for Libby and his girls would be? Why would she not have insisted he was here? He was as much a part of the family as Patrick was, albeit not by law. If Libby thought about it for a second longer, she would begin to panic. About what, she wasn't quite sure. She couldn't panic about nothing. Panicking could be catastrophic. Push it all away. Go to sleep, please, sleep it away.

A toxic mass spread through her chest. Her breathing gathered pace. Trying to calm down made it worse; trying to sleep made it worse. Think, Libby. Don't think. Not too much. Or maybe just enough to remind yourself of what worked last time you felt this way. What *had* worked? What hadn't worked?

She sat bolt upright, turned on the light and reached for her knitting, taking up where she had left off.

Rhythmic, satisfying, endless rows of beautiful loops, making a garment that would clothe her child. That was all she needed to think about. That was enough. Her breathing regulated. The sweat on her palms cooled and dried. Her thoughts became more manageable. She was on top of this. Her mum would be fine about Connor. She was going to be okay. She would have the chemo and she'd be better by Christmas. A good friend of Libby's had recently got the all-clear from breast cancer and her life had gone back to normal. These days it did not have to be a death sentence.

As a child, when her mother returned after a long tour, she would climb into her bed and Nora would whisper the words of her favourite picture book to her. *Once upon a time, there was a little girl who lived in a glass jar...* Her mum had known it off by heart and would carry on until Libby fell asleep. The story was about a fairy who had lost her wings and had made a home for herself amongst the moss and ferns inside a glass terrarium on a sunny windowsill. A huge ginger cat would try to get at her, but he never could. Then one day, the glass jar was knocked over by a strong wind and smashed to pieces. The fairy's contained, cosseted little world was gone, and she didn't believe she'd survive the new dangers around her. This was how Libby felt now. Mum's cancer had smashed her glass jar.

She tried to recall the story's happy ending, but her mind blanked and she couldn't remember. Not without her mum to tell her.

NINE

NORA

The curtains had been open all night. My phone was still lying on the duvet, where it must have dropped from my hand. I had his voice in my head still. The voice that had lulled me to sleep after that disastrous evening. The rising sun was now an orange disc, with its thick glow oozing into the sky, sticky-looking like marmalade, pushing its way up to warm the whole world. He would be seeing that same sun from a completely different perspective. It filled my soul, giving me the energy to deal with Emma at the market. I was glad she had asked me to go with her. It would give me an opportunity to make things right.

Predictably, she bossed me and Eliot about, flapping us out of the house as though we were both small children, but I held my tongue like a good girl. I said nothing when she began shouting and jabbing at the sat nav, insisting we wouldn't find a parking space if we got there a minute after 7 a.m. She looked comically irate with her hair scraped back at the front and her ponytail big and poufy at the back, frizzed up in the damp heat. But I knew why she was in a state. The truth was there between us; it simply hadn't been said. It needed to be said. Why was saying it so different from knowing it?

After we had parked up in the village square, she ushered Eliot into the first patisserie we came across, ordering him to buy – in French – a hot chocolate, two coffees, two croissants and a *pain complet*.

As we spied on him through the window display of giant breadsticks and salted pretzel loops, Emma began her inquisition.

'Did you sleep okay?' she asked, twiddling and fussing her fingers through her ponytail in the way she used to do when she was studying for an exam.

'Not brilliantly.'

'Me neither,' she said.

'That's unlike you.'

'Well, obviously, after everything last night, I—'

I interrupted. 'Oh, not now, darling.'

Before she could continue, Eliot emerged with our breakfast. For now, I was saved, but I braced myself for her upcoming cross-examination.

'What is this called, *en français, s'il vous plaît?*' Emma said to the stallholder at the vegetable stand, pointing at an artichoke.

'*L'artichaut,*' the man replied good-humouredly.

'Go on, darling, you say it too,' Emma said, putting her hand on Eliot's shoulder. When she had an agenda, she was merciless.

'*L'artichaut,*' Eliot parroted.

And on she went: star fruit, rutabaga, endive, curly kale. None of which Eliot would be required to say ever again, and was even less likely to eat. Poor kid. When she was stressed, she pushed him too hard. I admit I had to take some responsibility for how uptight she was being this morning, and I wanted to put an end to it.

'Look, Eliot, that guy's making leather wristbands. Why don't you go and get one?' I said, handing him a ten-euro note, knowing what I was risking but unable to bear watching Emma torment him any further.

He scuttled off.

Predictably, she didn't waste a second of our alone time. She stepped closer and said, 'So, I wanted to go through some of the details, if that's okay?'

Already I regretted handing her this opportunity. At dinner I had been a coward, and as I much as I hadn't wanted to be one today, I was still feeling extremely wimpy. Right now, never talking about my cancer with any of them again seemed the most appealing option.

'Aren't these lovely!' I said, linking arms with her and ambling over to a table of linen. From a folded pile, I pulled out a maroon-and-grey-striped tablecloth. 'And this is simply divine.' I opened it up. The lady behind the stall asked me if I wanted to buy it, and I handed it back to her, shaking my head. Her wares were only a foil. She snatched it back and refolded it, muttering at us. I remembered how bad-tempered my father had been with the children who had disrupted the displays of dolls and games in his shop. He had never said goodbye to those who'd left empty-handed, re-stacking everything they'd touched, grumbling about them being tight-fisted time-wasters, even the sweetest little ones, whose uniform blazers were too long for their arms.

Watched eagerly by the stallholder, I carried on fiddling with the linens. 'It's all going to be fine. You don't need to worry about me. Look at this, it would match your curtains back home!'

Emma stared at the pillowcase as though it were a mucky dishcloth. She would not be derailed. 'It would really help if you could give us a bit more information, though I know it's hard to talk about.'

Opening up my diaphragm, I inhaled and exhaled. 'What information do you need, my darling?'

Looking almost startled by my capitulation, she stuttered. 'Er,' she began, 'how long have you known?'

'I don't remember. A few months.'

She swallowed. 'What tests have you had?'

I noticed a bolt of toffee-coloured lace and checked its price tag. 'An endoscopy and a CT.'

'And the doctors could tell what stage it's at? Or do you need a laparoscopy?'

I smiled wryly. 'Have you been googling?'

'I did do a bit of research, yes.'

'No, I don't need one of those.'

'So they've told you what stage?'

'Stage three.' The lie just came out.

'Three. Okaaay. Not great, but not the worst. And you're going to have chemo?'

'They do want to schedule some chemo, yes.' It wasn't a complete lie. They did want to do these horrid things to me.

'No operation?'

'No.'

'That's good, isn't it?'

'I have no interest in them cutting me open, so yes, I guess it is.' It wasn't quite an answer. Emma's need for certainty was suffocating. '*Merci, au revoir,*' I said to the stallholder.

'*Au revoir, mesdames,*' she said, managing a small smile.

At the stall across the way, Eliot showed me his new black leather wristband. It had his name pressed into it. Emma followed me, puffing her cheeks up and blowing out a shallow sigh – she needed to work on her pranayama breathing techniques.

After some wandering about, buying a bag of rainbow pasta and a pot of olives, I led Eliot over to the cheese counter. 'Darling, would you please order me some cheese?'

'*Du fromage, s'il vous plaît,*' he said, scratching his red, very

British forehead, leaving white stripes shooting from his eyebrows.

I beamed at the stallholder, who wore a jolly bow tie.

'Which cheese?' he huffed in English, as though we were inconveniencing him by shopping at his stall.

Emma pointed, talking over Eliot in shrill Franglais. '*Quel est...? Le Camembert?* That one? *Oui?*'

The bow-tied man unwrapped the circle of cheese. The waft of *fromage* turned my stomach. While Emma and Eliot were engaged at the counter, choosing some for Patrick, who loved cheese, I looked around for an escape route. Behind the drinks van that was parked next to the cheese counter, I would be hidden. I nipped off and was quietly sick.

A mangy old cat sniffed at me through the metal fencing. 'It's rude to stare,' I said to him. He meowed, hooked his claws onto the wire and stretched his body out long and lean, blinking his green eyes at me slowly. 'Don't look at me like that, silly cat. You know exactly what it's like, with all your horrid fur balls.'

I was used to being sick. It was part of having stomach cancer. Diarrhoea was another delightful symptom. But as I stood straight, dabbing my mouth with my handkerchief, my head swam and I doubled over again with a nasty cramp. Although it was only 9 a.m., it was already getting too warm for me.

Or maybe it wasn't the heat. It might be the cancer worsening. Dr Altmeyer had warned me it would; said my decline would be rapid, that I had been lucky up until now. Yes, he'd actually used the word 'lucky' to a woman he had diagnosed with stomach cancer six weeks before; lucky me, Nora Fitz, whose cancer had advanced to stage four with only a bit of heartburn and some blood in my stool to show for it.

He had described what I would go through with a slightly harsh edge to his voice, unless I was imagining it, but I had fought back the tears and held my head high, even managing a wry little smile for him. I'd understood why his attitude towards me had changed and why he seemed hostile. Don't get me wrong, his professional veneer was in place, but I was intuitive, and I knew I wasn't just another faceless patient to him. He liked me more than the average, had enjoyed my stories of theatre life, had wanted to save me. If I were to flatter myself further, perhaps he had fallen in love with me during that very first consultation. Quite simply, he might have seemed cross with me because he cared. I had that power over men. I did something to them. It was the little boy in them: their need for a maternal figure to take charge and draw them into her bosom. But then they resented it! Such a confused sex.

'Mum! *Mum*!' I heard Emma from around the other side of the van. The cat scampered off, leaving a puff of dust.

'I'm here, sorry.' I stepped out. The sunlight seemed to burn into my stomach, directed like a torch's beam. I winced, and Emma frowned.

'Oh! We found you. Are you okay?'

'Yes, yes, sorry. Just a little woozy.'

'It's getting hotter. We should go.'

'But I haven't...' Eliot began, and then bit his lip and looked at the ground.

'What's that, darling?' I said, holding both his hands, wanting to sink down to my haunches, but fearing I wouldn't get up again if I did. 'Did you want something else?'

'No, it's nothing, Nor-Nor.' There was a wobble in his voice. Emma was about to fuss, but I shook my head and held her back. It was her fault he was feeling emotional. Pushing him to speak French all morning!

'Come on, you can't kid a kidder. Tell me,' I said brusquely.

He looked up at me. 'It's just I saw some crystals over there and I thought I could buy one each for Hazel and Amber before we go. I have some money left. But not if you're feeling poorly.' He held out his change.

'A little bit of cancer isn't going to stop me from accompanying my grandson to get presents for his big cousins now, is it?'

We helped him choose. I enjoyed the sensation of the cool stones falling through my fingertips. It distracted me from my pain and from Emma's concerned sideways glances. I loathed being watched all the time.

Emma's phone bipped. 'Oh!' she said, reading a text, shaking her head. 'Wow.'

'What's that?'

'Libby's texted. Connor wants to jump on a flight out here. She wanted to check it was okay with you.'

I stepped away from the table, took a slow sip from the bottle of water Emma had bought me and concentrated on swallowing it straight down without choking. 'Oh really?' I said.

'Typical of him to turn up at the last minute, isn't it. I had a feeling he might.'

The sun was now on my back, and I felt frustrated that it wouldn't leave me alone. 'Did you?' I said, as though I hadn't thought the same.

'Sadly, yes.'

I spoke breezily. 'Well, I've always said the villa was big enough for the whole family. I've never excluded Connor.'

Emma looked at me as though she were about to say something else, but I patted my sick, sweaty brow and she held her tongue.

'I'll text her and tell her it's fine.'

'Yes, darling, you do that,' I said, nodding. 'I'm happy if Libby's happy.'

Eliot chose his crystals. He seemed satisfied. After that, Emma declared it was time to go.

We headed back to the car park and my mood sank further. The more I thought about Connor arriving, the more drained I felt. And I could sense Emma's itch to know more about my diagnosis, her dissatisfaction with my vagueness. She wasn't done yet, I knew that much.

Across the street, a couple of teenage boys were playing *pétanque* in the dappled shade of the plane trees; a handsome older woman in a polka-dot dress strode past them carrying a baguette in her basket. She waved at the boys and they dropped their boules and lolloped after her. I imagined they were her grandsons. The injustice of it sliced through me; guessing she would see her grandchildren grow up while I would not. I felt a pang of such regret, my knees almost crumpled under me.

Eliot climbed in the back of the van and slammed his door. The reverberations went through my hand and up my arm and tripped my thoughts like electricity up a live wire. I pressed my hand into my chest.

Over the van's roof, Emma said, 'Mum? Are you okay?'

I could not hold my feelings in for one minute longer.

'I wanted this holiday to be perfect,' I said, hating the crack in my voice.

She put her hand up to her forehead, shielding her eyes. 'Connor won't get in the way of anything. He'll probably just slouch about looking cool and handsome and tortured, and we can just ignore him,' she said, sounding dead certain.

Her schoolmistress earnestness, her desire to manufacture perfection was a version of my own need to create simply the most marvellous holiday every single day, and I saw that she was more like me than I had ever wanted to recognise. But our desire to dress up the worst was like me trying to put nice clothes on those dusty old dolls in my father's shop. The prettiness on the outside was only a superficial fix and wouldn't last.

'Maybe Connor *should* be here,' I murmured, thinking aloud. Through the back window, I could see that Eliot had his earphones on. He was listening to Phil Collins on Spotify. 'Maybe it's right that everyone is here on my last-ever holiday.'

Emma removed her hand from her forehead. Her eyes were

no longer shielded, and I could see the naked terror in them. 'What do you mean, your last-ever holiday?'

I bowed my head and studied my blue-veined feet and pearlescent green nail polish: a dead woman walking. I wanted to push the fear onto someone else. 'Oh, I thought you of all people would have worked it out,' I said. An imaginary string tugged my head up from its crown, and I found myself staring straight at her. 'The cancer's spread to the lymph nodes and elsewhere. I lied about it being stage three. I really don't know why. I suppose I felt under pressure and wasn't ready to tell you the truth. The truth is, it's...' A small choke stopped me before I continued. 'It's a bad stage four. They could cut me open and pump me with all the chemo in the world, but it will make no real difference. The point is, whatever they do – or don't do – it'll kill me before the year is out.'

'No,' Emma breathed hoarsely, horror-struck. Her skin flushed from forehead to chest with an instant redness, like a rash. 'That's not what you told us last night.'

I guess I deserved that. 'I understand why it's hard to believe me now.'

'It's not that I don't believe you.'

'As Oscar Wilde said, my darling, "The truth is rarely pure and never simple".'

I got into the van and closed the door, shutting in the truth, both impure and complex. I was good at that, slamming it all away. With Eliot there, I was extra safe. Emma wouldn't be able to talk about it any more. I was too tired to go over it with her. She had been haranguing me all morning for facts, and now that she had some of them – if not all – she didn't want to believe them.

Her torso, dressed in a pink denim sundress, was framed by the window like an abstract photo. The softness of her curves had been chased out by discipline. Had she never savoured the sugary mouthfuls of a second cream cake? Or had a long, boozy cheese and wine lunch, just for the hell of it? Or lolled about on a sofa or under a tree doing nothing much, thinking about even less? She was always achieving, always bettering herself or martyring herself to a cause, but if she were ill like me, she would regret her self-flagellation and wish she had ripped off the sackcloth and enjoyed life more.

It took her a few minutes before she got into the van next to me.

'Sorry, Mum,' she said, glancing at me shyly, tugging her earlobe.

She started the engine with a couple of twists of the key, and as we shot off, I was jerked forward. I glanced over at her, ready to tell her off for driving too fast. Her shoulders were up around her ears, her fists tight on the wheel, holding it together for Eliot in the back, always holding it together for everyone else. I bit back my complaint. My heart ached for her.

I held my forehead, propping it up in the heel of my hand, trying to catch the world passing by: the bright yellow sunflower fields and purple strips of lavender and deep green points of cypress trees, and the domed blue sky above us, but not one damned fluffy cloud for me to sit on in heaven.

We arrived at the villa and parked up in the garage. For a few minutes after Eliot had climbed out and run off to give the girls their crystals, Emma and I sat in silence in the car. It was cool and dark. Emma's arms hung limp from the steering wheel.

I rested my hand on her knee. 'I know it's hard to take in.'

She looked at me imploringly. 'I'm sorry about my reaction earlier. I don't know why I questioned you.'

I smiled. 'I know, I know. I'm the queen of exaggeration.'

She let out a little laugh, with its endearing snort, then dropped her hands into her pink lap. 'I wish you had been exaggerating this time.'

'Me too, my darling. Me too.'

'You need to tell Libby.'

'Yes. But I'm scared for her. She's so fragile. Remember when Moggy died?'

'She was only seventeen then.'

'Two whole weeks she was in bed for. She wouldn't eat. She wouldn't talk. She wouldn't sleep. *You* were at Manchester by then. You have no idea what it was like.'

'Lying won't help her, though.'

'I won't lie!' I hadn't meant to sound ferocious. 'Sorry.'

'It's okay, Mum. All of this is so hard. But at least Connor'll be here soon. He'll be able to look after her.'

The agony of that and of having to tell Libby twisted inside me. I didn't know how she'd cope. It terrified me more than the cancer itself and I hoped I'd have the strength to go through with it. 'I want to find the right moment to tell her. You must let me do it in my own time, okay? Promise?'

'Okay.'

'I'd like us not to talk about my cancer any more today, if we can. I would much prefer to appreciate this wonderful weather and my darling grandchildren without having to think about it all the time. I have to live with it in my body every minute of every day and I do need a break.'

'Why don't you have a nap in the shade while I make lunch? Libby should have been to the supermarket.'

'I'd appreciate that,' I said, glad of her understanding. 'Thank you.'

I brushed my thumb under her eyes, wiping away the salty tear marks, wanting to say 'I love you'. I was out of the habit. All through her childhood, I had told her I loved her, but at some point in adulthood she had stopped automatically saying it back, and I had been wounded each and every time. I was grateful for her gentleness now. It reminded me of how caring and considerate she had been as a teenager. While most teens slouched about, Emma had been a bossy little mother hen, making me and Libby surprise breakfasts in bed, running baths or tidying bedrooms. It had been quite unnecessary, above and beyond, and I had lovingly chided her for it, telling her she was giving herself too much work to do – she could be a terrible martyr about it. Such was the pattern of her life.

Her unstiffening today gave me hope, and I felt realigned, sensing that my plans for this trip were back on track after its rocky start. The unexpected curveball was Connor's arrival. It wasn't going to be easy to have him here. But there were advantages. Many. And I'd had nothing to do with orchestrating it. Maybe I'd wait for him to get here before I told Libby the truth about my cancer, soften the blow a little, for both our sakes. Emma had promised to leave me to do it in my own time, so she'd have to respect that and be patient. I knew what was best.

It was *my* cancer. *My* life. *My* death.

Outside, under the umbrella, I felt listless, and I sank back into the sunlounger and slept lightly. Memories of my past littered those strange minutes between wakefulness and sleep. Most disconcerting was a dream about a shadowy figure stealing my exercise book out of the vanity table drawer and reading it out to the whole family over lunch. It stirred me up enough to wake me, and it took a few discombobulating, sweaty minutes before I was reassured it wasn't real. When I dropped off again, I dreamt once more about a stranger coming to the villa to expose my deepest secret.

TEN

LIBBY

Libby had fallen asleep again after receiving Emma's return text:

Mum's fine about Connor flying over. We'll be back at the villa at around 11.30. E x

It was now noon. She turned onto her side, looking through a slit in the curtains at the silvery sea. Libby was determined to be optimistic. Dead swaying trees aside, her mum had said she was going to get better, and so Libby was trying to stick with that. Anything Emma had to say to the contrary would be unendurable. Her mind sent a shutter across the thought. Things that horrible weren't worth knowing.

Her feet were cooled by the stone steps as she walked upstairs. The sun streamed through the white net curtains. She liked moving through the villa slowly, taking in the view, tasting the salt in the air.

Emma was in the kitchen, unpacking the various oddities she'd found at the market. Libby felt guilty for lying in and wondered if her sister would consider it strange and unnatural that she had slept well.

When she said good morning, Emma jumped out of her skin and dropped a bag of rainbow pasta. The packet split.

'Oh, whoops! You scared me!' Her skin was blotchy, like she had been crying.

'Are you okay?' Libby asked, experiencing the sudden onset of a roaring, rushing din in her ears.

'Yes. Why?' Emma began sweeping up the pasta shells. Libby bent down to help, scooping handfuls back into the packet.

'Where's Mum?'

'Having a nap.'

'What did you find out?'

'Not much. Did Connor book his flight?'

'Not sure yet. He said he would,' Libby replied absent-mindedly, fixated on Emma's red-raw eyes. 'Did she tell you exactly what the doctors said?'

'Umm, not really.' Emma opened the fridge. 'Haven't you been to the supermarket yet?'

Oh, shit. The supermarket. 'I'm going now.'

'For God's sake. Mum needs some lunch. We only got cheese and olives at the market, but we need the basics—'

'Emma. Anything else I should know about Mum?'

Emma pressed her hands into her temples and made some kind of growling noise. 'Do I really have to go out again?'

'I'll go now and be back in an hour. It's fine,' Libby said, putting her coffee cup back in the cupboard, unsettled by her sister's rancour.

As Libby descended the narrow staircase to her bedroom, Emma called out after her. 'When will Connor be arriving?'

'I'm not exactly sure yet. He said he'd get the next available flight, which would be the nine a.m. from San José tomorrow. It takes seventeen hours, so he'll get here on Tuesday, around ten fifteen our time. But first I need to find out if he's even booked it. I'm waiting for his text to confirm.'

Emma was standing at the top of the stairs with a broom in her hand, but her expression was gentler. 'I hope he does.'

'Thanks, sis. Are you sure you're okay with it?'

'Of course! He's my brother-in-law.'

'Technically he's *not* your brother-in-law.'

'It's shocking you haven't made an honest man out of him,' Emma said, smiling.

Calmed by the playfulness of her tone, Libby laughed and quoted their mum: 'Honesty's overrated.'

'There's no helping some people,' Emma teased, clicking her tongue. Before she turned away, she added, 'Oh, by the way, I'm just going for a walk, but I'll be back in time to make lunch, and then Patrick and I want to take Eliot to the Château de la Napoule. Do you want to join us? Mum's coming, I think.'

'Sure,' Libby said, trying as hard as her sister to sustain the positive vibes between them, even though a chateau visit was the last thing on earth she wanted to do. It was only day two of the holiday, and she wasn't sure she had the strength to galvanise the girls into a cultural experience.

Once she was dressed, she returned to the kitchen. As she grabbed some bags for life from under the sink, she noticed a red pasta shell that had escaped Emma's broom, and revisited the image of her sister's nervous, tear-stained face. Mulling it over, she decided to focus on the smiles and jokes instead.

Outside on one of the terraces, Nora was lying on a sunbed in the shade of a large umbrella. Libby crept past, anxious not to disturb her. Her eyes were closed, and she was snoring a little. Her lips fell loose and damp into the cushion. The aroma of her expensive suncream was more like a taste, a comforting flavour. Asleep, without her personality to act as a distraction, she looked smaller and older. The thought of a tumour metasta-sising inside her was hateful. Libby wanted it to be out of her body as soon as possible. Tiptoeing over, she covered her mum's bunioned feet with a sarong, then carried on down to the pool.

'Hi, Mum!' Hazel shrieked.

'Shh,' Libby said, pressing her finger to her lips. 'Nor-Nor's asleep. What do you want from the *supermarché*?'

Their orders were embarrassingly un-French. Hazel, whose eyes were already red from the chlorine, shouted from her position straddling a watermelon inflatable, 'Frosties, please!' Amber, lathered in oil and flat out on her sunlounger, opened one eye and ordered Pringles. Eliot stopped his lengths and asked for some *crevettes*, which Patrick, who was reading in the shade in a T-shirt, informed Libby were shrimps.

Libby wrote the items down, and was poised to tell the girls about their dad's possible arrival when a speedboat zoomed into the bay, churning up the water below them. Wave after wave slapped the rocks. Hazel and Eliot jumped up and down and yelled hello as it whizzed around the promontory and away.

The unexpected commotion allowed her to reconsider sharing the news about Connor with the kids, deciding she should wait for his confirmation text. He was known for his *definitely, maybe* kind of decisions. Definitely, maybe not.

On the way up to the garage, with Hazel's calls for chocolate brioche falling away behind her, she texted him. Given the time difference, she knew it was too early to expect a reply, but she wanted him to see it as soon as he woke up.

Hi babe, let me know when you've booked your flight. There's a 9 a.m. from SJ tomoz? L xx

She drove through the narrow, cobbled streets of the village, negotiating the Sunday-lunchtime bustle. Her thighs were sweaty by the time she parked up in the supermarket car park. Once inside, though, she was freezing in the air-conditioned aisles as she worked carefully through Emma's exhaustive shopping list.

Still her phone lay mute in her shoulder bag.

The queue at the checkout was long. She didn't mind. It gave her time to open her banking app, make sure she had enough money. The expense of Connor's flight had set off her anxiety about their finances. Simultaneously, she had a brief, irrational fear that he might change his mind about coming over, never text back, never call, never come home to them again. The idea of being unattached and single shot through her mind. It wasn't a new thought. She imagined the rejection, more financial worries and the loneliness. Then wondered whether it would be any different to how she felt now.

Straight after lunch, Emma, Mum, Patrick and Eliot got ready for their trip to the chateau.

When Libby thought they had gone, Emma reappeared.

'I left these,' she said, waving her sunglasses. 'By the way, Mum's decided to stay behind.'

'Why?' Libby's heart skipped a beat. 'Is she feeling okay?'

'I think she might want to talk to you.' She saw a terrified glint in the brown of her sister's eyes before she slotted her sunglasses over them.

After Emma had left, Libby felt edgy. Having checked on her mum, who was resting in her room, she played about with the girls on the inflatables, acting as though nothing was bothering her, marvelling at the beautiful water and the blue sky above them, eating crisps and drinking Coca-Cola with ice and lemon. Secretly, though, she dreaded Nora catching up with her.

Her mum was an ethereal presence in the villa, barely there. Occasionally Libby wondered whether she had imagined the fleeting coolness of a shadow between her and the sun as Nora nipped past; or the spiky ends of her hair blowing in the wind as she disappeared down the stone steps to the sea; or her humming on the breeze from a window flung open. Real or not, she didn't approach Libby for a chat.

As the afternoon wore on and the sun dropped, Libby became increasingly anxious about why her mother was avoiding her, and what she and Emma hadn't told her. Connor's text, when it finally arrived, didn't help her feel any more certain about anything.

Hi babe, sunsets are blowing my mind. Waves are the size of mountains. Will book the flight when I get back to SJ. Reception terrible here. Give the girls a kiss from me. See you soon.

She texted back:

Cool, let me know when you have. Love you x

By supper, the trepidation had become more like a dull pain in Libby's bones than a conscious feeling. Her mum had continued to ignore her and had been drinking more than usual, regaling the family with some of her self-aggrandising stories, old favourites of theatre life and her humble beginnings above the toyshop. Details emerged about Grandpa Morris's bad business practice: how his outmoded stock had stopped selling and the loss of customers had led to a hike in prices and the failure of the business.

'It was ghastly when the shop was boarded up,' Nora groaned. 'It didn't only mark the end of Fitz Toys, it marked the end of hope for our little family. I'll never forget my mother's mood when we packed up our home to move into my aunt's spare room. That horrible tower block in Pimlico! Only then, only when there were nasty men lurking in the corridors and a permanent whistling noise through the crack in my bedroom window, did I realise how lucky I had been. But it was too late.'

They'd heard it all before. So many times, it was hard to muster any sympathy.

'Okay, we're turning in.' Emma yawned, stretching her arms

above her head. She'd barely finished her last mouthful of chocolate mousse.

'Really?' Patrick said. It was still early.

'Yup,' she replied. It was a 'yup' you didn't argue with.

Libby and her mum would be left on their own. It was important that she find out what had been discussed at the market, but every inch of her screamed that she wasn't ready to hear it.

Patrick swigged back his tumbler of Amaretto. 'Early night it is, then.'

'Even the kids aren't in bed yet,' Libby protested. They were watching a movie after a late swim. The girls' hair was sopping wet down the backs of their nighties, and their toes were prune-like. Emma had been sensible enough to protect the sofa in the snug with layers of towels.

'I was up at five thirty, remember,' Emma said, as though her decision to get up at dawn to go to the market had been Libby's fault. She stood up, stacked the pudding cups and kissed Libby and Nora goodnight. 'Eliot's sleeping in Hazel's room tonight. Would one of you make sure they're in bed at some point?'

'Of course.' Nora nodded, then watched Emma go with a little furrow between her eyebrows.

There was a loaded silence. Libby looked out at the inky view.

'How about a sneaky midnight swim?' Nora said.

Libby checked her phone. 'It's only nine thirty.'

'I never took you for a pedant. Let's go and see how cold it is.'

'But I'm so... *dry*,' Libby said.

'How often do you get the chance to walk from the dinner table straight into the sea?'

Nora picked up her glass of wine, handed Libby hers and

trotted down the steps to the water's edge. Libby followed her flowing skirt, almost grabbing onto it like a kid.

The sea was black and oily. Libby kicked off one sandal to test the temperature. It was bath-like.

'Come on. Kit off,' Nora ordered, swigging back her wine and leaving the glass on a step.

'I'll just go and get my swimming costume.'

'Don't be daft.' She whipped off her clothes and stood in her pants and bra.

'Oh, okay.' Libby chortled and pulled her dress over her head.

They grinned at each other, then Libby stepped slowly down into the water. It became colder and colder, but she forced herself to keep going. When the sea lapped at her middle, she squealed. Submerging the rest of her body would take a big brave burst of energy that she was warming up for. Just as she was bracing herself to make the final push, her mum shoved her from behind and she was thrown under. Through hysterical laughter and gulps of seawater, she splashed Nora back until she too was in.

They swam side by side, fast at first, and in circles mostly, but then they relaxed into their strokes as their bodies adjusted to the temperature. They twisted onto their backs and bobbed there, floating in silence for a long while, making the odd remark about Patrick or Emma or one of the children; feeling the roll of the waves beneath them, staring up at the velvet sky and the splashes of clustered stars. Connor would love this, Libby thought.

'I'd like to believe we become part of all this when we die,' Nora said. 'The sea, the sky, the wind. It's a comforting thought, isn't it?'

'But you're not going to die,' Libby said stupidly, blinking up at the twinkling universe, wishing on every star in the sky that it was true.

'I will some day.'

'But not yet.' *Please not yet. Please don't say it. Please don't make it real.*

A horrible pause. The watery sounds in her ears. A swell of black fear gathering inside her.

'Not yet.'

The power of the unsaid, those unconscious cues that Libby had been absorbing over the past few months, seemed to weigh her down in the water. Information her mum had been dropping like coins into her pockets, precious little hints that all was not well, now threatened to drown her. Her muscles felt dog-tired.

'I'm getting chilly,' she said, and began swimming back to the steps.

The villa glowed white against its home of rugged rocks. Nora was slow behind her, and Libby felt bad for abandoning her. She waited, and held her mum's hand so that she didn't slip on the slimy film over the steps.

'That was so lovely,' Nora said, squeezing out her hair.

They scooped up their clothes, teeth chattering.

'Gorgeous,' Libby said.

The cotton of Nora's T-shirt and skirt clung to her limbs. Looking at her thin arms and distended belly, bloated with illness, it was obvious to Libby now that she was sick. All of her mother's life, dieting had been anathema to her. She had loved her fuller figure. If she'd ever 'overdone the butter a little', which was her way of saying she'd been eating too much, she would simply eat less of it for a few days. Never would she have wanted to lose weight to fit into a new swimsuit. Back home, Libby should have asked her why: why her invites to Sunday roasts at her place had stopped, why she had begun turning down offers of her favourite chocolate biscuits, why there had been an acid smell on her breath some mornings.

And today she had intuited from her mum's light-footedness and Emma's inscrutability that there was still more to know.

'You're okay about Connor coming over, aren't you?' she asked, creating another diversion, putting off the truth for as long as possible. 'He hasn't booked his flight yet.'

'Of course I am, darling! Yes, yes, yes, it's wonderful news! I can't wait to see him!' Nora was overdoing it, perhaps overcompensating.

'I'm waiting for his text to confirm which flight he'll be on.' Libby pictured his deep tan and his sideways smile and his wide shoulders, and a pang of real longing punctured her earlier reserve.

'Lovely of him to come, but he doesn't need to. Not on my account.'

'He was very upset when I told him. He really loves you.' Libby collected both wine glasses, then, as she slid her feet into her sandals, she blurted it out. 'He was asking about your prognosis, and I said I didn't know what to say to him because I didn't really know anything. But I should... probably know. You know?'

Nora was ten steps ahead already, and there was a brief break in her step before she continued on, quicker. 'Oh, you sound like Emma. Certainties when it comes to this bloody disease are impossible. You know what doctors are like: they stick you in the system and send you endless letters and you're none the wiser.'

'That's as clear as mud, Mum.' Libby frowned as she followed her, talking to her back. 'What you said last night was that you'll have the chemo and you won't need an operation or anything. And they think... what? After that?'

'Oh, I won't need an operation, darling.' Nora flapped one hand in the air.

'Just the chemo?' Libby stopped climbing, sceptical still. 'Is that what you told Emma?'

'Emma knows.'

Libby had to jog a few steps to catch up. She spoke breathily. 'So what you told us at dinner was definitely true? You'll have the round of chemo, and the doctors say that's all you'll need?' She had to double-check. Or was it triple-checking by now?

'Well. That's what Dr Altmeyer said.'

'Wow, okay.' Libby was cautious of adjusting again, returning to the optimism of this morning, mistrusting it. Why was it all such a mess in her head? Nothing her mum had said just now felt grounded, but she couldn't very well suggest she didn't believe in the idea of her recovery. Discussing cancer wasn't easy at the best of times. Asking the right questions without being blunt and upsetting was a minefield. 'I've been worrying all day that it was much worse than you and Emma were letting on.'

'Uh-huh?' Her mum turned to face her at the door to the kitchen. There were droplets on her face still, moonlit, and her round brown eyes were shining like an owl's, wide and unblinking. She looked young, like a girl, and Libby sensed she was looking right through her. 'You mustn't worry about me,' she said. 'Let's just look forward to Connor's arrival.'

'And you're sure Emma knows all this? She seemed upset after the market.'

Her mum liked to wind Emma up. Libby wouldn't put it past her to be ambiguous, make it sound worse than it was, poke at Emma for some emotion, tears even, garner extra sympathy.

Nora tossed her hair. 'Yes, darling, she knows. But how she interprets it is anyone's guess.'

'Oh, right. Okay then,' Libby said.

Nora blinked finally and kissed Libby's cheek. 'Night, then. I'm so thrilled that Connor is joining us,' she said again, and disappeared upstairs, leaving vague, slippery footprints.

Libby stacked the glasses into the dishwasher, completely

baffled. She couldn't believe Emma had left her hanging all day; that she'd led her to suspect their mum was dying when it seemed there was hope.

Defiantly she discarded the rest of the clearing-up in the sink and went straight to her phone, dialling Connor's number. Now that both her mum and Emma seemed unreliable, she felt very alone and yearned for his presence by her side. This time, she wasn't settling for his flaky answers. What she needed from him was a definite 'I've booked the flight and I'm going to walk through those airport doors on Tuesday morning' kind of certainty.

His phone was switched off, but she wasn't giving up. She climbed under the sheets, still in her clothes, and did some research into available flights, then carefully composed a text that he couldn't squirm away from or misinterpret.

Hi Connor, there's availability tomorrow on the 9 a.m. from SJ. Book it asap. I'll see you at Nice arrivals at 10.15 on Tuesday morning. The girls and Mum will be over the moon. Everyone is dying to see you. Especially me. It doesn't feel right without you. Love you xxx

Asking for what she needed from him gave her a boost. She thought she might even talk to him about postponing the rest of his writing trip until next year, when her mum was recovered. Because she definitely, definitely wanted her mum to get better. And Connor was definitely, definitely going to get on that flight.

She longed to collapse into his arms, feeling they might be the only solid pair available to her for a while. Just until this cancer nightmare was over, when everything could return to normal.

ELEVEN

EMMA

By dragging Patrick away from supper early, it seemed she had inadvertently given him the wrong impression. He had a look in his eye she hadn't seen in years. The timing was way off. All day she had held back the truth from Libby, and it had given her a headache.

She was complicit in the secret until Libby knew.

As soon as she closed the bedroom door, Patrick moved towards her to kiss her on the lips, missing awkwardly. 'Sorry,' Emma said, pecking him on the cheek. 'I've had such a long day. I just want a lovely long bubble bath, really.'

'Maybe I'll join you?' he asked shyly.

'How about coming to talk to me instead?'

As soon as she got in the water, he tried to put his hand under. Her muscles seized up. Her whole being was full of what was going on with her sister and mum. There was nothing to spare. 'Sorry, love, not now,' she said, gently guiding him away.

With a hangdog expression, he pushed himself up to standing, and she felt terrible.

'Patrick,' she said as he turned to leave. 'I'm so sorry. It's just...' She stopped. She couldn't voice her mum's devastating news out loud, not until Libby knew. Everything hinged on that. 'I'm really tired. After everything... you know.'

'Yes, of course. It must be the last thing on your mind.' He blushed slightly and closed the door.

Unable to enjoy the huge double bath or the luxurious soap, she climbed out as tense as when she had got in – more so, perhaps – and wrapped herself in a robe.

Through the bathroom window, she spotted her mum and Libby bobbing about in the sea below. It seemed Nora had chosen to break the news under the stars, which was suitably sentimental for them both, and Emma felt glad of it, but apprehensive about Libby's reaction. Not only in terms of their mother's prognosis, but also because Emma had kept it from her. Over the last few days, she and Libby had to some extent recaptured their friendship, their sense of sisterhood and trust, and she was very afraid of losing it again.

She went back into the bedroom and got under the sheets next to Patrick, still in her bathrobe. 'Spoons?' she asked.

He snuggled his body around hers.

After lying there with him for a while, and knowing that Libby now knew, she mentally dredged up the news from that dark space inside her, taking him through her morning at the market. 'Part of me didn't even believe her, like she was just making it up to get attention. How awful is that?'

'You probably didn't want to believe it.'

'Should I be crying now?'

'Do you want to cry?'

'Not really.'

'You can't force feelings you don't have yet.'

She was reminded of his amazing ability to accept any human reaction as normal. He'd seen it all before.

'It's almost like it doesn't feel real until I've talked to Libby about it. Is that weird?'

'Not at all.'

'I feel so bad about not telling her today.'

'None of this is your fault.'

She hoped what he'd said was true, and she kissed the back of his hand. 'Thanks for saying that.' He snuggled his face into her hair. A stirring from his groin moved up against her back. It was flattering to feel it, but she was nervous he would take it further.

He didn't. He was Patrick. Patrick was thoughtful and sensitive, and he had not only listened to her, he had heard her.

'I can't believe Mum's going to die,' Emma whispered, as her eyes dropped closed.

He hugged her tighter. 'I'm so, so sorry, Em.'

She wanted to keep her eyes open for Libby, just in case she knocked on the door in floods of tears. But somehow she drifted off to sleep in Patrick's arms, and Libby never came by.

At the first sign of Monday's dawn, Emma removed Patrick's arm from her hip, crept out of bed and dressed in her running gear. Her plan was to get fresh croissants and orange juice and make a big family breakfast. They would all need it.

Libby would need it more than anyone. She had never built up the resilience to deal with bad things. Her sensitivity made her porous. Yet so kind.

Fondly Emma recalled how she'd once begged her to pull the car over for a drunk old man waving madly at them from the bus stop on the village green. He had asked them if they wouldn't mind taking him home, like they were a cab service. On the way to his little house, half an hour out of their way, he had aggressively insisted, with eye-wateringly strong whisky breath, that they volunteer to clean the pews of the village church at the weekend. While Emma marked him down as a drunk, silently reminding herself to donate some money to the local addiction centre, Libby's heart had apparently gone out to him, and she'd given him her telephone number. Every Saturday for a month, she had ended up on her knees in that chilly church with him, hiding her agnosticism and cleaning away the grime.

Deceiving her yesterday had been horrible. Emma had never before lied to her about anything important, but she would explain to her today that she'd promised their mum she'd allow her to break the news in her own time.

Her apology whirred through her mind as she ran through the dusty, chalky lanes from the villa. She resolved to make it up to her, hoping to laugh in a macabre way together about their mother's dead tree quote and her typical bending of the truth at dinner on Saturday night. Anything to lessen their terror about her dying.

She prayed for her mum as she passed olive groves, lavender fields and tumbledown limestone houses; she prayed for her as she ran through cobbled alleyways past courtyards and painted doorways and back gardens crammed with flowers.

In spite of running a Church of England primary school, and leading prayers for the children every day, Emma's faith had slipped over the years. She was comforted by the rituals and structure of the Church, but she hadn't been engaged in a spiritual sense. Her mother's cancer had changed that overnight, and she prayed fervently to God to perform a miracle and cure her.

She emerged into a small square, where there was a simple fountain and a boulangerie. The water from the angel's stone mouth was like nectar on her tongue. Her nose then led her to the freshly baked pastry. She bought four croissants, three *pains au chocolat*, a special strawberry tart for Libby – her favourite – and a baguette. Warm butter seeped through the paper bags as she nestled them into her rucksack.

A café with a zinc-topped bar was open. She shotted the best espresso she had ever tasted and then set off back to the villa, feeling strong enough to shut the drawer on her ruminations until she had talked to Libby.

Bathed in the glow of the morning sun, carrying warm, fluffy croissants to her family, she thought of that cuddle with Patrick last night. It had been years since they had been physically close like that, and she realised how much she had needed the intimacy. Considering the seriousness and magnitude of her mother's prognosis, it was odd to be uplifted by this small pleasure.

Emma was laying out the breakfast in pretty baskets when Libby came out onto the terrace. She was wearing stripy pyjama shorts that barely covered her bum, wrinkled up on one side. Her hair was wilder than ever. Emma admired her natural curves and fleshy body. Not a dimple of cellulite anywhere. She felt a rush of love for her, relieved that she was awake and the first to come down.

'Hi,' she said cautiously, picking up the strawberry tart, swallowing away a lump in her throat. 'Are you okay? I was waiting all night in case you wanted to talk, but I must have fallen asleep.'

Closer, she noted that Libby's eyelids were fluttering low, hiding the brown, reminding her of their sibling squabbles when Emma had stolen her sweets or told tales to their mother. This, in Libby's adult self, was rare and disconcerting.

'I spoke to Mum last night,' Libby said under her breath, ignoring the pastry, glancing back at the villa with its closed shutters.

Emma nodded and chewed the side of her mouth. 'I know.'

'Why didn't you tell me?'

'I'm so sorry, Libby. Mum really wanted to tell you herself.'

'You must have known how much I was worrying.'

'But she was the one who had to tell you, not me. I'm sorry, I really am. But I didn't have a choice. I had to respect her wishes.' Dismayed, Emma realised that Libby was as angry with her as she was upset about their mother. She understood, just as Patrick had understood her own dry eyes.

'I was going out of my mind thinking she might be dying, when you knew she wasn't, but all you could go on about was the bloody supermarket shop I'd forgotten! Didn't you for one second think about how much I'd be freaking out?'

'Wait. What?' Emma shook her head. 'I'm confused. What did she tell you last night?'

'That she doesn't need an operation, just chemo, and that she has a good chance of recovery.'

With a sense of horror, Emma realised that their mother had not been straight with Libby. She panicked, not knowing what to say next. The thought of having to clarify the mistake kicked at her brain, torn in two between what she'd promised her mum and what Libby should know. Furious with Nora for leaving her in this predicament.

'Libby, I think you might've misunderstood,' she said, hovering at the breakfast table, putting down the strawberry tart. Its aroma no longer smelt as sweet.

Libby perched her bum on the balustrade, with her feet up on the back of one of the chairs, watching Emma nervously rearrange the baskets. 'Yeah?' Her toes were candyfloss pink, clenched around the wrought iron of the chair, tipping it back and forth. 'How so?'

Emma's sweat was cold on her skin. 'Didn't Mum say *why* she wasn't having an operation?'

Staring at Emma, Libby leant over to the table and took a croissant from the basket. She began picking shreds off it and pushing them in her mouth, flakes of pastry falling down her singlet. 'Because they can shrink the tumour without it.' The croissant hung from one hand.

Emma picked up the bread knife and began sawing diagonal chunks off the baguette, deciding she would have to take responsibility for telling her sister the truth. It was cruel to leave her in the dark. 'What she meant was that the cancer has spread,' she explained, slicing each piece down the middle with precision. 'So that operating would be pointless.'

'No, no.'

The chair wobbled as Emma put the knife down and came around to her sister's side of the table. She held Libby's knee, which was soft and warm. 'I know it's hard to take in,' she said softly.

She waited for the denial to fall away. But Libby shook her head. 'No, no, she would have told me.'

'But she told me,' Emma insisted.

Libby pushed another bit of croissant into her mouth. 'Why has she told us different things?'

Emma remembered her own initial scepticism. *I understand why it's hard to believe me*, Nora had said, tipping her head to the side and widening her eyes, as though questioning who she had brought into the world.

'Maybe she's finding it difficult to come to terms with it herself,' she suggested.

'But it's so confusing, all this. There she is, telling me one thing last night, and now you're telling me another.'

'She might have been trying to protect you, Libs, and wimped out of going the whole hog. She's got a bad track record for that kind of thing. Especially if she doesn't want to face up to it fully.'

Memories of their parents' separation came up for air. Emma had been ten and Libby seven when their mother had told them that their dad wasn't coming home, that he had had a breakdown and had been sectioned at the Priory and wasn't allowed visitors. The lie had been a protection mechanism. A lie to others to avoid the truth that lay inside her: she'd been usurped by another woman and this had been unacceptable to her.

Thinking of it now, it had been quite a lie. Quite a colossal bloody lie.

'But did she actually *say* her cancer was terminal?' Libby asked tearfully.

Emma tried to recall Nora's exact words. 'She said it was her last-ever holiday.'

'That's typical hyperbole. What else?'

'Let me think. How did she put it? She said they could chop her open and give her all the chemo in the world, but that...' She broke off, trying to remember. 'But whatever they do to her – or don't do – it won't make a jot of difference.'

'That's weird. *Whatever they do or don't do?* What did she mean by that? Was she saying there were still options? Or was there a disagreement with her consultant, maybe?'

'Well, we're talking about Mum here. There's bound to have been one.'

'You don't think she's scared of surgery and said no in a reactionary way, do you?'

'No...' But Emma considered this. 'It didn't sound like that.'

'Or she's testing us, waiting for us to beg her to have it, find out how much we really love her?'

'Do you think?' The possibilities opened in Emma's mind like flower petals in spring, like the miracle she had prayed for. Any alternative to her death was welcome.

But Libby sighed. 'I don't know what to think. I'm probably overthinking it. Trouble is, she's told us both something different, which means she's definitely lying to one of us.'

They fell silent for a few minutes. The silver-green sea was flat and still. Emma was feeling frighteningly muddled. 'It would be good to hear it directly from a consultant, or read a neat NHS letter in black and white, signed by an oncologist, laying out exactly what the deal is.'

'Yeah.' Libby whistled and sat down on one of the chairs. 'If only.'

'There must be a way of finding out.'

'When we're home, maybe. Then we can try to get to the bottom of it. But for now, let's remain optimistic. It's the only way any of us will enjoy all this.'

'Hmm. Yes.' Emma poured some coffee into her cup, planning a new fact-finding mission. She'd been naïve. Interrogating their mother had been a wild goose chase. A clear outline of her prognosis from another source was needed, and Emma was going to get it. There had to be a way of working around the doctor–patient confidentiality issue.

Libby broke into her train of thought. 'Connor hasn't texted to say he's on his way yet.'

'Really?' Emma's attention turned. 'Are you serious? I thought you said he was planning on getting the Monday-morning flight.'

'Costa Rica's six hours behind. And he's been on a surf tour and wasn't back until late Sunday.'

'A surf tour? Isn't he supposed to be grafting away at his book?'

'He needed a break, I think. It sounded amazing. He went all the way from Tamarindo to Jaco to Dominical and back to San José.'

Emma sighed, irritated with Connor before he'd even got there. 'One per cent perspiration, ninety-nine per cent inspiration?'

Libby let out a rueful laugh. 'Probably.'

'So you don't know for sure that he's arriving tomorrow?'

Reaching for her coffee, Libby shrugged. 'His text yesterday said he was going to book it. But no confirmation that he had. Have a read.'

She scrolled to his message and showed it to Emma. *Sunsets are blowing my mind! Waves are the size of mountains!* And so on. Give me strength! Emma thought. He was ten years older than Libby and yet he acted like her teenage son. Out loud she said, 'I guess he didn't say he *wasn't* coming.'

'Definitely maybe,' Libby murmured.

'And you've tried calling him?' Emma would sometimes have to state the obvious for her sister.

'Straight to voicemail. I think he switches it off when he's surfing.'

'Infuriating.' Emma felt stressed for her. When it came to Connor, not knowing was a permanent state for Libby. Then again, perhaps she was used to it. Perhaps they had both grown up not knowing. Not knowing why their dad had left; not knowing when their mum would be off on another theatre tour; not knowing which au pair would be looking after them; not knowing who their mum would fall in love with this time; not knowing what mood she'd be in when it ended; never knowing. Never knowing where they were with her. And here they were again, scrabbling around for answers, because there was something not quite right about what she was telling them.

After an awkward breakfast where everyone talked about everything except cancer, Emma went straight upstairs and logged on to the villa's internet to do some more research. The first question she typed into the search engine was *How can I speak to a doctor about my mum's health?* She stopped and went back, deleting it and replacing it with *Is my mother lying about dying?* It felt like a leap into a dark, nasty place and not quite where her head was at, but with the relative anonymity of the internet, she decided she might as well go for the jugular.

After an hour of reading through disturbing stories about mums or daughters or boyfriends who had told their families they were dying when they were not, she was dazed and appalled by how common it was. She also felt a little sullied by how gripped she had been by their stories.

When Patrick came in, she jumped. 'Just getting this,' he said, taking his book from his bedside table. 'Everything okay?'

In the spirit of their closeness last night, she shared her suspicions with him.

'Hmm. I'm not sure she's capable of going that far,' he said.

'Libby clearly thinks she is.'

He sat down on the bed with his book on his lap and spoke in his therapising voice. 'Libby's always been good at burying her head in the sand.'

'Yes,' Emma said, tapping and scrolling randomly, embarrassed that she'd brought it up. 'I'll be down in a bit. Just finishing up.'

When he'd gone, she closed her laptop.

Patrick's instincts were usually right. His analysis of people was learned, studied, bookish. He'd grown up in a seventeenth-century cottage with low beams, wild roses tumbling over the pergola. John and Sarah were normal parents. When Emma had first met them, she had sat listening to them laugh and chatter about politics and plays – John carving the steaming roast chicken and Sarah pouring more wine – and exhaled, thinking how lucky she was to have finally found her place in the perfect family.

She opened up her laptop again, but couldn't bring herself to continue the search. To shake off her confusion, she logged in to her emails to see if there were any Monday-morning administration issues she could deal with remotely. Anything to put a lid on it.

Alarmingly, there were three messages from Samarth. The subject line in the first was *A leak.*

Before she had read down to the end of his second email, she had dialled his number.

'You should have called me straight away about this,' she said.

'If the parents had taken it further, I would have.'

Hearing his voice, she was transported across the Channel to St Thomas's. If it had been term time, the children would be neatly dressed in front of their purple exercise books, scribing their phonics; or sitting cross-legged on the story rug with their necks craned at the teacher, picking noses and licking shoes – daydreamers and square bears, popular and awkward, all of them with a quirk that she could love. All of them within her safety net. Right now, during the summer camp, she imagined it was chaos, and she didn't like being so far away.

'You're absolutely certain they're not going to take it further? I wouldn't put anything past the Jacksons.'

'Minor Injuries said it was just a bruise, so Mum calmed down.'

'And it was definitely the leak that caused her to slip?'

'Donna didn't actually see it happening – she was on the bars with Oscar – but she said that Sophie's PE shorts were wet through and that all her friends had pointed to the radiator to say that was where it had happened. That was when Donna noticed the leak in the roof.'

'Have you called the plumbers?'

'They're arriving after lunch for another patch-up job.'

Emma sighed. 'Only two grand more to raise.'

'How many more cake sales is that?'

'Thousands.' She laughed.

'Don't think about that now. Think about where you'll get your next croissant from.'

Talking to Samarth about their rainy, leaky, underfunded school facilities should have reminded her to appreciate the luxury villa and the sunshine, but it had the opposite effect.

More than ever, she longed to be stalking around the scratchy nylon carpets of St Thomas's, chatting to Samarth in the library as they tidied books away into the book tree. It was simpler there. Here, everything was topsy-turvy: routines were gone, reality seemed unreal, truths became untruths.

'There's the most incredible boulangerie in the village here,' she said.

'And everyone's behaving themselves?'

'Uh-huh. Yup.'

'Good.'

'But if I say the word, I might need you to send an email to say the whole roof has caved in and that you need me back at work asap.'

'Ah. That kind of good.'

Emma regretted making the joke. 'It's complicated.'

'I'm very good at complicated.'

'I wouldn't be so sure. Mum's taking it to a whole new level.'

'My mum would probably eat yours for breakfast.'

'No!' she laughed, wondering if it was possible to find a mother more troublesome than hers.

'Beat this,' he continued. 'My fiancée actually left me because she couldn't handle her. And the worst of it is, I was jealous because she could get out of the relationship with Mum but I couldn't.'

'Oh.' Emma wanted to laugh, knowing he had meant it to be light-hearted, but what he'd said was terribly sad. 'I'm sorry about that.'

'Don't be. I'm over it. You've just got to get on.'

She pulled her sarong over her legs and plumped up the cushion behind her head, watching the fluttering of a linen bow on the bedpost. Beyond it, she noticed a lizard darting across the terracotta tiles of the balcony. Further out, a cruise liner on the horizon. 'Yes, sometimes that's the only way. I have a brilliantly effective filing cabinet in my mind. It's where I store all my mother's crap.'

'Drawers sound good, as long as they have locks and sound-proofing.'

She chuckled. 'Believe me, it's a psychological Fort Knox in there.'

'That's what I like to hear. Head Teacher is in control.'

'And don't you forget it.'

They had a gossip about a couple of the teachers – lazy Mrs Harrington and jobsworth Miss Worrall – and she wished she could chat like this all day. Distraction worked. The original problem didn't go away, but the sense of confusion and doubt shrank in the face of a busy mind. She was grateful to Samarth. Her family could learn a few things from him. Dwelling on the negative was utterly pointless. Over-emoting might work for some people – for Libby – but it didn't work for Emma.

'Now get back to running my school, Mr Lakmal,' she said.

'It's all under control, Mrs Hooper.'

And she decided it was. She felt hot with shame about her internet search and decided to drop her previous investigation altogether. With a clearer head, she began with some more practical searches about doctor–patient confidentiality. What she learned was frustrating, but she was comforted by the factual nature of her findings. Unless her mother gave her permission, there would be no way of getting information from her oncologist.

Moving on, she clicked into some expert websites about stage four stomach cancer and read up about the disease, arming herself with knowledge from medical journals, cancer charities and organisations.

Then she stumbled on a medical paper about a ground-breaking trial in the US. It claimed that 63 per cent of their stage four stomach cancer patients had lived two years or longer. They were looking for volunteers for the second trial.

There were various organisations and doctors attached to the paper, and it wasn't clear where she would start, but she knew that this was the route her mother must try.

It seemed to Emma that, as per usual, she was the only one in the family who was capable of sorting her mum out.

TWELVE

NORA

'It's too late for that,' I said.

You're saying I don't have a say?

'Absolutely you don't.'

I will change your mind.

'Not about this.'

I've changed it before.

'And look how that turned out.'

I don't regret it for a second.

'I do. With every fibre of my being. I'm like a smoker. I've been addicted half my life, wishing I'd never taken that first puff.'

I don't believe you regret this.

'Nobody seems to ever believe me about anything.'

Poor track record?

'The cheek of you.'

THIRTEEN

LIBBY

'Mum! Is Dad here?' Hazel cried, running towards Libby with her big grin, tripping on her oversized towel, her wet curls falling into her eyes.

Nora looked up from her sunlounger, where she lay fully clothed with her bag on her tummy, ready to go to the beach.

'I think he must have missed it, sweetheart,' Libby said. It was Tuesday, and he hadn't come through the arrivals gate at 10.30. She pushed away the image of a mauled leg and a cracked surfboard. 'I'm sure he'll be on the next one.'

Hazel's face fell. Libby pulled her in for a hug.

Nora sat up. 'He wasn't on the flight? You waited in the right terminal?'

'There's only one. He wasn't there.'

'But he said he was going to be on it. Do you think he's okay? Those surf tours are terribly dangerous.'

Libby shot her a warning look. 'Of course he's okay. He probably missed the plane and lost his phone or something, or it's out of battery.' She spoke loudly and clearly.

'Yes, yes,' Nora said, nodding one too many times. 'He's lost his phone and missed the flight. It's easily done. I missed one of the most important flights of my life when I was supposed to be going to Prague to meet a well-known art director out there. I thought I'd lost the job, and believe me, that job ended up changing my career forever. But actually it worked in my favour.' A smile played on her lips as she lay back and pulled the brim of her hat over her eyes. 'The art director was on the flight I eventually got, and we struck up a conversation, not realising who the other was. When we found out, I did honestly *try* to stop flirting with him, to be professional, you know? Oh, he was quite divine and much younger than me and had thick black hair and was terribly intelligent, with these intense eyes, and we ended up having the most wonderful love affair.'

Her wittering suggested she was nervous. Everything that had been going on in the villa over the last few days was obscured temporarily by the fear that something had happened to Connor. Could fate deliver two disasters to one family in this way? Emma had once piously told Libby that God would never give you more than you could handle. But why was she thinking about God? She didn't even believe in him.

Emma came hurrying down the steps from the house.

'Uh-oh, here comes the sergeant major,' Nora muttered, pulling her hat further down over her face.

'Hi! Where's Connor? I've got everything in the car for the beach. I've just been waiting for you to get back. You've been ages! The sun's going to be gone at this rate,' Emma gabbled. She clapped her hands. 'Kids? KIDS! Come on, out you get! You need to get dry and get dressed for the beach. We're leaving in five minutes.'

'Aye, aye, Cap'n,' Nora jibed nastily.

There was more tension than usual between her and Emma. They seemed to be clutching at the opposite ends of the same string, and it was fraying and weak, ready to snap and throw them both violently backwards.

Libby said, 'Connor wasn't on the flight.'

'Oh, no! Really?' Emma squinted at her from under her black cap. Her skin glistened and her ponytail was silky-straight, and her eyes were filled with concern. 'He *missed* it?'

'I guess so.'

'Is there another one?'

'There are only two flights a day from there. Six o'clock's the next one. So I might take the other car to the beach, and I can go directly from there to the airport.'

'You don't mind trekking out there again?'

'No, it's fine. If he's lost his phone or something, I'm not even sure he'll have the name and address of the villa written down. And even if he did, he won't have the money for a cab.'

'It's a bit of a risk.'

'I'll go this one last time. I'll worry more if I don't.'

A trip in the car on her own, away from the hostility, was so appealing, she might have gone as far as fabricating a story to escape the atmosphere for a bit. Furthermore, Emma had warned her that she planned on talking to their mum about the American medical trial. Emma had presumed that Nora would embrace it as an idea, but Libby thought differently.

The beach turned out to be more than an hour from the villa, but no further from the airport. As soon as they had found a parking space, a few too many streets away, a strong wind picked up and Amber complained about being cold. On the way over the busy road running parallel to the beach, Hazel lost control of the inflatable and it skittered across a car bonnet and landed on a windscreen. The kids ran at it, nearly getting run over, but managed to pin it down with their lives intact. Their screaming was caught on a large gust of wind.

'This is lovely, isn't it,' Emma shouted, laden with the picnic freezer box and a huge bag of towels, struggling across the grey shingle.

The shingle got stuck in Libby's flip-flops. It wasn't quite what she'd had in mind when she had imagined sunning herself on the Côte d'Azur. She was sure she had seen sheltered sandy bays marked on the map within five minutes of the villa. At least the sky was achingly blue. More than she could say about the sky above most British pebble beaches.

'Mum didn't want sand,' Emma explained, even though Libby hadn't asked.

They tried putting out their towels, but they wouldn't lie flat. They had to anchor them with pebbles in each corner. The choppy sea seemed prescient, symbolising the foaming crests and tumbling violence of Libby's visions of Connor, and she felt jumpy as she watched the girls falling about in it. They were having fun, losing their bikini bottoms, coming up for air with great screeches, spluttering through their tangled hair like monsters from the deep. Patrick had swum underneath the waves to the calm bit further out, where he front-crawled back and forth as though he were doing lengths in a pool. Libby hadn't wanted to go in at all.

Emma and Nora were standing in the shallows with their backs to her. There was a huge amount of gesticulating from Emma. It appeared their mum was not as invested in the conversation as Emma would like her to be. She had her head turned away and one hand planted firmly on top of her hat, and occasionally she yelled, 'Careful, darlings!' at the children. The cotton of her maroon kaftan was plastered to one side of her, while the rest flew off to the other side, as though fighting to escape. By the looks of it, she hadn't warmed to the idea of the American trial. Libby debated going over to them to mediate, but she doubted they'd listen to her.

Beside her, Eliot built a tower of flat shingle. Every time it was blown over, he would diligently start another one.

'This wind is a mistral,' he stated simply as he balanced the smallest of the smooth grey stones on the very top. His rust-red hair was brighter than ever against the azure sky, yet his face looked translucent, marked by smears of SPF 50 million.

'Yes, I suppose it is.' Libby tried to rub away the goose-bumps from her legs, pulling her knees up to her chest. 'Do you think it will affect flights?' Her ten-year-old nephew was prob-ably the only person on this holiday she felt she could get a straight answer out of.

'Yes,' he replied. 'It might. But the weather app said it will stop at around six o'clock.'

Libby checked her phone. It was 4.30 already and she still hadn't heard anything from Connor. If he had found a seat on the next flight, she would have to leave in fifteen minutes to get there for its arrival at 6 p.m.

'These are called *galets*.' Eliot held up one of the stones. 'They make the sea bluer.'

'I didn't know that, Eliot. You're the cleverest little nephew I could ever wish for.' She ruffled his hair and kissed his forehead.

When Libby said goodbye to the girls, she warned them, 'Look, this mistral might have disrupted flights. And I don't know for sure he'll be on this next one. It's a bit of a long shot. So don't get your hopes up, okay?'

It was blissful to be in the car, out of the wind and away from her mum and sister. But as she sat in one traffic jam after another on the way to the airport, she couldn't generate the image of Connor walking through the gates towards her. It simply wouldn't bloom in her imagination, as though she were far-sighted, deeply connected to him, sensing more than any worldly facts could present her with. She began to doubt the sense in the journey, wondering if it was a wild goose chase. But she drove on anyway.

She parked up in a space near to where she had parked this

morning and walked the same path to arrivals, where she stood at the back, glancing down at a gut-wrenching news headline on her phone about a landslide in Bangladesh. Each person who had died would have family and friends in mourning now, and she felt tuned into their grief.

As the minutes ticked by, her panic began to build. She backed off from the throng waiting eagerly behind the cordon and found a seat next to a bin. It smelt of stale cigarette ash, decades old, and it turned her stomach. If he didn't appear, she would have to start calling around his friends, and suspected she'd be marked as the hysterical woman who wanted to tame a man whose spirit would always be wild. She had never wanted to be that woman.

Another half an hour passed by. A steady stream of people filtered through the doors, searching for their names on placards or hugging friends and relatives. She scanned their faces, desperate to see him.

She tried his phone again. And again, in a frantic, childish way, as though the outcome might be different two minutes later.

As she spoke into the nothingness of his voicemail, the images of him struggling in the sea came rushing into her mind again: a wave that tumbled him, a speedboat that didn't see him, a sudden cramp, a shark. The phone lying on the sand, or worming and twirling its way down to the seabed, her messages going down with it. Her imaginings were vivid, conflated with scenes from disaster movies, and they struck a chill in her heart. It was the only way to understand why he hadn't been on either of the flights today.

Was this how it happened? Would she remember this moment for the rest of her life? Forever, in her mind, sitting here in a plastic chair in an air-conditioned atrium, staring at the sparkles in the flooring, smelling cigarette ash, knowing instinctively that the love of her life was dead?

She hurried back to the privacy of the car to make the emergency call to Connor's South African friend Martyn, from whom he was renting the condo. She felt jittery, fearing what was coming.

Her screen displayed a text from Emma. *Hi Libs, mistral has disappeared. Found a beachside café with sardines. Gives you and Connor a chance for a romantic dinner on the terrace maybe? Or you could join us, depending on what happens. Em xxx*

Libby swiped the text away and dialled Martyn, no longer caring what he thought of her. She was too desperate to know something, anything about why Connor wasn't there to enjoy the romantic dinner that Emma had imagined for them.

'Ja, he's still got all his limbs. Ha! Just about. We're too old for it, man. But what a trip.' Martyn whistled, and a dog barked.

She rested her forehead on the steering wheel, its moulded plastic pressing into her skull. 'Right. Cool. D'you know if he left for the airport at all?'

'No, sorry, man, he didn't mention going anywhere. I've been sleeping mostly, and kinda guessed he'd gone back to his book. Or to bed, you know?'

Was it simply that Connor didn't care about them enough to get on the flight?

'It's just he was meant to be flying over to see me here in France for a week – my mum's not well. But he hasn't shown up.'

'Shame, hey. Sorry about your mum. Shame.'

'Thank you, that's kind. She'll be okay. Is there any chance you could do me a massive favour...' She hesitated, feeling awkward about asking anything of anyone, but deciding she couldn't be shy under these circumstances. 'Would you be able to go check on him at his place, maybe? Only if it's not too much bother.'

'Hey. Ja. Sure, hey, I can do that.'

'And tell him to text me?'

'Ha! Shame. No problem. I'm heading that way now. I'll beat him with a frying pan for you, mate.'

She laughed. 'No way, save that pleasure for me!'

After saying thank you and hanging up, she knew she should have felt relief that Connor was alive and well. But she found it hard to let go of the drama in her head. The picture of herself as a wretched widow was more appealing than being unloved and discarded.

An hour later, as she was chopping mozzarella and basil for a lonely supper of Caprese salad, waiting for the others to return, wondering how she could frame the story of another missed flight, she received a text from Martyn.

Hey! Bumped into a mate of Con's, said he missed the 9 a.m. flight from San José and then lost his phone charger. Hope he shows up in France soon.

Libby was so irritated, part of her wished the shark *had* got him. It would have made a better story. There would be other flights coming in from Costa Rica over the next few days, but she was damned if she was going to wait for them.

Libby lay in bed thinking about how happy everyone had been when they'd bustled in from the beach and supper out. Even her mum and Emma had seemed easier with one another.

The girls' hair had been matted from the wind and there had been sand in between their toes that had sprinkled over their bed sheets, which had then disproportionately upset them. They had been wired and hyper, bickering one minute and laughing hysterically the next, admitting that Nor-Nor had let them drink watered-down wine, like the French kids, and allowed them to order two desserts. They had been only momentarily saddened by the news that their dad wasn't here.

Libby knew she should have been pleased they weren't sad.

But sad children were ammunition, living evidence of how
selfish he had been. Her descriptions of their disappointment
could have been used to pluck at his heartstrings. In the absence
of their distress, she was left with her own. She didn't think she
could forgive him for putting her through this uncertainty and
layering on the worry while she had so much on her mind
already. She composed him an angry text, telling him not to
bother coming over at all, that none of them wanted him, that
she hated him. It was a mean, spiteful, revengeful text that went
on forever.

She didn't press send and threw her phone onto the empty
side of the bed.

It was late. The shadows of the room were becoming
overfamiliar. She had left the windows open to let the air in.
The white cotton curtains fluttered. She liked watching them. It
was meditative, allowing her to drift into a less fraught state of
mind. The sounds of the sea lulled her further, and she floated
away from her anger into a deep sleep.

When she woke, she heard a voice. A tall shadow rippled
behind the curtains and she screamed, her heart beating out of
her chest. Her limbs shot into a bizarre defensive position of a
star shape flat out on the bed, legs and arms splayed. There was
a laugh. She knew that laugh. Before she could see his face, he
was under the sheets, pulling her to him.

'What was the starfish all about?'

He kissed her ear and she twisted her head away. 'What the
fuck?' she cried. 'Jesus, Connor. You scared me to death!' She
squirmed, wanting him to let her go, but he held on tighter.

'I'm sorry for being late.'

'Get off me.'

'You still want me, don't you?' he murmured.

'No.'

'I want you.'

'I don't care. You're an arsehole.' Her heart was beating at double speed.

He nibbled her ear and spoke gently. 'I'm so sorry, Libs. I missed the connecting flight, and then my phone ran out of battery and I lost my charger and I didn't have your mobile number in my head, and I couldn't risk leaving the gate to make a call anyway or buy a charger because Montreal was fucking chaos and I was on standby for the next flight, but then I didn't get on that one either. It was hell. I was in the airport for over ten hours.'

She stopped struggling. 'I thought you'd been eaten by a shark.'

'Bet you wish I had been,' he said.

'Too right.'

He kissed the back of her neck and her shoulders and into her hair, and she softened, relenting, relaxing into his affection, unable to fight it.

'God, I missed this. Missed you,' he said, climbing over her, flattening her, pulling her shorts off.

She should have made him wait for it, but she was too thrilled by him to stop it from happening. As he held her, her whole being settled, and she realised how much she had missed him too. It was the same when he made her laugh in the middle of a row; she could never hold onto her anger for long.

But she halted him briefly and held his gaze. 'You know, I think Mum's got a good chance of recovery. And Emma's found this cancer trial in the States. I mean, it's worth looking into, isn't it?' She had needed to qualify it, to say it out loud.

'Yes, sure,' he said, closing his eyes, moving into her.

She was never sure if she should want him to look at her during sex, or whether it was something people did only in movies.

'I love you,' she said, but he was too far gone to respond.

FOURTEEN

NORA

I hadn't wanted him here. The mistral yesterday had been my dying hope – excuse the pun – and yet here he was, shirtless at the breakfast table. His tan was deep, and his chest lean and hairless. My eyes were drawn to every twitch of his muscles. In a moment of rare empathy for the male sex, I felt sorry for all the men who were forced to train their gaze away from a woman's plunging neckline. It gave me a dry mouth, putting me off my croissant. Eating with stomach cancer was enough of an ordeal, without this to distract me.

It was hard to know where to rest my gaze. I couldn't look Libby in the eye either, not while she was convinced with such charming, childish optimism that I'd get well. I suppose I was to blame, and regretted shying away from a proper discussion with her. That night, when we'd swum in the sea, I'd been so happy and at one with her under the stars. I hadn't wanted anything to spoil our time together. There was a part of me that took heart from her ignorance, which shielded her still. Shielded me, too. And the truth hadn't seemed to make any difference to Emma. In no uncertain terms I had told her I was dying, yet she was carrying around false hope in the form of a medical trial in the States.

Now she was twittering on about the Spanish architect who'd designed the cultural museum in Saint-Paul-de-Vence, which she wanted us to visit today. Maybe she was as flustered by beautiful topless Connor as I was. She and Patrick probably hadn't had sex in years, and Connor made Patrick look like a frail old man, even though he was four years his senior.

'Connor, darling, do put your shirt on at the table,' I said, interrupting Emma.

'Sorry, Queen Victoria,' Connor chided, grinning at me. Libby chuckled. She was turned to him, with her feet up on his chair and a cup of coffee resting on her knees. Her body was exposed by her short shorts and singlet, and I longed to have such peachy flesh again.

'And cover your ankles, Libby,' I joked, but part of me was serious. I wanted them to put it all away. This display of sex and fleshiness in middle age. Even the way Connor put his shirt back on seemed suggestive. As he lifted his arms, I could smell him. There was a sweetness to his sweat that filled my senses and boiled my blood. My envy of their youth felt close to malice.

He told us stories about Costa Rica, about rainbow-coloured trees, and strawberry poison-dart frogs as bright as Eliot's hair, and sulphur lakes and forests in the clouds, bringing the exoticism of the country alive for the kids, transporting us all there. In this context, abroad and away from the daily grind of his life back home, he was in his element. He wasn't the moody, monosyllabic writer I'd watched stalking around Ivydale Cottage dreaming of flying Libby's ridiculously messy nest.

He had always reminded me of Hugh. A strange thing that Libby would fall in love with someone so similar to her father.

Hugh had been appealing and interesting, with his long dark sideburns and velvet jackets. The way he'd tilted his head to the side when he listened to me, as though he were jotting down every word I uttered. It was the journalist in him. Most of the time, he hadn't been listening. His listening ears came out only for the famous people he interviewed in his profiles, or for the women he wanted to sleep with. Oh, yes. It was useful to him then. When he'd retired from the *Sunday Times*, a couple of years ago, I'd thought, who is he going to sleep with now?

His example should have been enough to put Libby off troubled men for life. Having a father like that couldn't have been easy. His absence was a blessing, yet I had a sudden yearning to do it all over again with him. How desperate it felt to know I could never be young again, fall in love with him again, have my babies again, love them all better.

As I sat basking in the sun, thinking about how complicated things continued to be at the end of my life, the voices around me disappeared. My mind scrambled back through the past decades, flying over the various memories, right back to where it had all begun. To the original secret. To the marbled notebook with the curled corners that was shut away in the narrow drawer of my dresser upstairs. Always the notebook, as though nothing else of any importance had happened in my childhood, as though I had been no other age and there'd been no other story than the one I'd scrawled romantically every night in those pages. I knew I often dragged out the familiar old sob story about my father and the toyshop and our money struggles, but in truth, that well-worn narrative was the theatre backdrop to my childhood, a vast, roughly hewn canvas of oily, painterly impressions. That was all. At centre stage stood the secrets in my notebook.

For once, I was grateful that Emma was our tour guide extraordinaire, coordinating our day with her minute-by-minute schedule. I could see she was driving Libby mad. Plainly Libby wanted to sit guilt-free by the pool again. But she was a good enough mum to recognise that the girls would benefit from some culture, from lifting their heads from their phones for five minutes.

'Connor talks about himself *all the time*,' Emma whispered in my ear in the long, tedious queue at the Fondation Maeght.

'Does he?' I asked.

As we shuffled forward, she whispered another insight into something he'd said or done, and tutted like an old fishwife.

Once inside, though, she was distracted.

'This place is marvellous, darling. Well done,' I said, truly in awe of where we were.

And with that, she leapt in again with her nonsense about America. 'Did you read that thing I sent you about the trial?'

'I haven't, darling, sorry,' I said. 'But I will.'

'You won't, though, will you?'

'Of course I will,' I said, sighing inside, wishing that she had been able to keep it cheery and that I had been able to be straight with her.

In modern times, oversharing had become indiscriminate. I didn't approve of that sort of splurging. There was no doubt in my mind that keeping certain things to oneself built resilience and willpower – I was convinced of it – and that my repression of particular experiences – my nursing of them – made me feel self-sufficient, powerful at times, almost invincible. So it shouldn't have been a surprise to me that I was finding it hard to be frank and open with her and share how I really felt and what I really wanted. Breaking a habit of a lifetime was going to be challenging.

So many secrets and so many lies, for so long.

Amber took endless photos of the Chagall mural mosaic, and Hazel wanted to swim in the Braque pool with the fish on the bottom, and Eliot adored following the white line around Miró's *Labyrinth*. The girls were gripped by his retelling of the Greek myth of Ariadne's thread, which the white line represented.

'She was also known as the Mistress of the Labyrinth,' he explained.

I could have used her thread to lead me through the maze in my mind. It seemed I was running in the wrong direction with my daughters, heading down one path and meeting a dead end, backtracking and trying another route, circling the truth, getting lost on the way. Emma believed I was going to die unless I did as she said, and Libby thought I was going survive. Neither of them was right.

I stood quietly in front of Giacometti's bronze sculpture *Le Chien*, most taken by it. He was starved and fragile and sad, with his head hung low as though looking for scraps of food that he knew wouldn't be enough. I wished he would come alive and plod after me, so that I'd have a companion on my journey.

A crow landed on his back and I flapped it away. I didn't like crows.

In the Saint-Bernard Chapel, I watched Libby and Connor linger for a while underneath the stained-glass window. Their faces were turned upwards and bathed in a green holy light, eerily beautiful. I saw Libby reach for his hand. He humoured her for a second or two, but then pulled away to look at something else, putting both hands safely in his shorts pockets, pushing his pelvis forward.

I left the chapel to look for Emma and Patrick, but I couldn't find them. They had barely spoken to the rest of us or to each other, listening only to their headsets, standing at each artwork for the required amount of time. Patrick was one of those relaxed, old-fashioned nerds with a thirst for knowledge that was instinctive, effortless. As a newborn babe, he'd probably sucked in more facts than milk. It wouldn't put him in a highly strung mood as it would Emma.

I wandered back outside to the Giacometti courtyard and settled in front of *Le Chien*, resisting the quite mad urge to pat it and speak to it soothingly.

I felt a presence by my side.

'Plagued by self-doubt?' Connor said, pointing to the plaque about the artist.

'Hmm. You can see some of that in the old mutt's face.'

'Strange if you think about all the praise Giacometti must've got in his lifetime.'

'You think self-worth can be attained through validation?'

He shrugged. 'It helps, no?'

'I've had some wonderful reviews in my time, and some real stinkers, and none have changed how I've felt about myself or my work, not fundamentally.'

'How *do* you feel about yourself and your work?'

'That I came from nothing and worked my way up and was marvellously lucky to be able to make a living out of my passion.' It was only a *little* dig. He deserved some punishment for taking so long to get here – not that I wanted him here. No, no.

'Judi Dench never reads her reviews.'

'I found it terribly hard to stick by that.'

'Because you craved the validation?'

'Oh, I suppose so,' I said, flapping my hand in his direction. 'The good ones were always a bit of a boost.'

'You can't do it for other people, though,' he said.

'But sometimes, darling boy, the ego is weak relative to the headstrong id, and the foolish impulse to get ahead of oneself can take over. It's arguably better to overpower that Freudian horse and harness your creativity for an audience.'

'You think I need to write a formulaic novel because I'm not a genius?'

'One's ideal self can be a standard set too high,' I said, turning to him, looking into his grey eyes playfully.

How nice that we weren't talking about cancer. He wasn't treating me differently as the others were. He never did. Our blunt exchanges were such fun.

'As feisty as ever,' he said, winking at me.

'You ain't seen nothing yet,' I said, and sauntered away from him and over to the *Standing Woman*, trying to make myself as tall and thin as she. She seemed to be surveying the world, and for a minute I felt small next to her. Given a karate chop, she would snap in two. I was made of flesh and blood, which kicked her bony bronze arse.

'Hi.' Emma had appeared from nowhere.

'Oh, hi.' I wondered how long she had been nearby.

She craned her neck to look to the top of the *Standing Woman* and spoke out of the corner of her mouth. 'What were you talking to Connor about?'

'We had a stimulating chat about Giacometti.'

'Oh?'

I guessed she was geared up for a bitch about him.

'Yes. I think it's wonderful that he flew all this way for me,' I said.

'For Libby,' she corrected.

'That's what I meant.'

'I heard him joking with the kids about the woman's boobs in the Léger painting just now. Ugh.'

She made me feel instantly cranky and tired. 'What was wrong with her boobs?'

'Nothing, Mum! That's not the point!'

'What *is* the point, darling?'

'That he can be such an arse?'

Two crows landed on the grass at the statue's feet. I stamped on the ground to scare them off. 'Can't we all,' I said.

Emma straightened her cap and her lips parted. Her big eyes were unblinking. Before she could say anything, I shut her down. 'And don't you dare bring up that cancer trial again!'

'Okay, Mum. Okay,' she said, backing off.

'You'd better find the others. I'm feeling a bit light-headed,' I said.

She hesitated for a second and then stalked off past Connor, who had lain down on the grass next to *Le Chien*.

I felt bad for snapping. With a deep breath, I took out my phone and reluctantly clicked into the email Emma had sent me about the trial. She had first brought it up on that godawful windy beach, and I had shut it down before finding out more details. The doctors back home had explored all possible avenues, and I was angry with her for thinking she knew more than them after a couple of hours on Google, peddling false hope.

As I read from the website, humouring her, I admit my hopes initially soared, but then they sank again, lower than before. I recognised the trial. Dr Altmeyer had indeed already been down this route on my behalf. Due to an autoimmune condition in the form of mild psoriasis, which I had suffered from on my scalp as a young adult, I had been disqualified from taking part. A wave of disappointment flooded me, worse than it had been the first time around.

I looked over at Connor again, who was lying in the same spot as before. His ankles were crossed and his eyes were closed. He looked comfortable in his own skin, and peaceful.

When his time came, I imagined he would be better at dying than most, with fewer regrets, having sought pleasure in his life, albeit selfishly. I had seen people die in many different ways. My mother had gone suddenly of a heart attack after a hot bath. Lucky devil. But my father's conventionality and martyrdom had got in the way of a good death. He had departed slowly, reluctantly, and he had been bitter and angry about it, as though it were unjust.

It was perhaps why the universe had sent me Connor this week. In spite of my resistance to his arrival, his purpose here was now clear to me. Unlike my father, he believed that suffering was unnecessary, that martyrdom was a mug's game, that we didn't have to accept fate's plans, that we could throw the rule book out and live how we wanted to live and die how we wanted to die. I had needed the reminder.

He had been right on the phone: I needed him here.

FIFTEEN

EMMA

The children were behind Emma and Patrick in the ice-cream queue. They were having a hot debate about which flavour won out as the absolute best ever. Emma's phone pinged with a text. Casually she glanced at it, but when she saw who it was from, she hid the screen from Patrick.

There was a burst of laughter from Nora and Libby, who were sitting at one of the round tables with Connor, having already put in their orders. Nora's head was thrown back. She tossed her hair a little, behaving as though she were the star on a movie set. The strip light from the ice-cream parlour blanched one side of her face, lending her an unreal, filmic quality.

Emma went back to the text.

Hi Emma, I forwarded the link you sent about the US trial to Rachel and she said she'd look into it for us. Call if you need to talk. Also, if you haven't seen the email, we raised £35 in the Save the Gymnasium Roof summer camp cake sale. We're right on target to raise two grand by Year 3021!! Sam xx

She imagined his long dark eyelashes blinking as he typed those two kisses, and experienced a rush of excitement. Patrick had never sparked this kind of feeling in her, not even in the early days. She wondered whether she should have worried about it more at the time.

Their meeting had been more about their minds than their bodies. They had sat next to each other at a local bookshop event and had struck up a conversation about the author, agreeing that her book about a love affair between an ex-con and an agoraphobic was unusual and provocative and incredibly pretentious. But they had both thought it a shame that there were only eight other people there to hear her talk about her writing process. Gripped by each other as much as by the author, they had exchanged numbers, and she had known that Patrick was going to become a big part of her life. But she would not have pegged them as husband and wife. They had grown into that. Perhaps they were still growing into it. Their pace was lamentable, and she wanted her burgeoning feelings for Samarth to slow down. Being away from him gave her an unnerving perspective on their day-to-day relationship and how much she looked forward to seeing him every morning. It was shocking to realise she missed him.

The kids' ice-cream debate was getting too loud. Eliot was arguing passionately for pistachio, whereas the girls fought for cookie dough and Nutella and sprinkles. Eliot screeched about how much he hated sprinkles.

'Keep it down, you lot,' Emma said.

She put her phone away, wishing she could text Samarth back to thank him for getting in touch with his friend who was an oncologist in an NHS hospital in Brighton. She hadn't mentioned it to Patrick, because he had been dismissive of the US trial idea, trusting that Nora's doctors would have ruled it out for good reason.

There was another cackle from her mum in response to something Connor had said. Emma returned her attention to Patrick, feeling conflicted and guilty about her secret exchange with Samarth.

'I can never tell whether Connor and Mum hate each other or adore each other,' she said as she watched Nora touch Connor's forearm.

Earlier she had caught sight of them in the courtyard at the Fondation Maeght, and had hung back, unseen. Her heartbeat had run ahead of itself. She had been looking at nothing, with a funny feeling that she had spied more than she should have. The way they'd held eye contact as they spoke, their proximity to one another, how her mum had abruptly walked away had been wrong in some way, but she wasn't sure why.

'They're certainly brutal with one another's feelings,' Patrick said.

'Mum seems to take crap from him in a way she wouldn't from anyone else. She almost enjoys it.'

'Maybe they recognise something in each other.'

'Yeah, the narcissism,' she scoffed, which was what she knew he had meant.

'Something like that.'

Dropping her voice, she said, 'It's sometimes like there's sexual tension between them, don't you think?'

'There could be some unconscious sexual tension there.'

'Ugh. What a thought.'

Patrick continued staring at them and said nothing more.

'She's so much *older* than him,' Emma added.

'The age gap isn't that big. He's fifty-something.'

'Fifty-one,' Emma clarified. 'Going on sixteen.'

Connor and her mum were thirteen years apart. In theory, putting aside the startlingly obvious moral indecency of it, an attraction between them wasn't unimaginable.

'And your mum's sixty-four – going on fourteen,' he laughed. 'But she's a beautiful woman. And the spit of your sister. And actually, personality-wise, they're more—'

'Blimey, sounds like you fancy her too.'

He chuckled. 'Well, if I'd met her first...'

'Ugh.' She harrumphed. 'You wanted some lemon sorbet, right?'

He kissed her on the lips. 'Yes, and I'd quite like some of you.'

'Stop it,' she said, laughing, unused to the public display of affection, snapping into action to place their order at the counter. She made sure everyone's chaotic requests were taken down correctly and that they had the exact flavours, sprinkles, cone, tub, single or double scoop of their dreams.

The whole family trailed back to the cars through the narrow, cobbled streets and courtyards of the town. Emma's coffee scoop was heaven in a tub. Eating it with her dinky little spoon took deep concentration, and she allowed each mouthful to melt slowly on her tongue. She rarely gave herself the time to enjoy moments like these, and her mind wandered indulgently back to Samarth's text. Her tummy fluttered, and then she felt weird about how thrilled she was to have heard back from him. Perhaps there were other people she should have asked advice from first? Her school-mum friend Pip was a nurse, and her dad's cousin worked somewhere high up in the medical field. Both of them might have helped her find out more about the US trial.

Before getting into the cars, they stopped briefly to mill about in the evening sun and lean on the railings by the car park. The sunflower fields below were smudgy yellow, and the pointy tips of cypress trees nicked the apricot haze at the horizon. It was too perfect, composed like a painting. She soaked it in for a few minutes and then asked everyone to gather together for a photo.

Through the lens, she admired their nut-brown tans, bright summer clothes and goofy hugs.

'Cheese!' she shouted.

She was taking a photograph of the perfect family. Running strongly through all the girls were Nora's irrepressible features.

Curly blonde manes, round, open faces and big owl eyes. Connor's darker characteristics and rangier limbs had come through in Amber and Hazel only in passing. The absolute stand-out exception, she thought proudly, was Eliot, who looked like he'd been adopted. Patrick's red-headed DNA, having fallen out of his own head, now flaunted itself in his son's.

'Come on, you lot, you look bloody miserable! Do it like me!' She demonstrated by striking a model pose and pulling out a comedy smile that was more of a grimace, then captured their laughter in the shot.

Connor flung his arm over her mum's shoulders. How comfortably her head was leant into him, Emma thought. Her hair was tucked into his elbow crease as though it belonged there. Emma's attention moved to Libby, who was hugging Amber and Hazel. For a second, the dynamic between her sister and nieces was a mirror of the past: of her mum, Libby and her. The closeness of the trio, the love, the absence of a male figure, the maternal figure in the centre who was both worshipped and worried about in equal measure. Another generation, and little had changed.

It wouldn't occur to Libby that there might be some kind of flirtation going on behind her back. Not even for a nanosecond would the thought cross her mind. Libby had always found it difficult to criticise their mother. She might complain in small ways, or roll her eyes, but it rarely had any heat in it. On the whole, she saw the best in people, as though even a brief consideration of the darker side of someone would flood her with unmanageable sorrow about humankind overall.

Most daughters couldn't suspect their mother of stooping so low, and Emma was ashamed of her suspicions. Perhaps it was easier to find fault in others than to confront her own dubious attraction to Samarth. She must stop being so friendly with him. He seemed to be getting into everything, even family photos.

· · ·

On the drive back to the villa, seconds before the sun disappeared behind the horizon, light shards shot striking patterns through the lime trees and onto the road. Emma was tired and could have closed her eyes and gone straight to sleep, but she was mesmerised by the disappearing day, and she clung to it with a sense that all the tomorrows from now on would be different.

But the shift from light to dark was rapid, and the daylight was gone before they had reached the villa.

The bedtime routine with Eliot was fraught. He was wild with sugar and tiredness, rabbiting on at high speed about the artworks and sculptures he had seen today, begging Emma for some time to put in more lengths in the pool.

'You're too tired, darling,' she said. He was heading towards a complete meltdown.

Thankfully he drifted off mid-sentence, and Emma went back downstairs to the dinner table. Amber and Hazel had already disappeared to watch a film, leaving the grown-ups alone.

Patrick looked droopy drunk, and Libby seemed giddy and pink and happy – painfully happy to have Connor's chair scooched up next to hers and to have his hand rubbing her thigh, up and down, up and down.

Nora was wan and ethereal.

'How are you feeling, Mum?' Emma asked, sitting down next to her, planting her palm on the back of her mother's hand, feeling the rope of her veins and their slow pulse.

'Oh, you know. It could be worse,' Nora said, flashing a quick, childlike smile at Connor, demurely pulling her pashmina across her chest to cover her low neckline.

Emma was eager to ask her if she had read the trial website yet, but she had promised not to and she would respect that. She would talk about plans for tomorrow instead.

As she opened her mouth to speak, her mum said, 'Don't go there tonight, darling, okay?'

'What?' Emma asked, both surprised and exposed.

There was a sudden tension in all the faces around the table.

'Oh, come on,' Nora tutted, scrunching up the side of her mouth, as if to say, *Don't kid a kidder.*

'I was only going to ask you what you wanted to do tomorrow!'

'I don't want to do anything tomorrow.'

'Fine!' Emma said, holding her palms up. 'Wow.'

She folded her arms and stared out at the view. A thickness formed in her throat.

Then Connor let go of Libby and clapped his hands together. 'How about a cheeky midnight swim?'

As he said it, he leant forward towards Nora, making her his sole focus, challenging her to cheer up. A twitch a smile suggested she might, now that he was asking. The two of them stared at each other. The rest of the world could have vanished around them and they wouldn't have noticed.

Maybe he had singled her out because of her cancer. Or maybe not. Maybe he was flirting with her, or maybe not. Maybe, Emma thought angrily, everyone in this bloody family looked to her for approval before they made a bloody decision about anything.

'A swim is a marvellous idea!' Nora said.

Upstairs in their bedroom, Emma and Patrick were changing.

'I hate swimming this late,' she said.

'Nobody's forcing you.'

'I'm not letting those two out of my sight.'

'Who?'

'Mum and Connor.'

'Don't be mad, Em.'

'Shh,' she said, putting her finger to her lips, even though he hadn't been loud. She whispered hoarsely, 'I thought I was being mad, but I'm telling you, I've got my eyes peeled.'

He dropped his voice. 'To see what exactly?'

Emma put two feet into one leg hole of her swimsuit and almost toppled over. 'Them flirting with each other.'

Patrick chortled. She wasn't sure whether it was in response to what she'd said or because she was hopping about the room naked with her swimming costume tangled around one leg. 'And if they do?'

'Are you *kidding* me?' She finally got the costume on properly.

'You can't police a bit of innocent flirting.'

'Innocent?'

Patrick put on his gentle, professional voice. 'I think this conspiracy of yours is better than having to think about your mum being ill.'

She wanted to strangle him with her swimsuit straps, but said calmly, 'It isn't about that.'

He held out a bathrobe, like a waiter with a coat. '*I* believe you, thousands of psychotherapists wouldn't.'

'Thanks for nothing,' she said, and shoved her arms into the fluffy robe. He twisted her around, knotted the cord around her waist and placed a kiss on her cheek.

'You're welcome,' he said. 'No charge.'

She refused to smile and wondered if she should forget about everyone downstairs and instead rip her bathrobe off and ravage Patrick. But the thought of Connor and her mum frolicking about in the pool in the dark was too compelling.

Their submerged limbs looked wobbly and green in the pool floodlights. They were all a little drunk. Nora and Libby were floating on their backs talking nonsense. Patrick and Connor were swimming lengths underwater to see who could hold their breath the longest – Patrick was doing remarkably well, which amused Emma, guessing it would have bruised Connor's ego.

At one point, Libby and Connor came together for a cuddle. Emma was relieved. It was what she had wanted to see between them.

'No heavy petting in the pool!' she shouted out.

'Get a room!' Patrick added.

Connor and Libby laughed and swam apart, and Emma regretted being silly. If she hadn't said it, they might have remained glued to each other and disappeared inside.

As it was, the five of them stayed up late, still in their bathrobes, damp from their swim, falling about like teenagers, downing the orange cocktails that Connor had mixed at the bar. Emma felt the weight of recent days drop away, and her worries about Connor and her mum seemed silly to her.

After polishing off the Aperol and the last crumbs of the supersized bags of crinkle crisps, they decided that a game of beer pong would be a good idea. Every time they missed the ball, they had to knock back a shot of beer. Nora missed too many and Emma drank her forfeits.

Libby was the first to turn in, but Emma stayed up, making sure Nora was okay, fretting about her being up this late – drinking too much, darting about, tripping herself up on her long flared trousers – and that tomorrow she would pay for it with more than just a hangover.

At around 1.30, Patrick dragged Emma away from the table, leaving Connor and Nora as the last ones standing, playing a best-of-three. They wove their way upstairs and collapsed on the bed together. Within seconds, Patrick was snoring. But Emma's head was too spinny to lie flat, and so she mooched downstairs again to pop a paracetamol and neck a glass of water, hoping this would help with the hangover in the morning.

The glass she took from the sink was marked with her mum's coral lipstick. It was oily and thick, like a left-behind smile. As she scrubbed it away with the brush, she heard voices from somewhere outside. Tipsily, she zigzagged her way towards the open French windows.

She spotted their silhouettes through the cotton curtains.

Her mother and Connor were standing facing each other, inches away. Her mum's head was tilted back into Connor's cradled hands, as though he were stopping it from falling off. Her voice was high, mouse-like, but quiet enough to be unintelligible. His deep murmur in response had a reassuring tone.

A blink or two helped Emma to refocus, to double-check that her eyes weren't deceiving her. What she was witnessing became sickeningly real. She was about to launch herself through the curtains at them, interrupt this intimate tête-à-tête, when her mum made a sudden movement towards the open window. Emma froze as she watched her sit down on the bench on the other side of the glass, an arm-stretch away. From here, she could hear what they were saying.

'I shouldn't have told you,' Nora said, burying her face in her hands.

Connor moved to stand square in front of her. She craned her neck to look up at him.

'I'm glad you did,' he said, leaning down, cupping her face in his hands.

Emma let out a small gasp. Were they *kissing*? She recoiled and tripped on a small step down from the open-plan sitting area to the kitchen, disorientated by the darkness of the room, as well as by the alcohol racing through her bloodstream and the shock of what she thought she might have seen. She took the stairs two at a time, terrified about being caught.

Safe in the bedroom, she whispered right into Patrick's earhole, 'Patrick, are you awake?'

'What is it? Is it Eliot?' he asked groggily, opening one eye.

'No, no, sorry, he's fine. Sorry, I didn't mean to scare you.'

'What's up?' he said, propping his head up, yawning, reaching for his wristwatch. 'What time is it?'

'You've only just fallen asleep,' she said, irritated, itching for him to be awake enough to talk to.

'Ah. That's why I'm still drunk and hung-over all at once.' He rubbed his face and groaned. She handed him a glass of water from her bedside table. 'You're gonna need this.'

'I'd prefer whisky.' But he glugged it down and then closed his eyes, mumbling, 'What is it?'

She whispered, 'I think I've just seen something.'

'What?'

'I couldn't see them too clearly – it was really dark, and I could only see the back of her head – but I think Connor just kissed Mum.'

Patrick, who was never shocked by anything, coughed up the water he had just swallowed. 'Kissed how? A peck on the cheek?' He sat up straight, spluttering, wiping his mouth. They were almost nose to nose as she explained how Connor had bent down to Nora; that it had struck Emma as a kiss but that she hadn't seen their mouths meet.

'Okay, so their faces could've just been close,' he said. His eyes were as pale as the moon.

'Yes, maybe,' she said, but her heart was racing. Again she revisited what she had seen, trying to make it clearer in her own mind.

'There's wriggle room there,' Patrick said. 'What did they say to each other again?'

'Well, I heard Mum say, "I shouldn't have told you", and Connor said something like "I'm pleased you did".'

'Maybe they felt intimate because they were sharing something, so they became physically close but not sexually close, if you see what I mean. Could that be it?'

Emma screwed up her face. 'Could be. As I said, I didn't actually see their lips touch.'

'Surely he wouldn't be that much of a prick.'

She was not accustomed to hearing Patrick use language like that about anyone, and she found it really quite attractive. Rarely did she see anything other than a measured, well-trained response to an emotional crisis. He adored Libby. He'd once drunkenly told her she was the sibling he'd never had as an only child.

She felt anger build up inside her again. 'And Mum let him.'

'It really is unbelievable.'

Speculating about it some more sent waves of nausea through her. It was mind-boggling and, at this stage, wildly presumptuous. She settled on disbelief.

'There must be a logical explanation for it,' she said, thinking of Libby's lovely, innocent happiness. The burden of being the witness to an actual kiss, perhaps the messenger, opened up a pit in her stomach.

'Maybe talk to your mum?' Patrick suggested.

'Talk to *Mum*? She can't even give us a straight answer about her cancer diagnosis.'

'Oh Emma, my love, I know she's ill, and my heart goes out to her, but she really is giving you the runaround. She's not making it easier on you. Or herself, quite frankly.'

For this simple acknowledgment of how it had been for her, she had never loved him more. 'At least I've got you,' she said. 'Unlike poor Libby. I mean, was she aware they were having this cosy middle-of-the-night chat?'

'If she wasn't, let's hope she doesn't find out.'

'And anyway, I don't even know what I saw.'

'And your mum is going through hell. We have to remember that.'

'Yes.' Her brain felt squeezed. 'Do we need to do something, though?'

He rubbed her back. 'What if I talk to Connor? Get the measure of things subtly.'

'Not a bad plan. You can use some of your tricks.'

'They're not tricks.'

'You know what I mean.'

'I do,' he grinned. 'I'll find a quiet moment with him tomorrow.'

'What if he confesses to something?'

'No. He won't.'

'But if he does.'

'Okay, if he does, I'll find it quite easy to tell him to piss off back to Costa Rica, actually.'

'Yes. Good. I like the sound of that.' She smiled gratefully. 'For now, let's try and forget everything and get on with the holiday.'

'I think that's right,' he said, nodding.

She was amazed. 'I never thought I'd see the day when you'd suggest I bury emotional trauma.'

'Don't tell my supervisor, will you?'

She laughed and kissed him. On the lips. The intimacy of this moment, the trust between them, his empathy and his unwavering support combined to create an aphrodisiac more powerful than the text from the handsome young Samarth back home.

He held her, and she felt herself falling into him. She craved this tenderness, wanted them to be closer than they'd ever been, needed to be reassured that he would never break her heart in the way that Connor could at any moment break Libby's.

There was an edge of desperation when they began stripping off their nightclothes, touching as though trying to scrabble under each other's skin. Years of abstinence had not dampened their desire. It seemed it had been dormant rather than non-existent. But as he fumbled to put the condom on, it flopped. Emma carried on trying to excite him again, and he made noises that suggested he was as committed as before, but his body wasn't agreeing.

'Let's try again without this thing,' he said, pinging off the condom. And they did, with embarrassingly awkward attempts, but it didn't take long before they both knew it wasn't going to happen. He lay heavier on top of her, skin dampened from the exertion, and very much less desirable. However much she knew his mind had wanted her, it was a fact that his body had rejected her, instinctively, unconsciously and from the core of him, and this hurt. It didn't make her feel any better to know that he probably felt like a failure. Both of them would be humiliated by it.

Afterwards, they lay in each other's arms, having got dressed in their pyjamas like a good married couple, and settled down for sleep, ostensibly in a routine of companionship. But her body was cold with the dissatisfaction, with the anticlimax. A vortex opened in her mind and her mum's overheard words to Connor sprang out of it.

I shouldn't have told you.

I'm glad you did.

Her need to sleep fought with the recurring question: what was it that Nora should not have told him?

SIXTEEN

LIBBY

Libby found Emma and Patrick leaning on the railing of their balcony. They were in their towelling robes, nursing coffee cups. They hadn't heard her come in, and they both jumped back as though the railing had burned them.

'Oops. Sorry to barge in. I did knock,' she said.

Emma slammed her cup down on the edge of the saucer rather than its middle, so that it flipped and slid noisily. 'Oh goodness, sorry about that. Morning, Libs.'

'Feeling a little delicate, are we?' Libby chuckled.

'Not too bad. You're up early.'

'Connor woke me. He wants to talk to us both before Mum gets up.'

'Really?' Emma shot a look at Patrick as though Libby had suggested Connor was planning to kidnap her.

'He thought we could stroll into town to get a coffee.'

'What, now?'

'Yup.'

'But we're watching Eliot doing his pre-breakfast swim.' She pumped her thumb over her shoulder behind her, and Libby saw Eliot thrashing out lengths below. 'It's only a few weeks until his 5K,' she added.

'Please, sis. I think this is more important.'

'Do you know what it's about?'

'He wouldn't say, even though I begged him. He wanted you and me to be together. But I think he talked to Mum last night.'

'Whatever Mum has to say, she can say it to us directly,' Emma said.

'But that's the point, she's not saying it to us, is she?'

'And she's opened up to Connor?' she asked.

'I think so.'

'Actually,' Emma said, taking her sunglasses from her head and putting them on, 'Patrick wanted to talk to Connor anyway. Didn't you, Patrick?'

Patrick shoved his hands into his robe pockets and rocked back on his heels. 'No, no, it can wait.'

'Can it?' Emma said through gritted teeth.

Libby waited for Patrick to capitulate, but he stood firm for a change. 'Yes, it can definitely wait. You three go ahead. You can go to the boulangerie on the way back. I'll lay the table and catch up with Con later.'

He had never before called Connor 'Con'. Nobody did. As Libby closed their bedroom door, she got the impression that Emma would be having words with Patrick. She didn't have time to wonder what they might be discussing, though, and went back to her all-consuming worry about her mum and what Connor was going to bring to light over coffee.

Her stomach was in knots. She slipped her hand into Connor's as they walked along the row of cafés, waiting for Emma to choose one she liked. Connor squeezed her fingers, which usually meant he was about to let go of her. But he didn't, and she felt his love pump through her.

'What about this one?' she asked, pointing to one with pink napkins in fans.

'No. That's empty. This one's quite full, which is a good sign,' Emma said. But as they approached, she whispered, 'Actually, no, the croissants look horrible.'

This happened three more times. Libby was patient with her, looking out to sea, breathing in the salty air, knowing Emma couldn't help herself.

'This one looks good,' Connor said, sitting down at a table and picking up the menu.

Emma bit her lip and glanced over at the café next door. 'Not that one?'

Connor ignored her and gestured at the waiter. Emma sat down and began cleaning her knife and fork with a napkin. Libby brought out her knitting and started to sew the pink sleeve onto the body, stretching it out over the marbling of their little round table, which wobbled.

'That looks great,' Emma said, nodding at the yellow lightning bolt on the sleeve. Originally Libby had planned on two bolts, one down each sleeve, but she had decided that an asymmetrical design was more interesting.

The sweater caught the eye of a lady on the next table. She didn't seem shy about staring. Her bouffant hair was silver, and her diamond studs were as big as fists, and Libby guessed she had been a beauty in her day. She thought she'd suit a cashmere sweater with electric-blue and white Breton stripes, with maybe a little gold yacht embroidered on one sleeve. A stylish emblem on one sleeve of every jumper was going to be Libby's signature design. Her heart plummeted. It baffled her that she could be thinking about knitting while she waited for Connor to disclose his news.

Last night, Libby had been fast asleep when Connor finally

came to bed. This morning, before she had opened her eyes, he had put a cup of coffee on her bedside table. She had awoken to its aroma and to the feel of his big hand stroking her hair. His voice had come next, and she had opened one eye. A slit in the curtain had allowed in a narrow column of light. It had beamed onto his face, dividing it diagonally. His expression had been inscrutable when he'd told her he wanted to talk to her and Emma about Mum, but Libby had known – knew now – that it was not going to be something she wanted to hear.

After their coffees arrived, Connor put one knee over the other and sipped his espresso before speaking. 'I think your mum feels bad about the mixed messages she's been giving you.'

Emma said, 'I think it might be better if we hear this from Mum, don't you?' She smiled, but her teeth were clamped together, lips zipped straight.

'So why are you here then?' he asked her.

She wiggled her head, as though confused, unused to being challenged, and Libby felt tense, fearing a confrontation. 'I... well...' She paused. 'She hasn't been very forthcoming, and... well...' She stopped and smoothed a hand along one side of her ponytail. 'Okay. Fine. Go ahead.' But she refused to look at him.

'Your mum is very unwell,' he said.

'Oh gosh, no way, really?' Emma spoke sarcastically, taking an efficient sip of her cappuccino.

Connor closed his eyes, as though counting to ten. When he opened them, they were bloodshot. He spoke directly to Libby, ignoring Emma completely. 'I'm so sorry, but there isn't a cancer trial in the world that can save her now – and she's talked to her doctor about all of them.'

'Even the one—'

'Yes, even that one, which he's ruled out because of her medical history. They've scheduled her first chemo session for August the tenth, but it won't prolong her life for much more than a few months. Towards the end, it'll be about making her as comfortable as possible.'

His last sentence barely registered. It was too much for Libby's mind to process. Suspecting it was one thing, hearing it confirmed quite another. Terror surged through her.

'How long does she have?' she rasped.

'They hope the chemo will get her through till Christmas.'

Libby might have fainted if it weren't for Connor putting a glass of water in front of her. Going through the motions of taking a sip and then another kept her body occupied while her mind had a chance to adapt to the idea of living through this moment. When she came around from the shock, she and Emma clutched each other's hands. She looked deep into her big sister's eyes and recognised the depth of her distress. In that one glance, they were fused as one, two souls stripped bare, transported to their childhood selves as though there had been no time growing up and apart in between.

Through her tears, Libby said, 'We knew it. Deep down, we both knew why we were here.'

Emma gulped a few times before clearing her throat. 'I was actually *told*,' she admitted hoarsely, allowing a laugh of irony.

'Confronting it is the hardest thing,' Connor said, reaching out to them. Emma flinched, pulling her elbow away from him.

They were interrupted by the woman on the next table. '*Madame, vous l'avez laissé tomber*,' she said, handing Libby her knitting. '*C'est très jolie.*'

'*Merci*, thank you, thank you,' Libby said, taking it, wiping her tears. '*Merci.*'

'*Je suis vraiment désolée que vous soyez triste*,' the woman added, squeezing Libby's arm, nodding respectfully around the table. '*Au revoir.*'

As Libby put her knitting back in her bag, she felt the strangeness of making a connection with a complete stranger, and silently, sentimentally vowed to knit a sweater in her honour one day to thank her for being unusually kind in the worst, most overwhelming few minutes of her life.

She watched the woman go. When she returned her attention to their table, the air between the three of them had changed. It was charged with sadness and fear. 'I wish she'd been more straightforward from the beginning,' she said.

'She planned to be, but she said it just came out all wrong.'

'And she opened up to *you?*' Emma said.

Connor rose above her barbed tone. 'I guess I was a neutral person. She's scared. Or scared of you guys being scared.'

'I get it,' Libby said.

'Where do we go from here? Does she know you're talking to us?' Emma asked.

'She doesn't, and it probably wasn't my place—'

'No, it really wasn't,' Emma said.

'I'm sure she'll talk to you about it herself. She's got some day trip planned for the three of you, so maybe just hang back from bringing it up for a bit and enjoy being here with her. But I thought it was important it was cleared up. There's nothing worse than not knowing.'

'Thanks,' Libby said, fiddling with the zipper of her purse.

Emma remained silent. She took up her teaspoon and scraped at the sediment at the bottom of her cup.

'I thought I'd stay on for the rest of the holiday,' Connor said.

Tears gathered in Libby's eyes. 'That would be amazing. We'll need some moral support, won't we, sis?' She glanced at Emma, expecting her agreement.

Emma opened her mouth, about to say something, but closed it again. 'Sure,' she said, rummaging in her handbag, avoiding eye contact. She stood up, and the teaspoon clattered onto the floor at her feet. 'Sorry.' She picked it up, put it back on the table and pushed it over to Libby, as though it were a gift. 'I'd better get back.'

'Really? Now?' Libby said.

'Yes.' Emma bit her lip, tears wobbling in her throat. 'Sorry.'

'Em, are you okay?'

'Yes! Course! I'm absolutely fine!'

Connor guffawed and let out a small 'ha', which Libby didn't like much.

Emma took in a large breath, expanding her chest, composing herself, before stepping aside from her chair, pushing it in neatly, like a schoolgirl at her desk. 'I'll see you both back at the villa.'

When she had gone, Libby said, 'Why did you do that?'

'What?'

'Laugh like that.'

'Because she is so buttoned up. She doesn't know how to say what she really feels. Even after the news I've just given you, she can't just sit here and be with us. Be with you.' Connor's gaze followed the waiter, and he raised his hand at him, unable to catch his eye.

'But everyone reacts differently to stuff, you know?'

He watched Libby's mouth with a faraway stare, as though waiting for her to say something more. 'I get so much negativity from her all the time. It's obvious she doesn't want me here.' Again he waved at the waiter.

'Mum does, and that's all that matters.'

'Maybe it's best to just leave.'

'Without paying?'

'No, I mean maybe I should go back to San José. I don't want to cause any trouble. Not now. And if I'm upsetting your sister so much by being here, I'm not sure how much I'll be helping you or your mum.'

'But you have as much right to be here as anyone else in the family.'

'Do *you* want me here?'

'That's a silly question.'

Libby often forgot how insecure he could be. She was never sure where it came from. His parents doted on him, though they were bewildered by him. She couldn't say she blamed them. As a boy, he had been chucked out of two expensive boarding schools. At his first school, he was caught dealing marijuana from the 'shag hut' – the bike shed on the rugby fields. At the next school, he had demonstrated his anti-capitalist sympathies by setting off fireworks in the squash courts. At school number three, the art teacher had channelled his rebellion into her subject and he had thrived. Or so the story went. In Connor's family, every story, however troubling, had a happy ending.

'This was a bad idea,' he said, tucking his hair behind his ears, focusing on Libby intently.

It wasn't clear whether he was referring to this coffee or his trip over here, or both. Libby could never truly gauge his thoughts. There were layers to him that she continued to uncover, year on year. In this instance, she didn't care to find out. The last couple of days with him, lazing and goofing about, had been restorative and bonding, and she had found renewed hope for them as a couple. The distance that had stretched between them over the last few months, both physical and emotional, seemed like last week's news, faded by his response to their family crisis. She was keen to build on that, repair their relationship, lean on him more, demand more, share their memories of this holiday, especially now they knew how precious they would become quite soon.

'You were the one who said I shouldn't let Emma boss us about, so listen to your own advice and just ignore her.' A waiter brushed past her and she grabbed his attention. '*L'addition, s'il vous plaît.*'

Connor leant back to let the man deposit the bill in front of him. Libby picked it up and balked at the price of three drinks. She used some of the cash her mother had given her for the next supermarket shop to pay for them.

'Okay. I won't pack my bags yet, then,' he said. His eyes were smiling, and she read into them that he was amused by her assertiveness, but possibly sceptical of how long it would last. He thought he knew her, but she was easy to underestimate. She might not make the most self-assured decisions for herself, but if someone she loved was being wronged, she could be more headstrong than Emma and her mother put together.

SEVENTEEN

NORA

'Eliot, my darling,' I said, for the second time, kneeling on my old joints at the edge of the pool, splashing my hand about in the water, trying to get his attention. He must have been in some kind of swim trance. Or he was studiously ignoring me. I didn't want to think about why that might be.

Connor had insisted the noise had been a little bird – I hoped not a crow – or a small animal or a gust of wind, but I was less confident. Children were always sneaking about. It was in their nature. Emma, as a child, had often popped out of nowhere when I'd least expected her. She loved to snoop and listen in. I wondered if she remembered the time she had walked in on Stephan and me making love in my bedroom. She'd only been six years old, and it had been hours after her bedtime. Stephan and I had made a point of being terribly quiet in bed, but it had been an intense union, and I'd failed to hear Emma's bedroom door click open. It had killed the romance. I'd liked Stephan – he'd been a wonderfully talented playwright.

There was only one way to find out whether Eliot had been there last night, and that was to ask him directly. I left my towel on the side and waded in, physically stopping him in his imagined lane. 'Eliot!'

He spluttered with shock, his eyeballs filling his goggles. 'Oh! What happened?' he exclaimed.

'I've been trying to get your attention, darling.'

He grinned and took some sort of listening device out of his ear, showing it to me. 'So sorry, Nor-Nor, I was listening to the Beatles. Love, love, love!' he sang.

My heartbeat settled to its normal rhythm. 'Oh, wonderful.'

'Is everything okay with you?' he asked me.

'Yes, yes, quite okay. It's just, I can't find your mum or Auntie Libby. Or Uncle Connor, for that matter. Have you seen them?'

He looked up to the balcony. 'They said they were going for a coffee.'

'Only the three of them? What about your dad?'

'He's laying the table.'

'Oh yes.' I had seen Patrick on the way down to the pool when I had been looking for Emma and Libby, and had forgotten. He was a forgettable kind of chap, albeit rather unnerving sometimes. His quietness could be penetrative. He'd look at me in that considered way, psychoanalysing me, no doubt. I might be a fascinating case study, but if he thought he could get into my head, he had another think coming.

'It was only Mum and Auntie Libby and Uncle Connor who went,' Eliot clarified.

'Oh, I see.'

'I've only got two more lengths to do,' he added.

'Really? Your training schedule is gruelling, darling. Are you sure you don't need to have a break?'

'But Nor-Nor, you gave so much money to the cause, and it's going to help the school so much. So I've got to keep going.'

'Oh, of course, sorry to interrupt you. Off you go.'

Giving up on finding the others, I wrapped myself in my

towel, lay back on the sunlounger and read the news on my phone. The morning sun gently warmed my arms, its rays not yet burning, and I tried to blot out the memory of the sounds that had disturbed us last night, fearing a voyeur.

When Amber and Hazel pottered down, I was immediately on edge again. Amber slouched over to me, rounded shoulders, vacant expression. Her footstep was heavy, her hair was knotty and her bikini was too bright for her skin, but my God, she was beautiful. She settled on the sunbed next to me, saying nothing. Hazel skipped across, always full of nervous energy. She sat at my feet.

'How are you feeling, Nor-Nor?' she asked. There wasn't a scrap of accusation in her voice.

'Oh, your old Nor-Nor is holding up, my love, just about,' I said, aware of Amber's heavy presence next to me.

'If you need me to get you anything, anything at all, I'm here for you,' Hazel said.

'Thank you, sweet girl.'

She kissed my cheek and leapt up, bounding over to the poolside, catching Eliot's attention, stopping his swim with the instant success I hadn't managed myself.

'Hi, Amber,' I said.

She smiled at me. 'Want one?'

'What are you listening to?'

'Birdy.'

'Yes please.'

She handed me an AirPod. I laid my head back, experiencing a third wave of relief, reassured that my grandchildren had not witnessed an act they would never understand. The young singer's melodic voice stood the hairs upright across my skin. There was a theory that people who experienced goosebumps easily were more sensitive and empathic than those who didn't. I looked over to Amber's arms and they were covered in them. She had always been a self-contained child, inscrutable, but I imagined that what she contained ran deep.

In the middle of the next song, she took out her earbud and fixed her big eyes on me. 'Do you think it's weird to want to listen to music that makes you feel sad? I mean, like, I feel kind of sad listening to this song, and, you know, I'm not being joyful at all, and I know I should be enjoying all this, I mean, of course I am, it's amazing here, but sometimes it feels better to be sad. You know? Is that bad?'

My heart doubled its size. 'It's not bad at all. If music makes you feel sad, then that's a beautiful thing. You're responding to it viscerally. It's what the lovely young Birdy would surely want. Don't hide from any of your emotions, my darling. It's natural to feel sad. I feel sad too. Terribly sad about having cancer. But strangely, as I talk to you now, I feel terribly happy. Just looking at your beautiful face makes me happy.'

She grinned. 'We're happy *and* sad.'

'Yes, why not. Let's feel all the emotions in the world. Or, I know, let's go one better, let's name every single one of our feelings right now.'

And we did, laughing as we went along. She expressed her anger about being sprayed with pool water by Hazel, and then her guilt that she had begrudged her little sister some fun. I felt relieved that the sun had come out again today and fearful that it would rain tomorrow. Or was I fearing sadness again, or even death itself? And on we went. So many emotions named, simultaneously felt, both ridiculous and profound.

'I love you so much, Nor-Nor,' she said, in conclusion.

'I love you too, sweetheart,' I said, holding her hand, feeling more alive now than ever.

When Emma appeared, I resented it. She stalked along the poolside, saying something to Eliot, who promptly got out of the water. Hazel was left bobbing about on her own. I felt instantly

afraid again. Not of silly old death, but of Emma's shouty ways
– much scarier. I exhaled, steeling myself.

'Come on, you lot. Breakfast is on the table. Out you get,
Hazel. Amber! Off your phone!' she said.

I turned to Amber and whispered out of the side of my
mouth, 'What have I done to deserve such a bossy daughter?'

Amber chuckled, accepting the returned earbud.

'Hi, darling,' I said to Emma as she approached. 'Where
have you been?'

It took only one look from her, and I knew. I knew that she
had been Connor's little bird last night, that she had been the
wind and the scuttling animal. My bones shivered.

'Oh gosh, I'm starving,' I said, trying not to grunt as I stood
up. It was such an old person thing to do, and I didn't want to
feel old right now. I wanted to feel young like the children and
skip off to be fed, taking zero responsibility for anything.

'Can I have a word?' Emma said, with her right palm
hovering at my chest.

I stared down at it. She was not the boss of me. My sights
were set on the breakfast table, where she could not harangue
me. I swerved around her.

'Mum. I don't think you want to have this conversation in
front of the others.'

'To what conversation are you referring, darling?' I asked
airily.

'I think we should go into the house, so we're not disturbed,'
she said. There was matronly disapproval in every syllable. I
could almost taste it coming off her breath.

'I'm terribly hungry. Any chance it could wait until after
brekkie?'

'No, Mum, this can't wait.' She was walking ahead already.
I plodded behind, off to the gallows.

She led me to the study on the ground floor. The room was

small, filled with a large faded-white bureau and two uphol-
stered chairs in white linen, which faced one another ominously.
Emma sat down on one of them. Refusing to yield, I lurked by
the window, behind the desk, pretending to be interested in
what was outside. There was nothing to see except shrubbery
and a garden hose. A crow swooped in. Or was I imagining that?

'What a delightful room,' I remarked, moving to the bookshelf. 'But how odd it is to cover them all in funny white dust
jackets. Books are such lovely, colourful things to look at, why
lump them all together like this?' I waved a paperback at her,
still hoping we were here for a friendly chat. Her eyeballs had
frozen over. I promptly slotted the book back in with its friends.
There was no getting away from it. I was here to be interro-
gated, so I plonked myself down, feeling the nausea rise and fall
and then swing up my gullet as I waited for her to tell me what
she thought I'd done.

And waited. Directly above us, the maid was hoovering in
Amber's room. Having a maid was one of the many luxuries of
staying in a house like this. Another hidden cost. It staggered
me that people who *weren't* dying would pay such an eye-
watering amount for a holiday. I couldn't help feeling it might
have been better to put some of it towards a hospice charity, or
WaterAid, or even a cat home.

Emma still hadn't said anything.

In her running gear, her legs looked thick and hard, like a
man's.

She turned a paperweight round and round on the desk,
appearing sweatier by the second. The diamond on her engagement ring had slipped sideways to rest heavily on her little
finger.

'I don't really know where to start,' she began.

'Start at the beginning,' I said, holding my ground.

She rubbed her hands up and down the shiny Lycra.

'Firstly, I want to apologise for hassling you about the US trial and giving you all that false hope.'

'Because, as I told you at the market, there is no hope,' I said. Her face fell, and the rubbing stopped mid-thigh. I regretted the brutality of it. Not of what I'd said, but of my cancer.

To her credit, she pulled herself together. 'Yes.' She looked up to the ceiling, squinting at it, and I wished the maid's clattering about was our only problem here. 'But I want to talk about something else.'

'If you like,' I said.

She threw her muscular little arms in the air and shouty-whispered at me, just like Hugh used to do. 'No, I don't like it,' she said. 'I don't like any of this. And, quite honestly, I didn't think it could get any worse, but then I saw you and Connor last night.'

'Saw us?'

'I think I saw the two of you...' She made a sound that was rough at the back of her throat. 'Actually, I'm not exactly sure what I saw.'

I pressed into my breastbone. 'Well, then. Why are we here?'

She dropped her voice even further. 'I thought I saw Connor kiss you.'

'And what of it?'

'*What of it?*'

'I was upset.'

'So he did actually kiss you on the lips.'

'Lots of my friends kiss me when I'm upset.'

'He's not your friend, he's your son-in-law.'

'Not "in law" at all, in fact.'

'Oh my God... Okay, sorry, he's your daughter's long-term partner, lover, soulmate. Whatever. Or shall we say he's your granddaughters' father?'

Her insolence angered me. I slapped my hand on my thigh.

'Bloody hell, don't treat me like an idiot. I know what they are to each other and I know what they are to me, and I know what you think you saw last night, but it wasn't like that. The whole thing was completely innocent.' My thigh burned and I was enraged.

Emma had never thought expansively. She had never understood the creative sensibility. Like her approach to art at the Maeght, it was something to be ticked off on her bucket list. There was no *passion*. No understanding of what an impulsive act could feel like. How liberating it could be to throw caution to the wind. She was bound only by rules and convention. When she was small, when the au pairs were off and I would have to collect her from school, she begged me to put on some nice shoes. By nice shoes, she meant I should ditch my fabulous leather ankle boots. But I'm afraid I was unable to mould myself into the twinset-and-pearls lot at that ghastly second-rate school they attended – St Dullsville. Those narrow-minded teachers had turned her into a square. Her conscientiousness had become controlling, her life so middlebrow. She fretted more about the upkeep of her washing machine or the colour of her wooden floors or the unsuitable tracksuits Eliot liked to wear or the market value of that little house they'd never sell than she did about the things that should *matter*. Anything outside of her neat and tidy life had become a threat.

My feelings burst up. '*I*, my darling, have lived my life steeped in culture, literature, travel, the arts, and they have thrown up more questions than answers and have liberated me from convention. You should try it. They are the kinds of influences that have taken me out of small-mindedness and forced me to embrace other people's differences, allowing me to grow and change in the world I move through and the choices I make. I give myself to others in the moment, *fully*! Every day, minute by minute, my giving is wholehearted, emotional, empathetic, rather than a moral, do-gooding obligation on a head teacher's to-do list!' My voice had grown loud, and I felt my whole being shake with the truth of it.

Emma bunched up the side of her mouth. 'Riiight. Okay, so this is the game we're playing here? Hurling abuse at each other?'

Oh, she was a lost cause!

'There's no game, Emma,' I replied. She would never hear me.

'Okay. Whatever it is that *isn't* going on, please can it stay that way? For Libby's sake?'

'Not all of us are the same, you know, not all of us are covered in uniform white jackets like these books.' I threw a hand in the direction of the bookshelf, pleased with a metaphor she might understand, making it simple for her, deciding to run with it. 'We're as diverse and distinctive as all those disguised paperbacks up there. An erotic novel might shock one reader but titillate another. It doesn't mean the book should be burned.'

'Stop talking in riddles to get yourself out of this.'

'Metaphors, darling, not riddles. What I mean is, I refuse to feel guilty about appreciating the sensuality and kindness of a platonic kiss from a friend. But I accept that you may struggle with it.'

'Too right! Yeah, I struggle with it massively. I mean, if I knew that Patrick had kissed you *on the lips*, I'd be livid.'

'Darling, he barely kisses *you* on the lips, so I think that's highly unlikely,' I guffawed, but as it came out, I realised I'd gone too far.

Like a button had been pressed, tears flooded the rims of her eyes. Her chin dimpled and she stood slowly, effortfully. 'Okay, well, either way, I think it's best that you tell Connor to leave.'

I shot up like a much younger woman. My head spun. 'No. I will not send him home like he's one of your naughty schoolchildren. He's done nothing wrong. He's family, and he has as much right to be here as you do.'

'As *me?*'

'Yes, as you.'

'Wow. Okay. I know where I stand now. Maybe *I'll* go then. If that's how you see it.'

'Maybe it's for the best,' I said haughtily. The red mist had descended.

'Fine!' she yelled, abandoning the whispery part of her shouting. 'I never wanted to come on this bloody holiday in the first place!'

At the very thought of her abandoning me, I put my face into my cupped hands and began to cry, waiting for her to relent and embrace me. She groaned.

Hastily, desperately, I said, 'I didn't mean it. You can't go, not yet, darling, I've booked a special day for us girls. A chartered boat trip off Les Calanques. Just me, you and Libs. The three of us, like old times. Please, Emma. Give me one more chance. Please.'

She stared at me for a second, but it wasn't the face of a forgiving woman. Her eyes were sharp with suspicion. 'You really are unbelievable,' she said, and strode from the room, slamming the door behind her.

She'd left me on my own, feeble and misunderstood. It was the story of my life. Everyone I loved abandoned me in the end. I didn't know why I thought it would be any different now, at my very real end.

EIGHTEEN

EMMA

'That's it,' Emma murmured to herself, barely able to see through her tears as she rolled the number combination on the lock of her suitcase. 'She's gone too far this time. If I never see her again, it'll be too soon.' The dial stopped at 9.9.9.9. That's appropriate, she thought. It did feel like an emergency.

'You don't mean that,' Patrick said, shuffling his feet, shifting around the room, following her to and from the wardrobe as she yanked her summer dresses from their hangers and threw them onto the bed. They lay crumpled there, innocent and dejected. They seemed to be saying, *What have I ever done to you?*

'I do! I do mean it!' But her throat closed up.

Patrick took up one of the dresses and caressed it in his hands. 'She was just on the defence, because she felt caught out.'

She grabbed it off him. 'Exactly.'

'But she said it was innocent, so maybe we should believe that.'

'*What?*' she yelled. 'Are you kidding me? You're actually defending her?'

'I'm not defending her, Emma. It's just... you can't leave.'

'Watch me!'

'You're being ridiculous.' He scooped up as many garments from the bed as he could carry and clutched them to his chest in a big silly pile under his chin. 'Stop this.'

'Sometimes, Patrick, there's a right and a wrong. Sometimes there's no grey area to analyse. Sometimes it's clear-cut whether you like it or not. And Mum is in the wrong. There's no way it was innocent – I'm sorry, you should have seen her face. She's fatalistic about sex even on a good day, let alone now she's got cancer. It's like she can't help herself around men. Like she's ill with it, or something. And if Libby can't see it, then what the hell can I do about it? She can float around in her stupid denial for the rest of her life for all I care. I'm over it.'

'But if your hunch is right, the plan was to get Connor out of the picture, not *you*. If he does the decent thing and gets on that plane and never sees her again, it wouldn't be the end of the world, but if you do the same, you'll regret it for the rest of your life.'

Hearing Connor's name spoken out loud was like an assault on her senses, and the rest of his sentence was white noise, obscured by her rage towards the man who had come between her, her mother and her sister, disrupting her family unit. 'Did you talk to him?' she asked.

'I didn't get a chance. He went snorkelling.'

'Ugh. That figures.'

'I'll have a word with him, okay? And then you can decide.'

'You said you'd do that last night. And you never did.'

'But this morning things changed, and that coffee was arranged. And now your mum has said that there was nothing in it, and I think we should maybe believe her.'

'I really, really would love to believe her, you know.'

'I'm not sure you mean that.'

She blew out her cheeks and released a noisy sigh. 'To be

honest, that's insulting.' Without looking at him, she began folding a T-shirt. 'You know, she accused you of not wanting to have sex with me.'

There was a pause, and his face fell, and she immediately regretted bringing it up. It wasn't exactly what Nora had said, even though it was what she'd meant.

'Well, that's not true,' he said, his eyebrows furrowed.

'What's not true? What she said? Or that you don't want to have sex with me?'

'Of course I want to have *sex with you*.' He said the last part of the sentence nasally and under his breath, looking around as though someone might jump out from behind the curtains.

'It has been four years, Patrick.'

'No, it hasn't.'

'Yes. Four years.' She looked away, to the floor, noticing his toes scrunch up.

'It's none of Nora's business,' he said.

'You're right. It's not. It's the most private thing between us, but somehow she knows about it, which really, really gets up my nose, especially as she's the last person on earth I'd ever tell. And she's probably been talking about it behind our backs for years. With Libby or with her stupid theatre luvvies. She'll have been all, like, *Oh yes, sweetie-darling, I'm just so worried about them*, and her sweetie-darling theatre friends would have been all sympathetic about it, secretly loving it, and then they'd spout their flower-power, peace-and-love crap, and let their boobs hang out and shag each other or something, because *Oooh yeah, we're so cool, but poor uptight, frigid Emma, my God, how does she live without it?* And then when we have a row, she uses it against me just so she can win an argument, just because she can't keep her hands off her own son-in-law! Yeah, that's really so peaceful and loving, *Mum!*'

She ran out of breath. Patrick was staring at her open-mouthed, with his brow in an arch. He must have loosened his grip on the pile of clothes, and a pair of her ugliest comfy knickers dropped onto the floor between them.

She snorted. 'Mum's luvvie mates would probably tell me to burn those sexy numbers.' Embarrassed, she guffawed and then smiled weakly.

He picked them up with one hand and gathered them into his pile, but in doing so, a blouse floated to the floor. Then a grey running sweatshirt. Giving up, he dropped the whole lot, giving them a little kick in protest. 'Yeah, Nora, stick your peace and love up a big frumpy jumper, sweetie-darling,' he said, unable to hold back a grin.

They both chuckled, but there wasn't quite enough joy in it, and their expressions fell back to serious.

'I don't mean to rant on and drag you into this. I'm so sorry.'

He stepped over the clothes and wrapped his arms around her. 'No, Em, I should've listened to you at home when you warned me against this holiday.'

She laid her head on his shoulder and enjoyed his hand stroking the back of her hair.

The adjoining door creaked open, and Eliot stood in the doorway. He was clutching his towel around his throat with one hand. His hair was rustier when wet, and had dried in tufts. His eyes were ringed by deep, angry goggle marks.

Emma glanced at Patrick, whose pale eyes displayed as much terror as she felt. If Eliot had heard, they were in trouble. 'Are you okay?' she trilled.

'Are *you* okay, more to the point?' Eliot said, surveying the mess.

Emma switched into the default mode of a fussing mother, papering over the unsettling mood in the room. 'I think you might need to loosen the straps on your goggles, darling. When did you get out of the pool?' She went over to him, brushing her finger across the grooves.

He jerked away. 'I heard shouting.'

'Daddy and I were only discussing something heatedly. We were talking about our friends who are going through some problems. We weren't fighting with each other.'

His red brows joined in the middle. 'Not you and Dad. I heard you shouting at Granny Nor-Nor.'

'Oh, right! No, sweetheart. Nor-Nor and I had a little disagreement, that's all. But we've made up now.'

'Was that why she was looking for you before?'

Her heart banged at her ribcage, almost painfully. 'Was she?' She was surprised by how much she hoped that her mum had been looking for her after their row. To apologise?

'When you were out having a coffee with Auntie Libby and Uncle Connor.'

'Oh, back then. Yes, probably,' she said, exhaling her disappointment, allowing the heavy fabric of resentment to cloak her shoulders once again. On Nora Fitz's gravestone, they should engrave, *She Was Always Right*.

'Could you give me and Daddy ten minutes, Eliot?' she asked.

'Sure.' He nodded sadly and backed out, staring at them as he closed the door.

Emma swivelled round to Patrick.

'Either he's a world-class actor, or he didn't hear us.' She massaged her temples. 'Come on, Patrick. Let's just leave. All three of us,' she pleaded. 'If we go now, I might actually be able to salvage the wreckage of my relationship with Mum. If I stay, I'm going to end up killing her.'

'Not an ideal outcome.'

'Honestly, I know it might not seem this way, but I don't actually want to fall out with her. In spite of this whole Connor thing, I do understand the stakes, and I do want to be there for her when it gets bad, you know? For the hospital runs and her chemo and for when she can't sleep. It's better to help her with all the stuff that really does matter, don't you think? All this shit, this beautiful bloody house and that blue bloody sky, it's suffocating. And it isn't reality. It's just Mum's bullshit.'

'Hmm,' Patrick said, perched on the edge of a chair, with his ankles crossed underneath. 'The thing is, everything was okay until Connor pitched up.'

'You know what? I'm able to walk away from what I might or might not have seen last night – I mean, maybe it was as innocent as she said – but I swear, if I see something else, I just don't know. I really don't think I can keep it in. And I don't want to end up blurting it out in the heat of an argument. That'd literally be the last thing on earth that Libby needs right now.'

'True.' He nodded.

'So. Shall we make our excuses and head off into the sunset and find a lovely hotel further along the coast, then focus on dealing with Mum when we get home?'

He looked like he was holding his breath, but then he blurted out, 'Okay, let's do it.' He picked up the clothes from the floor and dumped them back on the bed, and began folding. 'You can say the gym roof has finally fallen in or something.'

'Yeah, good plan.'

'Squashing a whole bunch of children!' he added excitedly.

'Going a bit far.'

'Sorry, yes, not that. But something bad.'

'I'll make something up.' Her hand found his in the pile of clothes and she held it for a second. 'Thank you,' she said.

'It's a bit like an adventure.'

'To be honest, Libby will probably be over the moon. I know I drive her mad.'

Patrick laughed. 'Nooo.'

'Yes,' she said, snorting.

They fell into a quiet rhythm of packing up. She thought about Samarth and his advice. He had suggested they stay here for only a few days. If she had listened to him, they might not have found themselves in this mess. The week had felt like an eternity; like they were in a doll's house with a big snotty child moving them into positions they didn't want to be in and closing them in under the painted roof at night, legs twisted and heads on the wrong way.

The doors to the wardrobe were open when Libby came in. The hangers were still fidgeting on the rail. Patrick scuttled into the bathroom.

'What's going on?' she said. A strip of burnt skin ran across her cheeks and nose, making the whites of her eyes seem brighter.

'There's been an emergency at the school,' Emma said.

'Right. Okay.'

'The gym roof has collapsed.' She wondered if she should add in some of Patrick's squashed children.

'Can't someone else deal with it?'

'The kids are okay, by the way,' she said pointedly.

'That's good.' Libby clearly didn't believe her about the roof. Only an idiot would.

'We'll be heading off in about an hour.'

'Were you even going to say goodbye?'

'Of course we were!'

'The girls will be devastated.'

Emma turned away to zip up her suitcase. 'I'm sorry,' she mumbled. 'I know. But we'll see them at home. It's only a week.'

'You're really leaving, just because Connor's staying?'

'It's not that.'

'What's going on, then?'

Emma clenched her back teeth. 'Mum wants me to go, so I'm going.'

'What the hell happened between you guys this morning? I thought things were settling down a bit. But she was really upset just now.'

She turned to face Libby, ready to spring forward in self-defence. Then the grainy, shadowy image of Connor and their mum came into her mind. 'She'll get over it,' she said.

Libby's tone changed. 'How can you be so hard on her?'

Here we go, Emma thought. Libby would be thinking she was an unforgiving, robotic pragmatist. Blah, blah, blah. She was just like Dad. Blah, blah. By leaving, she was being true to type, proof that she was a heartless woman, a callous daughter. Blah.

'I'm so sorry, I really am,' she said, as dry-eyed and angry as Libby expected her to be. 'But she's too much for me. You have to understand, I love her, but I can't cope being here.'

In the absence of full disclosure, it was the most authentic expression of how she felt. What she had seen last night had floored her, whether her mother had denied it or not. It was too complicated, too messy. She needed to make a clean break from their dysfunction.

But Libby wouldn't drop it. 'Sorry, but that's not good enough. You can't run away now, just because she said something you don't like. Yes, she handles things differently to you, and yes, she's a total pain in the arse, but she's dying, and this might be her last-ever holiday...' Her voice broke. 'Emma, she's *dying*. And she's our mum! Does that even compute?' Her face crumpled, crushing Emma's heart.

'Of course it does,' Emma said quietly, touching her shoulder, feeling the doubts flood in. 'And I'm going to be there every step of the way when we're home.'

'No! I need you here now! I can't do this without you!' Libby cried, wiping her face with the back of her wrist, wild-eyed and imploring.

It had never occurred to Emma that her sister might want her to stay this much. 'But I thought you thought I was really annoying all the time?'

'You *are*! But I love you to tiny pieces. I know Mum and I spend loads more time together, but you're the one we rely on.

You look after us. Like we're the stupid siblings and you're the mum.'

Emma shook her head, trying to shake away the tears. 'More like I'm a bossy cow who keeps you in line.'

'Yes, and we love you for it.' Libby sniffed, unzipping Emma's suitcase. Taking out one garment at a time, she started hanging them back up. She would not let her go. 'Now come on, we need you to go to the supermarket with one of your Emma-style anally retentive lists, so that we actually eat something other than Coco Pops. And we need you to make sure the candles are out at the end of the night so that we don't burn the house down. And *I* need you to make sure I don't push Mum off the deck of this bloody boat she's chartered. Okay?'

'Okay.' Emma snorted, and began helping to unpack her things, resolving to hold in all the truths in the world if that was what her little sister needed from her.

NINETEEN

LIBBY

'Bye,' Libby said, kissing Hazel on the forehead. Hazel was lying diagonally across Libby and Connor's double bed, having taken full possession of it for most of last night. Connor had moved to the spare room, angry with Libby for letting their daughter in, accusing her of being indulgent.

'Don't go, Mummy,' Hazel begged now. Her eyes were barely open, but she grabbed Libby around the middle, forcing her to sit down.

'Sweetheart, not this again.' Libby had talked to her half the night about how safe it was to take a trip on a sailing boat in the Mediterranean, and had soothed her to sleep after a nightmare, sleeping very little herself. There was nothing left of her to give.

'What if there's a mistral?' Hazel whined, burrowing into her, curling her body around Libby's. From the impression Nora had given them about the seriousness of her agenda, a mistral would be the least of their problems. But Libby didn't tell her daughter that.

'Look outside. The sea is flat as a pancake. And if there was one, they'd cancel it.'

'I wish I could come.'

'So that you can drown too?'

'No, Mum! So I can save you if you fall in.'

Libby laughed and Hazel hid her smile in her lap.

'I saw that,' Libby teased, brushing her daughter's hair back and kissing her again. 'Nobody's going to fall in. I'll see you later. I'll take lots of pictures and send you texts. I love you. Be good for Daddy.'

Hazel held her tighter and Libby tried to prise her off. 'Hazel, I've got to go. They're waiting for me.'

'I love you, I love you, I love you,' Hazel repeated as Libby untwisted her body from her grasp. A dozen calls of 'I love you' rang out as she walked away. It was a wrench to leave her while she was upset, but Libby had no choice. The boat her mum had chartered left at 9 a.m. from Port de la Pointe Rouge, two hours away.

Emma drove. The three of them were quiet. Nora hummed along to the radio, breaking off to pass comment on a roadside watermelon stand, and Libby talked a little about Hazel's anxiety and then nodded off, waking up with a cricked neck to hear the other two bickering about the directions to the harbour.

Groggily, she followed them out of the car to the jetty, wishing she'd had more sleep last night, guessing she would need to be fortified for the day ahead. She wasn't wholly pessimistic about it. An absurd, illogical part of her hoped her mum was going to admit to making the whole dying-of-cancer thing up and they'd be able to go back to normal again.

Libby took a long stride from land to the deck of their sailing boat. The skipper was a smiley, muscular young woman in a blue cap and belted shorts. She was called Zara, and she held Libby's hand as Libby rebalanced on unsteady new ground.

After some safety advice and a quick tour, she untied, retied, coiled, uncoiled ropes, ducking under the sail and over booms, in and out of the hold, before taking up her position behind her big steering wheel. The boat cut through the inlet and out into the darker open sea.

Libby, Emma and Nora edged their way to the bow, where there was a supersized beanbag. Nora slid into the middle. Libby and Emma lay either side of her. She pulled them in closer, and Libby imagined Emma initially resisting but then yielding to her affection.

The breeze was warm. Their hair was flattened onto their foreheads. It seemed they were heading straight for the empty horizon, but then the boat swerved left and hugged the shoreline, gliding through aquamarine waters and alongside the undulating limestone cliff edges and inlets of Les Calanques. From their new perspective out at sea, they saw villas like theirs embedded in the rock strata. The properties seemed to be sitting prettily and proudly in their positions, as though smug to have had permission from the rocks to perch there for a few hundred years.

Predictably, Emma ran a geography lesson, informing her mum and sister of the Messinian salinity crisis five million years ago, of interglacial sea-level drops and fluvial and karst processes, but it soon became an unintelligible background murmur. Neither Nora nor Libby put their hands up to ask questions like her schoolchildren might. They had their eyes closed, heads back, and were enjoying the ride.

For a short time, Libby forgot that they were there for anything other than fun.

She breathed differently. All around them there was blue, occasionally striped with the white-golden wisps of her mum's hair. Salt was on her tongue and stinging her eyes pleasantly, and the air seemed to run through her rather than over her. There was a paring down, a sense of disappearing from people and places, flying over the water into the natural world, empowered by the purity and simplicity of it. She felt Nora's body warmth down one side, and her stomach moved up and down with the waves like flutters of excitement.

After a while, Zara found a spot to drop anchor for a swim.

Libby jumped off the side, feeling the slam of water on her feet, seeing the shoals of silvery fish disperse and regroup, wiggling and nipping away. She and Emma swam into one of the narrower inlets, and Libby grazed her knee on the rocks and bled, and childishly feared the ocean and its creatures below them.

Neither of them openly questioned why their mum had chartered this boat for the three of them alone. Libby had started to believe it was simply a gift of experience.

Their lunch was served on a long table under a stretch of canvas in the centre of the boat. Zara had prepared baguette and Brie and red grapes, followed by cups of strong coffee, a slice of Montélimar almond nougat and some dusty chocolate truffles.

Afterwards, Libby lay on the bench with her knees bent up, feeling the sun dry her skin, wishing she could feel relaxed like this every day of her life, wondering if Connor's Costa Rican plan wasn't such a bad idea after all.

Nora offered them more coffee before pouring some for herself.

'This is just as healing for us as I'd hoped it would be,' she began. 'What I'm going to tell you now mustn't spoil your memory of it. I want you to keep it inside your heart.'

Libby dragged herself up to sitting. Her mum's elbows were on the table and her cup hovered where her lips should be, but her head was turned. Her profile was a pale statue against the blue. She had never looked so beautiful. Libby glanced at Emma, perplexed, and Emma frowned back at her. Her posture was excessively straight, and her fingers rested on the edge of the table, as though readied to push herself up.

All manner of absurd possibilities ran through Libby's mind: their father wasn't their real father; they weren't real sisters; Nora wasn't their real mother; she was a man; their dad was a woman; they were Macedonian orphans; they were the children of child-killers.

Nora turned her face towards them. 'I haven't been wholly truthful,' she said.

Libby's heartbeat sent vibrations to her fingertips. They throbbed with hope. Nora was going to tell them how sorry she was that she had lied to them, that she didn't have cancer after all and that she was checking into a specialist clinic for manipulative, self-obsessed nutters.

'We don't mind,' she interjected. A psychotic episode was better than dying.

Nora continued. 'I know Connor filled you in on some of the facts.'

Libby felt her mouth fill, and she avoided eye contact with Emma. The sun beat down on her back. Neither of them spoke.

'Basically, it will be a ghastly, slow death, painful and undignified. I'll lose all my hair. There'll be bedsores and green-nylon-clad nurses, and I'll be lying in an ugly hospital bed jammed unattractively in my lovely front room. Oh God, and one of those awful greying commodes, which will absolutely ruin my stylish little downstairs loo with the hollyhock wallpaper.' Her hand brushed down her throat and she fiddled with her necklace.

A tiny bird fluttered onto the table and then flew up into an eddy of air. Libby wondered whether she should say something reassuring, but she couldn't speak.

Nora continued. 'My body will waste away until I can't swallow food or even water, and finally my vital organs will shut down. I'll moan and groan and pee down tubes and soil the sheets, and towards the end I'll be high on morphine. At best I'll talk maudlin gibberish and at worst cruel truths that will leave a nasty stain on our relationship long after I've gone. I watched my father go like that, and I vowed I'd never let you see me die the same way.'

In this pause, Libby felt breathless, horrified by the indignities her mum faced.

They were further out now, moving fast through dark waters. The villas along the cliffs were tiny specks. Zara was sitting back, one expert toe steadying the wheel, squinting ahead from under her cap. In spite of her relaxed demeanour, it was obvious she was focused completely on the job, and Libby envied her.

'I want you to remember me as I am now,' Nora said, rubbing the coral lipstick print off her coffee cup with her thumb. 'Right here, right now. Look at me. I'm vital and present. And I want you to witness me living my best life right up until the minute I die. You see, darlings, I'm not scared of death. I'm scared of *how* I might die.'

She took a sip of coffee, leaving another lipstick mark. Libby wanted to snatch the cup from her. 'What are you saying, Mum?'

Emma nodded. 'Yes, what are you saying?'

Mum's moony, beautiful face and eyes were filled with light, ghostly and heavenly. She let her hair whip around her head, flicking it away occasionally, ensuring her gaze was trained on Libby and then on Emma, back and forth between them measuredly. Her voice seemed to come from deep inside her chest. 'I don't want you to see my fear and suffering towards the end of some horrendous chemo fight, ravaged and ugly with it. I'd like you to be able to enjoy one last perfect week with me and have a wonderful goodbye supper – a celebration of life. Then I want to go upstairs, run a bath, take the pills I've been storing up and end my life peacefully.' She finished her speech with a benign smile.

'Oh God... Mum,' Libby breathed, wanting to unhear what she had heard, horror-struck, dumbly tongue-tied. Emma's stare was fixed on their mum, but there was a sickly blankness to it, as though she were looking but not seeing, hearing but not absorbing.

Nora powered on. 'I'd like you to think about what kind of celebration we might have as a family, and how we might involve the children. I want to make it a happy reflection of my life rather than a sad one. I want to show them there's such a thing as a good death. One that I have chosen with all of us in mind.'

'How long have you wanted to do this?' Libby managed to ask, having to catch her breath twice, as though she were walking up a hill.

'A while now.' Nora looked from Libby to Emma. 'Emma, have you registered what I've just told you?'

Emma nodded first, and then shook her head, and her eyes darted up to the sky, anywhere but look at her mother. 'Sorry, yes. It's quite a lot to take in.'

'I know it is.'

There was a break in their exchange. Libby gazed out at the horizon and collected herself, pushed the panic down. Emma's chest was heaving up and down unnaturally fast. Nora looked from one daughter to the other. 'I'd like to know how you both feel about it,' she said at last.

'I don't really know,' Libby replied, thinking it was the most awful idea she had ever had to contemplate.

'Emma, you've said nothing, darling.'

There was a small pause. 'I don't know either, I really don't. How do you want us to feel?'

'I would very much like your blessing,' Nora said simply, looking down at her hands and then up at them both again.

Libby felt tears spill down her cheeks. 'I don't want to lose you at all. That's how I feel about it, I think. I just don't want to lose you, and by saying it's okay, I feel like I'm letting you go. And I can't do that.'

'Oh darling, it's so hard, I know that.' With these words came Nora's own tears. 'Emma, darling? Are you okay?'

Emma's cheeks had flushed hot pink. 'Yes. Sorry. Gosh. I'm just feeling a bit hot,' she said, flapping her hands in front of her face, clearing her throat more loudly than her voice had been.

Nora reached for her hand. Abruptly, Emma tried to stand up, banging her thighs on the nailed-down table, haphazardly shuffling out to the end of the bench. 'Sorry, Mum, I really am feeling a bit funny.' She went to the edge of the deck, peering over the side, as though looking for a place to be sick, steadying herself on the rail. The water was shooting away below them. They were no longer in the safety zone of shallower waters. There was nowhere for either of them to escape to, and Libby realised that this was why their mum had chosen a boat. They were a captive audience.

Emma spoke without turning. 'I just need a few minutes. I think I'll go for a swim. To cool down.'

Libby slid out from the bench and went to her, reaching out to her. 'Sis, come on, let's sit down. We're too far out for a swim.'

'I'll be fine,' Emma said, sidestepping her, quickly stripping down to her swimsuit. 'It's okay! I'll be back in a minute.'

Zara, noticing, was up, aghast, and moving towards her. '*Non! Madame! Attention! La mer*. We go very fast!'

But with one adept dive, Emma was over the side.

'*Madame!*' Zara cried, running to the rail to see Emma swimming away in a furious front crawl towards the shore. '*Mon Dieu!*'

The water looked choppy, irritable and bottomless. As the sailing boat careered on, Emma's tiny form was left behind in the vastness of the ocean. Zara hurriedly turned the boat into the wind and let it drift back. Without thinking, Libby ripped off her shorts to follow her sister in, but Zara put a hand on her arm and shook her head, then skilfully threw Emma the orange life ring.

'Take it!' she yelled down to her.

Emma continued on, head down, churning her arms through the water.

Nora was kneeling on her seat, hunched as though frozen, scooped out in terror, both hands clutching the bench, her jaw slack as she stared across the water. 'Do something!' she wailed.

'Emma!' Libby screamed through cupped hands.

Her mother began muttering something, but Libby couldn't hear what she was saying, and didn't have the headspace to ask her to repeat it. Gripped with fear, she watched Emma's stroke weaken. It was obvious she was tired. There was some splutter-ing, which could have been tears or water in her throat, or maybe both, and after a terrifying few seconds, she changed direction to swim towards the ring. Once she'd grabbed hold of it, Zara began pulling her in.

But Libby wouldn't be able to breathe until she was on board.

'The ladder, please, you drop it? *D'accord?* She is okay. *C'est bon,*' Zara said.

As Libby and Zara helped her up, Libby thanked Zara again and again. Emma shivered uncontrollably. At Zara's suggestion, Libby took her down into the hold. Nora tried to follow.

'Mum, don't worry, I'll sort her out. It might be best to give her some space. Sorry,' Libby said. Her mother backed off and sat down, pressing her hands into either side of her head.

Downstairs, Libby sat Emma down and wrapped a towel around her shoulders, rubbing at both her arms like she would for Amber or Hazel. 'You're okay, you're okay,' she repeated, feeling a protective swell of love.

Emma stared ahead, her chest heaving, her face a blank, wet

mask of shock. 'I didn't realise how fast we were going,' she mumbled through chattering teeth.

'I will make tea.' Zara appeared, shaking a battered blue tin at them. 'This tea is special, reserved for the crazy English who chuck themselves overboard.'

Libby laughed. 'She's not the first?'

'Er, she is the first who is not drunk.'

'I could do with a drink,' Emma said.

Zara chuckled. 'Okay, I have something stronger.' She winked at them, then, from a nifty little cupboard under a seat pad, brought out a small bottle of brandy and poured one finger's worth into three mugs. 'This is usually for me when I have rude Americans, so that I do not *push* them overboard.'

They laughed, and Libby was swamped by a combination of relief and gratitude and the ebbing away of fear.

'You want me to get your mum?' Zara asked.

Libby was about to say yes, but Emma said, 'Please, Libs, can we just have a moment?'

'Okay. Sure.' Libby looked right into her sister's eyes, saying, 'We won't let her do it. It's not going to happen, okay?'

Emma nodded. It was clear she would have cried if she had spoken, but Emma didn't do crying. Instead, she knocked back her brandy, then rested her head against the circular window behind her and sighed. 'Can we be your stowaways, Zara?'

Libby didn't want to go ashore either. She thought of their mum on deck above them, alone with her dark ideations. It must be hell inside her head. She had dressed her suicide up as a romantic notion, but it was likely she had been frightened and depressed after her diagnosis.

'We'll get her the help she needs. Okay? We can't deal with this on our own. Patrick will know what to do. He deals with this kind of thing every day.' Libby didn't feel as certain as she sounded.

'Yeah. Or we can drink our way through the rest of this holiday,' Emma said, shoving her cup towards the brandy bottle. Zara obliged and poured her some more.

'And one for Mum. I'll take it up to her. You can stay down here for a bit if you like,' Libby said.

As she climbed up on deck with her mum's brandy, something Connor had said last night sprang to mind: 'I'll stock up the bar. You're going to need it.' She had assumed he'd meant she'd be exhausted after spending a full day with her mum and Emma. Now she realised he must have known about this ghastly plan of Nora's, and anger surged up in her, too strong for the second hit of brandy to quell.

TWENTY

NORA

My bedroom had a comfortable white sofa that faced out to sea, and two charming wicker chairs either side of it. I had turned off the ceiling lights and opened the French windows to watch the sheet lightning that was silently electrifying the sky at the horizon. I loved the fresh air, but my shoulders were cold. I'd asked Connor to fetch me my pashmina, which was hanging on the bathroom door.

He draped it over my shoulders, 'There you go.'

'Thank you, darling,' I said.

He sat down on the chair to my right. I hadn't asked him to stay, but I imagined he wanted to talk over what had happened on the boat. Or at least I hoped that was why he had knocked on my door a few minutes ago.

'Supper was awful,' I said. I took up my cup of herbal tea and curled into the deep cushions, wondering why I'd wasted my whole life huddled next to radiators and tramping under slate skies when I could have been sitting like this, sun-kissed and windblown and meditating on the endless drama of the sea view.

Still, however stunning it was tonight, watching it had not

given me the answers. It could not help me with Emma and Libby, whose reactions had shaken me. I didn't know how I'd gather the strength to go through with the week ahead if I didn't have their support. Having been so determined yesterday about what I wanted to do, I was now tied up in knots, bouncing my worries around in my head and doubting the wisdom of my intentions, which wasn't like me at all.

'Libby told the girls that Emma didn't feel well, but I don't think they believed her,' Connor said. His T-shirt flashed white with each lightning strike, like a brief strobing, while his arms and head seemed to have no substance. He leant forward to roll a cigarette.

'My granddaughters are wonderfully intuitive.'

'Did you try to talk to her again?' he asked me.

'To Emma? She said there was nothing to say about it and went straight to bed.'

'It's so typical of her to rail against you.'

'Hmm. She was cross with me, of course – as you say, she always is – but this kind of thing is bound to make sense to her. It's her pragmatic nature, you see. But maybe she'll never admit it, just to be contrary.'

'And Libby will just want what you want.'

'You think? On the boat, she said that if she gave me her blessing, she'd be somehow responsible for my death. But I suppose they both need a bit of time to work it all out in their heads.'

Connor crossed one knee over the other and bounced his flip-flop, blowing out smoke before he spoke. 'Libby's not happy with me either. She banished me to the spare room.'

'You? Why?'

He picked a bit of tobacco off his lip. 'She guessed you'd told me what you were planning.'

'That's not your fault, darling.' I put my cup down and covered my feet with the embroidered hem of my dress.

'How do you feel, now that they know?'

A need to cry punctured my outer calm and I sought out his eyes in the dark. 'You know, that's the first time anyone has asked me how I feel.' My mouth filled with tears. A dark mass of terror drew nearer. 'I never wanted to get terminal cancer, you know. I didn't get the disease to cause trouble. This plan of mine was meant to lessen the agony of it all, and it benefits them too, arguably more than me.'

'It doesn't sound like they're going to see it that way.'

I released my hair from its clip, shook it out, shrugged off the encroaching fear. 'Oh, it's easier for them to paint me as some kind of ogre in all this, isn't it? But if I take myself off and do it quickly, it will be so much more humane. Like cats who go away to die quietly in the undergrowth somewhere.'

How haunted I was still by Dad's suffering, by the remains of bones and skin that had mocked his continuing heartbeat, by his faraway eyes that had stared towards nothingness, by his cold blue lips that had moaned and muttered his regrets. I had waited for him to offer up some profound gems of wisdom that I could cherish when he was gone, to help me understand life better – what he'd learned, what he had been proud of, what he had loved most, what his journey on this planet had meant to him – but if he'd known those things, he hadn't shared them with me. There had been nothing beautiful about my father's last days, nothing to be philosophical about. All I had learned was to be afraid of dying, that his life had not been worth living. Never would I leave my children with that legacy. Never would I let them witness me like that.

'To be honest,' I told Connor now, 'in my death, there'll be less drama for a change – and they're always going on about all my drama and how sick of it they get. What I'm doing is a gift, really.'

'A gift?' He snorted. 'All tied in a bow?'

'Well, why not?' I laughed. 'So I can rest easy for all eternity in my silk-lined coffin! It'll be covered in beautiful bouquets with all your pretty messages!' Their words rewriting who I was, I thought. I coughed, feeling the pain in my stomach radiate through me. 'Look. I haven't been the easiest of mothers, I know that better than anyone, but...' I broke off, wondering why ribboned memories from my past and present were criss-crossing. Suddenly, I didn't want him here; I wanted to be alone and sitting at my dresser, surrounded by my things: my father's enamel pill box, my mother's hairbrush, the photographs of my girls when they were little, and my notebook in the drawer. I wanted the comfort of its curly corners between my thumb and forefinger. 'Oh, I don't know now. I don't know anything any more. But I know I want to do this for them.'

There was a pause. I wondered whether he was questioning my sincerity. At last he whispered his response. 'It would be an unbelievably brave act,' he said, and attempted to reach for my hand, but I picked up my empty cup so that I was unavailable. My rings clinked when they met the china.

Twirling my fingers in the air above my head, I said, 'Oh darling, not at all.'

'Will you be scared?'

'Not in the slightest,' I replied instantly, before adding, 'Can you get me something, darling?'

'Anything.'

'My notebook, you know the one. It's in the drawer of my dressing table.'

He brought it over, but he didn't hand it to me straight away. He sat on the opposite end of the sofa with one hand on top of it. My mother had once pinned it underneath her own hands in a similar fashion, as though locking away what was inside. The vision of her in that moment became strong in my mind. Her hair had been in a black hairnet over her pink foam rollers. There had been a red patch on one of her cheeks from where she'd pressed her bunched-up fingertips as she told me off for writing such filthy stories.

'Give it to me,' I said to Connor. He paused for a second before doing as I asked.

'Your sudden attachment to that notebook makes me think about the pharaohs' tombs,' he said, eyeing it.

'Oh?' I rolled the right-hand corner of its paper cover. The words I'd written inside had a life in my head. My handwriting materialised as actual letters, floating in disjointed clumps or drifting through as a sentence or an oversized capitalised word.

'You know, the stuff they buried with them.'

I looked down at its dog-eared pages. 'Not rubies and gold for me, then?'

'The murals that were painted on the walls of their tombs were of wars won and decapitated enemies. It wasn't always pretty. That notebook would be part of your story.'

'Oh darling, how wonderful to be compared to kings and gods!'

He brushed his sea-salted locks back from his forehead. 'I'd like a painting of a stormy sea.'

'I'd much prefer beautiful things in mine. No storms or mummified cats or depressing tales in old notebooks. In fact, I brought this here to make peace with it somehow, to do something ritualistic. For closure. You might have some ideas.'

He blew out smoke and said, 'I went on this crazy creative-writing-stroke-therapy retreat once, where we took a psychedelic African plant to open up our creative minds. We wrote all this shit down, trauma from childhood and stuff, and then at the end, we had a big fire and we had to burn what we'd written. It was wild.'

'That kind of thing might work,' I said vaguely, fanning the edges of the pages with my thumb.

'Yeah. Get rid. Make space for rubies and gold,' he teased.

'Ruby studs and gold brocade. From some of the beautiful

costumes I've made.' But as I said it, I was reminded of the dusty, unsold china dolls that I'd found in my father's garage after he died. 'Or an intricate mural of tiny figures – heads intact, of course! Ha! – depicting the stories of my favourite plays. How about that? Far more interesting than my own life. They'd keep me busy in the afterlife. Like a dead person's *Desert Island Discs*.' I chortled, warming to the idea.

'But you don't believe in an afterlife.' He arched an eyebrow. The repeated flashes outside accentuated the lines in his skin, the shadows deepening the grooves, the light bringing out the youthful shine of his eyes.

'If I'm an Egyptian pharaoh I do,' I said lightly. 'There's something theatrical about how they went about it, don't you think? I understand completely why they liked to believe their souls lived on. I don't myself – it's the opposite kind of method to my man Epicurus, who believed everything stopped. But ultimately, it works the same way.'

'How's that?'

'Overcoming the anxiety, my darling. These days, we're terrible at death. Modern medicine likes us in denial. It loves the doctors patronising us and deciding our fate so we don't have to think for ourselves. But seriously, what the hell do they know?'

'More than I do.' The flame of his lighter burst, illuminating his eyes, which danced with mischief.

'But their fancy degrees have taught them nothing about people, nothing about how we feel. They peddle their euphemisms – "options for treatment" or "to make you more comfortable" – in their palliative care speak, pretending there's such a thing as a pain-free death, and we're supposed to roll over and let them take charge of our lives, willy-nilly, like they know it all and we have no agency in our own existence. If that isn't paternalistic codswallop, I don't know what is. Look at Emma and Libby. They were shocked by me today. Angry, even. But I bet you a million dollars they'd hang on every word of some male psychiatrist back home who'd sit with me for barely an hour to explain why I wanted to take my own life, and then prescribe pills for depression or an anxiety disorder or some modern nonsense like that. And then I'd be left at the mercy of some overeducated oncologist with a personality disorder who'd ply me with legalised poison and avoid my calls. And you know what? Shock, horror, I'll die anyway. Who knew?'

He shuffled a little closer and rested one knee on the sofa between us. 'They just want you to be around for a bit longer.'

'I understand that, Connor, but while they faff around with all that, they'll be wasting time with me while I'm still alive. And who said a long life is more valuable than a short one? It's so reductive. I know eighteen-year-olds who've left better legacies than people who've lived eighty years longer. It's what you've *done* in life that matters, especially when we have such little control over when we go. They don't seem to see how lucky I am to know what's coming. Think about it, there's some poor woman out there who's about to be killed in a car accident – in a minute's time, or tomorrow, or next week – but she doesn't have the foggiest. And she's bound to waste her last moments alive. Shouting at her kids or refusing sex with her husband, you know how it goes.'

He smoked and I watched the fumes curdle in the air. I waited for him to offer his excuses and say goodnight. When he spoke next, the mood shifted.

'Patrick knows,' he said.

'Of course he does. Emma would have told him everything.'

'No.' He dropped his voice. He was leaning forward, and I found his eyes shining at me, a fleck of light carved out of the grey. 'He knows about what happened between us.'

'Emma's already berated me about that,' I said. 'I tried to convince her it was the most innocent of kisses.'

'Not just about last night.'

A shadow like black wings crossed my vision. 'He can't know about that,' I insisted hoarsely.

'I think he does now.'

'You *told* him?' I rasped.

I had drilled our mistake out of my mind years ago, neatly extricating the memory of it, separating it from my relationship with Libby and the others, but Connor seemed to be handing me a rotten piece of it now.

'I didn't need to. He just seemed to know,' he said.

'Well, he's speculating then, isn't he? Deny, deny, deny.'

'I almost couldn't be bothered,' he said sulkily.

'You wouldn't dare hurt Libby like that,' I growled, sitting forward, stabbing my finger at him.

'I wouldn't. No.' He stood up and went over to the window, elbows sticking out like black wings. 'Not now.'

'Not now that I'm dying? Exactly right.'

The sky lit up silently behind him. 'I don't want you to die,' he said plainly, and I felt my insides dissolve.

'Don't be silly. You'll be fine,' I replied, trying not to gasp. I held my chest, pressing at the knot, massaging away its ache. 'And so will the girls,' I started to say, but the words caught in my throat.

He came to sit by me, stubbing his cigarette into my cup, which was marked by my lipstick. It sizzled before going out. I stared down at it, refusing to look at him, feeling and smelling him near to me. I couldn't move a muscle away from him.

'You don't have to stay here with me. I don't need you to be here,' I said. He was too close. My flesh was stinging, coming alive with the prospect of being touched.

'Everyone's asleep,' he whispered. 'We could lock your door and I could stay a while longer.'

A famous writer once said that people didn't change; they were revealed.

Twelve years ago, we had betrayed Libby, and there was

nothing we could do to take it back. While Hazel's baby mouth had been permanently latched onto Libby's breast, Connor and I would sneak out for drinks at the local pub to commiserate about how excluded and unloved we felt. We had become great friends, which had seemed wonderful for everyone.

One evening, he had dropped by mine to collect a favourite cuddly toy belonging to one of the girls. I'd been lonely and had offered him some chilled Sancerre. After a few too many, he had admitted he hadn't wanted a second child – he hadn't wanted Hazel.

After confessing to such a thing, our conversation had deepened, and at some point in the evening, I had dug out my notebook. I had read him the juicy bits, curling its corners, laughing as though my teen musings were funny. He had been horrified and I had teased him for being prudish, and he had kissed me as though to prove otherwise.

I'm not proud to admit that this intimacy had led on to sex that night – an overstep of an otherwise platonic friendship, before and since – but when I was diagnosed with cancer, he was the first person I called. You see, I had first-hand experience of how good he was at listening, how good at understanding, how good at keeping secrets.

Saying no to him now would not erase that one blip years back. Neither would it purge me of the wrongdoings laid out in my notebook. Saying no would not make me a good person. It was too late for that.

I leant my head on his chest. 'Apart from that one mistake, we've always been well behaved, haven't we?'

'I never saw it as a mistake.'

He put his arm around me. We watched the sky together, intimately and treacherously. Some day he would leave Libby. He had always wanted someone less cosy. Someone like me, I suppose. It didn't matter now. Hovering between life and death, normal rules need not apply. I wasn't going to be here to suffer the consequences.

He took my right hand and stroked his thumb across my skin. 'Tonight, let's forget anyone else exists,' he said.

With his permission for make-believe, relief washed through me. Until then, I hadn't been aware of how much effort reality required. His adoration was satiating, replenishing my reserves, dissolving the doubt my daughters had planted.

All week, I had strived to be authentic and genuine. But maybe not tonight.

'Lock the door,' I said.

As he stood up, the notebook fell from the sofa. I heard the beat of a bird's wings flying away, and I felt stronger. Like the pharaohs, this villa could be my mausoleum, a mental burial chamber for all my secrets. This lapse with Connor, and the long, tatty string of others that had gone before it, would rot alongside my bones, my casket closed on them forever.

TWENTY-ONE

EMMA

The sea was flat, pond-like. Emma was gliding along on a paddleboard she'd found in the pool room, off into the morning light, peachy on the water's surface, when she noticed Libby on the steps. She was waving at her, beckoning her back to shore.

She pushed the oar to turn the board.

'Is everything okay?' she called out.

'Yes. Sorry, nothing's happened. Just... Can I come with you?' Libby asked, panting, her face glowing with sweat.

Having convinced herself she wanted to be alone to sort through what must be done next, Emma smiled at her sister in her silly pyjama shorts with the frogs on and was relieved to see her.

'You look like you've just run a marathon.'

'I saw you from my window and wanted to catch you.'

'Why don't you get the other board?'

'I can't paddleboard!'

'Okay, hop on the end, then. It'll make it harder for me, but maybe that's a good thing.'

The board wobbled as Libby climbed on. She slipped off

the other side, making a wave. She did this three times, until Emma fell in too.

'Oh my God! What are you like?' she yelped, gulping in a mouthful of seawater.

Frantically they sculled in the water, laughing, dripping eyelashes and big wet faces bobbing about above the surface. It was difficult to stop the hysteria once it had set in, even though they were almost drowning and everything inside Emma was sad. It was laughter for the sake of it, in its purest, most pointless form, which felt odd and necessary and sisterly, and such a release.

'I have no core strength,' Libby spluttered, swallowing a wave.

After several more attempts to clamber back on, Emma managed to stand up and paddle, while Libby sat cross-legged on the end.

Their serious moods took over. Emma silently questioned whether she should share her true feelings with her sister, whether she would understand or think her a psychopath. For now, though, Libby's quiet company, her comforting weight and the rhythm of the paddle went a little way to settle her inner turmoil.

After a while, and inevitably, they began to talk about their mum. Out there alone in the middle of the sea, nobody in the world would hear them. Everything they said would be lost on the wind, which might be the best way for Emma's thoughts to go.

'She's saying she's doing it for us,' Libby said.

'And for herself,' Emma replied, chewing over the brewing scandal in her mind.

'It's like when she used to miss sports day every year, and she would say she really wanted to be there but didn't come because she knew it would put us off our races. But she's since admitted that in fact it was because she couldn't stand the thought of spending a whole afternoon with those other mums. It was nothing to do with us and what we might want. I know it's silly, but I always wanted her to run the mums' race. Just once, you know?'

'Me too,' Emma said automatically.

'And like when Dad left. She lied to us about him being at the Priory, and all the while he was living at Annie's in Shropshire and Mum was sending her hate mail on squares of loo paper.'

'Then remember that poor guy who was head of that record company? Oh my God, she basically said he was the love of her life, but when he'd had enough and couldn't take her abuse any more and announced he was leaving her, she turned the tables and basically accused *him* of abusing *her*.'

'His slip-ons were a bit much, though, right?' Emma said, feeling a smile come on.

'Oh my God, he was such a pretentious git. But you know what I'm saying.'

'She had the worst taste in men.'

'The actual worst instincts ever. I wish I'd thought about it more often when she was dishing out all her advice to me over the years.'

'I've never listened to her.'

'I know, and I wish I'd been as sensible as you. She's always said I should give Connor his freedom and support his trips abroad whenever it takes his bloody fancy, and I've actually believed that. But look at her own track record!'

Emma would usually jump at the opportunity to give her sister a lecture about Connor, warn her off repeating history, be more demanding of him, less scared of being a nag. Those were the days when she had wanted to save their relationship. Not any more. She said, 'Well, I don't know, needing him is one thing and wanting him is another. And, you know, if he doesn't want to be around, what can you do?'

The momentary pause before Libby replied suggested she was confused or surprised by her sister's atypical response. 'Honestly, I've always wanted to be tougher with him,' she said, treating Emma's reply as a blip, charging on, 'and I've always wanted to do exactly what you've told me to do, but then when it comes down to it, I wimp out and need Mum to pick up the pieces. It's pathetic.'

'Not at all. Connor's a tricky one.'

'He actually knew about all this before Mum told us. Not that he admitted to it.'

Emma's stomach twisted. 'Hmm. Maybe,' she said vaguely. Now wasn't the time to think about the supposed kiss and all the suspicions she was keeping from Libby. In fact, she didn't want to talk about Connor at all, but she understood that discussing him was Libby's way of avoiding thinking about their mum's suicide. 'Mum loves to confide a secret.'

'And to piss me off even more, he said he understood why she wanted to do it. And how brave she was and that he would do the same in her situation.'

Emma glanced back at Libby. Her legs were crossed, and she was hunched over them, pulling one eyelid over the other as though she had something irritating in it.

'I'm sure it'll all work out,' she said, wanting to move the conversation away from Connor. She doubted Connor would have the guts to do what their mum was planning, but, infuriatingly, his thinking on the subject wasn't far from her own. This didn't make her feel better about it.

After a while, she spoke again. 'Libby, how do you think *you* might want to die?'

'Umm,' Libby said, seemingly unfazed, 'I know where I want my ashes to be scattered.'

'Where?'

'You know that beach we used to go to as children? In Scotland.'

'Tralee?'

'Yes, there.'

'Okay. I'll remember that. But before the incineration stage, how do you want to actually go?'

'In my sleep.'

'And that's exactly what Mum's choosing.'

The board wobbled. Emma steadied herself, centring her core, twisting around to see that Libby had changed position and was now kneeling, squinting up at her with her hand as a visor. 'Please don't tell me you think she's doing the right thing.'

She fixed her eyes ahead. 'I did some research online last night and read a *BMJ* report that said the family members of cancer patients who'd died by assisted suicide coped better.'

Libby made a whistling sound. 'Wow. Unbelievable. You're actually going to be on her side. That's a first!' The board wobbled again, but Emma did not turn around to look at her sister this time. She did not need to see her face to know how appalled she was.

She continued. 'There was an article about this Dutch guy who had motor neurone and who'd chosen assisted dying, and he'd told his daughter that he wanted to die standing up, healthy. I think Mum wants to die standing up, so to speak.'

Emma wanted to go the same way, standing up and in control of her faculties. A clean, controlled end-of-life plan appealed to her. It was why she couldn't outright condemn her mum's idea.

'Note the word "assisted",' Libby said. 'I'm guessing that guy would've done it properly, if there *is* such a thing, with doctors who'd first of all checked he was sane and who'd made sure he knew his options, and then, when they were like one hundred and ten per cent sure, after planning with counsellors or psychiatrists or people like that, they would've handed him the proper drugs and dosage.'

'Yes, true. That's pretty much how it panned out. But we're not Dutch, so Mum can't do it like that here.'

'But what if it goes wrong and she doesn't die and she's left in a worse state? Her suffering would be ten million times worse.'

'I'm sure she's done her research,' Emma mumbled, skating over the risk, ploughing on with what had obsessed her all night long. 'In the papers I read online, it's proven that the bereaved have fewer stress symptoms if they're given the chance to say a proper goodbye to their loved ones. And they suffer fewer post-traumatic symptoms than the relatives of patients who die from natural causes.'

'Emma! Can you even hear yourself? Mum isn't a statistic in a research paper. We're not "the bereaved"! We're me and you. And we need to convince Mum not to do it!'

'Some people believe that forcing a patient to stay alive when their life has no value is inhumane.'

'Who says her life has no value?'

'The patient. Mum, in this case.' Emma glanced back at her sister.

Libby had drawn her legs together and put her forehead on her knees, and was talking into her lap. 'Sorry, Emma, I'm finding this all a bit weird. Yesterday you were freaking out about it completely and jumping into the sea like a crazy woman, and now you're all for it. I can't get my head around it.'

'I know, sorry. Even I realise how awful it sounds. I don't even know if I believe it's the right thing for Mum to do, I really don't. It's only that some people actually do think it's a better way to die. And I'm wondering if we should be open to that. Should we?' Emma genuinely wanted an answer. She was split in two. Feeling as much empathy for Libby's argument as she did for their mum's.

Tearily Libby said, 'Is it because you don't get on with her any more? Like you've become emotionally disconnected or something?'

Her words stung. Emma stopped paddling and lowered herself to the board so that she was sitting facing Libby. Her ankles were dangling in the water. 'I don't want her to die. I love her. But she *is* dying,' she said, clearing a bubble in her throat.

'What if there's a chance, even if it's only a tiny chance, that she might get better? Surely it's worth hanging on for that?'

'Like a miracle?' she asked vaguely.

'It happens! And if she fights, she might just be that rare person who lasts for years and defies all the doctors. And if she doesn't, not all cancer deaths are grim. They have palliative care doctors and people like that to manage the pain with meds and make them comfortable right up until the end. And there'll be loads of meaningful moments in that time. Many we'll cling to when she's gone.'

Emma watched the water move around her feet. 'But that's obviously not how she wants it to go.'

There was a long pause before Libby said, 'I really can't believe I'm hearing this. You've always been so anti-suicide, saying it's the most selfish act and that it goes against all your beliefs. I mean, you believe in God and heaven, don't you? But she won't go to heaven this way.'

Last night, Emma had read about the Dutch doctors who had refused a patient's request for medically assisted suicide based on their religious objections, and had wondered whether she should be opposing it for the same reasons. 'Should' had been the word she had fixated on. 'Should' suggested certainty and moral clarity. When faced with a dilemma like this with her own mother, she was learning fast that there was no such thing as clarity.

'He'd forgive her. He's God,' she replied glibly, but she grappled with it still. She had spent the past hour putting forward arguments that condoned their mum's decision, because it would be a compassionate thing to do, but she had never been less certain about anything. 'I'm not saying it's clear-cut.'

'I tell you what's clear-cut. If she goes ahead with it and the authorities think we knew about it, we could go to prison. For being accessories. I saw a documentary about it.'

'That won't happen.'

'None of it's going to happen. Because we're going to make sure she doesn't do it.'

'Don't shut her down, Libby.'

'I'm not shutting her down!'

'I know I reacted badly yesterday, but having thought it through properly, I believe Mum's being strangely sensible for once, planning it all out, wanting to talk about it. I mean, we have birth plans for our babies, don't we? And that's considered normal – even though it never pans out the way we hope. But we don't have death plans. It's this thing that we're all destined for with absolute certainty, but we can't even talk about it with each other. Remember that mum at school, a few years back, the one whose youngest died of cot death? There she was, going through the most unimaginable, unbearable pain anyone could ever go through, and yet most of the mums in the playground avoided her, not because they were mean people, but because they didn't know what to say, they just didn't know how to talk about it. But that's so—'

Libby interjected. 'You know what? I don't want to talk about it either. Can we turn back?'

Emma understood why she was reacting like this and stood back up, doubting her own words even as she said them, noticing with an exhausted feeling that they had drifted quite far out.

'I'm just keeping my mind open to it, that's all,' she said.

There was an expanse of silence as wide as the horizon. Her muscles burned as she pressed on through the water. The sun was higher now, and she felt it scorch her shoulders.

After forty-five minutes of solid paddling, they arrived at the villa's boat launch. Every muscle in her body was quivering.

Libby climbed onto the solid ground of the steps, then turned back. 'I'm sorry, Emma, I know you've always been able to argue me into the ground, but this time you're not making any sense. Just think of the kids for a minute and forget everything else. If Mum goes ahead with this, they'll spend their whole life wondering: what if? What if they'd done something differently, what if they could have saved her? What if, by saying this or saying that differently, or giving her more cuddles or being less rude, or doing this better or not doing that naughty thing, she'd still be alive? And we could tell them until we're blue in the face that there was nothing they could've done to save her, but they'd still feel it and they'd harbour memories of all those little regrets and have that guilty feeling living inside them forever. And that's just totally crappy and I'm not having it. Okay? And I really do believe that this whole thing is a cry for help and that all she actually wants is for us to beg her not to do it.'

Her impassioned speech was destabilising. Emma imagined Eliot feeling shame and remorse for the rest of his life, and she regretted putting forward her argument, wishing that her thoughts had floated out of her head and into the breeze, never to have been heard by another living soul. But she couldn't yet let go of them completely, reminding herself that Libby was often overemotional, overanalytical, and was terribly mollycoddling of the kids. Resilience and straightforwardness were also important qualities to foster in your children.

Emma returned her paddleboard to the pool room, but she didn't want to go back to the bedroom and have to talk to Patrick, who had kicked into extreme psychoanalyst mode in response to the news and wouldn't give his opinion either way.

She took her phone off the charger in the kitchen and wandered out into the garden to find a quiet spot. Beyond some bushes, there was a hidden path she hadn't noticed before. As she battled through the fronds, she dialled Samarth's number. It was a reckless decision; barely a decision, more like a knee-jerk reaction. She didn't think about how inappropriate it was, or the implications of not seeking out Patrick to confide in instead; nor did she consider the knock-on effect of it back at school. There were no compartments to put this in. The urge to talk to him flooded every sensible drawer in her mind.

He answered after two rings and gave his usual spiel about how on top of everything he was, before reeling off all the problems he was solving. She responded cursorily, barely pretending to care. When he finally asked her if she was okay – as she knew he would – the whole story of her mum came tumbling out.

'I don't feel like myself at all. I don't know what to think. It's like my head is going to explode. I just don't have any answers.'

When she finally looked up, with the phone pressed into the side of her head, she became conscious of her surroundings. She was standing under a small gazebo covered in flowers. There was a bench, which she perched on as she looked out at the view. Its beauty had an unreal quality, hazy and ungraspable.

'Okay, let's talk it through logically. What are the pluses and the minuses?'

Instantly Emma liked his objectivity. 'Pluses are, she won't suffer long-term. And she'll die in a place like this, which is as close to heaven as you'll get.'

'And minuses?'

'It could go wrong. She might be left brain-damaged or something.'

'That's a major minus. Next.'

'I'll miss her.'

'But you'll miss her anyway, whether it's in three months' time or next week. Think of another minus.'

'It's the kids, I guess.'

'How old are Libby's girls?' Samarth asked.

This was comfortable ground to cover, and she thought about them as though they were her pupils. 'Hazel is only twelve. She's a nervy, oversensitive little thing. She wouldn't cope at all. Year 7 has been hell for her, and her attendance is abysmal. And her anxiety levels are through the roof. She's still scared of Scooby-Doo films, for God's sake! But she's a darling girl – she's so empathetic, you know. She actually gets physically sick before Eliot's galas. And she was the one who first called Mum Granny Nor-Nor.'

'That's such a cute name.'

'Too cute for Mum, believe me.'

There was a clatter. 'Ow, shit. Sorry, I just picked up a pan of milk and the handle was hot.'

'Oh, God. Are you okay?' Emma asked, feeling maternal towards him.

She knew he lived in a flat in the local town, and she imagined it with high ceilings and an open-plan kitchen bar. Like in a romantic book, she pictured herself padding across the floorboards, bare-legged, wearing one of his white shirts.

'Yeah, yeah. Sorry,' he said. Emma could hear him running the tap. 'Sorry, go back to what you were saying.'

She re-engaged with her assessment of the children. 'Then there's Amber, who's fourteen. She's one of those brooding, self-contained types, and I always worry she's storing up this massive mountain of anger, but it's hard to tell what's going on in that head of hers – she's on her phone the whole bloody time. But she'll suddenly, out of nowhere, become furious about some cause or other, especially when TikTok has fired her up. She loves being outraged by the disturbing posts on her feed: like, you know, what kind of knot works best for a noose, or how to be a clever anorexic, or special household tools for self-harm and many other useful little tips. There's always the feeling that she's on the edge, and a small thing could tip her over. And this ain't no small thing.'

'And Eliot?'

Her stomach flipped. 'You know what he's like. He'll pretend to be more grown up than the grown-ups and intellectualise it, then when he actually becomes an adult, he'll grow his hair too long, develop a weed habit and never leave the couch. He'll end up on an actual Freudian couch being psycho-analysed by one of Patrick's colleagues, and Patrick and I will have to sit down and apologise to him for not protecting him as a child.'

Samarth didn't laugh. 'It'll be hard on them, that's for sure.' He paused. 'It's all very well for her to get all Sleeping Beauty about it and want to die a lovely romantic death in a castle-like setting, but she's dumped it in your laps so suddenly. And us grown-ups can maybe rationalise it, and research it, but the kids can't.'

'She used to do this to us when we were young, dump all sorts of grown-up stuff on us, assuming we could deal with it. Like the time one of our au pairs legged it in the middle of the night, saying she was running back to Catalonia or somewhere with her boyfriend. Instead of Mum rushing home from the production she was working on, she told us we'd be okay for a few days before Dad could come and pick us up.'

'How old were you?'

'Fourteen!'

Emma recalled her mother's babyish voice on the phone. 'You're my special little Mama Hen and so much more capable than that silly little flibbertigibbet Nuria could ever be. You told me she can't even boil an egg or make her own bed!' She remembered clutching the receiver, twisting the springy cord around her fingers until there was no circulation left.

When she had told Libby about Nuria leaving, Libby had cried and cried and cried, inconsolably, and Emma had realised why her mother had said she should keep quiet about it. In desperation, she had given Libby one of Mum's sweaters as a comforter, reassuring her that if a burglar or sex attacker came to the door, they would hide in the loft. It had meant to make her feel safe, but Libby had wailed even harder. So they had made a den in the television room, where they had slept and eaten, jumping out of their skins every time they heard a noise outside.

The relief when Emma had seen their dad's beardy face and heard his jolly voice had provoked a rush of tears, but she had bitten them back, desperate to prove how mature she was. Their father had laughed like a drain when he had seen their child-cave. Annie, with her rust-red bottle-dye hair, orange lipstick and paisley floor-length skirt, had been like an autumn leaf, and had tutted while clearing up their crusty plates and old sweet wrappers, muttering how shocking it was that Nora had left them here alone. Secretly Emma had agreed with her and had felt quite sorry for herself, but also vowed she would never wear paisley.

'It's all too much too soon,' she said now, feeling over-whelmed. 'You're right, she's made it into a fairy tale. Nothing out here feels real. We just need more time to adjust to it. The kids need more time – at home, in the real world, when they're settled in their own beds.'

'Can you talk to her about it?'

'Trouble is, she's so bloody stubborn. She'll be more gung-ho than ever if she gets even a whiff of my disapproval.'

'You don't have to diss her plans completely. You could maybe do the whole reverse psychology thing and say you absolutely support her decision, which in truth part of you does, but then question the timing of it – for her grandchildren's sake. You know, pull at those grandma heartstrings of hers.'

Emma contemplated this. 'Yes, maybe,' she said, an idea dawning. 'Maybe I could use Eliot's swimathon as a negotiating tool, suggest she at least stick around for long enough to see him through it. She knows how much it means to him. It would give us more time to make sure this really is the right course of action for her.'

'Emotional blackmail works like a charm with my mum.'

'Hmm. It might be a good way forward. Then we'd have the chance to talk to the doctors when we get home. And maybe we'd all have time to find a way to make peace with it and know for sure that she's thought it through properly. Or not. You never know, after all this, she might change her mind about the whole thing altogether.'

'She could be depressed, you know. Suicide ideation is common in cancer patients.'

'She might be.'

'So, we have a way forward, then.'

'Yes, the game plan is to ask her for more time, citing the kids' well-being. So they're properly prepared if she finally goes ahead with it.' After talking all this through with practical, unflappable Samarth, Emma felt in charge again. 'I knew I needed to speak to you.'

'Who knew my fucked-up relationship with Mum would come in handy one day?'

'Oh, Samarth. We should set up a therapy group and call it MA. No, wait, NMA.'

'Nutjob Mums Anonymous?'

She smiled. 'I was thinking more Narcissistic Mothers Anonymous.'

'Sounds more legit, I admit.' He laughed.

She remembered a recovering alcoholic friend of hers telling her about the serenity prayer, which the group had chanted at every AA meeting. She mumbled out loud, 'God, grant me the courage to change the things I can.'

'Amen. I have every faith in you. You're amazing.'

She felt the danger of this intimacy with Samarth and added brusquely, 'I'll talk to Patrick now. And the others. Thank you, this has been very useful. I'd better get on.'

'Make sure you get it all down in the minutes,' he said.

He was laughing at her, and she blushed a deep shade of purple, and was grateful he couldn't see her.

It was convenient that her mum had suggested Emma, Patrick, Libby and Connor take themselves off for supper in town – 'Mum's treat' – without the children, whom she'd babysit, giving them some grown-up time for a change.

Emma leapt at the chance, ignoring Libby's remonstrations, and accepted on behalf of the four of them. She wanted to talk to them.

'I promise not to bite your head off this time, Connor,' she said, straining to sound fun and forgiving, neither of which she felt. She viewed this dinner as the perfect opportunity to explain to Libby the turnaround of her feelings, put their differences aside, bury her anger towards Connor and discuss Samarth's way forward.

It didn't go according to plan.

Connor and Libby weren't the problem. It was Patrick. He was being stubbornly thick-headed, as though he somehow instinctively knew that Samarth had influenced her.

'But Patrick, don't you get what I'm trying to say? We need to slow the whole thing down by using a bit of emotional blackmail, by suggesting the kids won't cope with the suddenness of it all.'

'I get it, one hundred per cent. But I think it's better to stay out of it altogether rather than play emotional games with her. Narcissists like your mother can be dangerous. They don't play by the same rules as the rest of us, and she's in a volatile state right now.' He rested his professional gaze on her, the one she hated.

'But that's what I'm saying, that we play by her rules for once!'

'And you think you'll beat her?' he asked, mockingly.

'Yes.'

'Patrick's right,' Libby said. 'I'm not sure about playing games either. Maybe she just wants us to beg her not to do it?'

'Look,' Patrick said doubtfully, 'if your mum's determined to go ahead with this, there's nothing either of you can say or do to change it.'

'So you're saying we should both back off completely,' Libby said, picking at the skin around her thumbnail.

Emma didn't let him answer. 'I don't agree at all. I think there's a lot we can say and do.'

Patrick brushed his hand across the tablecloth, then sat straighter and looked at her directly. 'It's not your responsibility to stop her from doing it. This is on her.'

Emma felt tearful and misunderstood. 'But we need to try!'

'He's got a point, Em. If we get involved in trying to stop her, we'll become too wrapped up in it.' Libby seemed to be persuaded. 'And then we'll feel responsible for her death if she goes ahead with it anyway. It'll be like we somehow failed her. And you know what Mum's like. She does what the hell she likes, when she likes. Why should we think we suddenly have any power over her now?'

Patrick nodded. 'Exactly.'

'You've changed your tune since this morning, Libby,' Emma said.

'Not at all. I still feel exactly the same way. I desperately don't want her to do it this way. You're the one who's changed her tune – this morning you were going on about the Dutch.'

'This morning I didn't have a solution. I was desperate. In

effect I was giving in to her, which is what you guys are doing now.'

'It's really unfair of you to say that,' Libby said.

Patrick interrupted them. 'Nobody's giving in. Talking to her frankly about how you feel and continuing an open dialogue is important. But what's vital is that you separate yourself from having any agency in her final decision.'

'You're being so bloody defeatist.' Emma was furiously disappointed in him.

Connor, who'd stayed quiet up until now, leant forward on his elbows and shrugged his shoulders. 'What we're saying here, Emma, is that you can't control her,' he said, self-satisfaction dripping from his lips.

'Just you watch me,' she retorted, absolutely determined to prove them wrong. 'With or without your help, I am going to make sure my mum walks out of that villa alive.'

TWENTY-TWO

NORA

The children were gathered on the rattan corner sofa between the two palms. I sat opposite in the bamboo chair whose back resembled a large shell like in Botticelli's *Venus* – though I doubted Venus's full belly had been turned inside out by an hour of vomiting.

Meanwhile, Libby and Connor and Emma and Patrick were walking into town to drink pastis and watch the sun go down, dressed up for a rare night out without the children. When I'd kissed my daughters goodbye, insisting I'd be okay, they had been shiny from too much sun and a little glassy-eyed from the pre-dinner cocktails Connor had made. They needed the break. My revelation on the boat trip yesterday had been like a mallet to their heads. I could almost see the circling of cartoon stars. Trying to have a normal conversation today had been nigh on impossible.

Emma had put up a busy force field around herself, and Libby had been distant, in a dream state, going through the motions, talking but saying nothing. I hadn't brought the subject up and neither had they. If we went through the week like this, there would be little fuss and bother to contend with, which was an appealing thought, but neither would there be any engagement in what was happening, somewhat defeating the object of my plans for transparency.

Eliot had mixed me a G&T. It was more of a prop than anything. I wouldn't be able to keep a sip of it down. My stomach was a fire pit of pain. The symptoms had been gruesome this morning. It was remorse; sordid and shaming and tormenting, like a hangover after a raucous night. Abstractly, I fantasised that Libby might understand what I'd done to her, as though she were magnanimous enough to bracket it away as a dying request, an indecent proposal, where morals were put aside for me: the sad, selfish old woman whose life was at an end, who had borrowed Connor for one night of sensual pleasure, knowing that within days I would never feel anything again. But I was aware that the reality of her finding out would be more like a nuclear explosion, wiping out, in one go, the many wonderful years of our relationship. Mothering Libby had been one of the major joys of my life and I couldn't countenance the thought of her finding out what I'd done to her.

The smokescreen would remain, always there around me, as thick as ever, acrid and suffocating, as though I were dying of that rather than cancer. I briefly wondered how Connor was feeling this evening. Whichever way his mind took him, he would have to live with the scrunch of his bad conscience for many years longer than I would. Apt penance, some might say.

I surveyed my three grandchildren and lit the candle in the lantern on the coffee table between us. They were old enough to hear the truth. Not about Connor, no. I meant about my death. It had been the point of bringing them here: to share real goodbyes.

Their parents had not sanctioned the conversation I was about to have with them. I didn't need their permission. They were *my* grandchildren. I knew it was the right thing to do. Never would I let them feel like I had as a child, when the truth had been too messy and upsetting to confront. Left to her own devices, Libby would no doubt sidestep telling them at all, never find the right moment, wait until they were thoroughly confused about what they weren't being told, having overheard snippets of grown-up whispers. Or they'd hear second-hand through Eliot, whom Emma would have informed in her trademark no-nonsense style, in the voice that said: don't you dare show me your messy feelings.

The strip of burnt skin across Amber's face was like war paint under her heavy-lidded mahogany eyes and thick brows. Her hair was twisted up into a barrette, with the tips fanned out and sticking up, ready for battle. Or so I liked to project. I was the one ready for a battle, one of words and ideas, a philosophical war game.

Hazel, on the other hand, seemed less of an opponent. Her delightfully pale hair and paler big brown eyes topped by white-blonde eyebrows were softer on the eye. Her burnt nose was like a pink button. She had her knees together. Balanced upon them was her glass. She played with the ice in her drink, twirling the cubes around with her forefinger. Eliot was picking at a scab, digging into the translucent skin at his elbow. The smear of blood was livid, like his hair.

I held eye contact with each child, ensuring I made a connection with them that went beyond politeness, burrowing right into their psyches.

Then I began. 'A wise Greek philosopher called Epicurus once said, "Death does not concern us, because as long as we exist, death is not here. And once it does come, we are not here." What do you think about this, each of you?'

There was a long wait before anyone spoke. 'Say it again,' Eliot said, as though it were a riddle he needed to work out.

I repeated it.

'It kind of means we're not thinking when we're dead,' Eliot said.

Hazel said, 'When I'm dead, *I'd* be thinking loads about how good I've been. Because I'll be in heaven.'

I laughed.

She added, 'Or if I was an indigenous American, I'd be an eagle and I'd be flying around your heads thinking about ways to protect you.'

'Or you'd come back as a little ant that I'd squash,' Amber said.

'You totally suck,' Hazel said, punching her in the arm.

Rubbing at it ostentatiously, Amber added, 'But what about us going into a different dimension, like being in a k-hole or something?'

'A k-hole?' I spluttered.

'This girl on TikTok was talking about it. She had this weird near-death experience on ketamine, and she, like, went into this long bright tunnel, or whatever, and she knew she was going someplace else, leaving her body behind and moving into a' – she mimed speech marks – 'different consciousness.'

'That sounds better than coming back as an ant,' Eliot chortled.

I imagined my consciousness re-emerging inside an ant or, worse, in the body of a paedophile in Broadmoor or a woman of the Finnish Sami tribe living in a carpet-lined tent in minus-thirty-degree temperatures. Fates I felt lucky to have dodged in this life and hoped to escape in the next. But even if I ended up as an alien species with blue skin in the phosphorescent glory of a more evolved planet, or simply in the body of a lovely young girl from the Home Counties who was loved more than I was a child, I wasn't comforted. In any guise, the thought of my consciousness rolling on and on for all eternity was bloody exhausting.

'I saw a ghost once,' Hazel said. 'She was sitting in the corner of my bedroom with a handbag on her lap. She looked very nice.'

'Don't lie,' Amber said.

'I'm not! I swear it!'

'Coming back as something else is a lovely thought, a magical thought to comfort us, to help us fear death less,' I said, skirting over the ghost issue. 'But Epicurus wasn't a religious man. He felt it was the wrath of the gods that stopped us from enjoying life, stopped us from pursuing happiness and being the masters of our own universe. Heaven and hell suggest there's some kind of moral reckoning or a judgement from God. But if death really does end our conscious thought and stops our awareness of being alive, and the sensations in our bodies stop – which includes suffering and pain – what is there to fear?'

'The devil's pitchfork poking into my chest!' Hazel said.

'Haaazel,' Eliot said, tutting.

I grinned at her tightly. 'Okay, darling, but let's think like Epicurus for a minute, let's imagine we're *not* aware of being dead and that we're not reincarnated.'

'Okay,' she said.

'Like the joke "What happens after you die?"'

They looked at me blankly.

'"Lots of things happen after you die, they just don't involve you."'

They did not crack up. I felt a cough coming on, which I suppressed with a sip of gin and tonic.

Amber mumbled into her lap, moving into a cross-legged position and pulling out one side of her hair to pick at her split ends. 'But the people who are left behind are still conscious, and they'd be aware of those people dying.'

I drank some more. It was like pouring acid on the fire down there, but it helped smooth over my growing anxieties. 'They would, and they'd suffer, that's true,' I agreed. 'Because they'd miss that person.'

'I want everyone to live forever!' Hazel cried.

'If we all lived forever, would each life be as special and as valued? Would *I* be?' I probed.

Hazel said, 'Yes, of course you would!'

'You're a sweetheart, Hazel, but imagine hundreds of years of me. You'd go crazy with it. What would be the point of it all? You appreciate something much more if you know you're only getting it for a short time, which in my opinion means we'd better damn well enjoy being alive and not fear death, however near it might be. Right?'

'I guess so,' Hazel said, looking worried.

'And if this is the case, if you only had a week left on this earth, how would you choose to live it?'

There were a few ums and ahs before Amber piped up. 'Chuck in school and experiment with psychedelics,' she said, chortling.

'Your mum would be so proud,' I said, winking at her.

Eliot said, 'I'd swim the Channel and raise lots of money for cancer research.'

'Very commendable,' I said, perhaps wishing he'd wanted to take psychedelics and chuck in school.

'And you, Hazel? What would you do?' I asked her.

'I'd get a massive flat-screen TV in my bedroom and watch Netflix all day long and eat Marmite sandwiches and chocolate digestives and never get out of bed. And maybe I'd send Frank a Valentine's card.'

All of us laughed.

'And all those things would make you happy?'

The two youngest nodded and shouted, 'Yeah!' Amber grinned. 'For sure.'

'Then you are true Epicureans. As am I. Which why we're all here in France. Because being here with my family in this beautiful part of the world is everything to me. It means more to me than any of the drugs I've taken,' which provoked a shocked titter, 'more than every prestigious theatre project I've ever worked on, more than all the wonderful love affairs I've had, more than anything I've ever done in my life. You lot and your marvellous parents are my world. And that's why I don't want you to watch me die in a hospice bed surrounded by nurses, in terrible pain and horribly scary to look at. I want to spend my last week on this earth here in this wonderful place with all of you, happy and sun-kissed.' My glass juddered in my hand as though it were full and too heavy for my muscles, but it seemed I'd knocked the liquid down without noticing – it was as light as a feather.

Hazel looked to Amber, and Eliot stared agog at me. I could see they were working through what I'd said, wondering if they'd heard right.

'Sorry, Granny Nor-Nor, but why did you say it was your last week on this earth?' Eliot said with the sort of politeness he might reserve for a stranger. His sweetness tugged at my heart and I had to take a breath before I could speak again.

'Well, I'm not going to be coming home with you, darlings. I'm dying from this blasted cancer. And I'd prefer to die from it here by slipping away peacefully in my sleep, saving your parents a lot of aggro and heartache.'

After last night, I felt more passionately than ever that this was the right thing to do; that it would make up for my flaws and my rotten errors.

'I'm not leaving you here on your own. I'm staying too,' Hazel whimpered. Tears fell from her eyes.

'Nonsense,' I replied croakily.

Eliot was almost translucent, turning into a ghost before me. He said nothing.

Under Amber's eyes were scoops of black. 'Is that why Auntie Emma stayed in her room last night?' she asked.

'Oh darlings, yes, she has been rather cross with me,' I said, joining them on the sofa, squeezing in between Eliot and Hazel, blinking back the tears. 'But you three mustn't be. You must be stronger than that. More intelligent about it. Your mothers are bound by a doctrine of denial. But you are the TikTak genera- tion – you are progressive and forward-thinking and open- minded. You are my allies.'

'Tik*Tok*,' Amber corrected in a flat tone. She would usually laugh at my deliberate social media malapropisms.

Desperate for something positive to cling onto, I looked to Eliot, and waited eagerly for his analysis of the ethical conun- drum I was in. Nothing. The only reaction I had anticipated correctly was Hazel's; she was crying and holding my hand. I reached one arm behind her and the other behind Eliot and stretched my fingertips to reach Amber's far shoulder, pulling the three of them under the umbrella of my outstretched arms, clutching at their little bodies.

'I'm so sorry,' I whispered. Their sadness was as pure as it could be, and it was excruciating. I felt hollowed out, and I ached greedily for decades more time with them.

We stared across the sea. On my inner arm, I felt wetness from where Amber's cheek touched it, but I didn't hear her cry or see her wipe her tears away. Eliot's head was like a dead weight grinding into my bosom.

But they were being more grown up than the grown-ups, and had instinctively understood that sadness was the principal emotion. They hadn't overcomplicated it with insecurities and denial and anger and recrimination. Those were a waste of time, dispensable extras. For the children, it was simple: I was going to die, and it was either going to be a good death or a bad one. And they had accepted I wanted a good one. Their accep- tance was what I had wanted. So why did I suddenly and fear- somely regret that I had told them? Why did I feel more burdened than ever, despite finally letting go of the weight of my secret?

TWENTY-THREE

LIBBY

'I'm drunk,' Libby whispered into Connor's ear as they went downstairs to their bedroom.

'No kidding.' He pulled her closer. They stumbled down the last few steps, fused at the lips like teenagers.

He was untying the cords of her blouse as they lurched through their bedroom door. She was desperate to shed her clothes, as though it were the cottons that weighed down her heart. Still entangled in each other's limbs, they stopped dead. Both Amber and Hazel were sprawled across their sheets, fast asleep. Taken aback, Connor and Libby floundered around, doing up what they'd undone, then taking a moment to marvel at the beauty of their sleeping children.

Before they backed out, Libby tiptoed over to the window and closed the gap in the curtains. She was about to lean over to kiss the girls on the forehead when she lost her footing, slipping on some paper. Strewn around the bedside table were A4 sheets covered in drawings. Sharpies rolled around with their lids off. She gathered them up, unable to decipher the images in the darkness.

Connor put a finger to his lips, then took her hand and

dragged her out and upstairs to Amber's bedroom, where he resumed undressing her. But Libby had not yet let go of the drawings and wanted to take a closer look, hoping the poor light on the way upstairs had given her the wrong impression of them. She sat down on the bed in her bra, scrunched her chin down to stop Connor kissing her neck and turned on the bedside lamp. His desire would have to be put on hold.

She took a sharp in-breath. 'Look at these.'

He sat next to her. 'Whoa. Shit. That's weird. Are they Amber's?'

'I think so,' she replied.

The drawings were anime, a style that Amber had got bored with years ago, but it was the subject matter that alarmed Libby. Ageing, small-waisted action heroines with long, curly white-blonde hair and exaggerated wrinkles were hanging from nooses in trees with protruding eyes and bloody mouths. Notes on their chests said *Sorry*. For a flicker of a second, Libby feared that her mum had told them, but she dismissed it as soon as it popped up.

'Do you think Amber's overheard anything?'

'But we only talked about it openly for the first time tonight, at the restaurant,' Connor reminded her.

Over dinner, they had argued about Emma's reverse psychology tactics. Poor Patrick had tried to make his alternative view heard by suggesting that game-playing was unnecessary, manipulative and potentially dangerous. But Emma hadn't wanted to listen.

Libby flicked through the drawings. 'Such a weird coincidence, as though she's had some kind of psychic premonition.'

'I guess the unconscious messages we've been throwing around today could have got through somehow?' Connor suggested.

They held each other's gaze, both grappling for anything

other than the only logical explanation. 'Mum wouldn't have, surely,' Libby asserted.

But Connor didn't immediately agree with her.

She needed to convince herself. 'She wouldn't do it without telling us first.'

He fell back on the bed with his feet planted firmly on the tiles. His hands were in his hair. He groaned. 'I don't know, Libby. She might have let it slip.'

'She's not *that* bad, Connor,' she said wearily, feeling beleaguered by a whole evening of Mum-bashing.

Connor startled her by getting up suddenly. His tall frame loomed above her. 'No, she's not,' he said, walking over to the window. There was something murky and peculiar in his tone, and Libby didn't like it.

Misgivings about her mum filtered through the shield she had been holding up all evening to deflect criticism. She pictured Amber and Hazel sprawled asleep across their bed and felt a surge of dread. If they knew, they would be distraught, and Libby would have to put them back together. The idea of them being holed up here with their Granny Nor-Nor's imminent suicide ahead of them was inconceivable.

'Amber's probably just seen some horror film or something and they've spooked themselves out,' she said, needing this to be true.

'Yes, definitely,' Connor said, shutting himself into the bathroom, leaving Libby alone with Amber's drawings. *Definitely, maybe.* She wondered if she should nip across the corridor to Emma's room to ask her what she thought. Or better still, get Patrick to analyse them. But when she stopped at the door, taking one last look, she recognised there was little subtlety or subtext to unpick. There was no way of hiding from these drawings. The girls knew. It was obvious.

She imagined poor Amber processing her feelings; Hazel, too, in a fug of Sharpie fumes, seeking comfort in each other, waiting for their parents to return from dinner and explain the truth away. She felt utterly stupid for defending her mum's character.

Her last hope was that Eliot had been spared. In spite of his many talents and achievements, he was younger than his cousins. Libby prayed he was sleeping innocently in his bed, blissfully unaware of it all. Unlike her two girls.

Connor came out of the bathroom and climbed into bed, turning his back on her. She closed her eyes to sleep, and knew she wouldn't. A coil of miserable rage wrapped itself around and around in her stomach. If she had been skilled enough to draw anime, she would have scrawled a drawing that depicted innocence being ripped from children's throats.

Sometime later, she was woken by Connor slipping out of bed and creeping towards the door.

'Where are you going?' she asked groggily.

'Just getting a glass of water. Go back to sleep,' he whispered.

But she noticed he had his sweater in his hand.

TWENTY-FOUR

NORA

Everyone was asleep. I retraced the path through the bushes to our secret meeting spot at the gazebo. Leaves scratched my cheeks, nasty little creatures scuttled away from my footsteps, and there was the chill of the dew on my hemline. A vertiginous feeling.

Connor had insisted I bring my notebook. It was a strange request, which he wouldn't explain until I got there. I guessed he'd come up with some idea about a suitable ritual for it.

I wasn't ready.

Apprehensively, I sat on the bench and waited for him. He appeared five minutes after me with two glasses and a bottle of red. He kissed me on the forehead and glanced at the notebook on my lap. 'Good, you brought it.'

I put it aside while I drank my wine, took in the view and discussed the children's heartfelt reaction to what I'd told them earlier. But in truth, we were skimming across everything else to get to the main event.

I had to ask. 'Why did you want me to bring this with me?'

He swivelled his knees to face mine.

'In the spirit of all this honesty, I want to do something for you.'

'Is this an intervention?' I grinned, looking over my shoulder for the others to leap out of the undergrowth.

'Can I have that?' he said, pointing to the notebook.

'Why?'

'Please?'

'No. Not until you tell me what you're going to do with it.' His lighter was sitting on top of his tobacco pouch.

He must've noticed where my gaze had fallen. 'I want to read it. Not burn it.'

I couldn't let go of it. 'It's the only proof I have that I didn't make it up.'

'Please, trust me.' He put his hand out, palm up, staring right into my eyes. 'I know you didn't make it up.'

I chewed my bottom lip, feeling tears spring up. 'Hearing you say that is very important to me,' I whispered. 'I don't know why.'

'Because you blamed yourself for it.'

'It was my fault,' I breathed.

'Would you blame Amber if her teacher did the same to her?'

'That's disgusting! She's not like that.'

'Please. I want to read some of it out to you,' he said, again proffering his hand. As a compromise, I put the notebook in the space between us. He picked it up and smoothed his hand over the marbled cover before opening it and glancing nervously at me. 'Thank you.'

He turned the pages, scanning my words, and my heart bounced. He paused at one place. 'Now, I want you to imagine that Amber wrote this.'

'I can't do that!'

But he began reading anyway. I covered my face, wincing

into my palms, unable to get my granddaughter's sweet imaginary voice out of my head.

The sickening smell of resin filled my mouth and the discordant notes of a botched piano scale rang in my ears. My mind was filled with the vile images of my history teacher's long, cold fingers unbuttoning my blouse and the thud of a crow hitting the music room window like a bad omen. That three-second flashback was more devastating than the many frilly words being read out to me now. I experienced the dazed shock you feel after a fall, before the real pain sets in. A new comprehension, a new understanding.

As I watched the moon controlling the tides, my memories were being pushed and pulled, becoming clear and close one minute, regressing again in the next, swallowed up by my greedy, overprotective subconscious.

'Enough!' I cried, drilling my forehead into my knees.

Connor stopped reading and I began a faltering confession, fighting for breath as I remembered how terrified and suffocated and trapped I had been, and how confused I was now about why I hadn't run. Occasionally he relit his roll-up. My account was far darker than what was written in the notebook. By comparison, my juvenile diary entries were pathetic fairy tales: how the man had wooed me with compliments; how excited I'd been when he'd first touched my knee; how bowled over I had been by his thoughtful presents.

'I thought it was love,' I admitted.

'And it was the opposite.'

'Like all the others,' I said sadly, recalling a litany of disastrous affairs that had followed.

David, a conductor with the London Philharmonic, had been there for me when Hugh left me, but he'd had this ghastly high voice and had kept me a secret from his Jewish mother for four years, then dumped me for a woman who would become the

Jewish mother to his own baby nine months later. Then there was Harold, with his red curls, who'd had to shower straight after sex because he was convinced his wife had a superhuman sense of smell. And Oliver, a record company executive with ridiculous slip-ons and collarless jackets, who had lasted a whole two years through the worst of my menopause. Everyone had thought he was a living saint for putting up with me, but they hadn't known that he was a sociopath underneath all that charm – industry bosses so often were – and had openly shared me with male prostitutes.

These men had been echoes of that first dirty, shameful secret.

'And you're another case in point,' I said, only half joking.

'Don't say that,' Connor rasped. Surprising me, he stretched one hand across his face, half covering his eyes, squashing his nose, digging his thumb and fingers into the hollows of his cheeks. 'I feel so terrible about it.' His hand fumbled for mine, but it did not warm my cold, sweaty palm, and the reminder of our betrayal slid like cold water through my veins.

I remained still. He recovered himself, wiping some wetness from his eyes. 'Sorry, I didn't mean to put that on you right now.'

The diary was still open across his thighs.

I took it from him and closed it, then hugged it to my chest, returning my gaze to the sea, steadfast, blocking out my fear and guilt, returning to the past, feeling raw about that and nothing else, allowing myself a moment of pure misery about a destroyed childhood. And genuine pity for that girl who was me.

'Nobody will ever know what we've done,' I whispered, holding his chin, coaxing him out of his self-pitying state. 'And nobody will ever understand what you've done for me tonight.'

. . .

In bed later, I replayed our conversation, which was more like an experience, and reviewed the whole of my life through the prism of what had happened to me in those music rooms. Facing it prompted such a profound and sudden shift in my psyche, I was strangely elated, perhaps like a feverish child with unnaturally rosy cheeks and bright eyes, and I contemplated aborting my plans for this week, backtracking, eking out a few more months of this funny old life.

Would I be able to tell the girls? Was this my opportunity for a reset?

It was amazing, quite amazing, but the revelation of it had reignited an urgent desire to live.

TWENTY-FIVE

EMMA

'He knows jolly well that he's not supposed to swim unsupervised,' Emma said, peering down from the balcony, spotting Eliot's red head bobbing about in the blue. 'He's getting up earlier and earlier every morning,' she murmured, checking her phone. She was talking to nobody. It was only 6 a.m. Patrick was out cold in bed, mouth open.

She pulled a dress over her head and nipped down to the pool, wishing she had time to make a coffee on the way, feeling groggy from the wine the night before. It had not been a successful evening. Without everyone on board, she was not as confident as she had sounded about making sure her mum walked out of the villa alive.

She waited at the deep end and tapped Eliot's head. He reeled up as though confronted by a shark.

'Eliot. What do you think you're doing, young man? What is the *one* rule?'

He spat out a fountain of water and somersaulted into a turn, sliding up to the surface and slapping his skinny little arms in an unruly, angry front crawl away from her to the other end. Emma jogged to meet him.

'What has got into you?' she said, trying to grab his arm.

He slipped from her grasp and continued his swim.

Short of yanking him out bodily, she had no choice but to watch him attack the water, length after length. Tired and a little shivery, she lay back on one of the sunloungers, which was still damp from the morning dew. She forgave her son's defiance. In truth, she was proud of his dedication and endurance. There weren't many ten-year-olds who had his stamina. He'll be swimming for the county at this rate, she thought as her eyelids drooped.

Emma was being nudged awake.

'Auntie Emma,' Hazel whispered.

She jolted up, checking on Eliot in a panic, mortified that she'd nodded off on lifeguard duty, reassured that her son was safe.

'My goodness, Hazel, what are you doing up so early?' She rubbed at her hung-over face.

'I couldn't sleep.'

'Was it this little guy splashing about and making a racket?'

'No,' Hazel said loyally.

'The whole household will be up in a minute.'

'I'm going to make a hot chocolate. Would you like one?'

'I'd kill for a coffee, sweetheart. While you're up.'

'At your service,' Hazel said, saluting.

But Emma noticed that her eyelids were unmistakably pink and puffy from crying. Before she had a chance to ask her if she was okay, Hazel had scampered up to the villa.

It dawned on Emma that leaving the three children alone with their Granny Nor-Nor last night had been chancy. But the risk factor had been overshadowed by her eagerness to talk freely with Libby and the other two, out of the children's earshot, to bring them on side with her methods of persuasion.

Hazel returned carrying a cup, the coffee spilling over the white china rim, leaving puddles on the flagstones behind her. With slow, deliberate concentration, she handed it over, not for a second lifting her eyes from it, not even when it was out of her hands and safely in Emma's.

As Emma took it, she asked, 'Was everything okay last night, poppet?'

Hazel shook her head and ground her little heel into the top of her other foot, almost toppling over. 'Not really.'

Emma held her steady by the arm and glanced over at her son cutting through the water at a furious pace. Lurching out of denial, she instantly understood what had gone on last night. The realisation was like a door slamming her into a dark room.

'Granny Nor-Nor told you, didn't she?' she gasped.

Hazel's pale brown eyes, bulging with restrained tears, finally made contact and she nodded.

Blood rushed through Emma's head, and she blurted out, 'Well, it's not true. The medicine sends her a little gaga sometimes. Just ignore it. It's absolute rubbish.' Instinctively she knew that lying was a huge mistake, but she wanted to provide on-the-spot comfort for her sweet, distraught niece.

'Really?'

She mumbled an indistinct 'yes', and then said, 'Did she tell all three of you?'

Hazel nodded again.

'Oh, darling. That must have been very scary for you.' Emma pulled her in for a hug and stroked her back, while watching her son over her shoulder.

'It was,' Hazel sniffed.

'Granny Nor-Nor is very naughty sometimes. Very, very naughty indeed,' Emma said, suppressing an urge to charge into her mother's room and give her a piece of her mind. A few days ago, she might have.

Eliot came to the side of the pool and climbed out, staring at them curiously, shivering and dripping. His skinny chest heaved in and out rapidly with disturbingly shallow breaths.

'Hi, darling, I've just heard what your crazy Nor-Nor told you last night. What a loony-tunes she can be, getting you caught up in her fantasies.'

'It's not true?' Eliot said, pressing a bunch of fingers into one wet eye to rub at it, leaving the other blinking at her like a wink gone wrong.

'If you'd got out when I'd asked you to,' Emma chided, 'I would have been able to talk to you about it.' Telling him off was easier than lying straight to his face.

'Sorry,' he said, and she felt rotten. 'Why did she say it then?' he asked.

'She's on a lot of painkillers right now,' Emma replied, which explained nothing.

Eliot began waggling his head to the side, hitting out the water from one ear. 'And she didn't mean it?'

'Absolutely not.'

'You sure?'

'Absolutely sure.'

'I did think she looked a bit spacey.'

'How's Amber feeling about all this?'

'Fine, I guess,' Hazel said. 'She's still asleep. We slept in Mum and Dad's room.'

'I'm so sorry you were put through all that worry unnecessarily. I just wish I could have been here to stop it.'

'That's okay,' Hazel said simply, before asking, 'Can I go in the pool now?'

Emma wondered whether she should say no to Hazel, wake Libby up and tell her what had happened, but she needed a few more minutes to prepare.

'Yes, I'll stay here and watch you for a bit. Off you go.'

The two of them ran into the pool as though they could walk on water, and Emma thought how strange children could be, how superhuman. They seemed to have absorbed this new truth as a matter of fact and were getting on with it. She liked to believe they were displaying resilience. She didn't want them to dwell on what had been said last night.

When they screamed or bashed their woggles about noisily, she did not tell them off as she might usually. They were delighting in their play, lighter as a result of her white lie.

They'd now also have to lie to Amber, who was still asleep. This would fall to Libby. Emma felt sick about layering more distortions on top of a hoard of others. But having done it now, her instinct was to sit on it and push on through, adopt the children's hardiness and continue hoping for the best. What astounded her was how her mother's dysfunction was trickling down to affect her grandchildren's lives, how the rot wasn't stopping at Emma and Libby, how the lies were breeding as though they had minds of their own. It was what she had always tried to mitigate against, and yet here it was, happening with such intensity and speed she felt out of control, overwhelmed, trapped, like she was holding her hands across large cracks in a boat that she knew would sink.

So as not to disturb anyone, least of all her mother, Emma crept barefoot along the corridor towards Amber's room, where she assumed Libby was sleeping, hoping she could rouse her without getting Connor involved. It was already seven, which meant he was probably in a downward dog or meditating on his tatty yoga mat that reeked of mould and incense.

She had been right about the yoga, but wrong about the mat. Through the French windows that led on to a small balcony at the back of the house, she could see him sitting cross-legged on a towel. His face was tilted to the sky, and he had adopted a straight-backed pose that represented a calm, controlled mind. His knees were high off the ground, suggesting his hips weren't as agile as they once were, and the sacks under his closed eyes created shadows down his cheeks. He claimed he didn't suffer from hangovers.

She tiptoed over to the bed to wake Libby, whose eyes were covered by a mustard-yellow batik eye mask. Before she nudged her, she noticed a horrible cartoon drawing lying on the bedside table next to her pillow. It was of a woman hanging from a noose on a tree. She tried to remember if Libby could draw that well.

'Libs,' she whispered. Close up, the mask smelt the same as Connor's yoga mat. 'Wake up. We need to talk.'

Libby pushed the mask off, skew-whiff above one eyebrow, scrunching her face up as though she didn't recognise her.

Emma put her finger to her lips. 'Shh, come with me.'

Libby woke quickly, and unquestioningly followed Emma out of the bedroom and through the villa's front door, along the balustraded walkway that led to the garage. Behind it, they stepped over the plant borders and along the hidden pathway, down a couple of steps to the small gazebo smothered by honey-suckle that Emma had discovered when making the call to Samarth.

'Just look at that for a minute,' she breathed. It was impossible not to comment on the view, made more beautiful by the tangled frame of flowers.

'I didn't know about this spot,' Libby said, pacing about nervously.

'Don't tell anyone about it, will you,' Emma said, sitting down on the semicircular bench.

Libby bit the skin around her thumbnail. 'Mum told the girls, didn't she?' Her eyes darted about and she ruffled the front of her hair into a quiff.

'How did you know?'

'Didn't you see Amber's awful pictures on my bedside table?' she said, crossing her ankles under the bench.

Centimetres away from her toes, there were two wine glasses. Emma was about to warn her to be careful not to knock them over when she noticed the unmistakable smear of coral lipstick on one of the rims and the red wine sediment at the bottom of each.

'Oh dear, yes, I wondered who'd drawn them,' she said, hoping that Libby wouldn't see the glasses and wonder too hard about who had been sipping from them.

'I'm guessing Eliot knows.' Libby swivelled to face her.

'Unfortunately, yes.'

'Jesus Christ.' She threw her head back, catching a host of leaves and petals in her hair.

'Come here a sec.' Emma beckoned her forward and began picking them out. 'I saw Eliot and Hazel by the pool and they seem okay about it.'

'They can't be!' Libby cried, incredulous.

'I told them a little fib.' Emma scrunched the leaves between her fingertips, reducing them to scratchy flakes that stuck to her thighs.

'What did you say?'

'I told them Mum was a bit foggy from the medication she was on and that it was a silly story she'd made up.'

'Emma!'

'I know, I know.'

Libby's knees were jiggling and her feet were flat on the floor, poised to run. 'Amber won't be so easy to convince.'

'We could tell her the truth, but she'd have to keep it secret.'

'She wouldn't be able to do that, not from Hazel,' Libby said.

Emma couldn't bear to look at her sister in that moment. 'It would be awful to force her into that position,' she murmured.

'I just can't believe Mum's done this!' Libby said. It was a

strangely self-conscious spurt of crossness, as though she understood that she should feel anger but couldn't exhibit a genuine
display of it. 'I literally want to kill her!' she added, even less
convincingly.

'Don't worry, she's doing that for you,' Emma joked darkly,
her eyes dropping to the two wine glasses, perhaps dirtied by
deceit. Libby didn't have a clue about how angry she was entitled to be. And Emma didn't want to imagine what it would
look like if she was enlightened. 'Seriously, though, however
pissed off you feel right now, you can't go getting all tearful and
overemotional with her for telling the kids. It's what she'll
expect you to do, and she'll feed on it.'

'Yes, okay,' Libby said, looking glum. Her so-called fury
hadn't lasted, and Emma pondered this, not for the first time.
She herself had gone through their sisterhood competitively,
questioning how Libby maintained such composure. In her
meaner moments, she had accused her of apathy and passive
aggression, but now she reconsidered it, wondering why Libby
seemed unable to be angry at their mother when there were so
many good reasons to feel that way.

'I'm taking your heart from your sleeve and putting it in
your pocket, okay?' Emma said, plucking an imaginary heart
and slotting it into a pretend pocket, making sure that this
wasn't the moment her sister finally decided to get in touch with
her rage. 'Just for now, we have to be a little bit dishonest, for
the kids' sake.'

'But Patrick said—'

'I know, I know what Patrick said, but we know Mum better
than him.'

'We do.' There was a glint of hope in Libby's eyes, as though
she knew this might work.

'It's worth a try,' Emma said. The understatement of this
was huge, and she felt a rush of her own fresh anger. 'If it
doesn't work, and if everything we say falls on deaf ears and she

continues peddling all that maternal self-sacrifice bullshit and craps on about killing herself on Sunday at nine o'clock sharp, or whatever, then I will actually leave this time, even if I have to walk home, and I'll take Eliot with me, and there'll be no cosy goodbyes, I can assure you.'

'I'll come with you,' Libby said.

'Good. Whatever happens, we'll have each other, okay?' Emma said, shuffling along the bench to give her sister a cuddle.

'Love you, sis,' Libby said, resting her head on her shoulder. 'Sorry for being all aggro earlier. I think I'm just so tired. Not helped by Connor getting up in the middle of every bloody night to get some water or go for a walk to clear his head because he says he can't seem to sleep in this villa. I'm having trouble sleeping in it too now!'

'Oh dear! That can't help,' Emma said, trying not to imagine where Connor had been going, or to whom. While her suspicions were shut up somewhere dark, where they couldn't hurt her sister, she could allow some of her mother's better qualities to filter through. 'We'll get through this. And as insane as Mum is, I'm certain she loves the kids enough to do the right thing and really give them time to process it before she makes any decisions. Sometimes I think they're the only ones she's ever been able to love unconditionally.' She paused, then repeated, 'She'll do the right thing. And the right thing is to come home with us. With her family. So we can get through it together.'

It scared her a little to reconnect with Nora as a woman, as a person. Not as an absent mother, but as an ambitious, independent, irreverent spirit and a fearless female who would fight to the death for her kin. As someone who had not shied away from taking risks, who had lived life how she had wanted to live it, ridiculing its absurdities with a devil-may-care toss of her hair, unapologetic about the toes she had stepped on along the way. Emma couldn't help admiring all this. And her eyes swelled with unshed tears. A chasm would be left when Nora was gone.

The vision of the three of them sitting in a row on the plane bloomed in her mind. They were heading home together, sipping champagne again and laughing as Nora told the air steward what a difficult baby Emma had been. *Please, can I have the opportunity to groan at that annoying story just one more time?* she begged God.

TWENTY-SIX

NORA

In the morning, I remembered the two wine glasses we'd left and retraced my steps to the gazebo, planning to retrieve them and smuggle them back to the kitchen, where I could wash them and put them back in their place in the cabinet.

We couldn't slip up now.

The children were occupied in and around the pool: Amber on her phone – drier than she had been in England; Hazel rootless on the inflatables; Eliot engrossed in his lengths. The grown-ups were busy too. Patrick was reading his Booker Prize-winning novel. Emma and Libby had gone for a walk and Connor was on a paddleboard. It was encouraging to see that life could carry on after I'd told them that I would not be coming home with them this coming Sunday.

None of them knew about last night or about the new doubts that plagued me. Three months of steely resolve was unravelling in my mind.

As I got closer to the gazebo, I heard a voice. Unmistakably, its shouty tone belonged to my darling elder daughter.

I stopped to listen. '...and craps on about killing herself on Sunday at nine o'clock sharp, or whatever, then I will actually leave this time, even if I have to walk home, and I'll take Eliot with me, and there'll be no cosy goodbyes, I can assure you.'

I was winded by her words. Not even a physical blow could have been more unexpected or injurious. Their conversation continued, but I could no longer hear through the pounding in my head.

How mistaken I had been to predict she would respect the cleanness of my death. It seemed she would prefer to suffer. I had underestimated how desperate she would be to wipe my bottom and clean my bedsores as part of some gruelling, martyrish rite of passage.

There I had been, seriously contemplating opening up to her about what had happened to me as a child, while she and Libby derided me and disrespected my choices.

I could have fled, scared of what I might hear next, but I revealed myself to them.

'Oh Jesus,' Emma said, slapping her hand to her chest. 'You scared the living daylights out of me!'

'Hello, you two. You didn't get far on your walk,' I said haughtily.

Libby shook her head and Emma nodded. Part of me relished Libby's flushed, blotchy skin. *Yes, I did hear you, if that's what you're worried about.*

Emma managed to say, 'We decided it was too hot.'

Such a good liar. Always such a lack of respect. At only two years old, she had been stonily indifferent towards me. The way she had surveyed me with those large, glassy eyes of hers – chilling from someone so young. I'd hoped that nurture would win out, that my influence would shape her, that she was simply wilful and bright.

'This is a heavenly spot, isn't it? I had no idea it existed,' I said, moving to the very edge. The drop was perilous and there was only a flimsy railing between me and a fatal fall. From behind me, Emma said, 'Okay, okay, Mum, let's drop the act. You know we were talking about you.'

She was playing the honesty card. Clever.

'Oh?'

'We're pretty upset that you told the kids,' Libby said, then began to ramble. 'Well, not upset, we understand why you did it, we just felt that maybe we could talk the whole thing through.'

I swivelled to face them, fortified by the children's reactions last night, sick to death of my daughters' resistance and denial and lack of support. 'Their sadness is literally living inside of me now,' I said, reminding them and myself that the right path wasn't always the easy one.

But before I had a chance to go on, Emma scowled at Libby and said, 'What she's very clumsily trying to say, Mum, is that we found it all a bit shocking and we needed time to get our heads around it, but we're getting there and we're really trying to understand and you know, we feel, more than ever, that we have to be respectful of your decision and learn to accept it.'

'I appreciate your understanding.' I was relieved we weren't going into open combat, preferring to play along while they humoured me, while they pretended to champion my cause. Blah, blah, blah. Her earlier rant was the rub. Her support might be superficial, but it would do for now. I knew enough about acting to know that if one inhabited the role, like an actor on one of Stanislavski's stages, the character's traits become entwined with one's own emotional experiences. It was why great actors were such royal fuck-ups. 'The kids were wonderful last night. So supportive. You would've been proud of them,' I added, making my point.

The redness on Libby's chest spread further up her neck. I looked away, finding eye contact with her difficult, petrified that she'd see in my expression what had happened last night with Connor. My gaze returned to Emma, whose smile was fixed.

'Good, yes, I'm sure they'll be okay,' she said. 'Good, good, we're all good then.'

Her pretending was amusing, and as transparent as when she would hide behind a curtain as a toddler with her little toes showing. I said, 'Let's sit down this evening as a family and plan my celebration of life ceremony.'

'Celebration of life?' Emma asked, both eyebrows raised.

'Yes, darling. It's all part of the plan.' Playing dumb could be fun.

'Umm, I'm not sure,' Libby said, biting her lip. 'It might be a bit soon. Maybe we should wait a few days.'

'But then the kids won't have a chance to organise anything. Eliot is bound to want to draw a picture. And Hazel and Amber might want to bake something special for me or write a poem. They know how much I love poetry.'

Emma said, 'Libby's right, Mum. Let's give them a couple of days.'

'We don't have the luxury of a couple of days,' I said, trying to sound sweet but making it clear that I was in charge here.

There were a few more rather pathetic remonstrations, which I fought off, knowing I'd win unless they decided to be more honest with me about how they really felt.

I was feeling smug until Emma looked down at my feet and said very slowly and deliberately, 'Oh gosh, look... Seems we're not the only ones who know about this place. I wonder who the lovebirds were?'

She bent down to reach for the two wine glasses under the bench, and my heart stopped. One was stained with my coral lipstick.

'That's your lipstick, Mum,' Libby said, sounding confused. 'I thought you said you'd never been here?'

'Ha! Like I'm the only person in France who wears coral lipstick!'

'Funny coincidence, though.' She wrinkled her nose.

'I agree,' Emma said.

I blushed. 'Well, I can't explain it, can I?' I might have sounded a little defensive.

Libby scratched at a mosquito bite on her hip, bunching her shorts up. 'Odd,' she said, tilting her head. A thought seemed to blow through her mind. Whatever it was, it was short-lived. 'Someone must've used one of your dirty glasses without noticing,' she said conclusively. Who that someone might be was left unanswered.

'Yes, probably,' I said, finding my breath.

Emma's eyes were on me. It had been a warning shot. She would be willing to use this to get what she wanted from me.

'Okay, well, it's only Monday morning, we can think about the celebration of life discussion at another point. Now, I'd better get back to the pool. I promised Eliot I'd time him.'

'Eliot's still swimming?' Emma gasped.

'Patrick's there, I think.'

'But he's been in the pool since dawn,' she said, and gaped at me as though it were my fault. 'I've got to go,' she said, tearing off.

Libby plodded along the path in her wake, and I followed behind, unspeaking.

A soreness in my gut escalated into severe cramping. Experience told me I needed to get to the loo fast. But I was nervous of hurrying Libby along, engaging with her on any level, sparking a confrontation. So I carried on, trying to hold it in.

My hesitation had humiliating consequences.

Fully deserved, some might say.

TWENTY-SEVEN

LIBBY

'Oh Mum, please don't worry,' Libby whispered, devastated for her. 'Stay there a minute, I'll make sure the coast is clear so you can nip in and get cleaned up.'

'I'm not sure I'll be nipping anywhere,' Nora said courageously, gripping Libby's elbow for balance, shuffling along the path like a concubine with broken toes.

Libby helped her across the courtyard to the front door and into one of the downstairs bathrooms without being seen. After a few minutes of loitering outside, she said, 'You okay in there, Mum?'

It was quiet except for the taps running. Then, 'All good, darling. No need to wait.'

She did wait, though, knowing she risked embarrassing her mum further, but worrying more that she might collapse while she was inside.

When Nora emerged, holding a rolled-up towel with her knickers tucked discreetly inside, she said, 'I do so love the French for their fabulous bidets.'

They both chortled. Libby linked arms with her and

escorted her to the washing machines, and then upstairs to her bedroom.

'I'm fine now, honestly,' Nora insisted weakly, looking pale. Her lower eyelids were quivering and damp, exposing the red veins underneath, and Libby recognised the strain that the last week had put her under. She felt responsible for making it harder on her, and made a secret promise to be more supportive, to try to genuinely accept her terms of death. The gulf between what she herself wanted and what her mum wanted stretched wide and black, and she knew she would struggle to bridge it with any sincerity, but she'd try, even if it took everything she'd got.

'Maybe have a little nap?' she suggested.

'Yes, I might. I can't seem to sleep in this villa.' Nora shut her eyes, as though she were going to take it standing up.

A fleeting image of Connor holding his jumper came back to Libby. Her mum closed the door, leaving her in the corridor with a nasty feeling in the pit of her stomach.

Clutching the handle, listening through the panels for concerning noises, she stood there for a few minutes. Her mum's sandals made a soft slapping sound away from the door, and Libby left her to it, drifting back along the corridor feeling dazed and hungry. *I can't seem to sleep in this villa*. Connor had used exactly the same words to her.

There was no time for Libby to recover from the fright her mother had given her. Loud yelling came from outside. She sped up, tripping on the snapped strap of her only pair of flip-flops. Down by the pool, there was a commotion.

'But I haven't done enough yet!' Eliot screamed, shivering on the side, scowling at Emma.

'Yes, you have! Look at you. Your lips are blue! Enough.'

'*No!*'

'Upstairs, now!'

'*No!*' Eliot ran to the side, slipping on the edge, recovering and diving in. His stroke was weak, his arms were smacking the surface, his little mouth was gasping for air when he turned to breathe.

'Patrick! What are you doing just standing there? We have to stop him!' Emma yelled.

'I don't know what to do,' he said, staring desperately into the pool.

'We have to get him out!'

'By physically pulling him out?'

'Yes, if we have to.'

'But he keeps getting in again! And what then? Drag him by the hair and lock him in his room?'

'Maybe? *I* don't know, *do* I? I don't know what to do! He won't listen to me!'

Behind them, Libby hurried over to Amber and Hazel, who were squashed onto one sunlounger together.

'What's going on?' she whispered to the girls under cover of the din.

'He's been swimming lengths for about four hours!' Hazel said, distraught.

'Four hours?'

Amber elaborated. 'He gets out sometimes to have a five-minute rest and a drink, but then he gets straight back in again.'

'I heard him being sick in the loo,' Hazel added. 'And one time Patrick got him out and hugged him super-tightly on the lounger while he screamed—'

'It was more like pinning him down,' Amber interjected.

'Yeah, it was horrible,' Hazel continued, 'but as soon as he let go of him, Eliot jumped straight back in!'

'Jesus,' Libby breathed, feeling tearful, pressing her fingers into her lips, staring uselessly at Eliot. Her head throbbed with the enormity of her nephew's distress, and also with everything they'd had to contemplate and process and confront on this so-called holiday.

'I've never, ever seen him not do what Auntie Emma asked,' Amber said, sounding quietly admiring, as though she viewed her little cousin in a whole new light.

Hazel said, 'I think he's upset about what Nor-Nor said.'

'But what Nor-Nor said isn't true, sweetheart.' Libby inhaled a sip of air as she said it, squeezing in between the two of them. Their gazes were fixed on Eliot charging up and down the pool. His manic behaviour seemed to be the manifestation of everyone's anguish. 'I know what she told you, but the drugs are making her go a bit wonky in the head. She has all these awful ideas, but she doesn't know what she's saying half the time,' she said, pulling them close and kissing them.

Hazel was the only one to reply. 'That's what Auntie Emma said.' Amber stared on.

'Auntie Emma and I are going to sort her out.' Libby watched Eliot's tumble-turn and decided that if he did one more length, she would be getting in herself to stop him.

'But what if you can't sort her out and she kills herself?' Amber asked.

The baldness of that sentence horrified Libby, but she shouldn't have been surprised. Amber was saying it how it was, learning at her grandmother's knee.

'No, no, no, it won't come to that.'

'There was this girl I followed on TikTok who killed herself,' Amber said gloomily.

'Let's try and think positively.' Libby's words sounded hollow. She had never felt less positive about anything. She wondered when Connor would be back from his paddle-boarding excursion. It was an absent-minded thought, knowing that it was like asking herself how long a piece of string was. Her mum was the only person who could help Eliot.

At that moment, as though a vision had been conjured, Nora appeared by the pool.

'What's all this hullabaloo about?' she hollered, flapping her kaftan wings. A gust of wind blew her hair out. The weak, wan figure of before, who had washed herself in the bidet, had been replaced by this maternal goddess.

'Oh Mum! Thank God you're here,' Emma cried tearfully. 'He won't get out of the pool. I don't know what to do!' Her voice was pleading and childlike; simply a girl asking her mum – the sorter-outer of all things – for help. All their hostilities rubbed out.

'Silly boy,' Nora said, taking off her kaftan to reveal a purple swimsuit, stepping into the shallow end.

Libby got up and moved over to the pool, anxious about both Eliot and her mum. Nora was putting up a front, performing a role as saviour, and this act of strength became actual strength. Libby was envious of it, and by comparison felt like a pale, unimpressive daughter.

Nora enveloped her grandson in her arms and held him while he wriggled and cried. 'Enough, Eliot, that's enough. Shh, darling. Come on, let's just lie on the lilos for a bit, have a rest, yes? You must be exhausted. All athletes need rest.'

Miraculously, Eliot flopped, like she'd pressed his stop button.

She waded further out for the two inflatables. While she was busy helping his fragile little body onto the blue one, she made a shooing gesture with her hands at her open-mouthed audience. Quietly Libby gathered the girls and crept away from the pool area, and Patrick collected Emma and encouraged her to let go. They left the pair of them floating in the water.

Libby went to her room and peeked out at the pool from the window. Her mum was lying on one inflatable with her hand trailing in the water. Her lips were moving. Bobbing next to her, Eliot was on his tummy with his face buried in the crook of his elbow, his goggles still in position on his head, his little ankles crossed backwards.

She thought, if that little boy's broken heart can't persuade her out of a fatal act on Sunday, then nothing can.

Hope pinched at her heart.

TWENTY-EIGHT

NORA

Deciphering the mumbling from underneath his arm was challenging. I paddled nearer to him. 'Say that again, darling?'

When I caught it the second time, I wished I hadn't tried to.

'I thought that if I trained really hard, you'd be so impressed and know how well I was going to do and then you'd want to live because you'd want to see me in the swimathon so much,' he said.

The shame of it. I could have drowned myself in it. My flesh flushed hot and then cold, until the chill set in and I began to shiver, rattled by what he was asking me to do.

My teeth were chattering by the time I said inadequately, 'I'm so sorry, my darling.'

'That's okay.'

There was nothing more to say. We lay there for a little while longer, and then I persuaded him out of the pool and placed him under the umbrella with a towel over him like a blanket. 'Sleep here for a bit.'

. . .

I closed myself into my bedroom. Regrets about last night, firstly
for telling the children and then about what I'd confessed to
Connor, bombarded me, and each dragged me further back in
time, bringing me lower and lower into despair. At the bottom,
or I hoped it was the bottom, I thought of my fourteen-year-old
self, and that diary. Those sordid words. It was no use trying to
be lofty, reinventing the person who had allowed that to
happen, cancelling out who I was. I was wretched to the core. It
was why I was incapable of delivering my grandson what he
wished for. Through naïve eyes, he had always seen me as the
woman I wanted to be, rather than the woman I was. While this
holiday was meant to embed my elevated self forever in his
mind, it seemed the opposite was happening.

'Thank you,' Emma said curtly, passing me the basket of bread,
and for a minute I wondered what she meant, considering I was
the one receiving the bread. But then she added, 'He's much
calmer, and we managed to talk before he fell asleep.'

I couldn't derive any satisfaction from being the heroine.
Eliot had sparked a doubt so profound, my nerve was bleeding
out of me at a rate. The empty space at the supper table where
he should have been was a more powerful presence than our
physical selves.

Looking around, it was obvious that everyone's mood was
subdued. Connor was hunched over his food, gobbling unattractively; Libby stared vacantly; Amber was watching something
on her phone on her lap as though nobody would notice; Hazel
was chewing nibbles of bread, lost in thought; and Patrick –
well, okay, Patrick seemed the same, as reserved and unreadable
as ever.

After a life of seeking out their respect and admiration –
insisting upon it – I had fooled myself into believing it gave me a
superior position, a more powerful role in the family, but I

couldn't have felt smaller amongst them. It seemed that Eliot's unassuming, quiet soul was the most forceful amongst us. Worrying about him now was a greater tug than any kind of scene I brought to the table.

A grim atmosphere was like poison in every forkful of the seafood risotto that Maria had made, and I resented it. It should have been delectable, served with a conversation about my life beautifully lived. But a discussion about my celebration of life ceremony would now be laughable. I could barely remember what life it was I might celebrate, let alone be deserving of anyone else's praise.

The sense of doom inside me and around the table was hellish. Their anger and my shame weighed us down. We were a collective physical presence, but completely separate in spirit. It was everything I had wanted to avoid this holiday. I tried to rally myself, wishing I could liven us up, and pulled out a courageous smile, saying, 'Isn't this place simply magical?' My voice sounded dead, but I was hoping to communicate how much I needed us to remain upbeat.

'Yes, girls,' Libby said. 'You know you should go and check out this amazing gazebo. We found it this morning. It's like something out of a film.'

Oh God. Libby, Libby, Libby.

Her teachers had always remarked on her caring nature and her extraordinary sensitivity to others, and here she was reminding the girls of the delights of this villa, which should have been the cheerful diversion I had craved. But her English teacher had once written on one of her reports, *Her essay writing is based more on intuition and empathy for the characters than it is a thought-through, fact-based analysis and exploration of literature, the latter of which she could work on if she wants to pass,* or something like it. And if her English teacher were to examine her response to me now, she would have made the same assessment. True, Libby had been empathetic, reading my face and understanding that my mood was sinking, and that some appreciation of what I'd given them might put me in better spirits. But she didn't have the facts, and she had brought up the bloody gazebo. Of all places. Mention of it couldn't have been less uplifting.

Then, to make matters worse, Connor said, 'Yeah, you'll love it, girls. It's round the back of the garage.'

My throat constricted. Stupid, stupid boy. If he had remained ignorant of the gazebo, he could never be identified as the drinker of the other glass of red wine.

'Oh?' Libby said. 'You knew about it too? Seems it's the worst-kept secret in France.' She laughed casually – she didn't sound like herself; none of us did, I suppose – and pointed to a glob of butter caught on his chin.

He wiped it away, leaving a greasy stain behind, catching my eye ever so briefly. I swore I could feel his heart thudding inside my own chest as he realised his mistake. I remembered how he'd dug his fingers into his cheeks last night, hiding his eyes with shame.

'Yeah,' he said. 'I forgot about it. I found it ages ago when I was trying to catch this gecko with the most amazing markings on his back to show the kids, and it scuttled up the back wall of the garage, which is where I hit on the path.'

He had rambled a bit, but his story had a kernel of truth on its side. While leading me away from there by the hand late last night, he had mentioned his escapades with the runaway reptile.

I studied Libby's face for signs that her much-celebrated intuition had picked up on his fraudulence and had identified him as the mystery wine drinker. If her suspicions had been roused, they weren't evident.

'I want to see the gecko!' Hazel said, showing signs of life finally.

'I'll find him for you tomorrow, sweet pea,' Connor said.

Tomorrow. Another tomorrow. I could count my tomorrows out with ease. Six of them left with Eliot. Six left with Emma, Libby, Amber and Hazel. It wasn't enough. I texted Connor to double-check he was meeting me again tonight in the gazebo. Seeing him would stretch the hours, make them count, keep those ghastly tomorrows at bay.

TWENTY-NINE

LIBBY

'This doesn't look right,' Libby said, cranking into first gear, gripping the wheel of the orange van to steady the tyres on the track as they climbed higher and higher through the dust and the trees. Her heart was galloping. It had been going at that rate since the early hours of the morning, electrified by what she'd seen.

'My ears just popped!' Hazel cried from the back.

'Me too,' Amber said.

'Me three,' Connor added.

'All will be well,' Nora said, breathing in and out from the passenger seat. Libby knew she didn't like heights. She should have worried for her.

'Why did you book a restaurant that was at the top of a hill?' she asked.

One of her mum's eyes creaked open. 'Because it's supposed to be the best.'

'Let's hope there are no windows with a view then,' Libby said meanly.

'I'm glad I'm not in that little car.' Connor twisted around to look behind them at Emma and Patrick in the red Cinquecento.

'At least this feels a bit more like a farm vehicle.' 'I think Emma was offended you didn't go with them,' Libby said.

'You sister's bloody terrifying.'

Nora snorted. In the rear-view mirror, Libby observed Connor's smirk and Hazel's tight jaw. Hazel adored her Auntie Emma and wouldn't hear a word against her, even from her dad. Amber, who was listening to her music, would have missed the slight. It wasn't the remark itself that was the problem for Libby, it was the conspiratorial air. As she contemplated it, a nasty prickly sensation ran across her skin and around her skull, leaving floating shapes over her eyeballs.

'I'm so hungry, I feel sick,' Hazel whined.

Libby felt sick too, and wished it *was* hunger.

'Even if it turns out to be a roadside shack serving fly-infested kebabs, I'm eating there anyway,' Connor said.

The restaurant couldn't have turned out to be less like a roadside shack. As they emerged out of the trees, they found themselves on the very top of the hill, its peak sliced off like the head of a boiled egg, allowing the restaurant to sit on top. An elegant grey canopy stretched over fifty or so spaciously laid out tables, each with a panoramic view of the Provençal country-side, tinted pink tonight by the dropping sun. The hushed chatter from the Tuesday-evening clientele died only momen-tarily as the eight of them snaked past, following the suited waiter to their table. The heavy-handled silverware clinked as they brushed the tablecloth with their knees to sit down. The glasses glinted in the candlelight and the smell of garlic made Libby's taste buds tingle. Even the warm breeze that messed up their hair was like a caress.

'Can we see the wine list?' Nora said brightly to the waiter. Her vertigo seemed to have disappeared, in spite of the dizzying drop on the other side of the railing.

'*Oui, bien sûr, madame,*' he said, whipping her napkin out of its ring and laying it on her lap.

When he'd gone, Amber said, 'That's the first time anyone has spoken French to us since we got here.'

That hadn't been true for Libby. She remembered the elegant lady in the café who had told her in French how much she'd loved what she had been knitting – the lady who had noticed that all wasn't well, the lady who would be seared onto her brain for the rest of time.

'They're a contrary bunch,' Nora scoffed.

'In Costa Rica...' Connor began. Libby turned down the sound of his voice in her head. All her senses were tuned into the more important nuances of his body language.

She watched them both. Connor and her mum. Every move, every glance, every smile, every frown, she noted down in her head. She watched for whose eyes they sought out when telling their stories, who they leant towards when listening, whose laughter captured their attention most.

The two of them were on form tonight, disagreeing with each other more than ever, loving every minute of it, commanding the table as though they were playing up to the extraordinariness of the restaurant. Its sophistication, its elevated position suited them. To them, the rest of the family were bit parts, unimportant as an audience.

To Libby also, everyone else paled next to the brightly lit Nora and Connor. Amber and Hazel's beautiful faces and their quirky little additions to the chatter failed to take centre stage in her attention. Patrick's interesting insight into the psychology of xenophobia was background noise, as were Emma's funny anecdotes about her adored little students. Usually, Libby would be laughing along to the stories of Alfie's antics, the naughtiest boy in school, whom she'd got to know over the years like a favourite character in a story book. Not tonight. Tonight she watched for something else.

She was not looking for clues to substantiate the unforgivably horrible suspicions that had been flickering through her head since seeing her mother nestled into Connor's armpit on the bench in the gazebo. She was looking rather for evidence that disproved them, for confirmation that this holiday from hell had taken its toll on her mental health, had sent her around the bend, cuckoo, nutty, out of her mind with paranoid notions. There was a cure for that: psychotherapists could talk her through her trauma symptoms and her mother's imminent suicide, and psychiatrists could dish out drugs. None of that fazed her. She wanted to be a madwoman who needed medication. What frightened her more was the alternative. If she was not going mad with paranoia, if there was something going on between her mother and Connor, there would be nothing in this world that could save her.

'*Moules-frites*. Yum,' Connor said.

'Oh my God, my favourite,' Nora said. 'That's what I'm having.'

Nothing odd there. They often enjoyed the same food. From the head of the table, Nora didn't look to Connor on her right. Libby dropped her napkin on purpose to check underneath the table. Amber had kicked off her stripy sliders and stretched out her legs. Nora's diamanté sandals were tucked chastely under her chair. Connor's buckled leather sandals were planted firmly on the tiled floor. Toe-tips were nowhere near enough for a game of footsie.

'There isn't an R in the month,' Patrick warned, referring to the mussels.

Nora shook her hand in the air, jangling her two gold bangles together, dismissing him. 'Oh, that's a myth, darling.'

Emma contested this. 'Not really. It's got something to do with the red tide in the summer months, when there's loads of algae in the water and it can have high levels of toxins. And there's some kind of spawning issue, too, but I don't really know much about that. I think if they farm them seasonally, it gives them the chance to repopulate.'

'Oh, nonsense. A restaurant like this wouldn't serve them if they were bad,' Nora said.

Connor pushed his menu into the centre of the table. 'I'm risking it. Too good to miss out on.'

'Can I have some too, Mum?' Eliot asked.

'And me?' Amber chimed in.

'No, absolutely not. The last thing we need is food poisoning,' Emma replied.

'I don't think it'd be a problem in a place like this,' Connor said, undermining her.

Libby was cleaved in two. So rarely did either of her children want to try different foods, it seemed a shame to steer Amber away from the mussels. But in a speedy calculation, she thought back to the many times – both important and insignificant, both in the past and recently – when she should have listened to Emma over her mum or Connor.

'No, Amber, you can't try them tonight. Auntie Emma's right. It's not worth the risk,' she said. Her voice sounded unexpectedly cross.

Amber looked over to her dad and laughed. 'Wow, Mum, okay. If you're sure.'

Libby was self-conscious about her outburst, while fully expecting to be ignored.

'*Moules* out of season is beyond rebellious, my darling. It seems now would *not* be the time to ask your mum if you could leave school so you can take copious amounts of psychedelics,' Nora said, winking at Amber.

Amber blushed and snorted, looking down at her menu. Libby didn't understand the in-joke, but worked out she was being mocked. 'Ha! Ha!' she laughed, slightly hysterically. 'Following in Granny Nor-Nor's footsteps then?'

Her mum's coral lips straightened. 'I left school at sixteen, darling, because my father went bankrupt and needed me to get a job.'

'Who paid for the psychedelics, then?' Connor said, deadpan.

There was a half-second pause before Nora threw her head back and hooted. 'Never you mind!'

Libby shuddered. What she saw now, after fifteen years of not seeing it, was the quiver between them, the excitement, the almost-flirtation. Before tonight, she had recognised only the light-hearted sparring of good friends. Going back twelve years now, she remembered when they had first truly bonded. Connor had felt usurped by the arrival of Hazel, who'd had colic and had needed Libby more than Amber had, and Libby had been grateful to her mother for getting him out of the house and cheering him up. Nora had described him as the son she'd never had.

The waiter came to take their orders. When it was Amber's turn, she glanced at her dad briefly, then said, 'Can I have the hake with dauphinoise, please?' A small victory. Libby wanted to high-five both Emma and Amber and felt tearfully grateful for having them in her life, which went to show how hyperreal and amped up this evening had become for her.

Living with her suspicions trapped inside her mind last night and throughout today had been difficult. There had been nobody to tell. Strangely, the only person she felt close enough to confide in was Amber, whose emotional intelligence would have been useful right now, but obviously she couldn't and wouldn't ever do that – she wasn't like her mother. Patrick was the only other person she'd consider sharing them with. But she knew Patrick would tell Emma, and Emma would flip the fuck out.

So far, her hunch was based on nothing more than a shadowy cuddle.

She had followed Connor last night after his story about the lizard. It had been a small lie, but it had set off a series of links in her head, like clicking the mouse again and again into inappropriate sites until you finally stumbled on something grim. A sensible person didn't go there. But Libby had never been sensible. She had never used her head, only ever followed her heart. And she had followed her heart last night all the way to the gazebo, where it had found a new, frantic beat.

'Oh, here we go!' Nora said, clapping her hands as the food arrived. 'Wonderful, look at this.' Each dish elicited a series of wows and claps, and Libby could see Amber sharing a cheeky giggle with Hazel about it. Since time began, she remembered being embarrassed by this clapping habit of her mother's.

Connor stared at his *moules-frites* in silent reverence, clocking Nora's next to his. But there wasn't even a split second of eye contact between them, or acknowledgment of them sharing the same meal.

'Dig in, kids,' Nora said.

'Can I try one?' Amber whispered to her Granny Nor-Nor.

Depressed by the predictability of it, Libby watched her mum show Amber how to pick the meat out with the pincered shell. If Emma had noticed, Libby guessed she would have stepped in, but Emma was elsewhere, absorbed in telling Eliot about the political history of *Les Misérables*, and Libby decided she didn't have the energy for the less revolutionary battle of *Les Moules*. They were probably right. A restaurant as fancy as this one was unlikely to serve dodgy seafood.

But it was gratifying to see Amber's face scrunch up in disgust.

'You don't like it?' Nora said, sounding perplexed, as though there might be something wrong with her. 'That's very odd. There's nothing not to like, is there?'

She was a dying woman, yet she couldn't help herself. What would it have taken to make her granddaughter feel good about trying one of the rubbery little morsels?

'I don't like them either,' Libby confided in Amber, nudging her.

'My father wouldn't have known what a mussel was,' Nora continued, sighing. 'He would love to know I was here, enjoying things he could only ever dream of.'

Libby waited for Connor's comeback, for the cheeky jibe that only he could get away with. It was never delivered. Instead, he looked at Nora and said, 'He'd be really proud.' He used a maudlin voice, filled with awe. It churned Libby's insides.

Over the course of the meal, Libby caught her mum secretly depositing a sneaky mussel on Eliot's plate every time Emma wasn't looking, making him giggle.

'What *are* you giggling about?' Emma asked him.

Nora hadn't seemed to care that Libby had seen her do this, trusting that she was incapable of standing up to her, despite the fact that Libby had also openly objected to the children eating the *moules*.

'I went deep-sea fishing in Costa Rica,' Connor said, off again on one of his stories about a scuba-diving expedition. 'But I went a bit further out than the others, wanting to follow a stingray, and the next thing I knew, the boat was zooming off back to shore, leaving me behind in the middle of the ocean! It took an hour for the guy to notice he'd lost a client.'

'Were there sharks?' Hazel gasped, hanging onto her dad's every word.

'You can say that again.'

'I imagine you're going to tell us next that you wrestled one in the waves, is that right?' Nora chortled archly.

'With my bare hands,' he laughed, mocking himself. He went on to describe an action-packed, comedy-filled scene of how he'd wrestled the shark, which he animated by standing up to demonstrate exactly what had happened, including an iffy rendition of the *Jaws* soundtrack.

The three children were laughing their heads off, only half knowing he was making every word up. They grabbed at his shirt, begging him to sit down and stop embarrassing them. On the next table, an attractive woman of roughly Libby's age smiled at this sweet display of fatherhood. Patrick was almost laughing too. Emma was struggling not to. And Nora was guffawing as uproariously as the children, as though she were still a child herself.

Standard stuff when it came to one of Connor's better stories.

'Oh, stop it! You're giving me a stomach ache, and I don't need one of those right now,' Nora said, making everyone laugh even more – tragedy and comedy equalled pathos, didn't you know.

But it was here that she slipped up, where Libby noticed that her usual touchy-feely ownership of Connor, her squeeze of the arm or tap of the hand or pinch of the cheek, more Jewish matriarch than flirtatious lover, was missing. The deliberate restraint told Libby everything she needed to know. If they were cuddling in the dark together but unable to touch in public, they were hiding something. And there was only one thing that could be.

Daunted by this observation, her smile fell away, and her heart with it. She lost her ability to play along nicely, only capable of staring at her mum, staring and staring, taking in each crevice and quirk on her moony face as though they were the markings of pure evil.

'Are you feeling all right, darling?' Nora asked her, and Libby tore her eyes away, wondering if she would ever be able to look at her again. She was unable to talk or reply, fearing an explosion so distressing and out of control, the children would be scarred forever.

Calmly she unhooked her bag from her chair and looped the long strap over her shoulder, thinking frantically as she performed this simple task. Doing both took much out of her. Then she patted her tummy, which nobody would want to ask

more about, and somehow managed to find her way to the
loos.

Dumping her bag at her feet in the cubicle, hearing its
contents skitter across the marble, she knelt in front of the
cistern and stuck her finger down her throat. Nothing came up.
She remembered she hadn't touched her food. The noise of her
dry-retching rebounded around her skull and probably up and
out of the gap at the top of the door. Someone in the next
cubicle flushed and cleared their throat. A tap ran at full flow.
She heard two more people coming into the toilets, urinating,
washing their hands and leaving; perhaps someone knocked and
asked if she was okay. But Libby did not stop pushing her
fingers down her throat, until her eyes were streaming and her
stomach was sore. She wanted it out. Out, out, out of her.

In a crumple in the corner, too weak to continue being sick,
almost not strong enough to stand up, she gathered her things
and stuffed them back into her bag, deciding she could not
return to the table. Instead, she emerged from the cubicle,
avoiding eye contact with the woman at the sink, who was fixing
her make-up, and managed to wash her hands, studiously
avoiding her own reflection, then hurried out of the restaurant
to the van, planning to drive herself back to the villa. The kids
could be taken home in the Cinquecento and the adults could
order a taxi. Or whatever. She couldn't care less how they got
home.

After that, she would have to do something about it, sort the
problem out somehow: leave him, leave her, leave someone. Do
something. She didn't know. She couldn't think that far ahead.

She turned on the ignition, silencing the radio that blared
out, and reversed out of the space, swinging onto the track that
led down the hill. As she made her escape, every bump of the
rocky surface juddered through her. She pushed down on the
gas, deliberately gathering speed, enjoying the fearful lightness
in her stomach. On each bend, she was flung from one side to

the other, occasionally banging her head on the window. Her eyes and throat smarted, dry from the billows of dust the car's tyres chucked up, making it hard to see and to swallow, but making it easier not to think.

At the bottom of the track, she skidded to a stop at the T-junction, letting the dust settle for a moment, giving herself time to regain her composure. It had been an exhilarating, horrible few minutes, and the adrenaline charged through her.

Before turning left towards Mandelieu-la-Napoule, she decided she should text Emma to tell her that she was going home with an upset stomach. She'd lie that she wouldn't have been able to make it back to the table without risking a mishap.

As she reached for her phone on the front seat, the van slipped forward, jutting out further into the main road. Too late, she realised the handbrake had not been pulled up fully. She didn't have time to correct it. There was an almighty bang inside her head, like her brains had exploded and her eyes had been punched out, followed by the sensation that she was being spun around so fast her heart and lungs were being left behind somewhere. It could have been her brain playing tricks on her, or she could have been literally going round and round. It wasn't clear. She could neither see nor breathe nor think. She could only feel. And the feeling was of overwhelming relief that there was something far worse happening to her now; something that she could do absolutely nothing about.

THIRTY

EMMA

'I'm sorry, but I'm going to check on her,' Emma said finally, ignoring her family's cries to 'Leave her be!'

As she unhooked her bag from her chair, a waiter came over to the table.

'*Excusez-moi, mais possédez-vous un véhicule orange avec l'immatriculation ZT 458 CB?*'

He spoke in a hushed, urgent tone, which scared Emma. For once, she wanted the guy to mock their French and speak perfect English.

As she tried to work out what he was saying, Patrick jumped in, '*Oui, tout va bien?*'

'*Non, monsieur, il y a eu un accident, en bas de la colline. Une de nos serveuses – qui sortait de son service – l'a vu se produire. L'ambulance a emmené la conductrice à l'Hôpital Pasteur de Nice. Souhaitez-vous le numéro?*'

He was talking too fast. 'What the hell is he saying?' Emma demanded, trying to decipher his French.

'Is she okay?' Patrick said, standing, phone in hand.

Emma shot up. 'Is who okay?'

'What's going on?' Nora cried. 'Tell me what's going on!'

'*Je suis tellement désolé, je ne sais pas. Nous avons le numéro ici. Suivez-moi.*'

Patrick said, 'You guys, stay here, everything's fine. I think they just need me to move the car.'

'Oh gracious, I thought someone had died,' Nora said, slumping back in her chair.

Emma didn't believe Patrick. She followed him.

'What's going on? Tell me,' she said, jogging after him. He was trying to keep up with the waiter, who hurried to the front desk.

Patrick spoke over his shoulder. 'There's been an accident with the orange van at the bottom of the hill. One of the waitresses at the end of her shift witnessed it happening. She must have been behind Libby in her car.'

'Libby? How do you know it's Libby?'

'Who else would be driving the van?'

'But how do you know it's the same van?'

'He told us the registration,' he replied, and then turned his attention to the waiter, who relayed the hospital number. '*Merci. Merci,*' Patrick repeated, punching it into his phone, immediately pressing call.

'But... but... what was she doing driving away? She only went to the loo. I need to check the loos.'

Emma's brain was running at high speed. In disbelief, she made her way to the toilets and banged on the locked cubicles. 'Libby! Libby! Is that you in there, Libby?'

A mumbled '*Non*' and a '*Je ne m'appelle pas Libby.*'

She ran back out to find Patrick pacing in the car park on his phone, speaking French to someone down the line. She stared at him from the entrance, not wanting to follow him into the dark, needing to put off knowing what he had found out. He approached, pocketing the phone.

'The ambulance hasn't arrived at the hospital yet, but they're expecting it in the next ten minutes. They said something about a collision with a motorcycle. But she was apparently unconscious at the scene.'

'Oh my God!' Emma breathed, hugging her bag to her chest. 'It was Libby?'

He nodded. 'But that's all they know. We should get the kids back to the villa and one of us should go to the hospital.'

'I'll go. Of course I'm the one to go. I'll take the red car.'

'Do you want me to come with you?'

'And leave the kids with those two reprobates? No way. You stay and keep Mum's hysteria away from them, and make sure you tell those two girls that their mum's fine, okay? Say she's got a bit of whiplash or something. Until we know otherwise.'

'Yes, absolutely.' He leant forward and kissed her on the lips. 'I love you,' he said. 'Now go. I'll take care of the others.'

'I love you too,' she said, and had never meant it more.

Everyone at the hospital spoke English, but even English was becoming difficult for Emma to understand. Her fear had stopped her from thinking straight. Her mind raged with horrors. A blonde nurse led her through the white corridors, telling her nothing. As she rapped on the door to a consulting room, Emma wanted to shut her eyes, too terrified to look.

The door opened. She put on her bravest face. A doctor with a large paunch and small round glasses towered over Libby. Her left forearm lay limp by her side and was bent at a strange angle, like she had a second elbow. It was absolutely all wrong to look at, and Emma's stomach churned. But she couldn't concentrate on that now, she was too relieved that her baby sister was not connected up to machines, that her eyes blinked open, that she was alive.

'Libby!'

'Hi, sis,' Libby croaked over the top of a neck brace.

'Thank God you're okay. Oh my God. I thought... Oh, Libs. What have you done to yourself?'

Their faces were close, like when they'd been young girls whispering after lights-out under the duvet with a torch. Tears fell out of Libby's eyes. 'I'm not sure what happened,' she sniffed. 'I think I broke my arm.'

You can say that again, Emma thought, daring to glance once more at its mangled form.

'Hello, my name is Dr Celal,' the doctor said in a thick French accent, continuing in faltering, mild-mannered English. 'She is very lucky... she have a little concussion and she hurt the neck a little, but not too bad, and she have X-ray. You see, she broke this bones... *le cubitus et radius*... many places...' He made a chopping movement in the air over Libby's arm. 'I think you say radius and... how do you call it?... ulna... many pieces. We operate, put some pins in here, and here. Not today, tomorrow. We do this and hope she has the full *mobilité*. And we straighten it now... This will be... you know...' He made a face that was very un-doctor-like.

'Painful,' Libby croaked.

He looked at her kindly. 'Yes, I'm sorry, but I put in the ketamine and *pouf*... your brain is far away from this pain. Best if your sister not here.' He laughed, with ominous humour.

'I'm not leaving her,' Emma said.

The blonde nurse entered brusquely. 'You have to go now, madame,' she barked. Emma realised it was an order.

The nurse led her to an area down the corridor, where she joined other patients and their families milling about. She called Connor to fill him in. He was tearful, irritatingly tearful, and she suspected he was drunk. Then she called Patrick, who was strong for her. After hanging up and another ten minutes of pacing, a terrible wail rang out through the double doors from the direction of the consulting rooms. It was a gut-wrenching cry that seemed to express pain from a wound that went deeper than a bone fracture, and it penetrated Emma's soul. Everyone around her stopped for a second to acknowledge it. Emma knew instantly that it was Libby, and ran back to the room, catapulting straight into the nurse.

'That's my sister, isn't it?' she said.

'*Oui*, this is normal,' the nurse said, shrugging. 'It is finished. *C'est bon*.'

'I need to see her now.'

'*Oui*,' she sighed, as if this were an unreasonable request. Emma became self-conscious about her Englishness, and worried the nurse had not been kind to Libby because of it.

'She is noisy, *non*?' Dr Celal laughed, as she hurried in.

'Not usually,' Emma said, smiling, sitting on the stool next to Libby's head. 'Hi, Libs.'

Her forearm was in some kind of temporary cast, like a stiff bandage, and looked reassuringly straight. Emma could only imagine the agony she'd experienced.

Libby spoke up to the ceiling, so Emma stood up and looked down on her. Her eyes blinked madly and she began to babble. 'Oh, Emma, it's so good to see your face. I had this nightmare, but it was so real. I was going down this long tunnel towards a light and Mum was there and she was smiling and I forgave her, and I said goodbye to you all, to the kids and everything. I thought something had gone wrong, like I was... I really thought it was the end.' She sobbed, digging her fingernails into Emma's arm, making little sense. 'I could hear myself screaming, like I was trapped inside the pain and nobody could hear my cries, yet I couldn't actually feel the pain, but I knew something horrible was being done to me. It was horrible. I'm so happy to be alive. So unbelievably grateful for everything. I love you so much, so, so much, Em.'

'I love you too, you loon. You weren't dying. It's okay,' Emma said, reassuring her, stroking her forehead gently, wondering what the infusion of ketamine had done to her brain and what she was forgiving their mother for.

Libby slept until it was time for her to be wheeled somewhere, first to a corridor, where they waited for an hour, then to a clean, bright room with shuttered windows. There was a view of the black night sky and the lights and rooftops of Nice. Emma felt better about having to leave her here.

'This isn't so bad,' she said, helping her to sit up in her new bed. 'Want this up?'

She pressed the button to elevate the bed, and then fussed over the pillows and covers, getting them straight. She wanted it to be as perfect as possible because she loved her so much.

'Phone?'

Libby shook her head.

'I'll put it here for you, just in case,' Emma said, placing it on her side table, noticing the five missed calls from their mother. 'Call me if you need to talk, any...' a yawn interrupted her sentence, '...time. Jeez. Time to get going, I think, or I won't be able to keep my eyes open on the drive back.' She gathered up her things. 'I'll see you tomorrow after the op, yes? I hope you don't get too hungry between now and then.'

'I don't want to see anyone tomorrow,' Libby mumbled. 'Except you.'

'Yes, it's probably best the kids come when you're in less pain,' Emma said, yawning again.

'I don't want to see... Mum or Connor either.'

Emma remembered Connor's tears and paused before replying, tucking a corner of the blanket under the plastic mattress. The noise that came out of her mouth was like a grunt, the sound effect of effort, of holding in what neither of them could broach right now.

Libby swallowed repeatedly before speaking again. 'I don't... want them... near me.'

'Okay, okay,' Emma whispered. 'Don't worry about anything now.'

Libby closed her eyes and drifted off again. Emma kissed her forehead and wished her luck for tomorrow.

Having dragged herself away from her sister's bedside, she plodded through the corridors and found a loo before going out to the car. She was so tired she didn't even hover over the loo seat. She sat right down on the grubby plastic with a big sigh. Her memories of supper were thick and slow, and she waded through them, trawling for clues to the suspected affair between her mum and Connor, guessing that Libby had seen something, heard something she shouldn't have. Nothing came to mind. The two of them had seemed the same as ever, and she couldn't work out how Libby had found out. If she had. She guessed she had.

In the car, she drove with the music loud to keep her awake.

It was 2 a.m. by the time she pulled up in the garage at the villa.

Before collapsing into bed, she trudged up to the top floor and knocked on her mum's door.

Nora's footsteps were rapid, but the door opened only a crack. 'How is she? She won't reply to my texts. I've been worried sick,' she jabbered, stepping out into the corridor, closing the door behind her, stumbling a little. There were red wine stains on her lips, and her eyelids drooped.

'It's okay, there's no more news. She's fine. Just a bit nervous about the op tomorrow. She's got a nice room, though. You go to sleep. It looks like you need it.'

Her mother pressed her hand into the middle of her breasts and burped. 'Oh, you have no idea how worried I've been. No idea.'

'It's only a broken arm,' Emma said, maddened by her.

'I want to see her. When can I see her?'

Emma had already worked out her line, which she delivered

officiously. 'We'll find out tomorrow after the operation. The doctors said they'd call us.'

The following day, Emma left the villa at one o'clock to the sound of her mum and Connor's vomiting, endless loo flushes and the faint smell of shit.

'They deserve everything they got for ordering the *moules*, and for everything else,' she mumbled uncharitably as she drove off towards the hospital. Conveniently, their sickness put off the dreadful task of having to tell them that Libby did not want to see them.

When she arrived, Libby looked and sounded worse than she had yesterday, but the doctors explained it was the after-effects of the anaesthetic and reassured her that the operation had been a success. Full mobility in her arm would be restored. Or at least, Emma hoped that was what they had communicated.

'Google Translate for me: the pain is worse,' Libby croaked.

'*La douleur est pire,*' Emma said, reading from her phone. 'Is it? Worse?'

'No, not really...' Libby licked her lips and spoke slowly and sleepily. 'But they said I needed to tell them if it was... Most of the nurses don't speak a word of English.'

'It's so weird, isn't it, that the nurses and doctors don't speak English, but every waiter in the south speaks it better than half of England.'

Libby let out a sound like a laugh and then pressed her morphine button.

They spent a good while translating some medical terms and practising the French sentences: 'Doctor, I've got an itchy haemorrhoid' (*Docteur, j'ai une hémorroïde qui me démange*); 'Doctor, will you do a boob job on my post-breastfeeding flat-breads?' (*Docteur, ferez-vous un travail de boob sur mes pains plats post-allaitement?*); 'Doctor, how can I stop weeing in my pants when I laugh?' (*Docteur, comment puis-je arrêter de faire pipi dans mon pantalon quand je ris?*). They were giggling childishly, until Libby flagged again.

While she rested, Emma took out her phone and stared at the screen, remembering that Samarth had texted her last night five minutes before the waiter had informed them of the accident. She reopened his message and read it.

Hi Emma, I hope everything is okay. Rachel got back to me and said she'd be happy to talk you through what she knows of the US trial, if it would help. A few of her patients have been eligible for it, but there are some caveats. Her number is 07567 332 000. Sam xx PS Melody in Year 2 went to the toilet only once today! Result.

She texted back:

Thanks so much, Samarth. Sorry for not getting back to you. Libby was in a car accident last night. Don't worry, everyone's alive! But she broke her arm quite badly and went in for surgery today, which went well. I'm in the hospital now. Speak soon, Emma

Typing it brought home the magnitude of it. On top of everything else, this had happened.

Her mobile buzzed. It was him. She crept out and answered it in the corridor. 'Hi, Samarth. Sorry. That probably sounded a bit dramatic.'

'My God, Emma. How is she?'

'Honestly, she's fine. Sleeping. Poor thing, though. She's in a lot of pain.'

'Not surprised. How did it happen? Was she the one driving?'

'Yes. She was at a T-junction on one of those winding French roads, and a motorbike came whizzing around the corner and she just didn't see him coming. He's fine, not a scratch.'

'I guess with everything going on, her concentration would have been off.'

'I suppose so.'

'Are *you* okay?'

Tears blurred her vision. The nurses at the station a few metres away looked like green blobs. 'I'm fine. Really. It's just...' She gulped. 'It's just it's all been quite a lot to deal with.'

'I'm guessing you have to be the responsible one for everyone, as usual.'

She turned away from the nurses and spoke quietly into the phone. 'I'm not sure it's that. I don't mind really. The bigger issue is Mum. I feel like everything that comes out of my mouth is winding her up and making the situation worse. Part of me thinks that every disagreement will mean she's now more likely to go ahead with... you know... on Sunday.'

'Okay. So you have to put all that self-blame away in one of your drawers. They are not useful thoughts. If they're not useful, there's no point having them. Right?'

'Uh-huh.' The drawers weren't closing.

'Everything is going to be okay.'

'Yes.' Was it?

'And I'm guessing the sun is shining?'

'Er...' She looked for a window, but there were none. 'I imagine so.'

'Well, that's something, isn't it?'

'Yes,' she said. She did not feel like crying any more, which *was* something, but she wanted to get off the phone. 'Okay, thanks, Samarth, you're very kind. I'd better get back to Libby. Thanks for the stuff about Rachel. I'll call her when we're home.'

'Happy to help. Any time. A positive point for Mrs Hooper's good attitude!'

The joke about her head teacher stoicism fell flat. But she was polite enough to laugh before saying goodbye and add in another thank you for good measure. He would have gone away thinking he'd made her feel better.

She crept back into Libby's room.

The evening sun streamed in across the rooftops, leaving wide stripes on the walls. It was beautiful and yet not at all uplifting.

Libby opened her eyes and smiled. 'Hi.'

'Sorry, I didn't mean to wake you,' Emma said. 'That was Patrick calling.'

The lie was unnecessary. Libby wouldn't have asked why she had been out of the room.

'How is he?'

'He's going to call the car rental people and the insurance companies today and sort out the claims, and also get your NHS medical card sorted.'

'And the insurance will cover all this?' she asked groggily.

'The NHS will.'

'Because I couldn't even afford a plaster.'

'Don't worry, Patrick'll sort it.'

'Lovely Patrick. Thank him from me.'

'Will do.' He *was* lovely, Emma thought. So very lovely. She stared guiltily down at her phone screen, clicking it on and off, replaying the conversation with Samarth.

'Em? Was it awkward? Telling Mum and... you know... that they couldn't come?'

Emma turned her thoughts away from Samarth. 'I didn't have to say anything in the end, actually. They've both been struck down with food poisoning and can't go anywhere. Serves them bloody right.'

'But...' Libby swallowed. 'Was Eliot sick too?'

'No, remember, he didn't have the mussels, he had the hake.' Emma tutted.

'He did... he did have some,' Libby said, pointing to the water cup on her bedside table.

Emma helped her drink with the bendy straw, deciding not
to correct her. Her memory was bound to be off. 'Don't worry
about any of that. You must focus on getting that arm of yours
better so you can carry on knitting lots of beautiful jumpers.'

'More like use it for a left hook,' Libby retorted hoarsely,
before closing her eyes and wincing. The slightest movement
seemed painful and tiring.

Emma was unable to laugh with her. 'It's four thirty
already. We'll talk about this when you're out the other side,'
she said fearfully.

When Libby drifted off again, Emma whispered goodbye
and left her for the night. She went through the motions of
finding her car in the car park and driving through the traffic of
Nice, and then along the dark, winding roads back to the villa.

Later, after supper, Patrick brought down a half-full bottle of
red wine from the kitchen to the sunloungers, where he and
Emma lay stretched out side by side. He unscrewed the cap and
poured two glasses. Before drinking, they made a solemn cheers
by touching rims silently.

'This wine is off,' he said, making a face.

'Is it?' she said, sipping it, staring up at the night sky,
wondering if Libby had woken and was looking out of her
window at the same time. She was still shocked that all of this
had happened. 'Tastes all right to me.'

'Don't drink it. It'll make you sick as a dog,' Patrick said,
grimacing after a second sip.

'Like we need more patients in this villa.'

'Who opened it?'

'No idea.' She put her glass down. She was less worried
about drinking it, more in need of a moment of calm in the cool
of the evening, alone with Patrick, away from the day's stresses.
Her eyes were dry with exhaustion.

'Strange, because I didn't. And you didn't. And it was unopened last night before we went out to the restaurant, which means someone drank it after Libby's accident.'

'I guess so,' Emma murmured absently.

'Definitely. Because I contemplated opening it myself but decided a hangover wouldn't be a great plan.'

'Wise choice.'

He picked up the bottle and gave it another sniff. 'Strange. Really strange.'

'Maybe the girls chugged it to drown their sorrows?'

She had been joking, but Patrick remained serious. 'They were asleep before I'd even left their bedroom.'

'Eliot, then?' she teased.

'It was obviously your mum and Connor.' His face was grimly animated. 'And they've both been violently sick. You know, I was always suspicious of the food poisoning crap. Eliot wasn't sick, and he ate some *moules*.'

'He did, did he?' Emma said wryly, remembering Libby had said the same. 'Behind my back?'

'Your authority is slipping.' He grinned, before getting back to business. 'But it means that Nora and Connor came home and drank this before bed last night.'

'That makes sense. She was drunk when I went to tell her Libby was okay.'

'Was she with Connor?'

'Could easily have been.' She remembered how her mother had pulled the door to. 'Yes.'

'Okay. That's stooping to a whole new level,' Patrick said gravely.

They lay in silence contemplating this.

'What are we going to do?' Emma asked him, sitting forward over her knees, feeling distraught, everything piling in on her. 'If Mum... if she... if she does this, if she...' She couldn't even say it. 'She won't, will she?'

'I can't tell you either way, Em. I wish I could. But Libby won't be out of hospital until the weekend, earliest, and it might have changed your mum's whole perspective.' He stroked her back. 'Maybe Libby's accident was the best thing that could have happened.'

Emma exhaled and lay back down. It was something to cling to. 'I hope so.' She reached out to hold his hand, feeling close to him.

After thinking their own thoughts for a while, Patrick said, 'Let's go to bed.'

'But I'm not tired at all,' she said.

'Neither am I. Not in the slightest.' He leant over to her sunlounger and kissed her gently on the lips. 'I wasn't thinking of sleeping.'

'Oh, weren't you now?'

'Nope.' He pulled her by the hand all the way inside, upstairs and into their bedroom.

They were nervous at first, and undressed slowly and awkwardly, and then their desire took over and with ridiculous speed they broke their four-year hiatus. Patrick didn't last long, but neither of them minded. The connection was deeply pleasurable, consoling, life-affirming.

Afterwards he said, 'Why the hell don't we do this more often?'

'I have no idea,' she replied, blissed out but amused by the timing of it, in literally the worst week of her life.

'I guess there's nothing like a relaxing holiday to get you in the mood.' He chuckled. Then they both pressed their faces into the pillows and laughed, smothering the sound in the cushiony feathers, shoulders juddering, their tears soaking the Egyptian cotton.

Her mascara would mark her side of the bed, and she would normally have cared about the linen, but sex had reduced everything to the essentials, to what really mattered, to their loving

and living and dying, to the moment as it was: messy and imper-
fect and raw. She had missed this feeling. She had missed loving
Patrick this much.

Though she realised it was odd to feel less uptight now,
when she had so much more to worry about, something had
loosened in her and she didn't know how to explain it.
Tomorrow she would have to break the news to her mum that
Libby didn't want to see her, but she didn't have a useful
thought in her head as to how she'd go about it or how she
would control the outcome. One thing was certain: there was
literally nothing she could do about her mum's reaction. Absolutely nothing. So what was the point in fretting over it?

THIRTY-ONE
NORA

'I've done them a favour, you see,' I said to Connor.

We were both dressed and ready to go to the hospital, idling at the table in the shadows of the palm tree, waiting for Emma, who was playing water pistols with Eliot.

Amber, after a week glued to her sunlounger, was dangling her legs in the water and actually smiling – without using her phone. Hazel was next to her.

'How do you figure that?' Connor said. He was slouched forward on his chair, elbows on his knees. He'd been in a mood with me since the wine had poisoned us, suggesting it was my fault for not listening to him when he'd told me it hadn't tasted right. I had accused him of being a wine snob. More than I'd cared about its quality, I'd needed to drink it to cope with the worry about Libby.

'Look at Emma,' I mused, massaging my temples to soothe a headache. 'There she is, playing with Eliot finally, which is quite funny, really. I mean, at the beginning of this holiday she would have been shouting at him, herding us out of the door and snapping at us about going for a wee-wee before we left.'

'Come back, anal Emma, all is forgiven,' Connor grumbled,

swiping his phone screen for the fifth time – 13.32 – and jiggling his foot. I was as keen as he was to visit Libby, but I knew that a five- or ten-minute delay wouldn't hurt. Anyway, I was getting far too much pleasure out of this new playful Emma.

I continued thinking aloud, 'I've done them a favour by bringing them all here. Look at them. They're all happier. Neither of the girls is on their phone, which is a miracle. It's the honesty, you see? It releases people.'

'Right, yeah, they're thrilled that you're...' He stopped. 'And that Libby was in a car crash.'

'Libby did it on purpose, you know. Not consciously, you understand.'

He turned his head in my direction. 'She almost died on purpose?' I couldn't see his eyes through his sunglasses, but I knew they were full of fire.

I laughed lightly, though that hurt my stomach, weakened by the vomiting. 'She only broke her arm.' I sipped the iced water Hazel had brought down for me.

'It could have been much worse,' he said.

'Which proves my point. It was a cry for help.'

'How's that?'

'She was sabotaging my plans. It's textbook. Freud could have used it as a case study.'

'*Are* your plans being sabotaged?'

This sent a sharp pain through my head. I didn't respond to it. 'We've always been close, Libby and me. Too close. I suppose I blame myself.'

He got up suddenly and went to the girls.

'Emma, we need to go,' he called out from the poolside, tapping his wrist.

I was open-mouthed at him, affronted. How dare he leave our conversation hanging. Did he expect me not to talk about her? Did he actually believe that his sensitivities about the situation between us were more important than how much I loved my own daughter?

'Sure, in a minute. Visiting time isn't until two thirty,' Emma called out, spraying the girls at the same time, provoking a scream and a tidal wave as they leapt into the water after her.

He raised his voice, trying to be heard over the giggles and screeches. 'But the traffic is always terrible into Nice!'

Nobody paid him any attention. If it hadn't been for this building headache, I would have said something wry. Everything was upside down today: Connor was angry and Emma was being chilled.

'I'm going,' he said. 'If she wants to come, she can. You coming?'

'We can't go without her.'

'I can.'

He stalked off. Within seconds, Emma was out of the pool, dropping her pistol, slapping steps towards me. 'Where's he going?'

'Oh, so you *were* aware we were sitting here waiting for you then?' I said, piqued, putting my hat on.

'Stay here and watch the kids, will you?' She stamped up to the villa and returned a minute or two later with her rucksack on her shoulder, seemingly ready to go, except for the fact that she was in her swimming costume.

I looked her up and down, at her hard curves and her now wild tangle of hair. 'You're going to the hospital like that?'

Connor charged over to us before she had a chance to reply.

'Can I have the car keys, please?' he said, holding out his large hand to her.

She gripped the strap of her rucksack with both hands. 'No.'

The kids stopped goofing about and looked over. Fun auntie was gone.

It was time for me to stand up, although I felt terribly light-headed. The cancer was never far away. 'Frankly, I'm losing my patience now, Emma. Connor and I have been sitting here like lemons waiting for you, but you don't seem to be making any move to get going. And it's now almost one thirty. If we don't go now, we'll miss visiting time.'

'I told you last night, we're not going,' Emma said.

'What?' I said, with an extra whoosh to the 'wuh' sound.

'I told you,' she repeated, clutching at her hideously practical backpack. 'She doesn't want any visitors.'

I thought back to yesterday evening, when Emma had blathered on about how unwell Libby felt after the operation and how she'd requested we stay away and have fun in the villa until she was feeling up to it. I hadn't had the energy to argue with her about it – wiped out by a day of purging the bad alcohol from my system and heavy with regret.

'And *I* said we'd call her in the morning.'

'You've spoken to her?' Emma asked, with less firmness in her tone, plainly taken aback. She pressed her fingers into each eye socket to dry them.

'I left a message saying we'd see her there at two thirty. She'll be expecting us.'

A smile twitched at the corner of her mouth, but she covered it with her hand. 'She won't have heard that message, Mum. She doesn't listen to her messages abroad because it costs too much.'

'Darling, she might've *said* she didn't want visitors, but you know what she's like. She was just being kind. She probably didn't want to put us out and was thinking about us missing all this.' I swept my hand across the view. But the blue of the sky looked solid and unfriendly, and the sun blinding.

'I'm not sure kindness was at the heart of this,' Emma said, wiping away the drips from her nose with the back of her hand. 'For once.'

'You've never understood her like I have,' I said, glancing

over at Connor, who had one hand in his pocket and one fiddling with his top shirt button.

Emma widened her feet and crossed her arms over her chest in a manly fashion. 'Really?'

I stood a little straighter, inhaled right into my belly and spoke in my gentlest tone. 'Okay, darling, let's not be like this with each other. It doesn't get us anywhere. All I'm saying is that I know you feel you need to stick rigidly to plans all the time, but sometimes it's not about that. I want you to imagine how she'll feel if we don't turn up. She might have said one thing yesterday, but she'll certainly feel regret and loneliness today. Do you think you can see it from her point of view? Maybe close your eyes and imagine it. Can you try and feel what it might be like for her, all alone in a hospital bed, surrounded by foreign nurses, in pain and needing a hug from her mumma?' If I coaxed her to take a trip into Libby's head, she might be less black and white about what was said yesterday and more flexible for us today. She nodded, but said nothing. So I continued into the awkward silence, going a little deeper. 'People's emotions are ever-shifting, darling. The movement of time through yesterday, today and tomorrow isn't any more linear than the world is flat. The past, present and future is wrapped in the now, and the now slips away before we have a chance to hold it. There is no point in trying to control us all the time.'

Connor closed his eyes and breathed in. 'I think that's right. And for my part, I'm sorry for bringing my own feelings of frustration and anger into this situation just now.'

Emma stopped nodding and cocked her head at us both. Her gaze rested on me, as though taking seriously what I had said, and I felt I'd made a breakthrough. Then she let out a loud 'Ha! Sorry,' before pressing her fingers into her smile and chewing at her lip. A strange nervous giggle came next, and she hid her face behind her hands, 'Sorry, sorry, I shouldn't, but... Oh my, oh my...' she chortled, snorting through her closed hands. I couldn't tell whether she was laughing or crying. Connor and I shuffled about, waiting for her to compose herself.

'Could you let us in on the joke?' I said, feeling humiliated by her reaction.

She dropped her hands, which I noticed were quivering, and her voice was a whisper. 'The joke is, you two actually think you're getting away with it.'

The instant tension felt like a fusing of my joints. My mind wiped out, and I became unable to send messages along the usual pathways to remind my body how to hold itself up. I might have toppled over had it not been for Connor's arm, which steadied me. Motionless and stiff, I rasped, 'I don't know what you're talking about.'

'No, of course you don't.'

My throat constricted with tears and my voice became small. 'I'm feeling quite upset by your aggression, darling.'

'Yes, sorry, Mum, you're so sweet and delicate.'

Anger stirred inside me. 'I think you'd better go and get a drink of water or something and calm down.'

'Always playing the victim, aren't you, Mum?'

My eyes dried. I'd heard enough. The flapping of black wings flashed across the sun, leaving imprints of their vile silhouettes across my vision. 'I'm not playing at anything,' I rasped.

'No, that's right, sorry, correction, you actually *are* the victim.'

Unfamiliar and sudden rage charged from nowhere and coursed through me. I pointed a shaky finger into her face and erupted. 'VICTIM? *VICTIM*? HOW *DARE* YOU! I'VE NEVER BEEN A VICTIM OF ANYTHING IN MY WHOLE LIFE!' I bellowed, blinking away visions of being trapped underneath the hair and sweat in the music rooms. 'MY FAMILY CAME FROM *NOTHING*! BUT LOOK WHAT WE HAVE NOW! BECAUSE WE'RE FIGHTERS. LIKE

MY FATHER DID FOR ME, I FOUGHT FOR EVERY SINGLE CRUMB ON YOUR PLATE. AND I DID IT ON MY OWN WITH NOBODY TO HELP ME. I DIDN'T NEED ANYBODY ELSE BECAUSE I'M STRONGER THAN ANYBODY AND I'VE GOT MORE RESILIENCE IN MY LITTLE FINGER THAN YOU DO IN YOUR WHOLE BLOODY BODY. BECAUSE I'M A FIGHTER! A *FIGHTER*, YOU HEAR?'

My voice was like a stranger's. The sensations of being ripped in two by a man's desire revisited my body, literally as though he were inside me now. I could barely stand straight for the tremors of fear and fury and confusion that juddered through my being.

Emma's eyes blinked rapidly. The kids stood in a row behind her, wide-eyed with horror, arms clamped across chests, bottom lips loose.

Connor put his arm around my shoulders. 'Come on. You're not well enough for this. I'll take you up to your room,' he said.

I allowed him to guide me away. My teeth chattered. Three different lives, three different Noras came crashing in on one another: the past, the present, the future. Yet I didn't know who any of them were. It was the beginning of the end. Or perhaps this *was* the end. Perhaps this was what nothingness felt like.

THIRTY-TWO

LIBBY

The relief of seeing Emma's face poke around the hospital door was enormous. It felt like being rescued.

Libby's second night in this place had not been traumatic exactly, but she had felt isolated and scared and unable to sleep. There was a woman in another room who had wailed throughout both nights. When Libby had asked the nurse what was wrong with her, she had explained with hand gestures, miming and broken English that she was old and had fallen, resulting in an inoperable brain injury. Knowing of her tragedy made the eeriness of her cries that much worse, and agonising to listen to.

At home, if she couldn't sleep, she'd get her knitting needles out, but she wouldn't be knitting through her worries any time soon. The doctor had said it would be six months before she had her fine motor skills back. He had been unmoved by her teary explanation of how knitting grounded her and kept her sane, and how she didn't know what she'd do without it. Especially now.

Generally, the medical staff's professionalism was cold and efficient. The night nurses had been particularly bad-tempered and had delivered the morning painkillers early, while it was still dark, but Libby had felt grateful that she and her pain had not been forgotten about. The first crucial dose of the day had reduced the high-pitched screeching agony of the nerve pain in her arm to a more manageable murmuring ache.

'So sorry I'm late,' Emma said, stepping through the door but not hurrying to her side. She was untangling the caught-up straps of her bag for life from her rucksack.

It surprised Libby to see that Emma's hair was out of its ponytail. Her curls had frizzed at the roots and knotted at the ends. The T-shirt she wore over a blue cotton skirt was wet in patches and oversized. It looked like one of Patrick's.

'You're *late*? Who even *are* you?' she teased.

'I've no idea any more,' Emma said, finally separating the two bags and looking up at Libby and then down at her bandaged left arm. 'How is it feeling?'

'Not great.' Libby could feel every pin and screw in her reconstructed bones. The radiation of pain from each one was like an echo of the drill and hammer the surgeons would have used to rescue her mobility. But she bore the pain more fearlessly than any pain she had felt before. Because it held her hatred for her mother at its core and gave her purpose.

'I've brought you some magazines,' Emma said, reaching into her bag. 'They're in French, but they might be educational. And some lavender sweets from Hazel, which I'm sure are revolting. And then this from Amber.' She handed Libby a ring. 'What's the significance?' she asked.

'It's an elephant with its trunk down.' Libby showed her its emblem, deeply touched by her daughter's kindness. 'She bought it last year in Camden Market because the guy on the stall told her the elephant symbolised pushing through obstacles. She's worn it every day since.'

Emma paused before taking out the next item. 'They're missing you terribly.'

'I miss them too.' Libby slipped the ring onto the third finger of her right hand.

Next, Emma presented her with a packet of cheese biscuits. 'Eliot insisted I give you these. He's eaten half of them. Do you even like them?'

Libby laughed, rearranging herself and sitting up a little. 'Not massively. It's a joke between us. I caught him eating them one night,' she chuckled.

'Oh yes? Why didn't I know about this?'

'He begged me not to tell you because you always get so cross about the crumbs. But we both agreed that eating in bed was worth the odd scratchy crumb or two.'

'Cheeky sod.' Emma snorted. 'I do hate that feeling on my skin.'

'Remember how you used to brush the sheets with the Barbie hairbrush every night before bed?' Libby said.

Emma snorted and sat down on the visitor's chair, slowly folding up her empty bag for life, smoothing it flat on her knees. The absence of knitting and a get-well present from her mum or Connor was keenly felt. 'This room's lovely and cool,' she said.

'How is it out there in the real world?' *How is Mum?* Libby wanted to ask but wasn't yet brave enough. To have separated from her, to be silent in the face of her texts and calls, to be unavailable to her both physically and emotionally felt like the tearing of flesh.

'The fact that it's better in here says it all really,' Emma said.

Libby left this hanging in the air, not ready to tell her sister about why she had left the restaurant that night, knowing she would want to know at some stage. The mind-boggling spinning of the van hurtled at her again, less like a memory and more like a reliving of it. While she breathed through the giddiness, she could see Emma sitting forward. She felt her hand on her good arm.

'Are you okay, sis?' she heard her say as though they were underwater.

Libby couldn't speak. She was comforted by her sister's touch. They sat in silence for many minutes. Or were hours going by? She wasn't sure. What she was sure of was Emma's love and support, and how much it meant to her. She must have said out loud, 'I'm so glad you're here,' because Emma said, 'So am I, sis.'

As Libby drifted off to sleep, she was perversely thankful for the accident and for this hospital and for the nurses who didn't know about Connor and her mum. She was sheltered from them, could avoid them, and she could sleep and heal.

When she woke up, Emma was texting on her phone. 'Oh, hi,' she said, looking up eagerly. 'How are you feeling?'

'Bit better. How long did I sleep for?'

'About fifteen minutes or so.' She put the phone down on the side table. 'I was just texting Patrick to tell him how you are. Everyone has been so worried.'

A need to cry blocked Libby's throat. 'Sorry...' she began, and then she did cry. 'I'm such an idiot.'

'Oh, Libby. No, you're not. Don't be sorry.'

'Sorry... sorry,' she said, wiping her eyes with her working arm.

Emma plucked some tissues from the box and wiped Libby's whole face with them. It was something their mother would have done.

'How was Mum about not coming?' Libby managed to ask.

'I did as you said and told them you weren't feeling well enough.'

'Did they accept it?'

'Umm...' Emma paused, seeming to think back and assess it. 'Not exactly.'

'What happened?'

'Umm,' she repeated, and balled up the tissue in her fist,

swapping it from one hand to the other, squeezing it each time as though it were a stress toy. 'I think I know why you were upset at the restaurant.'

Libby's heart seemed to scramble from her chest. She could do nothing more than stare into her sister's face, mesmerised by what she had said.

Emma continued, 'And I think they know you know.'

Two worlds collided: the unproven secret inside Libby's head and the abstract external reality of it. 'How?' she whispered.

'I noticed things that didn't seem right between them. It was only a hunch. But I sort of confronted them about it.'

'Oh my God.' Libby twisted her head away and stared out of the window, humiliated.

'I couldn't have said anything to you, Libs.' Emma got up and stalked back and forth at the end of the bed, rubbing her forehead. 'I saw them together, late, just once, but Mum swore it was platonic. And I couldn't mention it to you because if she had been telling the truth and if it really had meant nothing, then I would have upset you for no reason. Especially when Mum's cancer... I mean, you know, everything was so tense as it was... But then there was the wine glass and that bullshit that Connor came out with about chasing the lizard, and I just knew they were hiding more, but I didn't know how much, you know? So I couldn't say anything because none of it was anything more than wild speculation. I'm so sorry. I'm so, so sorry.'

Libby could see her out of the corner of one eye, while the tears dripped out of the other, leaving a pool in the indent of plastic pillowcase where her ear was. She was entitled to feel angry with her sister, but she couldn't drum it up right now. Had it been the other way around, had Libby suspected Patrick and their mum of an affair, she might also have kept it to herself. The idea of Patrick with Nora was laughable; the idea of Connor with Nora was not. Only Libby could have been stupid enough to have fallen in love with a man capable of it, and then let it happen right in front of her.

'Say something,' Emma said eventually.

Libby turned her head and looked at her. Emma was now leaning her shoulder blades against the wall, with her hands interlocked behind her neck, elbows pointing out.

'It's okay,' she sniffed. 'I know why you didn't say anything.'

Emma let her hands flop by her sides. 'Trust you not to be angry with me.' Her eyes were wide and raw. 'I don't deserve you. I'm so, so sorry.'

'It's not you who should be sorry.'

She sighed and shook her head and then nodded, then rubbed her face. 'What are we going to do?'

It was the question Libby had asked herself a hundred and one times. 'I was hoping you had some ideas.'

'Under normal circumstances, you'd be able to tell them both to fuck off and never darken your door again. But...'

'Yes. Exactly. But.'

'I know. But.' Emma's gaze flicked around the room. The issue of their mum's suicide schedule lurked in the recesses like a cornered creature ready to attack if approached.

Libby already had an idea. 'The doctors have said I'll be out of here by Saturday, after they've fitted the cast. And that I'll be able to fly home the same day. So I can go directly from here to the airport.'

'You don't want to go back to the villa?'

'No. I want to fly home early with the girls. I was going to ask you to look into flights.'

'And you're okay with it... if Mum...'

'Yes, I'm okay with never seeing Mum ever again,' Libby said, communicating only some of her anger.

'Okay, I understand,' Emma murmured.

'Will you look into changing my flights, then? My phone's

in the drawer. If you log in and search through my emails, you'll find the ones from BA.'

'Umm, okay. Are you *sure* sure? That'll be quite final,' she said, bunching her bottom lip under her teeth.

'If you don't do it, I will,' Libby said, trying to sit up, feeling increasingly uncomfortable, waiting to see if Emma was on her side or not.

Emma relented. 'Okay, look, don't be silly. I'll do it. I was just making sure you were set on it.'

She called BA, who told her there weren't any flights available. Dozens of other airlines said the same, until she finally managed to find three seats on an Air France flight.

'She says there are three seats in business class, leaving at eight p.m. from Cannes and flying to Manchester,' she said, muting her phone. 'Which would mean you'd have to get the train down.'

'That's okay. Amazing. Book them.'

'There's a snag. They're almost a thousand pounds each.'

'A grand *each*? Are you kidding me?' Libby cried. 'Are you just saying that so I can't leave?'

'No, Libs. I wouldn't lie to you about this, would I?'

Libby wanted to say, 'I don't know, would you?' but she said nothing at all.

Emma waggled her mobile. 'D'you want me to tell her to go ahead?'

'Obviously not. I can't afford that.'

Emma unmuted her phone and told the woman on the other end that they would not be booking the flights. After hanging up, she said, 'It'll only be one night in the villa.'

'I can't spend all that time with Mum and Connor, I can't. I just can't do that,' Libby said. She wanted Emma to fully comprehend the magnitude of this fresh, dangerous loathing for them both, and felt annoyed that she wasn't getting it straight away.

'Okay,' Emma said, adding glumly, 'What about a night in a hotel?'

'I've already looked into it, and everything affordable is booked up.'

'You can't drive back, not with a broken arm.'

That gave Libby an idea. '*You* could, though. We could rent a car.'

'There's no way I'm taking you on that hideously long journey with your arm in that state. It would be unsafe and irresponsible. And it would still be expensive.'

Libby was stifled by her sister's refusal to help. 'The villa's like the Hotel California. *You can check out any time you like, but you can never leave,*' she said angrily. Pain shot through her arm and she wriggled into a new position that was no less uncomfortable. Moodily she accepted Emma's help to straighten the pillow behind her.

Once she was settled, Emma sat down again next to her. 'Maybe it's fate, you know. Maybe if you're forced to see them, you'll be able to make some kind of peace with Mum before...' Her voice trailed off.

'Fate? Jesus.' Libby glared at the wall clock, biting back a tirade of abuse. Discovering that her sister was not invested in her escape had been a shock. She had hoped for one hundred per cent loyalty from her, but it seemed Emma was only at eighty per cent. 'Look, I'm tired. And it's four thirty,' she added, reminding Emma that visiting time was over. It seemed her sister had only pretended to understand how it felt to be cheated on by the two people she had trusted most in the world. Seeing them would burn her eyes out. Having a magnanimous little chat about it was out of the question.

'For your sake, not theirs,' Emma backtracked.

Libby now wanted to be left in peace to eat the strange hospital food, stare out of the window and be looked after by impassive foreigners. Emma expected her to do what she was incapable of doing. It wasn't possible to find a resolution with the woman who had both given her life and then with God-like jurisdiction decided to rip out her beating heart. A reconciliation with a mother who did that was out of the question.

They said a stiff goodbye, which felt nothing like their heartfelt greeting.

Two minutes after the door closed, Emma reappeared and stood there pink-faced and pretty in the middle of the sterile white room, twisting her hands. 'I'm so sorry for saying it was fate. I can't even imagine what it would be like to have to face them again if it were me.'

'I hate them,' Libby rasped, with a vile mental picture of her mother naked with Connor; her own mother having sex with the man she loved, with the father of her children. 'I won't be sad at all when she's dead.' Tears sprang up out of nowhere.

'Okay,' Emma replied gently. 'We'll sort something out. I'll talk to Patrick.'

'As long as I don't have to see them,' Libby murmured, squeezing her eyes shut, shocked by what she had admitted to Emma.

The door latch clicked closed.

The consequences of not saying a final goodbye to her mum came filtering into her thoughts. Libby imagined being left in an unresolved state of doubt, swinging back and forth between love and hate in angst-ridden flux for the rest of her life.

Lying there pinned on her back, pushing Amber's elephant ring round and round on her finger, trying to choose between the two extremes, felt like the beginnings of madness.

And the wall clock kept on ticking, each second taking her further away from a solution and closer and closer to her mother's death.

THIRTY-THREE

EMMA

As Emma opened the door to the villa, Hazel jumped up off the hallway sofa. She must have been waiting for her. 'Auntie Emma! How's Mummy?' she cried, rushing up to her.

'She's doing really well, poppet.'

'Did she like her sweeties?'

'She loved them.'

'When can we see her?'

'Guess what?'

'What?'

'She'll be out of hospital the day after tomorrow.'

'Really?' Hazel said, tearing up, throwing her arms around Emma and then clutching her hand and pulling her along. 'I can't wait to tell Dad when he gets back.'

'He's gone out?' Emma dumped her bag and keys and took off her shoes.

'He went to the supermarket.'

'Oh, right.' But it didn't sound right at all. Since Connor had arrived, he hadn't once been to the supermarket.

Hazel added, 'But he'll be back soon, don't worry,' as though picking up on Emma's concern.

'Has he been gone long?'

'Ages.'

'He might've got stuck in traffic somewhere.' She wished she could tell her niece not to bother relying on her father any more. 'Come on, let's see what Uncle Patrick's cooking up.'

They headed towards the aroma of onions, where Patrick stood at the hob stirring a big pot.

Hazel trotted up to him. 'Uncle Patrick?'

'How can I help?' He turned around, waving a wooden spoon. He was wearing Maria's frilly apron. 'Oh, hi!' he said, startled by Emma, missing Hazel's question about Connor. 'I didn't hear you come in!'

'Fetching,' Emma said, kissing him hard on the lips. They lingered there.

'How was she?' he asked.

'Tired, but coping,' she said, nosing into the pot of potatoes and then the mince. 'Cottage pie?' The bubbling sound comforted her. Cottage pie wasn't the sort of meal you'd associate with a holiday in the south of France, but it was exactly what they all needed.

He nodded and gave her a taste from the wooden spoon.

'Where are the others?'

'Amber's watching a film with Eliot. And your mum's in bed.'

'Did you speak to my dad?' Hazel asked again.

'Oh, sorry, Hazel, no, I didn't manage to get hold of him. I'll try him again for you.' Patrick glanced anxiously at Emma.

'Thanks,' Hazel said.

'Now off you go and tell Amber the good news about your mum coming home.'

'Okay.' She ran off to the television den, calling over her shoulder, 'Tell me when you speak to him!'

As soon as she was gone, Patrick dropped his cheery expression. 'Connor's gone AWOL.'

'You didn't believe the supermarket line either?'

He shook his head.

'Bloody hell.'

'Hazel keeps asking me where he is, and I don't know what to say.'

Emma's stomach clenched. 'It's probably for the best that he keeps out of our way for a while. I couldn't bear him cringing and skulking about the place.'

'As long as he comes back.'

She reached for a glass from the cupboard. 'How's Mum been?'

'I've been up to see her, but she won't eat or drink anything I give her. She looks really awful. Like she's completely out of it.'

She glugged the water down, swallowing away a trace of sympathy. 'I'm not surprised.'

'But I've thought of a plan.'

'Oh good, I've been short on those. Go on.'

'The kids need to go home.'

'But there are no flights left in the whole universe!' Emma cried, letting out some of her earlier frustration.

'I know, I've looked into it. So I thought we'd go on the train instead. I've always wanted to do it, and it would be a real experience for the kids.'

'But it's too soon after surgery for Libby to cope with all that jostling about in the crowds.'

He pulled the pot from the stove and poured the potatoes and water into the colander. 'I didn't mean that Libby would come too. I thought she could stay here with you and your mum.'

Steam billowed around his head.

'You think it's a good idea the three of us stay here alone?'

'Well, I thought—'

But Emma couldn't listen to what he thought. 'No. Libby doesn't want that.'

He tried to continue, 'I know it would be hard, but it might be for the—'

'We either leave together or not at all. I promised Libby I'd sort something out.'

'What, though?'

'A hotel room? Or an Airbnb?'

'When I was looking into options earlier, I found nothing suitable. There were either windowless dives or super-posh hotels that cost over five hundred a night. Or places too far from the airport. That's why I landed on the train idea.'

'What's Libby going to do then?'

'There's only one option.' He began mashing the potatoes with methodical focus.

'She can't!' Emma was a loyal ambassador, faithful to her little sister's message.

'Remember, you two don't need to be all nicey-nice and forgive them or anything. It's not for me to say how you should or shouldn't feel. But I do think it would be a mistake to just walk out. I guarantee it won't be the clean break either of you want it to be.'

'I know what you're saying, and I was thinking the same until I spoke to Libby. But she's so angry, there's just no way.'

'But if we give her time, she might change her mind. People have been forgiven for worse.'

'Not in the space of twenty-four hours.'

'Who knows? Perhaps they have. And look at Connor, skulking off out somewhere, avoiding his responsibilities to the kids. I bet you he's at the airport. And if he is, did *he* do the right thing?'

'Don't you dare compare me to that man,' she shot back.

'I'm not comparing you,' he said, drying his hands on his apron. 'Look, Emma, I can't make you stay, and I'm not sure I'd

have it in me to do that if it was my mum who'd behaved so
badly, but as the person whose job it is to know what will be
better for your mental health long-term, and Libby's, I would be
failing you if I didn't strongly advise you both to try to make
peace with your mum before she dies.'

It was a more strident version of what she herself had spon-
taneously suggested to Libby in the hospital, and rued. Patrick
sounded urgent and prescriptive, almost parental. She realised
that she'd never had good advice from an actual parent. It
wasn't a thought that made her feel sorry for herself; it was
simply an acknowledgment of fact. And like the teenager of a
Patrick-style parent, she felt both bolshie and terrified by what
he was asking her to do.

'You've booked the train tickets already, haven't you?' she
said. It was clear he had made up his mind.

His mobile phone interrupted them. He scrabbled around
the kitchen looking for his reading glasses. When he finally had
them on, he read the text. His shoulders slumped. 'Oh shit.
Read this,' he said, handing the phone to her.

Emma's heartbeat picked up speed as her eyes darted across
the screen.

*Hi Patrick, I'm at the airport, heading back to CR. Tell the
girls for me. I can't face them. Sorry for everything. I fucked up.
Connor*

'What a dick. Running off and leaving his kids like that. It's
pathetic,' she spat, shoving the phone back into Patrick's hand.

He handed her the glass of wine he had poured for her,
knowing he no longer needed to persuade her. 'Yes, Emma, I've
booked the tickets already. I was going to tell the children
tonight. And we'll now have to break the news about Connor
too.'

The thought of them leaving her alone with her mum and
Libby made Emma feel ill. She left the wine dangling in the air
between them. He put it down on the side.

'How much are you going to tell them?' she said, making a point of saying 'you' rather than 'we'.

'I guess we could say he had to leave suddenly because of a visa issue in Costa Rica. It's lame, but it'll do for now. He hasn't left us much choice.'

'Hmm,' Emma murmured. 'And the reason Libby and I are staying and they're going?'

He carefully spooned the mash on top of the mince. 'I think we should tell them that your mum's not well enough to continue having a proper holiday, that you and Libs need to look after her for a few days to get her better before she flies home for her cancer treatment. And I think they should say goodbye to her, properly, in case she goes through with it. Mum and I said a proper forever-goodbye to my Grandma Nim about ten times in the hospice before she actually went. We'd only snuck out for a cup of tea, and off she popped. But we had all those other goodbyes to fall back on, so it was okay.'

Emma had loved his mum's mum, Grandma Nim, believing she was one of life's characters, but she couldn't bring herself to tell Patrick that right now. She picked up her wine and walked over to the window, noting the bench, now empty, where she had seen her mum and Connor kissing. 'And when they're saying their goodbyes, might Mum tell them everything?' she asked him.

'Either way, we risk that. But my feeling is she won't want to. It would leave her looking bad, remember.'

'Her narcissism works in our favour for a change,' Emma said bitterly.

'They'll have to be closely supervised throughout all this.'

'We've learned the hard way on that front.'

'I was thinking we tell them over supper – what do you think?'

They shared a look of absolute dread.

'Sure.' She nodded. 'Yeah. You've obviously thought it all through.'

'It's all I've been doing.'

'I'll just have to tell Libby she has no choice.'

He put the pie into the oven. 'I don't envy you.'

As she served up big dollops of comforting cottage pie to the three children, Emma worried that it would forever spoil their enjoyment of it.

The equivalent for her had been spaghetti carbonara, which had once been her favourite meal. Thirty-four years ago, aged ten, she had ordered a big bowl of it at a chain pasta restaurant on the evening her parents told her that Dad had fallen in love with Annie and that he and her mum were splitting up. To this day, she remembered the aftertaste of slimy garlic sauce and the bloating fattiness of it moving about in her stomach. She hadn't been able to touch it since.

Her heart went out to Amber and Hazel, who were going to go home without their dad and their grandma. Their world was about to fall apart, just as hers and Libby's had all those years ago.

THIRTY-FOUR

Libby was on the verge of tears as Emma led her to the villa's front door. The world outside the hospital was noisy and frantic, and the mixture of emotions about seeing her mother warred in her head. She had been eager to be discharged, desperate to sleep in a normal bed, but she had been safe in that white boxy room. There had been a stream of experts who could tell the difference between the kind of pain that was normal and the kind that wasn't. Right now, she wondered what the doctors would say about the sharp twisting in her abdomen, which had rendered her mashed-up arm, bent into a cast of electric blue, pain-free.

Before she and Emma went inside, she read again, for the millionth time, the messages the kids had written in multi-coloured Sharpie on her cast when they had visited her in hospital:

Love you to the tiniest ~~peaces~~ pieces. See you back home. Love you, Eliot xxx

Your the best mum in the whole world. Best ever. Love from your favourite daughter, Hazel xxxxxxxxxxx

Miss you already, Mum. See you at home. Loving the blue. Love you so much, Amber xxxx

They fortified her, gave her the strength to step over the threshold, fearing her mother might be waiting there, defying her instructions to stay in her room, to leave her alone. To back the fuck off.

When Emma had told her of Patrick's plans to take the children home early, she had been almost crushed by terror. Returning to a house full of people had at least offered her some camouflage. Some love, affection, noise and distraction from her mother. Without them, she was more vulnerable. Yet she understood that the children needed to go home. The villa was no longer a safe place for them to be, and she appreciated Patrick's good sense in making the decision.

She'd laughed at Emma's joke about him being the dad the two of them had never had – though she had said it in a way that made her sound like an aggrieved teen, and Libby guessed they'd argued about the arrangements. Libby was yet to hear the full details of the children's reactions to Connor's abandonment of them or their goodbye to Granny Nor-Nor, which had taken place this morning and had apparently gone as well as could be expected. Each time she thought of them perched on her bed or hovering near it, waiting to kiss their grandmother's cheek for the last time, regret seared through her. One parent, at the very least, should have been there to hold their hands and console them during the saddest moment of their young lives. They had both let them down. Connor the most. The thought of his pathetic text to Patrick sent a shot of white-hot pain through her arm.

'Oh. Amber's left her sunglasses,' she said, focusing on their solid black form on the hallway table rather than dare look beyond them to see if her mum was there.

Emma glanced at them and then furtively through to the

kitchen. Her shoulders dropped in relief. 'Oh, right, yes. I told her we'd bring them home for her.'

Libby yearned to give her daughters a hug. Earlier this morning, she had tried to call them, but both their phones had been switched off, which was a first for Amber, and she imagined Patrick had had a hand in that. Her phone would be the worst place to hide. Grateful once again for her brother-in-law, she had decided to try his mobile later and speak to the girls then. For now, she had to trust their emotions were in expert hands. It was a hard lesson for her to learn that not every moment of a child's life should be overseen by their mother; that a mother was not always the best person for the job.

And wasn't that the truth in the context of her own mother. The mother she had been tied to throughout adulthood, as though still clinging to her leg like a toddler. A lifetime of signs she hadn't paid attention to, little tensions that she had ignored, put aside and decided not to think about. She had witnessed moments between Nora and Connor – tiffs, glances, laughter, flirtation – yet had wilfully missed the meanings and nuances, leaving the little signs to accumulate into this huge chaos of feelings. Into this catastrophe.

She didn't know how she would react when she saw her. She wanted to put it off forever. Imagining it happening made her want to turn and run.

It was only a few hours later when it happened in reality.

Libby could not have forgotten it was coming, obviously, but still she was taken by surprise.

Her mother stood at the bottom of the stairs, stunning in a long white cotton shift dress, white-blonde hair tumbled around her shoulders, no jewellery or make-up, full, high cheeks fiery red on her waxy skin. Raw and all woman, both beautiful enough and wicked enough to sleep with the man Libby loved.

They stared at each other. Neither one knowing how to start walking through the debris following the explosion. It was too late to put back together what they'd lost. But somehow they had to see themselves through the next twenty-four hours.

Her mother's large eyes blinked, shining like an owl's in the dark.

It was the end of a relationship whose past was irrevocably changed, and it was the beginning of a relationship with no future.

What did that look like? What did it feel like?

It felt like death before death. Like her mother was revisiting Libby as a ghost, briefly conjured in shocking, petrifying splendour. The sight of her brought back everything Libby had loved about her – the embraces and the gleefulness, the bickering and the heart-to-hearts, the soulfulness and the forgiveness. She wanted to ask her for a hug, to make it all better, and she wanted to run at her, fists flying. The contradiction was paralysing. The love was transitory, almost gone before she had blinked, before the hate charged in to solidify her mother as a very human and frightful enemy.

It was Nora who spoke first.

'I'm making soup for supper. It'll be ready at eight.'

That was all.

THIRTY-FIVE

NORA

Tomato soup and white crusty rolls. My last supper.

My brain seized. *Might I please live for eternity after all?*

I focused on the small things. Bringing out the pan. Pouring the soup. Counting out three knives and three spoons. I'd once known an actress who had pretended right up to the last minute that she wasn't dying of cancer. She had told her visitors she was about to fly off to Bali for a holiday of a lifetime, or audition for a part in the upcoming David Hare at the National, and many other pipe dreams. She had barely been able to swallow, yet this was how she had wanted to continue. Her loved ones had withered away in the corner. They had not been allowed to confront the truth, had not been permitted to tie up loose ends and say goodbye. It had been an agonising denial, where her false positivity had become corrosive and destructive for all those around her. Inevitably she had died, and nothing had been in order. The family had fallen apart.

In my family, after my death, there was going to be unity, a coming together.

Three glasses. Three napkins. Three places on the outdoor table for supper.

Good and bad feelings moved through me, and I observed them come and go, calmly, without wrestling with them. I wasn't disconnecting from them or from myself or from the world around me. Quite the reverse. As I listened to the soft noises around me, to the hum of the generator, to the chatter on the next-door neighbour's veranda, to the buzz of a bee, I felt more grounded than ever, like I'd joined in on something, become part of the whole, tapping into a swell of feeling that was bigger than me. My individuality and independence, my free will, seemed to have been one big joke all along.

Once the table was laid, the artificial bright blue of the pool shone in my peripheral vision, so very still. It hadn't been used today. My longing for my grandchildren was excruciating. Their sweet, harrowing goodbyes this morning had ripped a hole right through me. They believed there was a chance I might come home if I got better, but the 'if' had been emphasised. I think they knew the truth.

'I'm going to put all the sponsor money from the swimathon into Cancer Research and make you better,' Eliot had whispered in my ear.

When I'd said to Hazel that she must promise to go to school, she had sobbed. 'I'll go every day for the rest of my life. Just for you.'

Amber had been less gushing. Her self-control had drained the colour from her skin. I had said to her, 'Come off your phone for at least an hour a day and use the time to read a book. Do it for me, darling. Won't you?'

She had nodded gravely and hugged me tightly. 'I love you, Nor-Nor, I love you so much.' I had remained holding her, hoping my embrace would see her through the rest of time without a care in the world, and then I had checked myself. 'And remember our chat, my darling girl,' I'd added. 'About how we must observe our feelings and allow them in, even if they're sad. Never push them down. They won't overwhelm you if you let them in as they come along.'

'I'll be listening to a lot of Birdy.' She had smiled. I had been left breathless by this.

'Yes, Birdy,' I stammered.

They had jumped on the bed and hugged me all at once, crying together.

'Don't be sad for me,' I had reminded them.

If my life had amounted to anything, it was my love for these three. In that moment, I had not been afraid of dying – in the moment before it, I had been terribly afraid, and had been afraid again in the moment after that – but in that hug I had been reminded of the more permanent feelings that churned through me: the timeless, immortal, enduring nature of love. Mortality did not exist. I was forever. I was never. I was me. I was them. I was everyone. I was love. I was death. I was peace. Fear of the rain or of sadness, of dying or of nothingness, became something-ness. It hadn't been an end-of-life epiphany; it had simply been a lesson in a moment of time, caught on a breeze. Now gone.

The prospect of them growing up without me was surreal. I was already devastated that I'd miss their eighteenth birthdays, when they would wish for wonderful things to happen to them; their graduation gowns as they dreamt of their brilliant careers; their goofy smiles on their wedding days; their prideful tears as they held their beautiful, perfect little firstborns.

A surge of anger and regret coursed through me.

I was only sixty-four, goddammit. I was owed another twenty or even thirty years of loving them, of being there for their successes and failures, of guiding them through. But now they'd live on without me.

Before then, though, I had tonight to get through with Emma and Libby. There was so much to say.

While I waited for them, as the minutes ticked past eight, I wondered what I would do if they did not come down to the table. Would I knock on their bedroom doors? Corral them and coax them? Or would I leave them be? Accept that I couldn't have it my own way?

A letter left next to my body would suffice, I supposed. In it I could explain my will.

Yesterday I'd written a short note to Connor, apologising to him. I had tucked it into my marbled notebook, slipped both into an envelope, licked a few French stamps and sent it off to Costa Rica. Whatever he chose to do with it – burn it, throw it in the sea, whatever – I had asked him to keep it a secret from the girls. I didn't want them to feel bad about what had happened to me as a child, or think it exonerated me. There were no excuses for what Connor and I had done to Libby.

As I waited, my mobile phone rang. Connor again. He had called and texted a dozen times. I turned it off and waited for Emma and Libby, already wording a simple fact-based letter to them in my head.

I was grateful I never had to write it down.

They walked down the steps side by side. Poor Libby, with her bad arm and her gaze fixed at her feet and her hair tied back. I wished it was wild around her face. Emma had showered. Her skin was shining as though polished and her hair was wet and combed through, the curls slick and the wet patches spreading across her T-shirt.

They looked more similar than they had in years as they sat down to the left and right of me. They both stared down at the tomato soup.

'Remember our first night in the close?' I asked.

'No,' Emma said. She dipped her spoon in and swirled it around, then took it out and laid it on the tablecloth. The orange soaked into the linen. Libby stared at it.

'I thought that house was hideous back then,' I said. 'I thought it would be the worst time of my life. But because of you two, I think it might well have been my happiest.' I took my first sip of soup. It was less synthetic than tinned soup back home. 'When I finished on productions, I couldn't wait to put the key in the door and sit in our little kitchen with a cup of tea and hear all your news, and then tend to my garden under the apple tree.'

'Do you remember Mr and Mrs Spiegel?' Emma asked.

The name prompted Libby to look up for the first time. Not at me, but at her sister.

'Umm, I'm not sure,' I said, having a feeling it was critical I should.

'They lived next door and fed us breakfast when you forgot.'

'Oh,' I said.

Libby smiled. 'Frosties.'

'I think they died,' Emma murmured, picking up her spoon and playing with the soup again. I tried to remember more about the old couple who had lived next door, but I could only recall their car, which had been white. I didn't think this detail would help my cause.

'I wasn't a perfect mother,' I said quietly.

'Ha!' Libby snorted. She glared at me and we locked eyes. I had her. *I'm so sorry, my darling*, my look urged silently. *I'm so sorry*. But I couldn't say it. I couldn't be defined by my failure.

'Look, tonight wasn't how I pictured it going. I wanted the whole family to gather together. But that was not to be.'

'That's not our fault,' Emma said.

'That's not what I meant. I understand why Patrick took them home. What I meant was, this is a sadder event. But strangely, it is more apt. It has always been just us three. Always. The three of us eating soup in front of the telly when it's rainy outside.' I paused, feeling the tears come on. 'At least it's not actually raining, and the rolls aren't stale this time.' I tried to laugh, but I sounded strangled and coughed into my napkin. The red soup from around my mouth left a livid stain on the linen.

I tore open my fresh roll and spread it with butter. It melted into the warm white dough and tasted infinitely better than the microwaved corner-shop bread and own-brand margarine from the eighties. 'We've come a long way since then. I always wanted to leave you with more than I had. Whether you believe me or not, it was what drove me after your father left us.'

'Left *you*,' Emma corrected.

'Left me, Emma.' I sighed. 'Yes, thank you.' *And you*, I added to myself, reaching for my wine. The effort of trying to break through their wall of rage was wearing, and I wondered if it was futile to try. 'But I didn't let it break me,' I battled on, focusing on Emma, 'and there was fallout from that, which you obviously still feel keenly. But there comes a point when you move on and stop carrying around the anger. Or it will make you ill.'

On Emma's behalf, Libby's jaw fell open, but Emma shook her head very slightly at her.

'Did whatever made *you* so angry make you ill?' Emma asked.

'I have nothing to be angry about, darling. I've had a wonderful life.'

Out of nowhere, a bird with black wings dived towards my bowl. It circled back up and around our heads and hit the villa's window in a flurry – *thud* – and I jumped out of my seat and batted it away. 'Shoo! Shooo!' I cried.

'What are you doing?' Emma said, flinching.

'I hate birds.'

'There weren't any birds.'

Flustered, I sat down, my heart racing. 'It might have been a bat.'

It was Libby who spoke next. 'What is it with you and blackbirds, Mum?'

'It's crows. I hate them,' I said through gritted teeth, with a sense of it swirling around my face, even though I knew it was gone. My hands shook as I returned the bread from the floor to my plate.

'But why?'

'Because they're just horrible,' I said, shivering the thought away. But others followed, like a murmuration swooping into my head. I stayed very still, resisting an urge to scream or fend them off, telling myself they weren't real.

'There are no crows anywhere,' Emma said.

'Do you ever get confused between now and the past?' I asked them quietly, still shaken.

'Sometimes,' Emma replied.

'There was this field just behind the music rooms at my school where crows used to land and peck about, and I thought they brought bad luck.' It was half of the truth. Those crows had witnessed bad things. Around every corner, through every twist in life, I had seen them. They had become omens of my secret.

'It's quite ridiculous, being scared of those innocent little creatures all my life when they've done nothing to me. Absolutely nothing.'

'That's what phobias are. They're irrational,' Emma said.

'Irrational. Yes. Do you remember when you had a fear of wildfires, Libby? In the English countryside when there was barely a dry day!'

Libby picked out a roll and tried to carve into it with her one good hand and a blunt knife. Emma took over and did it for her.

'Arguably, what with the climate emergency, those fears were prescient,' I said, scrabbling around, aware that the chitchat was diversionary and getting me further away from where I needed to be.

'And you, Emma, were scared of not getting A's. Could that be considered a phobia?' I tried to laugh.

'You can't just focus on the fact that I *got* straight A's, can you, Mum? You have to criticise how badly I wanted them.'

'I wasn't! I was unequivocally thrilled by them.'

'You wanted to be. But nothing I did was ever good enough.'

'That's not true. Not true at all.'

'Saying it's not true doesn't make it not true.'

'I can't win.' I wasn't here to dwell on what we couldn't change. 'Please, darlings, let's not argue.'

There was a silence like a resentful grunt.

'I want to talk about my will,' I began, in earnest this time.

Another look was shared between them. Libby dropped a hunk of bread into her soup and began fishing it out with her fingers.

'I've put everything in order. The house will be in your name, Libby, and I've transferred all the bills over to you, but if you sell it, the money must be divided between the two of you. It's worth very little, but there's no mortgage. I didn't think Emma would want it, and I'm guessing it might be an especially attractive prospect for you now.'

I paused, realising my error, glancing nervously at her. Poking at her single status, which hadn't been the case when I had put my finances in order, was a step into territory we weren't ready for. Her bread sank into the soup. She stared at me, open-mouthed. The scandal of Connor must for the time being remain untouched. I hurried on. 'Upon my death, a large sum of money will be deposited into each of your accounts. Emma will have a little more, to compensate for the house. It won't be enough to live off forever; it will be more like a cushion. Rather a nice soft velvety one, I might add.' I smiled at them both, but their faces seemed to have lost elasticity.

'Where did this money come from?' Emma asked, eyes stretched as wide as they could go.

'Hugh – your dad – gave me a small chunk in the divorce and I was too stubborn to spend a penny of it on myself, because he was such a bloody bastard, so I put it into one of those trusts that you can't touch unless you give a hundred years' notice, or almost. It was as good as burnt, in my mind. But you see, my friend Wilf – remember him? – he was a darling and gave me some rather splendid financial advice, which meant it turned into quite a lot. And I decided you two should have it.'

Emma put both her elbows on the table, interlaced her fingers and pressed them onto her mouth. Speaking into them as though in a desperate prayer, she said, 'You've had all this money sitting there all this time and you've never thought to mention it?'

'I didn't want you to rest on your laurels. I wanted you both to find good careers and make your own way in life.'

'That worked out well,' Libby said.

'Well, it did for Emma, didn't it? And maybe now you can use the money to set up a little business with your knitting.'

'I'm utterly speechless,' Emma said, shaking her head back and forth.

I took it as happy surprise and said, 'I hope it will go some way to making all your dreams come true.'

'Blood money,' Libby murmured.

My heart stopped. 'No!' I exclaimed.

'You think I want to touch a penny of it?' The hatred in her voice sliced through me.

'Darling, please,' I said. Suddenly, I wasn't ready. I swallowed, feeling the soup slide back up my gullet. 'If you can't bear to accept the gift from me, can't you see it as money from your father?'

Libby shot up. The table wobbled. 'It's not, though, is it?'

'Okay, okay, let's stay calm,' Emma said, pressing the air down with both palms.

'There are no strings attached,' I insisted, the lump in my throat forcing me to stop talking and regroup. 'It is simply a gift. My final gift to you. A gift of love.'

'*Love*?' Libby spluttered, tears pouring down her face. 'What a joke!'

Emma got up and went to stand by her side. 'Libby, come on, let's go inside.'

Libby shook her off. 'No, Emma. I can't do it. I can't just stand here and say nothing. I don't care if I feel guilty about it every single day for the rest of my life. I can't let her get away with it. She has ruined my life! She's ruined the girls' lives!'

I breathed in. I deserved it. I would withstand it.

'Come on, Libby,' Emma repeated, trying again to guide her away from me.

'No. She's right. I accept whatever she needs to say to me,' I said, remaining calm. 'But Connor would never have stuck around. He thinks only of himself. Some of us are made that way.'

Libby covered her face with her hands and screamed into them. 'I *hate* you! I hate you *so much*! How could you have done this to me?'

There was a heaving in my chest, and it made a monstrous sound, like an animal in distress. I stood up, wanting to go to her, but stupefied by the imaginary beat of wings. I wrapped my arms around my chest. 'I'm so sorry, I'm so sorry, I don't know why, I don't know why I did it,' I cried.

Why had I hurt her? Why had I done it? Furious tears sprang into my eyes.

Reality had breathed on Connor and me and the spell had been broken. Our affection for one another had become infected and disruptive. The same ending on a loop of heartache and broken families, of broken people.

'I'm a terrible person,' I moaned gutturally, turning my back, hunching over, curling, folding up a life's worth of lies. Or was it just the one lie? Only one. So long ago. I wasn't brave enough to tell them, though the story burned in my throat. If they threw it back at me, accused me of trying to excuse what

I'd done or of being the filthy little girl my mother had thought I was, I would be left in purgatory. It would feel like stripping down to nothing and roaming naked forever through a jeering crowd.

Gathering my strength, I rose to face them, taller than I felt. 'What can I do to make it okay?' *What can I do if dying isn't enough?*

As though Libby had heard my thoughts, she dropped her hands from her face. I could almost see the ghastly idea forming. I waited, braced. After a brief, guilty glance at her sister, she delivered her terrible request. 'Give your grandchildren more time,' she said.

I was stricken. What she was asking me to do was too much. My bones ached with it. 'Is that what you want?' I breathed.

'Yes, that's what I want, Mum.'

I said, barely audibly, 'Okay. I can do that.'

Emma let out a little sob. 'Seriously?'

I nodded, confirming what I couldn't bear to imagine. 'I won't go ahead with it tomorrow, if that's what you both want.'

Emma rushed over to me. She stopped short of throwing her arms around me, but cried, 'Oh Mum. We do want that.'

Over her shoulder, I could see Libby's face. I shuddered. The appeal for a stay of execution wasn't for her children's sake. Hope wasn't on her agenda. She was asking me to do this because she wanted me to suffer, right up until the bitter end. This was my punishment. Proof of my failure as a mother. Payback for being a selfish woman, for never being good enough for them, for mothering to suit me rather than them. Us mothers got away with nothing.

Deep inside, I had always known I would fall short of what they deserved.

I remembered the day I had turned nineteen. Over birthday tea and cake at my aunt's, there had been a phone call. My aunt had taken it in the kitchen and had handed me the mint-green receiver. The man on the other end of the line had thanked me for my letter and offered me an assistant's job in the costume department on a short run of a theatre production in London.

Mum had winked. 'An admirer?'

Because it was easier, I had said yes.

The excitement had lit up her careworn face. She had only ever wanted a husband and children for me.

Later that evening, I had gone for a walk through the London streets. It was dusk, and the string of lights on Battersea Bridge had been lit already. Underneath them, I cried because I feared that some other lucky girl would swipe the job from me. I didn't want children; I wanted a career.

Hugh had been the one to persuade me I should want both.

On the cusp of death, I was being coerced once again. I was being asked to be the mother Libby wanted me to be. The mother I didn't feel capable of being. It felt like giving birth to her all over again, when I would have to lose myself in an act much greater than myself for the sake of this other life. Was it possible to change? Could I be their everything in the truest sense? Could I give myself up to them? *Should* I?

THIRTY-SIX

EMMA

Emma and Libby had their feet in the sea, sitting on the steps, hip to hip, tumblers of red wine balanced on their knees. 'I don't get it, help me out here,' Libby said. 'I want to understand why. *Why* she did it to me. How could she have slept with Connor? How could she have done that to me? She still hasn't given me any answers.'

The water was warmer than the air and its movement stroked Emma's feet. It was restful as she grappled for an answer. She contemplated Libby's anger now versus her display of cool selflessness at supper. Their mother's suicide, albeit macabre and difficult, would have allowed her immediate separation from some complex responsibilities towards her, but she had chosen the harder path and put the children first.

Over the years, Emma had not respected many of Libby's choices, believing she was too soft, a bit of a waster, failing to monetise her knits or get her kids through the school gates. But she had always put kindness first, which was paying dividends now. Thanks to Libby, their mum would have longer on this planet, perhaps have a chance to atone, and certainly gather many more precious moments with her family. If not years more.

Libby went on. 'Seriously, Emma. How was she even capable of it? It's doing my head in. I can't work out why she's so fucked up.'

'I don't know either, I really don't. I guess her childhood was a bit weird.'

'Sure, her dad was grumpy with the kids in the shop, and they didn't have any money, but that's all. Both her parents were devoted to her. She's always going on about how great they were, how they sacrificed everything for her.'

'Perhaps too much?'

'No. It's not that.' Libby shook her head. 'I can only think she did it because she literally hates me.'

'No, that's not true. Come on.'

'*Come on*? What? Pull myself together? Because, what? Because what she did wasn't so bad?'

'Don't put words in my mouth. What she did was unforgivable. But she didn't do it because she hates you. She did it because she hates herself.' Emma wasn't sure this was true, but she knew it was a robust psychotherapist's trope.

'But if her parents were so great, why does she hate herself so much? It doesn't make sense, does it?'

'I don't know, Libby. These things are complicated. Some people are just born that way – though don't tell Patrick I said that.'

'Maybe.'

'At least you've got a bit more time with her now. When we're all home, you could try to talk it through with her again.'

'Ha! You think she's going to come home with us?'

'She promised you she would.'

Libby swigged back the last of her wine, reached for the bottle behind them and poured herself more. She didn't offer Emma a top-up.

'Believe it when I see it,' she said, swilling the wine in her glass.

'I'm going to try and book Mum's flight home,' Emma said, standing up, nervous of this cynical new Libby, who might change her mind back.

'Go ahead. Waste the money. We'll be rich tomorrow anyway.' The bitterness in Libby's voice didn't suit her. What had they done to her? All her innocence had been sucked from her, all her trust.

'You coming up?'

'I'm going to stay here for a bit,' she said, putting the bottle where Emma had sat.

'Night, then. See you in the morning,' Emma said.

But Libby didn't reply.

Emma was lying on top of the bed covers, wide awake, stewing over everything Libby had said. She longed for Patrick. At two in the morning, it was too late to call and ask him how to get her little sister back. The one who was sweet and careless and naïve.

She tried to imagine what advice he would give her. He'd say that their mum had always been secretive, that maybe there was more to it but they'd probably never find out.

Inventing advice was what Emma had done as a child when her mum had been away working. *What would Mum say about Abigail telling me I'm ugly? What would Mum say about Peter, who looks like a potato, asking me out? What would Mum say?*

She had never called her at work on the theatre phone, even though she had said they could. But Libby had. Libby would leave messages with the receptionist about anything and everything. *Which sandwich would be better for the school picnic on Thursday? Marmite or peanut butter? Can I wear the blue dress to my friend's birthday party, even though the hem's coming down and there's a small hole in the sleeve? I got nine out of ten in my spelling test!*

Sometimes it took a couple of days before their mum would call back with an answer. But she always did, although often too late for the information to be useful.

Would the answers Libby craved now come too late?

Libby had always expected too much from her mother, believing her a better person than she was. Ironically, in the final hour, it was Emma who wanted desperately to believe that Nora, when faced with her own mortality, would be truly remorseful. Emma had plumped for trust and hoped her mother had learned her lesson. It was impossible to imagine her taking her own life when she had three such beautiful grandchildren to live for, albeit only for a short time now.

Her thoughts were interrupted by a knock on her bedroom door.

'Come in,' she whispered, expecting it to be Libby. She was taken aback by the sight of her mother, glowing white in her nightie. For a second, she wondered if she was real. 'What's wrong, Mum? Is everything okay?' she said, swinging her feet to the floor.

'Shush, shush, don't panic,' Nora said. 'Get back into bed. I just wanted to say goodnight.'

'Oh. Okay.' Emma's heart punched into her ribcage.

Her mother bent down to her and wrapped her in her arms. 'I have never said sorry.'

'For what?'

'For not being good enough.'

Emma couldn't breathe. 'But I've been so difficult—'

'Difficult?' her mother interrupted. 'You've been perfect. Feisty, maybe. Saying it how it is *always*, but nothing I haven't deserved. We've clashed because you needed so much more from me – and sometimes less – and I've let you down so many times. You and Libby and Eliot and Hazel and Amber have been the lights of my life, my every joy. Thank you for putting up with me. Thank you for being exactly as you are, my darling.'

Emma cried into her mother's nightie, feeling like the small child who had always wanted her mum to love her just like this, feeling like the grown-up who was mourning that very thing.

THIRTY-SEVEN

LIBBY

Her mother's smell was in her nose, her voice in her head, her arms around her. It was a dream. A dream that she didn't dare wake from.

'I wanted to be everything to you. Perhaps I believed I was, and that I could give and take what I wanted. But I was wrong. Things in my past made me the way I was. I was unable to change in time for you, my sweet girl. Learn from me. Don't be scared like I was. Don't let what I've done to you define you. Find a way to be free of me now.'

She let her mother hold her. If she woke up, she would have to be angry. And she couldn't be angry. She could only feel love. It was like when she was small, when her mum had woken her up in the middle of the night to say she was home and to say goodnight and to say go back to sleep and to say she'd see her in the morning.

'Go back to sleep,' she said now, and she stroked her head. Libby kept her eyes closed, pretending to be asleep, and waited for her to say she'd see her in the morning.

But she never did.

She had crept out, leaving Libby wide awake and staring at the moon in absolute terror.

If she had got out of bed and followed her mother to her bedroom, she might have been able to stop her.

THIRTY-EIGHT

EMMA

Emma woke the following morning and went upstairs. The water in the bath was cold, and her scream engulfed her whole being. She was unable to stop.

Her mother was dead, and she didn't want it to be true.

Libby followed her in, slipping on a tile, rebalancing only to collapse by her side.

'Oh, no,' she moaned. 'No, no, no, Mum. No, you didn't.'

Together they tried to drag her out of the water, spluttering encouragements as though she could hear them. 'Come on, Mum. Come on.'

She was too heavy and too slippery to move.

Libby ran downstairs and found her phone, fingers quivering as she called for an ambulance. She begged them to come as quickly as possible.

Emma cradled her mother in the bathwater, her arms aching. She became the mother, and her mother became the baby. From cradle to grave and back again.

· · ·

When the paramedics wheeled their mother's body out of the villa, Emma and Libby held hands, squeezing until there was no blood left in their fingers. They'd been given all the preparation in the world, and yet there was nothing that could have prepared them.

Before they closed the ambulance doors, Emma noticed that one of Nora's feet was sticking out from under the blanket. 'Wait!' she cried tearfully, running over to her, unable to bear this brutal and sudden separation from her mum. 'Wait.'

She pulled the baby-blue blanket over her mother's stone-cold foot, and as she tucked it in, the paramedic eyed her.

Emma spoke apologetically. 'It looked cold, but that's ridiculous, isn't it?'

The woman wore a long shiny black plait. She shook her head, then released the button that was raising the body off the ground, halting its ascent, and stepped towards Emma.

'In Hindu culture,' she said in a gentle Indian accent, 'the feet are sacred. In my family, we say to those who have passed, "Go with my blessing." Hold her feet now and say it. It will help her to leave.'

Compelled to do as the woman said, Emma squeezed one of her mother's bare feet, feeling the smooth undulations and gnarled edges where Nora had grounded herself to the earth and stood strong and proud. She was charged by this connection to her, as though channelling the many miles her mother had walked. Her tears fell onto Nora's skin, and she spluttered, 'Go with my blessing, Mum. Go with my blessing.'

Since she'd been young, she had asked too much of her mother. She had wanted her to live up to her impossible expectations. She had wanted her to be her hero. She had asked her to live forever. But she had died, and Emma now experienced the blow of her mortality and fully comprehended what she had never wanted to believe: that her mother had been human after all.

EPILOGUE

NORA

While alive, I had been convinced it was about to be completely over. And here I was, dead and able to see them.

Libby and Emma were hand in hand outside the crematorium. In my will, I'd asked them not to dress in black. Libby wore one of my favourite kaftans. It was orange, with mauve brocade. The cast on her arm was fraying around the edges and a little grubby. Emma's shirt was tucked neatly into high-waisted wide trousers. Both were wearing their hair parted down the middle and had brushed out their curls. Just the way I liked it.

Patrick and Eliot wore dark navy-blue jackets, which were dangerously like black, but I forgave them for it. They milled around with Amber and Hazel in tow. The girls were in a mixture of strange garments, including velvet swirly trousers and a fluffy zipped jacket. I admired their flamboyance and appreciated the effort they had made for me.

The room where the ceremony was taking place was terribly naff. If one didn't choose a church, the options were limited to these places with their dreadful pink plastic carpets and polished pine chairs – God's little punishment for rejecting him, perhaps?

The congregation consisted of close family only. I hadn't wanted anyone else there. The various friends I had made over the years couldn't possibly mourn me with any authenticity. They might have liked me and admired me sometimes – for my acerbic tongue and my amusing tales – perhaps some might even have thought that they were in love with me, but I'd made no real connections. Real bonds were formed when you opened up your heart and showed its wobbly human beat. I'd never been brave enough for that.

For the eulogy, I had asked them to keep it short and honest. I couldn't for the death of me guess what they might say.

Libby was the one to speak, which was my first surprise.

'I wish we'd known the real you, Mum,' she began, talking to me directly. 'But we loved what wasn't true. I could go on here about your eccentric ways and your fighting spirit and your talent for costumes, but it would be fluff. There was a massive gap between what you showed us and what you were coping with inside, what you were unable to talk about in life.'

The shock of what she was implying could have killed me a second time. Despite my banging on about honesty and openness, the holiday had been designed as a way of continuing the lie. The grandness, the expense, the luxury, the control of who knew what and when had propagated the myth of me, to make a legend of me. It had been orchestrated to keep the secret at bay.

'If you were here, you would be furious with me for knowing, let alone bringing it up. But when Connor sent me your diary, I was torn. Part of me wanted to burn it, pretend I didn't care, but I did care. I wanted answers. Needed answers to find peace. And to do that, I had to go back into your past to understand you.'

She surveyed the room, glancing at the coffin. Had I been alive in that casket, I would have clawed at the silk and scratched my way out, telling her to stop. I would fight and fight beyond the grave to keep the secret from them.

She carried on. 'You were right about so much. About how resilient we can be and how important it is to face death, how important it is that the children know the truth.'

I looked over at my grandchildren, who were ashy-faced and still. They were listening to Libby and I wanted to clamp my hands over their ears. How I wished I hadn't phonily encouraged this idea of truth!

'You thought everything would be easier for us because you believed you had tied up every single loose end. The finances, the bills, the funeral, your will, even what we should wear today. But these are superficial things. There was this one loose end that you had left untied. And it was the most important. It was buried deep inside your psyche, so deep you could never face it.'

She paused to take a sip of water, using her good arm. Her hand was trembling as she continued. 'What you went through was psychological murder. And for the rest of your life you pretended it hadn't happened like that. You were indeed a fighter, Mum. But you were also a victim.'

She stopped again and swallowed, and I became once again that tiny little curled thing, shivering in fright every time he had touched me.

Recovering, she went on firmly and confidently, 'You were both a victim and a fighter. A survivor, in fact. I think you would have liked that badge. Survivor. When I read your diary, when I learned of what you were put through, my heart broke. At such a young age, you had learned how to harbour shameful secrets and bury trauma. It was why you were unable to be the mother we wanted you to be. But you would be disapproving if I were to use it as an excuse on your behalf. It isn't an excuse, Mum, it is an explanation, a mitigation of responsibility perhaps. This is how I want to view it, whether you like it or not. I want to let you know, wherever you are – and I know you're somewhere, probably listening to me now...'

She paused to smile and to look up towards the ceiling, to the far corners of the room, where there were some cameras, and I wanted to wave and shout from where I was, saying, 'Hello, I'm here, my darling, I'm here!'

'...I want to let you know that I will always love you, Mum. Love you for the good and the bad parts of you. If you were alive, I hope we would have been able to have a relationship of sorts. One where I had full knowledge of the facts and was able to understand you better, where I was armed, where I was able to create proper boundaries, be less plagued by a need to please and by crippling self-doubt. These were the legacies of *your* childhood, leaching into mine and Emma's, and dripping even further through the generations to your grandchildren.

'But as much as I wished you had been able to open up to us, to confront what had happened to you, you did it your own way, as ever. By throwing that crazed, emotional roller coaster of a holiday, I guess you broke the cycle. I feel I should thank you for that, even though – and I can't believe I'm admitting it – it truly was a holiday from hell!' There was a snotty, teary chuckle from Patrick. 'But we learned so much, and I want to say that I appreciate you for that and I love you for being you. For entertaining me, for loving me in the best way you could, for making me think outside of the box.

'Mum, you were a legend, and despite everything, I can honestly say that I'm truly honoured to have known you.' She broke down. 'I love you, Mum. And I forgive you.'

Emma let go of Patrick's hand and stepped forward to hug her.

'Well done,' she whispered into her little sister's ear.

'Surrender' by Birdy began playing on a small CD player. Those who had remained dry-eyed were crying now. I listened to the song. Listened and listened, as though it was playing on a loop. Nothing that took place in that room was relevant beyond what Libby had said.

Little had been real in my life following Jasper Quinn. Yes, that was his name. I'd spent my life trying to forget, pretending I could escape him. I'd had nobody to save me from him. Not even my own mother, who had read my diary and chosen not to believe me. I had so desperately needed her to believe me. Connor had believed me. And it had ruined his life.

And now, at my funeral service, my beautiful family had been educated by Libby. She'd captured the dark heart of me, the essence of me, the me I had avoided all of my living years.

When it was all over, they filed out and milled about outside, reading the inane cards on the pretty flowers left in my memory on the paving stones. As the sun caught their hair and sparked off their tears, I longed to go back. Could I go back? Could I rectify my mistakes? Talk it through? Work it out? Get help? Ask them to love me for who I really was?

It was too late. I would be a long time dead.

The song played on and on inside my soul. Death had not been the ultimate surrender, as I had expected it to be. If only I had been able to surrender in the way that Libby had spoken of; surrender to my vulnerability, to my past.

But she was wrong about one thing. I was no legend.

True legends have philosophies to pass on, lessons learned from both their failures and their successes, from horrors and traumas confronted, human fallibility and mortality accepted. My endless need to hide my true self, to be admired, to be respected seemed so pointless now. It had caused so much pain.

Libby was the legend for writing such a brave eulogy. And I imagined that Emma had been supportive of her every step of the way. My two heroines, where the real truth lay.

·   ·   ·

I followed them in their cars to my wake. It was held in the little pub down the road from the close. They slurped tomato soup from mugs and ate crusty bread rolls, and they talked of me as though I weren't there. I wanted to tell them that I *was* there, and would always be there. But that was my last little secret to keep – you'll allow me one, at least; just a tiny one. The secret of the dead. The one pure secret that didn't turn to shit. The secret was that I had them forever. And they had me. I was in them and they were in me. I was everywhere. Like God. But, you know, elegantly bespoke.

A LETTER FROM CLARE

Dear Readers,

Huge thanks to you for reading *The Villa*. It was written during another terrible year of COVID restrictions. In lieu of an actual escape abroad, I set it in France and went on holiday with my characters! I hope you did too.

And I'd love to hear from you. Please do keep in touch by clicking on the sign-up link below, where you'll hear what I've been writing about next.

www.bookouture.com/clare-boyd

Too many of us have experienced losing a loved one in recent times. While writing this book, my husband lost his mum and our children lost their beloved *nain* (Welsh for grandma).

I spent much time considering our mortality and the meaning of life. Needless to say, I still have absolutely no answers! But I'm trying to work on the idea of living in the moment more often. A dear friend of mine once said that the small task of boiling the kettle and making a cup of tea, focusing on that one simple thing, was what had got her through an unimaginably difficult time in her life. So some days my goals are as basic as getting to the next cup of tea. And cuddles with my puppy. Oh, and a good book!

I'm hoping you liked reading *The Villa*. If you did, I would be incredibly grateful for a review. And please do follow me on social media for book news. See below for details.

Thank you again.

With very best wishes,

Clare

facebook.com/clare.boyd.14

twitter.com/ClareBoydClark

instagram.com/claresboyd

ACKNOWLEDGEMENTS

I wouldn't get through the emotional highs and lows of writing books without Jessie Botterill and Broo Doherty. You really do keep me going. Thank you. And to the whole team at Bookouture, who champion all their writers with such passion and determination.

Thank you to Ailsa Guidi, who corrected my Google Translate French!

And I want to thank my mum. She's just totally amazing.

Printed in Great Britain
by Amazon